Praise

"Tense and Exhilarating. It'll take you on a whirlwind of twists and turns, all while you flip the pages to find out what happens next. A real treat for anyone who likes a little adrenaline from their reading."

Adam Cantu, Amazon Review of *Fabricated Lies*

"Great book, awesome twists, loved the plot. A real page turner from a talented author. Highly recommended!"

Amazon Review of *Fabricated Lies*

"A thrilling crime novel that follows the story of a female police officer as she tracks down a notorious serial killer in a small town, this book is a must-read for any mystery fan that will keep you guessing until the very end."

Sylvia C. Hall, Amazon Review of *The Creation of Marla Adams*

"Marla is such a complex character that I fell in love with. Her surrounding cast is well developed and adds a great deal of depth to the story. Lots of mystery, suspense, and plot building. I'm hooked."

Amazon Review of *The Creation of Marla Adams*

"This was a very fascinating and informative read. I've actually never read anything quite like it. Lots of medical thrillers, but the stem cell twist was particularly interesting. I've been interested in stem cell therapy and research for a long time, and finding it in thriller fiction form was pretty cool. It's obvious the author is an expert in the subject which makes for an even more fascinating read."

Venus, Amazon review of *The Desperation of Marla Adams*

"Twisted Science. Twisted Motives. Twisted Fate. Twisted Lives. Unorthodox in every way Marla Adams is desperate and resorts to desperate measures! Like everything else is Texas, this thriller (set in Texas) will provide BIG arm-chair adventure with Big Intense Emotions."

Amazon Review of *The Desperation of Marla Adams*

PATRICK HANFORD

The Desperation of Marla Adams, my second excellent read from author Patrick Hanford, the follow-up to 2022's *The Creation of Marla Adams.* Well-written DEA fiction with characters & plot you can buy into with unexpected twists & turns.

Roger, BookBub Review

The Pursuit of Marla Adams

A Medical Thriller

Patrick Hanford

Savoy House Publishing

Cover design by KJ Waters Consultancy (kjwconsultancy.com) and Jody Smyers Photography (JodySmyersPhotography.com).

ISBN: (eBook): 979-8-9856939-6-6
(paperback): 979-8-9856939-7-3

Also by Patrick Hanford

Fabricated Lies
The Creation of Marla Adams
The Desperation of Marla Adams

Chapter 1

hooters on the line. Shooters set."

In a split second, two gun barrels simultaneously exploded clouds of gunpowder into the air. DEA Special Agent Marla Adams competed in fast draw competitions, and her competitor stood beside her at the Texas match, their faces tense and focused. Marla slid her modified Ruger Vaquero .357 caliber revolver into its western style holster and checked the times. Her shot clocked at .306 seconds, beating her opponent by a mere eight-thousands of a second. In this competition, that might as well be ten minutes.

The relentless Texas sun beat down against Marla's neck. The scent of saltpeter, charcoal, and sulfur lingered in the humidity, combined with the smell of sweat and soil, creating a distinct aroma unique to the event.

Instead of celebrating her time in the first of three rounds in the presence of everyone, she simply removed her ball cap to wipe her forehead with her shirt sleeve and tucked away a stray strand of dishwater blonde hair behind her ear before setting the cap back on her head. Without a word, she reached for the next wax bullet and dropped it into the chamber.

Half of her fifth finger was gone from an earlier gunfight, and the nub ached when she grasped the gun grip. She tried to ignore the innocuously named Pammy, who had consistently bested her in prior challenges. Despite the heat, the six-foot, full-boned woman dressed in full black attire except for the gold medallion on the side of her holster, flaunting her dominance at last year's world competition. Pammy tapped her chrome revolver against her leg, making sure the glint of bright sunlight hit Marla in the eye in case her smirk didn't get the message across that no one had a chance of winning against her.

Eight feet away stood two black disks set against the dry, dusty range, waiting to be hit. Rebuffing Pammy's loftiness, Marla concentrated on the center of the target, biding her time for the call. If she won this round, she could win the entire competition and quash her brash opponent and everyone else, alive or dead, who had ever doubted her.

"Shooters on the line. Shooters set," boomed a voice through the PA system, abruptly halting the chatter and laughter of the spectators. The air turned icy as every eye locked onto the stage.

Marla's hand hovered millimeters away from the Ruger's grip, her thumb poised to pull back the hammer and fire. The blood vessels in her neck throbbed against the sweat-ridden collar with each heartbeat, wide pupils fixated directly on her target. She caught the odor of saltpeter and sulfur again as she tried to guess the time for the light, a second went by, followed by another.

Lights flashed above the disks, and both shooters drew their revolvers as fast as a lightning strike, the wax charging straight ahead, leaving twin streams of smoke trailing in their wake. But when Marla fired, a searing pain shot through her finger, causing her to falter and miss her target. She looked straight up at the cloudless blue sky, struggling to hold back tears while tightly clasping her throbbing hand.

Pammy laughed aloud and raised her hands in the air. She beat Marla's first score with a time recorded at .302 seconds.

Marla fidgeted with her ball cap again, trying to block out Pammy's overconfident demeanor, which clearly intended to distract her.

With Marla and Pammy each winning one round, the stakes were high, with only a fraction of a second between victory and defeat. Marla's heart pounded in her chest while ignoring the sweat trickling down her cheek. She calmly loaded the final wax bullet into the chamber.

The tension in the air was thick, like the summer humidity, as the two competitors stood shoulder to shoulder, their guns ready. Marla's determination and concentration were palpable, while her rival exuded confidence and arrogance.

A hot gust of air tousled Marla's ponytail, but she barely noticed as she focused on the disk. She stroked the blunt tip of her sweaty, deformed little finger against the rough denim of her jeans, jaw clenched, teeth gritting, determined to prove herself in the final round.

The announcer called out, "Shooters on the line. Shooters set."

This was it. All that mattered was this one shot—a moment of validation. Like a camera lens, her vision cleared, her mind, eyes, arm, and hand aligned into a single point, like a laser beam shooting through a straw. When the light flashed, Marla drew in one fluid motion and fired. Sharp pains bolted up her finger to her hand and arm like a hammer hitting a nail.

Still holding the gun by her side, Marla raised her head to check the time—.293 seconds, the fastest she had ever drawn. Cheers and applause erupted around her as hands patted her back and shoulders. But glancing to her left, she realized the crowd wasn't applauding her victory; they were offering condolences.

The announcer declared, "Ladies and gentlemen, with a time of .291 seconds, Pammy is once again our state champion."

❖

Marla swung open the passenger door of the truck and pitched the gun belt and revolver on the front seat. She tasted the sting of disappointment and clutched the silver medallion for second place. Maybe her family was right. Maybe she was not that good. Part of her wanted to quit these ridiculous competitions, but another couldn't bear to let it go. If she could, she would give up everything she had and ever would have if only Crosby, her murdered husband, had...

Chapter 2

A former English Prime Minister once called Britain's prisons off the hook and out of order.

At four o'clock in the morning, in a London penitentiary, the night air reeked of desperation and despair. Dr. Hugo Wilborn, a female British doctor and brilliant experimentalist in her own mind, but a convicted extortionist sentenced to twenty-eight months to others. Her father demanded a son when she was born. Furious that the infant was not male, he named her Hugo anyway and then left, never to return.

The doctor brushed aside her uncombed, gray accented hair, revealing eye bags that aged her ten years. Broad shoulders and muscular arms honed from months of utilizing the limited workout equipment available in exercise yards. Despite the lack of free weights, prisoners used each other's body weight for added resistance, laying on backs during push-ups, pushing against others for bench presses, straddling someone's shoulders for squats, and innovating fixed horizontal bars from metal ladders for pull-ups.

Wilborn remained silent, standing outside a prison cell door while a middle-aged female guard slid a cold metal key into a door lock and turned it. After removing the key, she snatched the folded money between the doctor's fingers before shoving it into her shirt pocket with force. Without saying a word, Wilborn snapped her fingers, and the guard removed a flashlight from her belt and handed it to the inmate. She waited to enter until the guard disappeared down the hall.

Dr. Wilborn made friends in prison by finding special connections and buying the proper fags and snacks, burner phones, porno mags, and anything inmates and guards wanted, except for Billie Bagnulo. Nicknamed Bags, a previous long-term resident of Eastwood Park and Downview Prisons, didn't like Wilborn; she didn't like anyone, especially educated, egocentric snobs.

Wilborn hooked the handle with the index finger and partially opened the prison cell door, keeping it from banging against the wall. The stale air hovered, pungent with odors of sweat, urine, and scant personal hygiene. The almost two-hundred-year-old prison originally accommodated one person per cell, but now the overcrowding forced two inmates to share each cell with bunk beds. An overhead light attached to the ceiling automatically dimmed at nine o'clock, but the authorities never left the cell entirely dark.

A greasy smile stretched across Wilborn's lips. It was time for payback. Two women snored on the bunk beds. She nudged the flashlight against the woman's leg in the lower bunk, waking her. The inmate slipped out of the cell without speaking. Wilborn clanged the light against the metal bedpost before turning it on and aiming it at Bag's face in the top bunk.

The blinding light startled Bags, causing her to flip off the covers and swing her legs over the edge of the bed. "Bloomin' 'ell!" She promptly jumped off and stood straight, crossing her arms over her chest, smiling like she was still the dominant inmate. "Well, well. If it ain't the bloody wanker, Doc Wilborn. Heard you were gettin' released." She snatched a purple pencil from the wooden desk beside her bed and snapped it in half. "Want me to give your other foot a proper bashing before ya leave?"

Tacky sketches of naked and scantily clad women were taped to the wall.

"Last day, Bags." Wilborn loomed inside the cell with a stern expression written all over her face. "It's payback time for what you did."

"Bollocks," she retorted, cracking her knuckles. "You don't stand a chance against me, Doc. We've had a go before, and that didn't turn out too well for you, innit?"

There was a pecking order in prison. In the line for breakfast, the medical clinic, the library, who kicked the football first in a game, who bought the good drugs, and who you could talk smack to and dominate. Even with Wilborn's money, Bags ranked higher inside these walls.

Another prisoner, twice the size of Bags, entered the cell. Without looking behind her, Wilborn gestured with her head once. The brute moved around and trapped Bags in the corner.

"Wait," Bags said. "Let's talk this over. It was a blunder, mate. Everybody knows it was. You were new and full of piss. I had to show you the chain of command, who's who inside. Just a shove, I was meant to give ya, but you was such a weak bugger. Couldn't handle it, could ya? It was all your fault you tripped down them stairs and broke your bloody foot. But you should thank me. Because of that, you got special treatment, doctor visits, extra nosh. You commenced workin' out and got..." she motioned toward Wilborn, "you got all swole. Muscles now."

In prison, you learn when to fight and when to capitulate. Fighting when you were not supposed to would result in more broken bones than planned.

The brute spun Bags around and clamped her massive hand over the inmate's mouth.

"Have to be quiet in here," Wilborn said. "Mustn't disturb the guards."

The brute forcefully bent Bags' right index finger backward like a twig. The muffled scream never left the cell.

Bags collapsed to her knees, cradling her hand. "All right, you win. Happy?"

"Nah, not yet."

"Snag any of me drawings. They're worth a lot. Everyone says that."

Wilborn ripped several sketches off the wall. "Yer shite don't mean bollocks to me." The doctor motioned to the brute again. Without hesitation, a bear paw-sized hand latched onto Bags' right forearm.

"Now listen," Bags pleaded. "You broke my finger. We're even Steven now."

Wilborn glared at Bags kneeling on the floor. "My foot still torments me at night. I can't sleep well from all the pain you caused me. And you...you can still draw your rubbish pictures with a bloody broken finger."

"I got a hundred quid. It's yours if we call it quits."

"Not enough." Wilborn nodded to the thug. The back of a hand slammed Bags against the wall. The brute clamped onto Bag's shirt, pulled her up from the floor, and slammed her against the wall again.

Bags winced in pain. "This is all a cockup, I tell you—a bloody mess. Take what you want. Anything."

Wilborn gave another nod. The brute clamped a hand over Bags' mouth again, stifling any scream as the middle of the forearm cracked.

"All right. Stop." Bags huddled in the corner, cradling her broken arm. "In my left shoe. Two hundred quid in the shoe, just ruddy well take it."

Wilborn retrieved a wad of £20 notes from the shoe and gave it to the brute. "My friend here will keep a close eye on what you say about this...mishap."

Wilborn looked down at the other shoe, then back at Bags before picking it up and giving it a wobble. Two £50 notes tumbled to the floor. Wilborn didn't want it, so the brute grabbed them as they exited the cell.

♦

A prison guard rounded the corner at 6:03 AM and banged her fist twice on Wilborn's metal cell door. Each hard strike echoed off the cold walls of the compound as four hundred inmates began another day. With a thick cockney accent, she yelled, "Wilborn! Up ya get. It's time."

Dr. Wilborn had been waiting for this day for twenty-eight months. She sat beside the wooden desk, wearing a light blue t-shirt and black trousers. British prisons had no ridiculous looking American style, bright orange prison uniforms. Wilborn snapped back, her eyes fixated on the door. "I'm bloody awake already."

The guard peered through the 8X10 inch thick cell door window and saw the innocuous inmate dressed, ready to leave.

When the doctor could avoid the wrong people, she concentrated on science. Photographs taped to one wall with different angles of skulls and brains. A side view picture had a straight line drawn from the forehead to the front third of the brain measured in millimeters. She had a lifetime to decide how to save the world from itself, and she had the expertise to do it.

As Wilborn sat, the feigned pain in her foot, which she had strung out for the last two and a half years, suddenly vanished as she waggled it in rapid succession. After trashing a dozen letters addressed from the States, she held two documents that would dominate her future: the first, an acceptance letter from the General Medical Council, offering her a way back into medical research if she paid a fee and promised to stop her outrageous experiments, and the second, an aged newspaper article about Dr. Reginald McCollum, her lover and partner in research for nine years, who developed a technique to hyperstimulate stem cells to work in days, not weeks or months.

"Wilborn?" The guard banged on the door again. "Up ya get."

She rubbed her toes, pretending the bogus pain continued. "It will bloody well take a while to get up and out with my injured leg."

"You've played us long enough. That injury was over two years ago. Get your arse up from the chair and move." The guard snapped open the small rectangular cuff window and dropped it against the door for effect. The clang echoed off the cinder block walls. "Feeling lonely in there, all by yourself? You've been lucky without a cellmate for several months."

"Tell me where my cellmate buggered off to. She owes me money."

"How the bloody hell would I know? Scotland Yard is looking for her. There won't be no more escapes after what she done. The Captain here is combing every fiber of this place and still not found how she got out."

Wilborn smiled because she knew the answer and hoped no one else ever would. "That was months ago. Have the captain grab a mirror and look up her arse."

The guard glanced both ways before whispering, "I'm proper chuffed the tosser left. Bloody Yank was nothing but trouble around here." The guard clanked the door twice with the handcuffs. Back to her gruff voice, she bellowed out loud enough for the next cell to hear, "Get over here."

Wilborn rolled both pages together and stuffed them in her back pocket.

"Come on," the guard said, "don't be a bloody wanker."

"And you're a bloody rotter."

"I'll stick this key up your arse if you call me that again."

Wilborn knew the routine: turn around, hands behind her back, and stick her arms through the waist-high opening in the door. Her heart raced as the cold metal handcuffs clicked around her wrists. She refused to flinch, instead smiling slyly.

"You know the procedure. Go sit on the bed before I open the door," the guard barked.

The heavy sound of keys jingled from the guard's pocket before she inserted one into the lock and snapped it ninety degrees. The hinges groaned as the door creaked open.

Wilborn sat on the bottom bunk, waiting for the command.

"Up. Let's go unless you have a fancy to stay another year."

The doctor positioned herself between the bunk beds and the desk and stuck her bare feet into the year-old canvas slip-ons. "Right. Get me out of this bloody place."

The guard nodded toward the rear of the cell. "Do you want any of your pictures on the wall?"

"I got nothing else I need here because I'm never coming back."

The guard chuckled. "That's what they all say. I'll give you thirty days before I see your mug again."

Wilborn stepped out and noticed two guards at Billie Bagnulo's cell. "What happened down there?"

The guard nudged Wilborn forward. "Said she fell off the top bunk and broke her arm."

As she walked in front of the guard, memories of her former life began flooding her mind. The two doctors were set for BCR, Blooming Cells Research, Inc., to sign an exclusive agreement in their stem cell research, but the company backed away after they discovered a ninety percent mortality rate in the clinical trials. McCollum wanted to escape the bad publicity and the drying up of funded research money, so he disappeared from the British spotlight and secretly went off the grid in the US where he could fly under the radar, unfunded, but also unsupervised while Wilborn attempted to extort BCR for ten million pounds. A year later, when the news of Dr. McCollum's death in San Antonio, Texas, reached her, Wilborn blamed DEA Special Agent Marla Adams for it. She pushed aside the yellowed paper and vowed revenge. It's time for her bloody payback.

As they weaved down the hallway and the last metal door closed, the guard removed the cuffs from Wilborn's wrists and led her to a small room where a male correctional officer sat behind a half-open Dutch door and tapped his finger on a clipboard.

The officer presented a plastic basket that held her belongings. "Sign here and here."

She dug through her clothes and found a small key, Herring brand leather shoes, and the £15,000 Bremont watch. "Where's my money?"

"What money?" The guard held out a plastic debit card for her. "Don't forget this. It's a gift from His Majesty's Government, a farewell present to released prisoners."

"They should stick you in prison for thievery. I had several hundred pounds in my pocket when I was brought here."

The man smiled as he said, "Don't know what you're talking about."

Wilborn snatched the card, then tried to put on the clothes she wore when incarcerated. They were too small. "Give me some clothes that fit." After being given a shirt and pants two sizes too large, she signed the paper and dressed. She approached the exterior fence and extended her arm toward the gate before yanking her hand back. The buzzer had yet to make a noise. The electricity was still live. She laughed, "That would have been a bloody mess, leaving prison only to be electrocuted at the last second." The buzzer sounded, and the doctor hesitated when the gate popped open.

"You staying or going?" the guard asked.

Dr. Wilborn pushed the gate further open with the heel of her palm and stepped out—a free woman. Lifting her head toward the morning sun, it felt different, brighter, warmer than yesterday, the day before, and the eight hundred and forty-six days before that. The slam of the gate elated her.

Chapter 3

Hugo Wilborn removed a debit card loaded with £46 from her shirt pocket and flipped it front to back. There was a choice: spend the money on a taxi to stop at 10 Downing Street, bang on the gates, and demand to speak to the Prime Minister about her unjust incarceration of a world renowned doctor until the police arrested her again or go a different direction to Michael's Pawnbrokers to retrieve her stored possessions. The black taxi waited a few feet away, so she climbed in and shut the door.

Dr. Wilborn leaned back in the seat and observed the view outside the window, absorbing the sights of the bustling city she hadn't witnessed in a while. She inevitably felt a growing sense of excitement, reminiscent of a child on Christmas morning. People zipped about on bikes, mopeds, and electric scooters weaving precariously among each other. A red double decker bus passed an intersection. The city's pace moved faster than she remembered, but she welcomed any activity since she hadn't seen a moving vehicle in over two years.

When the vehicle crossed the River Thames, sunlight glittered off the water's surface. It was her last chance to change her mind. She said nothing when the driver steered toward the Limehouse district.

On the wide sidewalks were temporary tents permanently lined along the walkways full of retail clothing, cologne, and toys. A mixture of food carts from every region of the earth stood near the curbs. Dr. Wilborn lowered her window and took in a breath. The air was filled with curry, garlic and thyme, cinnamon and coriander. The aroma of fresh flatbread and olive oil brought a satisfactory smile. Butter sizzling on steel pans heated with propane burners made her mouth water. For the last two years, she ate stale bread, tasteless canned vegetables, and a brown sauce covering dry beef and chicken.

Boys stood on the sidewalks, whistling and waving as four girls in bright clothes with pink dyed pigtails and oversized sunglasses howled at each other in a red and white Mini Cooper convertible as they soaked in their fifteen minutes of teenage fame.

The driver stopped against the curb near the pawnbroker's shop, which had darkened windows and a sign with two letters missing.

"That will be twenty-seven pounds fifty-five."

Wilborn handed the debit card to the driver.

He swiped the card and waited for the transaction to be completed. "How long were you in for?"

"Long enough to know I'm not going back." Wilborn reached to retrieve the card.

The driver chuckled. "They all say that." He handed the card to his passenger. "Good luck to ya."

On the sidewalk, Wilborn bought a Moroccan flatbread, Indian Tandoori chicken, and a schnitzel the size of her hand. She squeezed half a lemon on it and ate the two meats inside the bread while listening to a near naked man with an unkept gray beard sitting alone, legs crossed, playing traditional Hindustani music with his sitar. A sudden pang of nervousness hit. She spit out what was in her mouth and dropped the last bite and the debit card in a public refuse container. What if her belongings had been sold, damaged, or destroyed? She shook off the feeling after pushing the doorbell at Michael's Pawnbrokers LTD. It buzzed until she pushed on the handle. After stepping inside, the door shut by itself, and the electronic bolt clicked. The dimly lit shop had shelves and display cases lining the walls, with narrow aisles leading deeper into the store. A sluggish ceiling fan circulated stagnant air smelling of old leather, moldy paper, and desperation.

A round-shouldered man with a slight feminine face and ear-length greasy hair perched on a stool behind his counter. A colorful, loose-fitting scarf wrapped around his neck while wearing gold rings on every finger and a thick gold chain with an oversized cross hung low on his chest. The doctor only knew this person as Michael.

"I'm chuffed. You've been out less than twenty minutes and are now arriving at my shop."

"How did you know when I got out?"

Michael pointed to his mobile. "People call me all the time."

Wilborn played nice. "We've been... acquaintances for years, and it occurred to me I don't know your last name. And, by the way, I see you've lost weight."

"Yeah, cheers. My doctor gave an ultimatum, croak young or shed three stones. And keep calling me Michael, no need for last names." He sneezed hard before pulling a facial tissue from the box, blew his nose, and pitched it into the wastebasket half full of used tissues. "How about some clothes that fit you better, Hugo? Over in the corner, there is a rack of old clothes."

The doctor shifted a round mirror on a stand aside and pressed her hands flat on the clear counter littered with jewelry, watches, and coins. After years of studies and decades of medical practice, it always irritated her when people called her by a given name: an insult, an attempt to lower her to the masses wanting desperately to be like her.

"Hugo? Do you reckon us bezzie mates? I didn't spend years studying and practicing medicine so that some pawnbroker could call me by my first name like an old pal. Where were you when I was eating slop and hanging around the bloody playground, dodging prisoners with their IQ ten points below idiot every day?" The doctor leaned in closer. "I'm Dr. Wilborn to you, and you can rush off to the back and fetch me my lot."

Still sitting on the stool, Michael moved his head slightly. "This is a business, Doc. I'm a pawnbroker, and storing something for two and a half years ain't cheap. You might be a doctor, but inside my shop, you're just another punter wanting help—and one who owes me a precious pawn for privately safeguarding your esteemed trunk."

Wilborn's eyes darted frantically around, ensuring no one else was in the building. "I gave you everything I had before I was thrown into that hellhole. I won't give you another quid."

A cruel smile spread across Michael's face. "No need for money." He reached out for her wrist. "Your ticker will do fine."

Dr. Wilborn wrapped her hand around her expensive timepiece. "This watch is worth more than all the rubbish in this gaff combined."

Michael swung around to the five-foot-tall safe behind him, flipped the handle down, and opened the door. Stacks of British pounds and American dollars stood in the back as the owner removed a bundle of cash and closed the door with his foot. "I'll give you five hundred quid," he set the money on the transparent counter, "or a grand in credit toward anything in the shop."

The doctor smiled wickedly. "I have something for you in my trunk instead of the wristwatch."

Michael nodded like a bobblehead doll. "A present? If I fancy it, I'll grant you eleven hundred in credit."

"Bring me my trunk, and we'll talk."

When the pawnbroker scampered to the back of the building, Wilborn delved into a box of tools in the aisle next to her, retrieved a long screwdriver, and discreetly held it behind her pant leg. Boxes scraped the concrete surface and metallic items clanged against each other. "Hey! Be careful with my belongings. It's bloody fragile, and I'll make you pay for any damage caused."

"Keep your knickers on!"

Moments later, Michael wheeled a black Seward trunk from the rear storage area, stopped near Dr. Wilborn, and lowered it onto the floor. "Satisfied?" He sneezed hard again, pulled another tissue from the box, blew his nose, and dropped the tissue in the wastebasket.

The doctor knelt beside the trunk and unlocked it with the small key before raising the lid. Inside was a sealed cardboard box. She popped the tape across the top with the screwdriver and opened the flaps. It was a second set of stem cell research equipment identical to what Dr. McCollum had used in the States. She lifted the centrifuge and positioned it on the floor. "Get me an extension cord."

Michael realized that the doctor had not removed the watch from her wrist. "Hand it over to me, or you don't leave. The entryway is electronically locked, so you'll never open it. And where's this gift you said you had?"

The doctor aimed the screwdriver at the man. "If this is broken, this will be your gift, and I'd be happy to stick it up your bloody bollocks."

Michael stepped around the counter, holding the end of a long, orange extension cord and a six-inch knife. He dropped the cord on the floor and pointed the blade at Wilborn. "Take off the watch. You know bloody well that I'm good at using this."

"And what if I don't?"

"Then I'll tell the bobbies you tried to rob me, and you'd be off to prison in no time."

"Fine. All yours." Wilborn slid it off her wrist and held it for grabs.

Michael's finger hooked a jeweler's cloth from the counter before he took the timepiece and held it toward the overhead light. "You should be happy you are out of prison. Why aren't you smiling?"

Wilborn shrugged. "I've been out less than an hour and I've been proper robbed." After kneeling beside the trunk and plugging the cord into the centrifuge, she pushed a button, and the machine spun, with an ultraviolet light changing the transparent lid to faint purple. She turned it off, unplugged it, and meticulously placed the centrifuge back into the trunk. Next to it, she opened a small plastic box, removed the screw top vial with a quarter full of clear liquid, and flicked the glass with her fingernail—the protein extract with a transition metal she and Dr. McCollum invented. This was a catalyst to hyperstimulate stem cell growth. The solution triggered fresh stem cells to develop new tissue growth in days, not months. She could eliminate people waiting years for transplants, instead, creating a new heart, a lung, or a kidney from their own body in less than a week, and guaranteeing her a Nobel Prize in Medicine plus a million pound prize, making her the most famous doctor in the world.

But to perfect her experiments, she must perform many medical trials on humans. It was essential that she travel to the States and retrieve McCollum's second vial in San Antonio, Texas, before continuing her life-saving research.

"I want my pressie, or you're not leaving." Michael held his phone in the air. "One call and you are back inside."

"Sure. Whatever you say." The doctor traded the liquid-filled vial for one containing white powder, removed a zip-lock bag full of multicolored tablets, and placed the bag on the glass surface.

"You kept rainbow fentanyl tablets in your trunk?" Michael asked. "And in my storage for over two years? What if a sniffer dog came in here and found it? I'd be shut down."

"Why would a dog come inside your shop unless they suspected you were hiding other drugs?" Wilborn opened the bag and spread ten tablets on the counter. When Michael made a move for them, the doctor slapped her palm on top of the pills. "You have one more thing to do before you can have these."

"What's that?"

She raised the bag of fentanyl. "Send this by FedEx."

"No. I'll go to jail if they find out it's drugs."

"You send dozens of packages every week, right? Send another. No one will be suspicious about a package from you." The doctor grasped a pen and notepad, wrote an address, and spun it around. "Ship it here."

Michael contemplated the note. "San Antonio, Texas, USA?"

"What time does FedEx come?"

Michael checked the wall clock. "Eleven o'clock. In eight minutes."

"Then I guess you should get this packaged promptly. After that, you may have the tablets."

Standing silent for a beat, Michael stared at the drugs and then scurried into the back room. Dr. Wilborn scooped up the ten tablets and placed them into her shirt pocket. An opened FedEx box sat on the floor near the corner of the counter. The doctor's foot spun it around, and then she read the shipping label. Of course, Michael had a last name: Smythe.

The pawnbroker returned, placing four packages ready to send on the glass surface with an empty box on top. He checked the clock on the wall: 10:57, then wrapped the bag of drugs in bubble wrap and taped the box closed before writing the San Antonio address on the shipping label. "What name do you want me to put?"

Wilborn pushed the box on the floor to the side with her foot. "I want to send another package. Go to the back and get a padded envelope."

"Bloody hell. You don't have time. The FedEx bloke will be here any sec."

"You want the fentanyl? Then go get the bloody envelope."

When Michael rushed to the back, Wilborn scribbled MICHAEL SMYTHE on the San Antonio address label, then slid it under the other packages. Stretching over the counter, she popped open the register and snatched all the banknotes. Inside the till, she recognized something. "Hmm. So, he likes cocaine." She removed two small vials containing white powder and closed the drawer.

The front doorbell rang, and the pawnbroker rushed to the counter with an envelope. "You don't have time for another package."

Wilborn waved her hand in the air. "Never mind."

"Where's the fentanyl?" Michael asked.

"The tabs are in my pocket. They're yours after the packages are picked up." She wandered down an aisle.

A man outside, wearing a FedEx uniform, cupped his hands around his eyes and gazed through the window. He waved and smiled. The pawnbroker pushed the button behind the counter, and the automated lock buzzed. When the courier entered, he ignored the customer on the other side of the building.

"Good morning, Ashton." The pawnbroker's hand gave a friendly pat to the sealed packages and box. "How's your day been?"

"Right proper." Ashton spotted Wilborn's Seward trunk. "Nice looking storage box. Is it for sale?"

"What?" Michael hunched over the counter toward the floor. "Uh, no. It's ...a new purchase. Swing by in two days once I've done a proper inventory."

Ashton handed him a business card. "Have a young one heading off to uni, and I could use it. Call me when you're ready to sell." He aimed the handheld controller at each package, scanned the addresses, and lifted them off the counter. "See you." He pointed at the card. "Don't forget to call."

Michael pressed a button near the cash register, and the entryway buzzed until the FedEx employee opened the door.

After Dr. Wilborn removed a shirt and pants from the clearance rack, she changed clothes and returned to the counter opposite the pawnbroker. "Michael Smythe, eh?"

"Who?"

Wilborn pointed at a box on the floor. "The name on the invoice label."

The pawnbroker shrugged. "Call me any name you want."

Wilborn patted the two vials she stole from the register in her back pocket while holding the other vial from the trunk, then tapped a row of white powder on the glass. "Well, Michael, with the last name of Smythe, here's a little extra for helping me."

"You had this in your trunk, too?"

"No biggie."

"Where are my tablets?"

The doctor placed them back on the counter while noticing her watch was already on display to sell under the glass. "Here. All ten." She nodded toward the line of white powder. "Go ahead, have at it."

Michael sized up the cocaine line, then nodded once. "You first."

"It's been twenty-eight months since I touched any drugs. Got to ease back into it." Wilborn touched a small amount on her index finger, then quickly placed her third finger to her nose and snorted. "Bloody well, good stuff." She motioned toward the line of powder.

"Leave it," Michael said. "I'll get to it later."

Wilborn shook her head. "If you're not interested...." She cupped her hand near the powder, ready to sweep it off the counter. "Fine. Don't."

"Wait. I didn't say I wouldn't." He nodded toward the vial. "Leave the rest here."

The doctor smiled. "Yeah, sure." The vial clinked against the glass counter beside the cluster of fentanyl tablets.

Michael used the edge of the FedEx driver's business card and straightened the line before snorting it. He rubbed his nose hard. "Oh, damn." He stumbled. His hands clung to the counter. "No. No." His eyes widened as everything blurred. Wobbling, trying to stay erect, he stuttered, "I...I..." His back slammed against the wall before falling forward to the floor.

Dr. Wilborn leaned over the counter at the motionless man. "You thought it was coke like the ones in your register. Bloody well wasn't. It was pure fentanyl, and you snorted enough to kill ten junkies." Tracking around the counter, she wiped her index finger on the man's shirt before removing his wallet and taking a credit card and British Driving Licence. She removed the scarf around Micheal's neck and wrapped it around hers. Holding the licence next to her face and looking in the round mirror, she compared Michael's face to hers. "Looks sufficiently close enough with no fret." She reached in and took back the Bremont watch. The safe door was closed with the handle down, unlocked, so she pulled it open, raking the cash out before closing it again and spinning the combination wheel. "Been a pleasure doing business with you, you twat." After pulling two disposable tissues from a box, her hand wiped the wallet and countertop clean of prints, then dropped it in the wastebasket. "It should be a few days before someone realizes you aren't answering the doorbell, and I will be miles from here."

Wilborn stepped back around the counter and hurriedly packed away cash while glancing at the door every couple of seconds. Stopping, she thought, *I've been rotting in prison for two years. That's a bloody long time.* After glancing at the door and ensuring there was no one, she crouched beside the dead man, rolled him from his side onto his stomach, and pulled the pants and underwear down to his knees. *A bloody long time indeed.* "Michael Smythe, I need something, and you are going to give it to me. A bit of practice not done in two years."

Turning to the aisle lined with power tools, she shoved items to the side and snatched a cordless hand power tool with a set of drill bits before returning to her trunk and removing a 50cc syringe. Clutching the hand-held drill tightly, she pressed the bit against the dead man's hip with an icy determination. The motor whined like a desperate cry as it tore through skin and muscle, sinking deeper into the bone until Wilborn found what she was looking for. "Fresh stem cells," she whispered. "I can still get what I want."

Chapter 4

Central Texas woke to summer refusing to relinquish its grip on triple-digit weather, with temperatures predicted to climb hotter by mid-afternoon. A heat wave continued to pound the state, spreading range fires throughout the surrounding counties. Smoke particles ricocheted red and orange sunlight into a wounded sky.

Despite the heat, Marla wore blue jeans, boots, and a long-sleeved shirt to protect her arms and neck. Sunglasses were stuck up on the brim of her Hildebrandt FD cap, ready to use when the blinding sun bore down its brightness.

Her house smelled new. It should. The builders finished a week ago at half the size of the previously burned dwelling—no need for anything larger, with never a prospect of another husband or children in her future. A coffeepot, toaster, and microwave sat next to plastic utensils and paper plates on the countertop in her kitchen. The pristine dishwasher and oven remained unused. Only a card table and chairs sat in the dining area. She couldn't force herself to buy furniture, a china cabinet, or pots and pans. It would signify she accepted her life without Crosby. Crosby, she thought. He crossed her mind ten thousand times a day, each time with a lightning bolt stabbing her heart. She knew he wouldn't pass through the doorway. He was dead. Killed. Murdered. Buried. But she felt his smile and his lips on her neck.

Marla Adams' naïveté died years ago. As a preteen, she never had the desire to hold a gun. The idea of shooting something, someone, taking the life of a man or beast was beyond her imagination. Now, with several family members murdered, that innocence would be impossible to resurface. The life of an agent was dangerous, every day, all the time, and even though she was inside her home, she wore her 9mm service weapon strapped to her belt.

Two previously frozen strudels sprang halfway out of the toaster before falling back. She stabbed the first with a plastic knife and slathered peanut butter over the top. She sighed and bit the corner. Halfway through her FMLA, Family Medical Leave Act, she had to decide whether to ask for an extension of time off or start planning to return to work. She sipped her coffee and took another bite.

Memories of her husband lying on the hospital floor, bleeding, raced through her mind. She wanted to help. She couldn't. Closing her eyes and turning the wedding ring on her finger, she hoped never to forget his face, his smile, his promise to love her forever. Forever ended weeks ago.

The strudel dropped from her hand to the floor. She cleared her throat and tried to clear her mind.

After cleaning the kitchen and disposing of the strudels in the trash, she proceeded outside to the front porch and watched the rooster standing on the chicken coop roof, crowing its morning alarm for his flock to start work. She headed to the barn and opened the door to find both horses looking at her. The mixed odor of fresh hay, fresh manure, and the apple orchard miles away hovered inside. Daisy scraped the muck off her front hoof. Blackie, once Crosby's horse and now hers, stood majestically in his stall.

"Daisy girl." She caressed the horse's forehead, then switched to Blackie. "And good morning, you fine-looking man. Hope you both slept well last night."

He snorted at her and swished his tail.

Marla reached into a bucket for a carrot and cracked it in two, giving each an equal portion. The horses ate them in a flash. She unlatched Blackie's gate and swung it open. He knew where to go as he pranced from the barn to the corral. "Sorry, girl. I can only ride one at a time. Your turn is next." Marla followed while slipping on work gloves. She squeezed the half-empty fifth finger of the right glove, adjusting the fit around what remained of the finger before breaking a hay bale into pieces and pitching it toward the horses. "Breakfast of my champions."

Riding to the opposite end of her land, she dismounted Blackie where a wall of dirt piled ten feet high stood with tin cans scattered from one end to the next. Wooden posts were stuck into the ground with paper targets riddled with a bevy of close-knit bullet holes. For her fast draw practice, to the side, eight feet away, was a metal pole with a flood lamp and a digital readout.

Marla unlocked a gun safe and removed boxes of .45 caliber wax bullets and 9mm full metal jacket bullets, along with her modified Ruger revolver and gun belt. She kept an extra set of guns at a separate place since her attempted murder at her home. Disappointed at not winning first place in the Texas contest, she skimmed her fingertip over the silver medallion attached to the side of her holster.

She had two different mindsets with the guns: a quick reaction time to a potentially lethal situation with the 9mm service weapon and a pre-shot habitual action taking several seconds before firing her competition revolver. After firing three boxes of wax bullets with the revolver one shot at a time, she changed to the 9mm Glock, firing rapidly two to three times at a target. For fun, she practiced her fast draw with the pistol, slower than her revolver but faster than anyone else on the force. The acrid bite of gunpowder in the air excited her, calmed her, and made her feel stronger against whatever the world threw at her.

Positioned on her horse, Cassie Chandler trotted alongside the shooting range. Marla hired her as a ranch hand for the ninety-four cattle she owned on a two-hundred-acre pasture. Cassie sported a straw cowboy hat, a Dallas Cowboys t-shirt, jeans, and boots. Because she had a glass eye and was deaf in her left ear from childhood cancer, certain people perceived her as weak and easy prey. She lost her previous job after pummeling another ranch hand unconscious when he made a poor life choice and patted her on her butt. At five-foot-ten and one-seventy-five pounds, with a spattering of fat, she could take down a man as well as a cow.

"Morning, Marla. Are we on track to bring in the cattle today?"

Marla locked her revolver and belt in the gun safe. "I bought twenty online. They should be here this afternoon."

Cassie yawned and shook her head. "Yeah, great. Okay."

"You all right?"

"Hmm. Can't seem to keep a guy," Cassie said. "Roger the Dodger hopped in his brown Silverado and left in the middle of the night."

"You mean the cowboy from the Johnson ranch? Heard about you dancing with him a couple of nights ago and the ruckus when another guy tried to cut in."

"Yeah, him. Thought there might be a possibility, but he only lasted a few days.

"Seems to be a real deal cowboy." Marla stroked Blackie's neck.

"Hazards of my job."

"What do you mean?" Marla asked.

"Whenever a guy finds out I'm punching cattle for a fast draw champion who is also a DEA agent, they split."

Marla placed her hands firmly on her hips and smiled. "So, it's my fault you can't keep a man?"

Cassie raised her hands. "Well, yeah!" She chuckled. "You tend to scare off all the beer drinkin', cocaine sniffin' dudes I hook up with."

"Hey, the last month, I'm just a cowgirl. On family medical leave or grieving leave or something like that." *Crosby didn't just die, the cartel killed him.*

"That is not how people in town see you. You're an ex-cop who's a bad-ass federal agent."

"I have a few weeks before I'm to report to duty, but not sure I want to return." Marla flipped the reins onto Blackie's neck. "You think you might hold on to a man if I don't go back?"

"Hmm." Cassie patted the neck of her horse. "Maybe, but the day you return full time is the last day I have a man in my bed. There's not a single guy who will buy me a drink. I might as well turn into a nun or one of those fancy poets."

"Poets get married."

"Not to anyone at The Broken Saddle Horn."

"Good point." Marla mounted Blackie. "Tomorrow morning, eight o'clock, we brand cattle."

"I'm heading to the bar tonight, and I'll make sure I'm done by midnight."

Marla chuckled. "I'm sure you have ways to encourage whoever you pick."

❖

Roger pushed open the solid wooden door to The Broken Saddle Horn. He found Cassie sitting at a table with three other girls. The band was on break, and country music blared from the overhead speakers. In the far corner, cowboys shot pool with balls clacking against each other.

Roger approached the table and smiled. Cassie relaxed against the chair with her legs crossed and returned the smile. "Hey, stranger."

"Did you forget I was with you yesterday?"

She uncrossed her leg. "Not at all, and I definitely didn't forget you snuck out last night."

Roger pushed his cap back a tad. "I...had something to do early this morning."

"Yeah? Other than leaving me cold in the bed, what else?"

"Something out of town. It's all good now. I'll head over to the bar and grab a couple of beers.

Cassie pointed at the waitress three tables away. "She'll be here in a bit."

"Yeah, I'm aware, but, um, they only have Lone Star for a dollar if you buy it at the counter."

"You know I don't drink Lone Star."

Roger swept his hand over the countertop at the bar, feeling its cool smooth surface beneath his fingertips. Trixi, the bartender, had messy purple hair reaching below her ears, uneven bangs fluttering when her false eyelashes moved, and a bright red beret perched at an angle atop her head like some kind of 1960s Paris revolutionary. She rocked a snug tie-dye t-shirt showing off muscular arms, wide yellow suspenders, and high-waisted black pants, far from the usual attire for a cowboy bar. She stepped forward while drying her hands with a white towel, then leaned against the counter across from Roger. "Hey there." She gestured toward the table where the girls sat. "Something serious? This is the second time you brought her here."

"Don't be that way, and I didn't bring her here. You know she's a regular almost every night."

Trixi scoffed. "She and all her girlfriends over there in the corner, sucking on beer bottles and hoping for something else, are eyeing you right now. You are the star of the show tonight." Her phone in her pocket rang.

"You going to answer that?" Roger asked.

"No. Not expecting a call, so I'll check the message later."

I just need a couple of cold ones. Lone Star for me."

"And the girl? What does she want?"

Roger casually scooped a handful of nuts from a bowl. "Hell, I don't know. You probably do."

"I do." Trixi reached into the bottle cooler for two beers and snapped off the caps while holding the bottles in one hand. "Staying with her tonight?"

"Don't fret, Trix. I'll come see you. How much?"

Trixi tilted her head a little before sliding the bottles in his direction. "You mean tomorrow morning, not tonight, right?" She wiped her hands on the towel again. "On the house."

Roger smiled and affirmed with a nod.

Chapter 5

When Dr. Wilborn entered the baggage claim area of the San Antonio International Airport, it knocked her back. In her mind, she was eight years old again, standing in a railway station that felt much the same. That day, they transferred her from her hometown to a London County Council Home specializing in preteens committing felonies. The memory, once buried deep inside, surged forward; it felt like yesterday, the shock, the dread, the unknown future, the sight of her foster parents lying in a pool of blood—victims of a kitchen knife attack.

A hand tapped her shoulder. She spun around and slapped it away. When an airport attendant asked her if she required assistance, Wilborn stopped momentarily and then said no.

The corner of Dr. Wilborn's mouth curled up as her black Seward trunk glided around the shiny conveyor system. A police officer meandered through the crowd. Wilborn smiled at the officer, seized the trunk, and wheeled it behind her as the automatic doors swished open. It was scarf weather in England, but with the Texas heat, she immediately wanted to strip off most of her clothes. With the last two years eating mostly cheap carbohydrates, she didn't mind the extra pounds in the cool, wet London weather, but she had a sudden urge to chuck the weight in this climate.

A row of yellow taxis lined up, awaiting fares. The doctor approached the next vehicle, an SUV with its tailgate open and the driver standing by. She signaled towards the backseat. "I don't want it in the boot."

The driver lifted the trunk into the rear of the SUV and lowered the tailgate.

"I said, not the boot. I want it bloody next to me."

"Oh, man. You're English. I never had one of them before. Whatcha say?"

Wilborn rubbed her fingers over her tired eyes and mumbled, "King George should have fought better." She climbed into the back seat.

"Yeah, I like your new king. Did you say, George? Thought his name was something else." The driver closed his door and shifted the transmission. "And I liked that queen, too. She was a nice lady. I mean, I guess she was. She never came around here. Only saw her on the television, but she looked happy most of the time, kinda like me. I'm happy most of the time." He threw a questioning glance from his rearview mirror while trying to decide if the passenger was a feminine male or a masculine female, choosing not to say, sir or ma'am. "Where are we going?"

After several minutes, the vehicle arrived at the hotel under the awning near the automatic doors. The driver continued to talk as Dr. Wilborn was on the verge of bounding from the vehicle and running to a quiet space.

"You sure you want to go here? I mean, it's okay, safe and all, but there's better spots around town. Hell, there's better locations about half a mile from here. Why don't I set you up in a place around the corner? Much better, and the daytime manager is real nice, if ya get my gist." He angled his phone screen toward Wilborn. "I could call her for you?"

Earlier in the day, the passenger on the plane sitting beside Wilborn complained about a place two blocks from his home. He had contacted the police repeatedly, and they did nothing. After they landed, Wilborn changed her 4-star reservation to a two-star hotel close by the drug infested shop. "No. Here is fine."

"Okay. Well, there's a sushi bar nearby and a couple of burger places...oh, man, I gotcha why you wanted here." The driver pointed down the road. "That watering hole, there. That's one of those English kinda pubs. I bet they got good English beers in there. I like Mexican but got to where I drank all day, so I quit. What kinda beer you like?"

"How much?" The heat was exhausting when the doctor swung open the back door and exited the SUV.

As the rear hatch lifted, the driver got out. "Twenty-six bucks." He placed the trunk on the pavement.

The doctor handed him thirty. "Good?"

"Yeah, thanks."

As the taxi drove away, Dr. Wilborn entered the hotel, and a blast of chilled air cut through her. The clattering of small plastic wheels against tile echoed in the empty lobby. A young boy with olive-colored skin, wearing a Polo shirt and jeans, stood silently at the check-in counter and looked intently at a woman dragging baggage behind her. "Mummy!" He finally cried out, and an older woman clad in traditional Middle Eastern attire appeared from the office.

The woman smiled warmly. "Hello. Do you have a reservation?"

"I called thirty minutes ago from the airport." Wilborn laid Michael Smythe's driving licence on the counter.

"How many nights will you be staying with us?"

"Two nights and I pay cash."

"Yes, of course..." the woman glanced at the identification again, "sir. I have a room on the second floor near the elevator. Is that all right with you?"

"No. I don't like crowds. I prefer the first floor in proximity to the rear exit, and I'll pay extra."

"Yes, of course."

Dr. Wilborn stopped at the last room near the rear exit glass door, pressed the handle down, and entered. It was a standard low-rent hotel accommodation, a square dwelling with a bathroom, a decade-old couch set against one wall, and a queen-sized bed with a wooden headboard and footboard against another. A single chair and a desk looked to be from the IKEA bargain bin with a television atop. Instead of a closet, there was a niche with a clothes bar, extra pillows, and blankets on the overhead chrome shelf.

After rolling the trunk near the desk, she stepped to the window and lifted the weighty cotton curtain back a few inches. Sunlight flared into the living area. The scenery was far from desirable—cars and pickup trucks parked between white stripes and a ten-foot, imposing tan-colored metal fence along the property line. She released the drapery, letting it cascade softly into place, drowning the room in shade again.

Kneeling before the trunk, Wilborn unfastened the locks and flipped open the lid with a creak. Inside were neatly packed clothes, shirts, and pants rolled tight and snug together like any experienced traveler would execute—or someone who had been in prison for two years. She mentally checked off several medical items on her list: hemostats, forceps, centrifuge, syringes, and probes, all intact. A square Styrofoam container made a squeaking sound when she removed the top to reveal a partially filled tube of a clear protein extract liquid, but she had to find the second vial somewhere in San Antonio. Dr. McCollum was better at producing the solution and promised to make more while in Louisiana, but alas, DEA Agent Marla Adams took that opportunity away.

After recovering the vial and killing Adams, Wilborn could return to England and prove their discovery could save millions of lives—proof that would be recognized by Queen Mary University of London, with the names of Drs. Hugo Wilborn and Reginald McCollum embedded in its newly founded stem cell research center.

The success rate of the experiments should have been better, but as with any experiment, failures were anticipated, expected, required before discovering the correct procedure. But this time, Wilborn would perfect the technique on a handful of druggies. Nobody cared about them. No one would notice them gone. The outcome of injecting stem cells into the front of the brain would be the anterior cingulate cortex producing not a superhuman but a smarter, more innovative, faster thinking, faster moving human. Fast enough to kill a DEA Special Agent.

Dr. Wilborn began by opening a small plastic case, removing the 1/8 inch drill bit with a distinct white tape marking, and measuring 1 5/8 inches from the tip. Too far, and her patients would be at risk of potential brain damage; too shallow, and the experiment would fail. Wilborn gripped the battery-powered tool she used on Michael Smythe and fastened the bit into the drill. She pulled the trigger and was met with a thunderous whine that filled the room. It had been two years since she'd last performed the procedure on a brain, and tonight she craved to hone her skills.

◆

The alarm in the digital clock sitting on the nightstand rang. Dr. Wilborn woke with the room dark and turned it off. The time display read 9:14 PM, which would be after three in the morning in London. When her Bremont watch slid down her wrist and she stopped it with her other hand, she remembered someone else latching onto her wrist.

Forty years ago, late at night, wearing ragged clothes, young Hugo sat with legs crossed in the center of the living room where she lived. A corgi rested beside her, flat on his stomach and chin down. On the floor, a knife lay inches away, covered with blood. A police officer who had known her since birth slid the weapon off to the side with the toe of his shoe, then crouched next to the preteen girl. The dog didn't move, but looked up at the man.

"Hugo, me young damsel, tell me what happened." He skimmed his hand over the girl's tattered back. "Did James do this to you?"

Hugo winced when she stretched her back with fresh streaks of blood and torn flesh between partially healed wounds. She kept quiet as her dog inched closer.

The officer gently grasped Hugo's wrist. "Your foster parents—what happened?"

After scooting off the bed, Dr. Wilborn moved towards the curtains and tugged an edge back. Overhead lights shone on the parking lot full of vehicles. She caught sight of her own pale reflection in the glass. Studying herself momentarily, she pondered the person who had aged a decade in the last twenty-eight months before releasing the curtain. After gathering items, she locked the trunk and exited the room, quietly closing the door until the latch clicked.

A block away from the hotel, she wandered down the sidewalk while gazing through the windows of the American interpretation of an English pub. "You have no bloody idea what a pub is." She turned at the intersection and waited for the light to change before aiming for the FedEx store that stayed open until 10 PM. It was a straightforward task getting her package of fentanyl and cocaine using Michael Smythe's stolen British Driving Licence. If she cleared the shop, then no one had suspected drugs.

With the box under her arm, she swung open the outside door and waited momentarily for the police to call out Michael Smythe's name. They never did, so she tore into it and stuffed the baggie full of rainbow fentanyl in one pocket and the two vials of cocaine in the other.

Her next stop was a permanently closed convenience store where drug addicts and prostitutes waited for a fix.

Three men and two women loitered near the abandoned building with graffiti painted on the outside. The plate glass windows were missing, and the counter and shelves were chipped and stained from years of leaky ceiling tiles eating away at the drywall. Stagnant air and the smell of piss lingered inside. A streetlight at the corner illuminated the ground as a plane above roared into the blackened sky. The doctor observed the men, with none ideal, but considering the circumstances, expected. One male had several bruises on his face. He would not be a candidate for stem cell injections. Dr. Wilborn had to be precise in the location of the inserted needle, and a swollen brain could result in incorrectly injecting the solution by a few millimeters. The second male looked mid-fifties and sat with legs extended and arms loosely crossed over his abdomen. His head leaned back against the wall and bent to one side. His hair was short, with days old scruff covering his face.

The doctor tapped the man's shoulder. "Hey. Got something for you."

The man never moved.

Dr. Wilborn nudged a little firmer. "Hey. Wake up."

The guy groaned, slid onto his side, and vomited.

"Bloody hell." There were better choices in life for her experiments. The last man, thin and gaunt, in his early twenties, with tousled shoulder-length hair, leaned against the storefront. He wore a Metallica black t-shirt and baggy jeans with cuffs bunching at his shoes. Wilborn studied the man's head. It seemed smaller than average. Would the drill bit marked at 1 5/8 inches, the length to the anterior cingulate cortex, enter too deep? A reduced head size meant a smaller brain.

"Bugger. I've no choice." The doctor approached. "Something to eat? Drink?"

The young man glanced up from a slouching position before dropping his head back down. "No, man. Not hungry." He slapped his forearm at Wilborn. "Got anything?"

The doctor attempted to hide her accent by speaking in short sentences: "Yes, at the hotel."

"Oh, man. No. I don't do that no more." He nodded toward the girl in the sequined red skirt. "See her? She'll do what you want."

"Not that," Wilborn said with a clipped tone. "A restaurant. I'll feed you."

The young man bunched his brow. "You talk funny." His eye caught a glimmer from Wilborn's watch. "Wow, man. Let me have that."

"Maybe another time." The doctor pointed down the street. "The pub. Food and beer."

"You want to feed me? Why?"

Wilborn shrugged. "Humanitarianism."

"No funny shit?"

"Honest."

The young man pushed off the building and staggered forward. Wilborn followed him to the street. As they drifted side by side, the doctor made an effort to sustain the conversation. With no one else around, she didn't care about her accent anymore. "What's your name?"

"I'm Jackie." The soles of his shoes scraped across the asphalt while he closely watched the person beside him remove a small glass vial from a pocket. "What's that?"

Wilborn ignored the question. "How old are you?"

"Twenty-four."

Wilborn mocked him. "You don't look a day over seventeen."

"Whatever you say, man." Jackie continued to stare at Wilborn's hand.

Wilborn held the cocaine vial out toward Jackie. "Hey, want a hit?"

"Sure." Jackie took the glass container, tapped some on the crook of his hand, and snorted it. "Good stuff, man." He held it out toward Wilborn without missing a step.

"No, you keep it." They turned toward the pub parking lot, and the doctor patted her back pants pockets. "Damn. I left my wallet in my room. Wait for me?"

Jackie tapped out the last of the powder and snorted it.

"I have extra in my room. Let me have the vial so I can top it up." She pointed toward the hotel. "I'm going over there to retrieve my money. Come on. I'll give you more."

"I don't do none of that sex stuff."

"No, no. Right. No sex stuff. My room is next to the back door. A quick in and out, then you can have anything on the menu."

Dr. Wilborn opened the door and flipped the light switch. Jackie followed. When the door slowly closed, the latch clicked. "Have a seat on the couch. I'll be right back." Wilborn headed for the bathroom as she pulled the baggie out of her pocket and removed a single white tablet, snapped off a piece, crushed it, and blended it with the cocaine in the second vial. She left the rest of the tablets on the counter, not the least bit concerned Jackie would steal it.

Dr. Wilborn meandered toward the couch and pitched it to him. "Have at it."

He stood while twisting off the cap. "Not much there." Jackie tapped out a mound on the back of his hand. "Looks a little different."

"Really? Different batch, different color, but all yours, go ahead."

Jackie sniffed it up his nose. He let go of the vial and coughed hard. "Oh, man, this is some heavy shit." He plopped down on the couch and fell to his side.

◆

Jackie woke naked on the floor, arms spread out and wrists bound to the sides of the top of the footboard with duct tape. Kneeling with both ankles on the carpet, his legs were taped to the bed frame. Every movement caused a piercing pain through his left hip as a sticky, warm ooze of blood dripped over his leg onto the carpet. Jackie's forehead throbbed unrelentingly. He sensed a liquid seep down his nose and a copper penny taste on his tongue. A blood-tinged sock wedged between his lips muffled any cries for help as panic swept over him.

The television was on with the volume high. A news reporter stood near a homeless shelter and reported about the triple-digit heat and people found inside the stormwater drainage system where the temperature was fifteen to twenty degrees cooler.

Dr. Wilborn reveled in the scene before her. Perched cross-legged opposite the young man as if it were merely an observation of a lab animal. Her British accent was laced with delight. "Don't be afraid. I'm a doctor. The part that would hurt is already completed." She gestured towards Jackie's hip with a sadistic grin. "I drilled a hole into your iliac crest, what the uneducated call a hip bone. Unfortunately, I had to dig deeper than anticipated for your stem cells."

The bed sheet on the floor beside Dr. Wilborn was covered with a horrifying array of medical equipment, from needles and syringes to IV catheters and even a battery-powered drill. Jackie screamed into his gag again, but only raw fear echoed back at him.

"And now we come to your noggin." Leaning in, she tapped his forehead once. "I ran a hole through your skull and into your brain! But first, I had to measure the circumference of your head." She gestured toward a tape measure on the floor. "Your head, almost too small, but in my experience, nothing unusual for a gadabout. I'm sure you will be chuffed to know the procedure went splendidly."

The realization caught Wilborn off guard. She was imitating her foster parents, who abused her both physically and mentally, and Jackie was her when she was a child. She clapped her hands to clear her head before leaning into Jackie's face. "I had to bide my time until you woke. The least you could do is pay attention to what I am saying." Wilborn gestured toward a small vial on the bedsheet. "This is priceless, more than your naff cocaine or fentanyl. I only use a drop of the solution that goes into your brain." She tapped it twice before laying it on the sheet again. "Can you feel anything, something buried deep within?" She reached for Jackie's head, where one end of an IV catheter tube, like the ones nurses used in people's arms, was inserted into the hole of the forehead, and the other end was secured to the skin with tape. "I've tried this on animals, but they couldn't communicate to me." Jackie recoiled when Wilborn handled the catheter tubing, causing the tip to slip out of the head. "You absolutely can't do that." The doctor gripped his patient's jaw, pressing the cheeks close together, then brandished a glinting scalpel mere inches away from Jackie's face. "This is very sharp. I could easily fillet you if I wish. Understand?" When she poked his chest, a muffled scream traveled no further than inside the room. "We are conducting an experiment, and you will hold still." Wilborn pushed the catheter tip back into the hole in Jackie's forehead. "You will not enjoy the consequences of what I will inflict upon you if you squirm and this catheter comes out again."

Jackie shivered while on his knees, naked and bleeding, tied to the bed. His worst fears about being lured into forced sex turned out to be not even close to what happened.

Wilborn saw her patient as applicable but ultimately disposable, a subject of apathy for her rather than another human soul. She paid him the same attention and respect as any other lab animal needed for research purposes. "Are you cold? As soon as the bleeding stops in your hip, I'll throw a sheet over your skinny arse. I didn't really look 'cause I was never interested, but FYI, once I saw that titchy knob of yours, I'll have you know you were in no danger at all." She laid the scalpel beside the drill. "Once you follow my instructions and I have completed this procedure, I'll set you free. Agree?"

Jackie nodded and squeezed his eyes shut.

Dr. Wilborn eased her grip on his jaw. "You might like this. You snort cocaine for gratification. This is no different, except..." She pointed her finger toward herself, "I insert a solution directly into your brain." Jackie sat motionless when the doctor tapped his forehead. "Good man. Don't move." She held a syringe filled with the stem cell mixture and connected it to the catheter. "Remember, you move, you die."

Dr. Wilborn slowly injected the solution through the catheter directly into the patient's brain. Jackie stayed rigid as a stone, sweat dripping down his neck as tears mixed with a drop of blood on his nose. His breaths were short and rapid as an uneasy feeling jolted through his head. "There." She stepped back. "All done. See? Bloody easy, right?"

Jackie opened his eyes and shuddered, lips curled in fear.

"Feel anything?"

Nothing but a groan emanated from Jackie.

The doctor dropped the syringe on the bed sheet and grabbed the scalpel, light glinting across the blade. "You must tell me. Did you feel anything?"

Jackie shook his head rapidly, tears forming a trail down his face.

"Good." She let the scalpel fall onto the bed sheet again. "We have a bit of time. If you participate in my experiment, the least I should do is tell you why. Right?" She continued to explain as if she were lecturing to a group of interested physicians. "I had a partner, Dr. Reginald McCollum, and we developed a way to make body tissue grow fast. After injecting stem cells every six hours, he recreated half a brain in four days. Bloody amazing, right? But that was months ago." The doctor patted Jackie's shoulder. "I understand your worries, but all this will go as planned. While I was in prison—"

Jackie let out a muffled scream through the sock stuffed in his mouth while struggling to free his wrist away from the footboard.

Wilborn grabbed Jackie's neck, forcing him to stare into Wilborn's eyes. "Don't interrupt me when I'm speaking." She let go and continued to explain. Her voice grew darker. "My theory is to allow the protein extract and the transition metal catalyst to sit, concentrate, and become efficacious. Do you know what that means?"

Jackie's reply was nothing but a feeble shake of his head.

Wilborn gestured her hands wide for emphasis. "It enables stem cells to multiply exponentially." She paused before adding an even colder tone. "My new protocol is capable of growing half a brain in two days. I could heal patients stricken with strokes within mere hours, not by injecting them four times a day as my partner did, but every thirty minutes." She pointed at the catheter. "I can enhance the growth of your brain many times faster than Dr. McCollum could." She smiled again and stared straight into Jackie's eyes. "Your brain would grow so fast it would ooze out of your eyes and ears. Like squeezing toothpaste out of a tube." Wilborn brushed her hand over Jackie's hair like petting a dog. "We will repeat this at the top of the hour."

Chapter 6

By eight o'clock the next morning, San Antonio was already moving at a fast pace. Sunlight streaked across windshields as vehicles sped down streets, racing in bumper-to-bumper traffic, their exhaust spewing elixir vitae into the atmosphere. Sparrows perched from suspended electrical wires thirty feet above the ground, watching others alight under concrete overpasses.

Jackie lay naked on his side outside the abandoned convenience store. Hair covered his face, and blood saturated the left hip.

A police vehicle pulled into the lot and stopped feet from the man. Red and blue lights flashed from the roof as the officer climbed out of the driver's seat.

"Hey, bud, where's your clothes? Can't sleep here. Got to move on." The officer gently kicked Jackie's foot. "Hear me? I said get some clothes on and move on." The officer bent down and rolled the man onto his back, with eyes fixed and dilated and a small hole in the center of the forehead.

✦

Marla recently repainted the barn white to forget what red meant—Crosby's blood, but the sun played a cruel game each morning by casting a bloody haze on the walls for a mere moment. She decided not to fight it and chose to believe it was Crosby saying good morning.

After penning the newly purchased cattle in the corral the night before, it was time to brand each one before releasing them to the rest of the herd. Marla and Cassie stood on opposite sides of the cattle crush, the cage that held a cow still while being branded and vaccinated. Three of Marla's heart brands were heating in the outdoor grill fueled with propane. Marla bent the top half of the right fifth finger of the glove back and forth and wished it would grow back.

"Did you get some sleep last night?" Marla asked.

Cassie let the first cow through the shoot and closed the cattle crush. "All night...by myself." She smiled. "Thanks to you."

Smoke poured as Marla held the brand against the cowhide. "I bet you'll survive one night without a man in your bed."

Cassie released the animal and brought in the next. "I'll try not to make a habit of it."

"No word from Roger?"

"Met him at the bar last night, and left again about four in the morning. He texted me. Said he left his money clip beside the bed and wanted me to give it to the bartender. Why the bartender? Whatever, but it's heavy, with an image of Montana on it with first place in the center. Not much cash in it."

"Montana?" Marla slapped the cow on the rump. "He runs the circuit up that far?"

"Not sure. We didn't talk much in my bed...didn't sleep much, either."

After releasing the branded animals out to the herd, they checked the stock tanks, windmills, and mineral feeders. Cassie headed back to her bunkhouse, and Marla returned home. After unsaddling Daisy, the horse trotted next to Blackie, lingering in the corral. Breakfast for her was four hard-working hours before the sun came up. Before feeding the chickens, Marla ensured the two horses had enough hay and water.

After a well-deserved hot shower, she perched herself on the porch with a glass of iced tea and finished an apple from Antone's Orchard on the other side of the county. A faint smile crossed her face as she gazed at the phone's background photo of her and Crosby on their wedding day, with his tuxedo clinging tightly to his muscular frame while her white gown hugged every curve of her body. Beaming with joy, a vivid reminder of how much they loved each other.

Her phone rang, startling her and causing her to drop it and clunk onto the wooden porch. Leaning over, she was surprised by the name BOSS on the screen. Assistant Special Agent in Charge Ronald Borland was calling her. She wondered why he would call while she continued on medical leave. She picked it up and answered.

"Hello?"

"Adams, this is ASAC Borland."

"Yes, sir. I recognized the number on my phone."

"Not asking you to come in, but we have a case concerning you."

"Excuse me, sir?" She stood, still holding the glass and wrapping her arm around the post near the steps. "What do you mean, concerning me?"

"We have a body that OD'd on fentanyl."

"Why is that a concern for me, sir?"

"The victim has a hole in the forehead where someone injected stem cells."

Marla threw the phone on the ground and dropped onto her butt. The glass bounced on the wooden porch, spilling ice and tea over her. He's dead. They're dead. Dr. McCollum, Bird, Wales. They're all dead. I saw them all.

She stood again and yelled out to no one, "I know damn well every one of you are dead!" Rushing down the steps and picking up the phone, she swallowed hard before continuing, "Where the hell is this body? I want to see for myself."

"The Bexar County Medical Examiner, your good friend, Dr. Berghoff, personally called me. He believes there is a connection and wants you to investigate."

"When?"

"He said you have his cell number and to call him anytime, day or night."

Marla stepped up to the porch and collapsed in the chair. "Sir, I have a hundred head of cattle. I can't pick up and leave."

"Right. I've already thought of that. I'll make a deal with you. If your ranch hand, Cassandra Chandler, and her boyfriend, Roger Hagen, will manage your cattle, freeing you up, they'll be considered off-limits."

Marla raised an eyebrow. "Roger skipped town, and how do you know their names?" She extended her hand upwards. "Dumb question, sir. DEA and FBI have information on everyone. You are assuming I will take this on?"

"I have enough evidence to put both of them in jail. It's up to you. I'm faxing you a redacted report from an undercover agent."

"Sounds a little like coercion."

"I have no idea what you are talking about. All I have done is request one of my employees to help me in a sticky situation. Marla, all kidding aside...."

"This is your attempt at kidding, sir?"

"Dr. Berghoff specifically asked for you, no one else."

With her hand stretched across her forehead, Marla squeezed her thumb and index finger against her temples. "I'll give him a call."

"Thank you. This is all yours, Adams. You head it up, run it, and form the team you want."

Before Marla could respond, the phone line disconnected. Marla called Cassie's phone, but it immediately went to voicemail each time. Inwardly, she groaned. "Damn it." She phoned again and left a message. "Cassie, you need to answer now. Call me back."

Marla waited half a minute and called again. Cassie's phone went to voicemail. "Call me now! It's urgent!"

She waited thirty seconds and called again.

"What?" Cassie sounded out of breath.

There was a rhythmic squeaking coming from the phone. "Where are you?" Marla asked.

Cassie straddled Roger in her bed. The only thing he wore was a smile and his ball cap. His hands slid across her breasts as she held the phone to her ear. "I'm in my bed, riding Roger."

"Thought you said he left town."

"He came back."

Marla heard a man's voice in the background calling, "Come on, a little longer." Oh, jeez. I'm acting like an old biddy. "Dismount Roger Hagen, and both of you get your butts over here."

The squeaking stopped. "I never told you his last name."

"My boss told me."

"Your boss, as in...the DEA boss?"

"Right. Get your clothes on and be here in fifteen unless the two of you want to go to jail."

Twelve minutes later, Marla leaned firmly against the porch column with her arms crossed as Roger's pickup rode over the cattle guard. The tires slid across the gravel driveway to a stop. As the two stepped out, Marla noticed he wore a brown leather holster clipped to his belt with a revolver inside. She left the front door open and entered the house.

"I knew you were nothing but trouble," Cassie told Roger.

"You didn't have to go with me, but you like your nose stuck in every-thing," Roger said.

Cassie side-kicked Roger's butt. "I have a respectable job and don't want to lose it. Why don't you get back in your truck and head out to wherever you were yesterday?"

"That's a damn good idea. Maybe the best damn thing you've ever said to me."

When he pivoted toward the truck, Cassie kicked him harder in the butt. He spun around and swung his fist at her head, which she ducked like a professional boxer, then slammed her fist into his abdomen.

"Hey. Both of you!" Marla said. They both turned back as she stood steadfast in the doorway. "Get in here. I'm not messing around," Marla said before disappearing inside again.

Roger patted Cassie's butt. She spun around and shoved him backward. He smiled at her. "Let's go back and rip each other's clothes off...and forget about this."

She returned a smile. "You tempt me, and I will make you suffer."

They shuffled toward the house as he wrapped his arm around her neck, and she extended her hand behind his back and stuck her thumb in his belt loop.

Marla heard boots clomping into the entryway. "Back here."

When Cassie and Roger entered, Marla stood at one end of the kitchen counter and pointed to the other end. "In here. Both of you."

Roger took his cap off and held out his hand. "Good morning, Mrs. Adams." He felt her firm grip when they shook, but said nothing about her deformed little finger, and neither did Marla. "I need to get back to my work at the Johnson ranch. He has some equipment that needs to be repaired. That old tractor of his always needs something fixed."

"Roger, it's the law enforcement in me. Slip the revolver out and place it on the counter, please. I have a strong aversion to armed people near me whom I'm unfamiliar with."

"Um, sure, Mrs. Adams." He unholstered the gun, landing it heavily on the counter.

"Thanks." Marla glanced at the holster with a fancy leather carving of the letters RH on the side and then the revolver. "Is that a Ruger Vaquero .357?"

"Yes, ma'am."

"Nice revolver, expensive."

"Bought it from a friend who needed some cash. I won a competition at the rodeo and had enough."

"We'll talk about that in a sec," Marla said before grasping Cassie's shoulder. "I have a favor to ask, and you won't say no."

Roger interrupted, "Is this a girl thing? I can leave." He reached for his revolver.

"No. Stay right there." Marla raised her eyebrow. "I need some help, myself."

"Listen, I have things to do." He reached for his gun again. "I'm out."

Marla slapped her hand down on the weapon before picking up a piece of paper and reading part of Borland's report. "You, Roger Hagen, DOB eleven-eleven-two thousand one, born in Topeka, Kansas, dropped out of community college after a single semester, then disappeared without a trace for three years before showing up in Hildebrandt, will shut up and sit quietly. If you interrupt me again, I'll cuff you and throw your ass in a cell. Got it?"

He nodded as he stood beside Cassie. "How do you know all that?"

Marla slid the weapon closer to her. "My boss, ASAC Borland, told me. He wants me back at work, and I want you both to watch the herd while I'm gone."

"What's an ASAC?" Cassie asked.

"Assistant Special Agent in Charge."

"I already have a job," Roger said.

"Mr. Johnson said he hired you a month or so ago, but you left last week," Marla said. "Where did you go?"

"I, uh, I decided to hit the road and the rodeo circuit."

"You haven't been on the circuit for a long time." Marla waved the paper at him. "Don't forget, I work for the DEA, and the Feds know everything about everybody, and you have not registered at any city or state rodeo in years. Where have you been?"

"Around. Small places. It doesn't make any difference. Mr. Johnson asked me to come back, so I did."

"But you said you came back because of me," Cassie said.

"He came back for something else." Marla glared at him, then flipped over papers freshly printed from Borland's email. "Roger Hagen, you bought four ounces of cocaine six days ago from a guy named Jiggy. Four ounces? That's costly on cowboy wages. But three days ago, you made almost twice that amount when you sold an ounce at a time to four people, but unfortunately for you, one was an undercover agent."

Roger moved for his knife hanging on the side of his belt. Marla beat him to it by drawing her pistol before he got it out of the sleeve.

"What are you doing?" Cassie shoved Roger's shoulder. "She's a fast draw champion."

"You are testing my patience, mister," Marla said. "Slip that knife out and gently slide it down the counter."

He did what she said. "What's your deal, lady?"

Marla holstered her pistol and swept the knife off the counter to the floor next to her boot. "My boss said he would bury your recent transactions, but you must stay here and stay clean." She laid eyes on Cassie. "And you? You are not the Princess of Nottingham. You were sitting in the passenger seat during each of his dealings. That makes you an accessory. For a woman who likes the feel of men, you are going to look awfully tense and stupid in a women's penitentiary."

"I didn't know what he was doing. I was just sitting...ignorant of what was going on."

"Bullshit." Roger shifted backward. "You handed me the baggies from the glove compartment, took the money I gave you, and hid it inside the console compartment. You knew exactly what I...we were doing."

"Marla," Cassie said. "I like this job, and I want to stay. I'll do whatever you tell me." She gave Roger the once over. "And dickwad here will do the same."

"You'll drop the charges?" Roger asked.

"There are no charges. This evidence has not been sent to the police or the district attorney...yet."

"What keeps you from bringing it up later?" Roger asked.

"If Borland says something, it's done, so it will be forever six feet underground if you do what you are told."

"Where am I staying?" Roger asked. "Mr. Johnson let me sleep in a room in the barn. If I leave, I'd have to live in my truck."

Marla shrugged. "Move in with Cassie."

"Hell no!" Cassie blurted. "He will not. I don't want him in my bed every night. Maybe some night I want a different guy?" She pivoted away. "And come morning, his ass is out of my house. I don't want no man anywhere near my stuff, or his food in my fridge, or his clothes in my washer. For all I care, he can buy a tent and sleep out in the pasture."

"I ain't got enough money to purchase a tent or anything. I buy Lone Star beer 'cause it's cheap. It's a buck at The Broken Saddle Horn. I sold those drugs so I could buy gas."

Marla shuffled the papers together. "Cassie, you stay with me, and Roger stays at the bunkhouse."

"Whoa, whoa, wait." Cassie stiff-armed Roger's chest. "You gave that place to me. I'm there. I like it. It's cozy, fits me."

"No!" Marla snapped back. "Jail time or watch the herd. Take your pick. Here's the thing, I have a camera in every room and a dozen outside the house." Marla pointed straight at Roger. "You stay out of my house and out of my bedrooms, or I guarantee you will be sent up for the max—ten years. Got it?"

Neither moved, like two middle school kids frozen in place as the principal laid down the law.

"Cassie, get your stuff and move into the second bedroom. You're my new roommate."

Chapter 7

The summer drought had been brutal for everyone in San Antonio. Dr. Wilborn wiped beads of sweat off her forehead. She had not sweated this much in her entire life. She needed to find a cheaper hotel closer to downtown near Central Library, one lined with people begging for donations.

The taxi stopped at a traffic light under an overpass as vehicles rhythmically clunked above like a bass drum keeping 4/4 time. Dr. Wilborn looked out the window at the Bluebird Motel, a single story, U-shaped building painted white on the bottom and navy blue on top. Aside from one vehicle, the parking lot was empty, which she guessed must belong to the front desk employee. A restaurant flourished on the opposite side of the street, with patrons sitting in booths next to plate glass windows as expansive as buses. A single waitress inside strode down the aisle with full dinner plates balanced on her left arm while holding a water pitcher with her right. Weather-beaten plywood covered the doors and windows of neglected one story buildings on each side of the restaurant. Wilborn motioned the driver to pull over.

The doctor reached the motel's front desk and laid Michael Smythe's credit card on the counter. Moments later, she stepped out holding a key chained to a diamond-shaped plastic tag with the hotel name emblazoned on both sides and wheeled the Seward trunk behind her until reaching the room. After unlocking the door and shoving it open with her shoulder, the air was heavy with mildew. The generic interior looked like the last place she stayed. She entered and adjusted the thermostat to sixty-eight degrees before venturing outside.

After locking the door, she made her way across the street to the restaurant, expecting the food to be dreadful. A waitress with a menu in one hand and silverware rolled up in a napkin in the other led the doctor to a booth.

"Big watch. Looks expensive. What would you like to drink, dear?"

Wilborn covered her hand over the watch. "Tea, please."

"Sweet or unsweet?"

"What?"

"Sweet or unsweet?"

"I don't understand what you're asking. I will stir the sugar in it myself. And bring milk."

"Milk? A glass of milk and tea? Want lemon with it?"

Wilborn rolled her eyes. "For Pete's sake. What is wrong with you people?"

The waitress returned with a glass each of iced tea and milk. "Have you decided on what to eat?"

"Jesus, bloody hell." She pushed the two glasses to the other side of the table. "I want a cup of hot tea, not this fretfully cold thing." She sized up her limited choices. "Do you have any English tea?"

"We have Lipton. One pot has sugar already mixed inside, and the other doesn't."

Wilborn rubbed her fingers over her tightly closed eyelids. "Forget it, just water...without ice. Do you have scones?"

"Scones? Hmm, no. We have sandwiches, ham and cheese, grilled cheese, and a turkey, ham, and cheese club."

"Do you serve breakfast? Eggs and bangers...sausage?"

"Sure."

"Okay then, I'll take two fried eggs, link sausage, and toast. Have you orange marmalade?"

"We have grape and strawberry jelly."

Wilborn wiggled back in the booth. "Any butter?"

"We have little squares of margarine in the fridge. Not too many people ask for them. They might be old."

Dr. Wilborn swept her fingers through her hair, curtly responding, "I'll choose the little squares."

The waitress wrote the order on her pad. "All right, be back in a bit."

From inside the restaurant, Dr. Wilborn peered out the window to observe a disheveled man in frayed clothes pushing a grocery cart full of aluminum cans along the sidewalk. The bottom of a knee-length overcoat flapped behind him as a car zoomed past. She wondered how anyone could wear a coat in this heat. Half a block past the hotel, the man abruptly turned and disappeared behind a wooden fence.

The doctor pushed the fork and knife to the side, bumping against the ketchup bottle and knocking it over, pouring the red liquid across the utensils. Her childhood flashed back when she wiped the red liquid off the knife.

At the tender age of eight, in London, Hugo sat in solemn silence inside the Crown Court with a judge roosting behind a gigantic desk while listening intently to two men arguing harshly over her fate. All three wore white wigs and black gowns. She understood nothing.

Exhibit A was a knife with blood partially wiped off the blade and Hugo's fingerprints on the handle. With both foster parents stabbed to death and her not uttering a word since being arrested, the prosecution barrister demanded a verdict of murder. The defence barrister asked the judge to dismiss all charges due to intentional infliction of emotional stress and self-defense.

Hugo wore a bland black dress and remained hushed on a cherry-stained wooden chair. With her forearms resting on a wooden table and slender fingers pushing a pencil back and forth, she made it a game, rolling the yellow hexagon instrument one complete turn, then two, then three. Anything to keep from picturing her foster father lying lifeless on the floor with his neck slashed and blood flowing out until the heart stopped. The foster mother, dead also, splayed on her side with multiple stab wounds in the stomach and chest.

Meanwhile, Clarise, her six-year-old sister kept still in the public gallery wearing a flower print dress, white eyelet socks pulled to her ankles, and black shoes, all recently bought by the defence barrister, the first she had ever owned.

Hugo glanced over her shoulder one last time at Clarise, who stared back in disbelief as they heard the word manslaughter declared by the judge. Within minutes, they whisked the convicted juvenile away.

There was a scraping sound of a plate across the table, startling Dr. Wilborn, and she shifted her gaze away from the window.

"Here you go, sweetie," the waitress said with a smile. "Enjoy."

Wilborn didn't realize how famished she was until she tasted the first bite.

Moments later, the waitress smiled again and cleared away the empty plate. "Might as well drink the milk." She placed the ticket upside down on the table. "You ordered it."

The dingy clothed man reappeared empty-handed without the cart, slogging along with a slight limp toward the hotel. Wilborn studied the uneven gait and concluded the man had torn a knee ligament, the meniscus, or both. Either way, it told her he couldn't run if he had to.

Wilborn slid out of the booth, dropped a twenty dollar bill on the table, and rushed out the front door toward the intersection. The man across the street had already passed the hotel.

Dr. Wilborn raised her hand. "Hey! You over there." She crossed the road and hustled down the sidewalk.

The man stopped and faced her direction, a black knit skull cap partially covered peppered gray hair down to his shoulders, a shaggy beard mixed into the facial hair, and ragged clothes not seen in a washing machine in weeks. "I ain't got nothing. No money. Nothing. Leave me alone."

The doctor smiled. "No, nothing like that. I want to help." She pulled a twenty dollar bill from her pocket. "Here. For your troubles."

The man took it, studied the bill, then the doctor's eyes, and then turned his attention back toward the bill. He smiled. "Thank you, sir. Thank you."

Wilborn fabricated a quick story. "Listen, I understand it's late, and my husband left me, so I'm staying at this motel. I have a six pack of beer in my room. Want to drink one with me?"

"You got a funny way of talking."

"Right. I'm from somewhere else. Fancy a beer?"

"I like a beer really cold."

Dr. Wilborn scrunched her nose, trying to hide her annoyance. Stupid Americans. They want ice in their beer. "Okay, cold. Probably six or seven degrees."

"Six degrees? That'd be frozen."

The doctor chuckled. "No. Six degrees Celsius. That's, uh, forty-four degrees Fahrenheit."

"Oh. Yeah. That's cold enough."

"We could drink them outside the room if that makes you feel comfortable. You don't have to go inside. I'm, uh, I'm wanting someone to talk to."

"What kind a beer is it?"

The doctor was getting agitated. "What kind do you like?"

He shook his head. "Most any kind, I guess."

"Well, that's exactly what I have. Tell you what…" She pulled out another twenty dollar bill and held it between her fingers—a further enticement to pluck an offer of companionship. "What's your name?"

"Everyone calls me Curvy." He stuck the money in his pocket. "Just one beer?"

"That's all. You can head on your way after one. As I said, I don't like drinking by myself." The doctor patted the scruffy man on the back and nudged him toward the motel. "Why do they call you Curvy?"

"I used to pitch the best curveball in the Majors." He shrugged. "Twenty something years ago; not as good now, but I can still throw one right over the plate."

Wilborn smiled half-heartedly. "All right, Curvy. Let's go."

Moments later, Dr. Wilborn inserted the key into the lock and nudged the door ajar. The lights were off inside the room. "Would you hold the door for me? I'll get the beer from the refrigerator."

Curvy placed one foot past the threshold and held the door open with a hand. Wilborn latched onto the man's shirt collar and pulled him inside the room.

◆

Curvy opened his eyes, taking in the dreary surroundings. A clock sitting on the nightstand ticked every second. His sunless body was clammy and pale while lying on his right side on a lumpy mattress wearing only blood-stained underwear and mismatched socks, hands secured with duct tape and tied to the headboard while the ankles were bound to the footboard. A partially filled 5cc syringe was connected to an intravenous port in the left forearm. Wilborn carelessly threw the man's pants and shirt in the corner of the room.

When Curvy twisted his wrists and ankles to break free, a pain shot from his hip to his knee, causing him to jerk back. "Hey, man. Let me go. I ain't got nothing to give you."

Dr. Wilborn squatted on the floor, legs crossed, while holding a scalpel firmly in her right hand. "You are the luckiest man in this stupid town."

She pointed at the man's bloody left hip. "Don't worry about that. It will heal very quickly."

"Hey, man. I'm going to yell. You need to let me go."

"Not likely." The doctor chuckled, then walked around the bed and jabbed the man's chest with the scalpel tip.

Curvy squirmed and yelled, "Ow! Shit, man. That hurt."

"Then you bloody well stay quiet." She aimed the scalpel tip beneath the man's eye. "Yell, and I will slice you like breakfast bangers." Wilborn poked Curvy's chest again.

"Shit, son of a bitch. Stop it. That God damn hurts. I want my clothes back."

Dr. Wilborn lifted the thin cotton blanket off the chair and draped it over Curvy's body. "How's that? Best I can offer for now." Before Curvy said anything, the doctor spoke again. "This is an essential operation. It requires a skilled surgeon with expert hands and a well-trained mind. I can transform the world and make all wounds temporary, with broken bones healing in mere hours, repair and regenerate a damaged heart or brain, and you will be very much a part of this experiment. Understand? It would be most advantageous if you cooperated fully. Trust me, and I shall execute what is necessary to help you."

"Fuck off, asshole. I don't need none of your fucking help." Curvy wiggled back and forth and tried kicking the blanket away. "Let me out of here." He tried to pull himself up to a sitting position, but his hands were still tied to the headboard.

Dr. Wilborn shoved her hand against Curvy's head and pushed him back down on his side, then leaned down and whispered. "I am in need of a participant for my experiment, and you are fortunate enough to be selected by me." The doctor stood straight. "One hundred dollars to you after all this is done."

"I don't want your shit money. I want out of here."

"Here is the best part," Dr. Wilborn said. "That syringe taped to your arm is connected to an IV line with a solution mixed with fentanyl. I inject it, and you have grand dreams. You wake up, and we will do it again, as often as you desire."

Curvy moved his arm. "No way am I doing that. That shit kills people!"

Wilborn leaned toward Curvy's face. "Don't you worry. I know exactly how much to administer to create wonderful dreams for you."

Curvy twisted his neck, trying to nudge the syringe away with his chin. He helplessly watched the doctor grasp his arm and ease the solution into his vein. His body felt limp while sinking into a relaxed state, while colorful flashes of light burst into his mind.

◆

Curvy heard water flow from a faucet nearby as he lay tied to the bed, with his body contorted in an open jumping jack pose and a makeshift gag in his mouth. His underwear reeked of urine. Too tired to move, he stared at a light flickering on the ceiling from the television on the dresser.

Dr. Wilborn emerged from the bathroom, drying her hands on a towel. "The operation went smashingly. Your stem cells are in your brain, growing, expanding." She pitched the towel in the air, and it dropped near the television. "I didn't quite reason this through. If I perform an injection every thirty minutes, when shall I sleep? Let's hope you will prove my theory is true very soon. Be a good egg. If you lay there for five minutes, I will inject the fentanyl before the stem cells."

When Curvy felt the syringe against his forearm, he remembered snorting cocaine a couple of times, but the fentanyl injection was the most intense sensation he had ever encountered in his entire life—better than his first strikeout in major league baseball. He wasn't sure if he wanted to stop the doctor.

Chapter 8

The sight of the County Medical Examiner's office building caused Marla's stomach to twist in knots, reminding her of the hometown murders that drove her to leave the Hildebrandt PD and join the DEA. She happily swapped out her manure-encrusted cowboy boots for federally mandated black shoes. Stopping at the rear entrance, Marla typed in the passcode Dr. Berghoff had given her months before, and the red light changed to green, giving her access. When she opened the door, rubbing alcohol, cleaning fluids, and air fresheners attempted to cover death. Vivid memories of Crosby surged back into her mind, forcing her to recall his murder and the autopsy conducted here. She asked Dr. Berghoff to recuse himself and let another forensic pathologist perform it because she knew she would never be able to look him in the eye ever again.

Her rubber soles squeaked with each step on the polished linoleum floor. A bevy of employees crossed the hallways, moving body parts from one place to the next. Some people recognized her, including an autopsy technician who waved with the fifth finger bent in reference to Marla's missing finger. She smiled, and then, like a punch in the stomach, would the tech remember her hand when she was supine on the cold steel table? When Marla entered the autopsy room, a shiver crawled up her spine, wondering which table Crosby's body had laid on and which ones once held her brother and sister-in-law.

A tinny sound of I Feel Good by James Brown played from the overhead speakers, an irony not lost in the medical field. When Marla arrived, Dr. Berghoff moved away from a body and discarded his gloves before waving his hand high in the air as if he were a magician finishing a trick.

"Officer Adams, it's nice to see you."

They shook hands, hers dwarfed by his. He remembered her missing finger and all it meant, what she left behind, and what she had escaped.

She gave him a faint smile, even though the presence of so much death weighed heavy on her shoulders. "Please, if you are going to make me come here often, then call me Marla."

"Marla, yes, thank you. My friends call me B."

"B?"

He shrugged. "Never quite took to my first name, Osgood. Kids called me Ozzy. Nowadays, when people think of Ozzy, they see biting bats and hear the song, Crazy Train in their head."

It was the first time she ever laughed in the autopsy room. "And what does your wife call you?"

"A great many four letter words when she's mad at me."

She chuckled and nodded in agreement. "B it is." Marla raised her hand like she was asked a question. "What do you have for me?"

"Agent Borland phoned me an hour ago and said you were coming in. I remembered you didn't like to see a body being removed from the refrigerator, so I asked one of my technicians to place it on a table over there."

"Thanks. I appreciate that."

They approached the table, where a fluorescent light hummed above them.

"Do you want the full view?" he asked.

"B, if I may. I'm not enthusiastic about viewing dead bodies on a silver platter. Let's just do what is absolutely necessary."

"Silver platter? Nice. Mind if I use that?"

She smiled and shrugged one shoulder. "All yours."

Dr. Berghoff pulled two gloves out of a box and slipped them on. "They found the body at an abandoned convenience store. Police ID'd the man through his fingerprints. His name was Jackie Samuel Binion. No bullet wounds or lacerations. Tox report is ending, but it's likely to be positive for drugs. With cardiovascular, pulmonary, and renal damage for a person only in his twenties, I suspect at least a decade of heavy drug use."

"My boss mentioned stem cells."

"Correct. Ready?"

Marla took a deep breath before exhaling. "Ready."

He lifted the sheet off the left hip to reveal a singular opening surrounded by shredded skin and exposed muscle. "My determination is someone drilled a hole into the iliac crest to extract bone marrow, the spongy substance containing stem cells. There are two entries into the bone, but only one into the skin. Whoever did this hit the first spot with little marrow, so he pivoted the drill bit further to the side without pulling it completely out and drilling another hole into the bone."

Marla felt sweat building in her armpits. "Okay, okay." She swept hair from her face. "You mean something similar to what Dr. McCollum did with my husband?"

"Very similar, except with your husband, he had two clean holes in the hip."

"Yes, he," her toes cramped inside her black shoes, "I rolled Crosby on his side and held him still while Dr. McCollum removed the stem cells. There were...were two holes. We did it twice."

"Dr. McCollum used a specialized medical instrument to remove the marrow on your husband. His procedures were professional. This..." He pointed at the purple and blue bruising with dried blood splattered over the skin, "... was brutal. Painful."

Marla wasn't sure what to say next. "Okay." She wanted desperately to hold or be held by Crosby just once more. "Do you know why this person did this?"

"To a point, I do." Dr. Berghoff covered the hip with the sheet before uncovering the face. "I removed the brain for analysis."

Marla closed her eyes. She had done this before; bodies in the morgue. The first time—was terrible; the second time, it was not as hard, but it was still not easy. She opened her eyes again. The scalp had been sewn with thick string to hold the skull cap in place, giving it a freakish Frankenstein look, and there was something odd on the forehead. "What's this?"

"This," Dr. Berghoff touched the forehead, "I have never seen before. There is a small hole in the forehead."

"Why?"

"Someone drilled a hole through the bone and into the brain with a smaller diameter bit than the one used on the iliac bone, an eighth inch in size. A cleaner procedure than the hip. After examining the brain, I determined the hole in the midline of the forehead correlates to hemorrhaging in the periphery of the frontal lobe and into the anterior cingulate cortex."

Marla furrowed her brow. "You lost me, B."

He held his hands out like he was holding an imaginary ball. "Imagine an orange, and someone pushed a nail through the rind and into the endocarp, the juice sac." He pointed at the corpse's forehead. "This is where the stem cells from the hip were injected." He touched the small hole. "I can tell you there were three injections with a mixture of stem cells, protein concentrate, and a unique metal compound similar to what your husband had in his brain. Whoever performed this procedure did so blindly, meaning without using a radiology-guided imaging device, and because of that, was unlucky."

"Unlucky? Why?"

"The three pockets of fluid were injected millimeters apart from one another, with one injection puncturing an artery and causing extensive bleeding, thereby inducing increased intracranial pressure on the brain and likely the cause of death."

Marla's fingers squeezed her temples. "Okay, why? Why in the hell would anyone do this?"

Dr. Berghoff pulled the sheet over the corpse's face before peeling off the latex gloves and dropping them in a nearby bin. "To access the precise point in the brain where decision making, pain management, awareness, anticipation, and error detection occur. That area is called the anterior cingulate cortex, which performs all those functions."

"You're losing me again, B. Whoever is doing this has to be crazy, right?"

"Probably, but I also see the potential for making this helpful in a legitimate setting with rational research boundaries."

Marla swung her arms out. "But this is neither. This person is a killer, a modern day Dr. Moreau, if you will, and must be stopped. But what could be the reason for doing such a thing?"

"This is speculative, but I believe I see what this person is doing. Someone with medical experience could be stumbling through these trials...these forced experiments, trying to perfect a smarter person if they don't kill all the human lab rats first."

"How can you tell it was forced?""

Dr. Berghoff pulled the sheet back, revealing the wrists and ankles. "There is adhesive stuck to the skin. This person was not a willing participant. He was shackled with tape."

The room felt like it was shrinking. Her feet shuffled a bit. "Still not getting why someone is doing this."

Dr. Berghoff laid his hand on Marla's shoulder. "It would take a highly educated person to copycat the stem cell injections your husband had, so that is not happening. And because of that, I believe the person performing all this must be a doctor, and for some reason, wants a smarter, faster person." He looked around before continuing. "In my opinion, someone somehow connected to Dr. McCollum, who performed the stem cell injections on your husband, is here for a reason. Marla? You are the only living person remotely connected to everything that has happened. Be careful. This person—this doctor may be coming after you."

◆

Marla closed the door to the pickup truck and pushed the ignition button. She squinted from the sun's glare through the windshield. Sexual Healing blared from the radio until she quickly turned it off, then shifted the transmission to drive and left the lot. When she merged onto Loop 410, she tapped the phone speed dial button on the dashboard screen.

"Hello," ASAC Borland said.

"Marla Adams, sir. You're right. Something's up. Dr. Berghoff is waiting for the tox report, but there's more."

"What about the stem cells he mentioned to me?"

Marla's throat tightened. She coughed to clear it. "Yes. Stem cells were utilized. This is a murder case. It should go to the city cops."

"Adams," Borland asked, "were they used like on your husband?"

She cleared her throat again. "Similar. The guy who did this took bone marrow from the hip and injected stem cells into the brain."

"Sounds exactly like your husband."

"Not quite, sir. Someone is not repairing a brain. They're messing with a fully functional one."

Chapter 9

Curvy's head lolled to the side like a child's doll. His eyes were half open and unfocused. Greasy strands of gray hair clung to the sides of his face. A thin cotton bath towel lay across his groin and upper thighs, hiding a pool of dark blood seeping into the bed covers. His left hip throbbed as he caught sight of a patch of red on the towel. The corners of his lips twitched, and goosebumps rose like weeds on his arms as fentanyl coursed through his veins. His thinned skin was covered in old scrapes and bruises, slowly wasting from years of drugs, unhealthy food, and sleeping on the ground or beneath overpasses. His parched lips mumbled, "Gotta piss, man."

Dr. Wilborn rolled her eyes. "You already pissed when I injected the fentanyl. I threw your filthy underwear in the trash." Dr. Wilborn wore blue surgical gloves and had one knee on the bed. She carefully administered the stem cell solution through the IV catheter lodged in Curvy's forehead.

"My head feels weird."

"I'm injecting medicine into your brain. It will bring you happiness." After the injection was complete and removing the syringe, Wilborn pushed back from the bed. "But this is the fourth one, and I should have seen a divergence by now."

Curvy crooked toward the voice and squeezed his eyelids tighter, trying to make the room stop spinning. "I gotta go, man."

"You're not going anywhere."

"I mean, I got to go to the bathroom."

The doctor pocketed the syringe. "You already pissed." She stood, went to the bathroom, returned, and laid another bath towel over Curvy's groin. "Go ahead and piss again."

Curvy half opened his eyes. "Let me go, man," he muttered.

The doctor scoffed. "Don't be daft. I can't untie you. No biggie, just piss on the towels."

Curvy opened his eyes wide and yelled, "Come on, man! I need to do the other."

The doctor stepped back. "Blimey. Why didn't you say that earlier? Yeah, okay." She cut the tape from one foot. "Don't go trying to kick me or escape. I found this revolver in your backpack." Wilborn held it up for Curvy to see. "What is it with all you Yanks and your shooters?"

"Why do you give a rat's ass? Hurry up. I gotta go. Cut the tape off my wrists."

Dr. Wilborn pushed the motel wastebasket closer to the bed. "I'm leaving one foot taped to the bed. You can defecate in this."

The doctor pressed the gun barrel against Curvy's ear as she cut the tape from one of his hands. "Leave what's on your head and arm alone. If you try to pull them out, I'll kill you right here."

When Wilborn cut through the tape around Curvy's second hand, he quickly sat up while rubbing his wrists. He reached toward the wastebasket and sighed. "I can't get it. Push it closer to me."

When the doctor leaned forward and nudged the basket closer, Curvy clasped his hands together and slammed them down on Wilborn's neck. The gun dropped from her grip and slid beneath the bed as Curvy lunged for the doctor. Wilborn kicked and scooted backward.

"I'm gonna kill you!" Curvy kicked the bed, trying to rip the tape off his foot. "Come here, asshole."

Wilborn scrambled to her trunk and grabbed the long screwdriver lifted from the pawnbroker's shop. She charged toward the bed, swinging the tool wildly in the air. "Get back down!"

With Curvy still bound to the bed, Wilborn pierced the tool deep into the leg. Curvy screamed as blood spewed across the sheets and splattered across Wilborn's face and neck. Curvy grasped the back of Wilborn's shirt, but his hand slipped away. With a desperate burst of energy, he broke free from the rope and kicked wildly at Wilborn, narrowly avoiding the screwdriver again as it pierced deep into the mattress. Standing naked, blood covering his hip and leg, with one last desperate effort, Curvy yanked the alarm clock off the nightstand and hurled it towards Wilborn with ferocious force, crashing it against her head and crumpling her to the floor. Curvy ripped out the two catheters and pitched them toward the doctor in defiance. He fled out the door, with blood pouring from his wounds and leaving a trail of red behind.

Wilborn regained her composure, rose to her feet, and wiped the blood off the screwdriver with the bed sheet. It was a failed experiment. She reached under the bed and retrieved the pistol, then methodically packed the equipment and drugs into her Seward trunk and locked it before hastily wiping the place clean of fingerprints. Opening the door, she looked both ways for any witnesses. Drops of blood trailed down the concrete walkway past a string of rooms. Dr. Wilborn dragged the trunk out of the room and headed in the opposite direction. With a final thud, the door slammed shut, leaving the carnage of crimson-drenched bedding and a broken alarm clock on the floor.

❖

The word BOSS appearing on her phone screen surprised Marla. They spoke only a few minutes ago after she left the medical examiner's office.

"Yes, sir."

"Adams. We may have a lead. Captain Helmsley from the SAPD called me, and they have someone named Dino Morelli in a room at the University Hospital. He can identify an individual who assaulted him using blood from his hip and injecting drugs in his head. The perp also stabbed him in the leg, but he should recover from that."

"I'm on my way. Text me the room number, sir, and a little bit about the man if you have anything."

"Adams, have you assembled your team?"

Marla scooted back against the seat. "No, sir. Not yet."

"I'm appointing Special Agent Angelo Rivera to the case. He will meet you at the hospital."

She fidgeted. This was personal, and she wanted to take care of it herself. "Yes, sir. I appreciate your help."

After parking in the visitor's lot and walking what seemed like a mile to the building, the automatic doors ceremoniously slid open, and cool air enveloped her. An empty reception desk stood to the left in the lobby. On the wall were graphic images of the hospital departments, Surgery, Emergency, Obstetrics, Pediatrics, Transplant, and Endocrinology. She skimmed through the lobby for Special Agent Rivera, but he hadn't arrived.

An elderly voice poured out from behind Marla. "Hello? Can I help you?"

She spun around to find a senior citizen sitting behind a counter, smiling while peering over her half-rimmed glasses at Marla. The lady smelled of Chanel No. 5 and cigarette smoke.

Marla smiled back and showed her phone screen to the elderly lady. "I'm here to visit Dino Morelli."

"Are you family?"

Marla flashed her badge toward the lady. "I'm here on official business, ma'am."

"Oh! I see." The lady pushed her glasses back up her nose and tapped her arthritic fingers on a keyboard. She studied the monitor screen before scribbling a name and a room number on a slip of paper. "Here you go, officer. Out past the lobby and to the left, an elevator is halfway down the hallway. I hope everything is all right."

"I'm sure it is. Thank you."

When the elevator door opened on the fourth floor, Marla stepped out to find Angelo Rivera standing in the hallway wearing a clean, crisp white long-sleeved shirt, black jeans, and black boots, with his badge and holstered pistol on his belt. He was pounding away on a piece of chewing gum looking like he was guarding the patient's door rather than waiting to ask him questions.

Marla smiled and held her hand out. "Rivera, good to see you."

"You too. Don't take it the wrong way, but Borland sent me to help in your investigation."

"Very thoughtful." She looked down at his boots. "Didn't I read in the manual about the department wanting us to wear black shoes?"

He glanced at the floor and then back at her. "Better to ask for forgiveness than all that other Fed bullshit."

Amused by his boldness, she smiled. "I'll have to remember that."

Rivera gave a slight nod. "Haven't seen you since...well, you know what happened with your husband." He shifted the gum inside his mouth from one cheek to the other. "I'm sorry about all that," he shrugged his left shoulder, "stuff."

Marla waved dismissively, not wanting to bring up unpleasant memories. "Right, thanks. Are you up to speed on what has happened so far?"

"Cocaine, fentanyl, some kind of medical malpractice."

"Definitely the drugs," Marla said. "Not sure about malpractice. I suspect this is a person without a medical license."

"Like the doctor helping you and Crosby?"

With a tiresome expression, she replied, "That person is dead. Let's find out what this guy in the room knows."

Air swished around the heavy wooden door as Marla pushed it open, revealing a man with a yellow-gray beard and almost shoulder-length hair propped up against several pillows in the hospital bed. A small square bandage covered the middle of his forehead. A sheet lay over his trunk and one leg while the other leg extended above the sheet, wrapped with surgical gauze from the knee to the foot, with a small round red dot midway. An IV bag hung on a pole near his right side, its transparent tube snaking almost to the floor before climbing back up to the forearm while a blood pressure cuff circled his upper left arm and a pulse oximeter was attached to a finger.

Marla held her breath for a few seconds, feeling an uneasy sense of familiarity, with the beeps from the monitor sounding like the ones when Crosby had been in the hospital.

"Who are you?" the man asked.

Rivera held his hand out. "DEA Special Agent Rivera." They shook hands.

He held onto Rivera's hand. "Dino Morelli. Call me Curvy." He eased the lawman's wrist over. "That's a cheap looking watch. Can't afford a better one?"

Rivera released his grip and tapped his watch. "My father's TIMEX."

"And now you have it. Why?"

"Drinking and driving don't mix well. After he died, It's all I wanted from him."

Curvy nodded. "Sorry about that."

Rivera changed the subject. "This is Special Agent Adams. Mr. Morelli—"

"Call me Curvy."

"Right. Curvy, we've come to ask you a few questions about your incident."

The bearded man fidgeted in the bed before straightening the sheet with a frown. "The cops beat you here. Gave all that to them an hour ago."

Marla stepped forward, extended her hand, and made sure of a firm grip. While holding her hand, he turned it to see a part of a finger missing, but before asking about it, Marla brought up his past as a major league pitcher. "I heard you used to be a big deal in the Majors."

A grin spread across Curvy's face as he released his grip. "Yeah. Been a while." His voice hung heavy with nostalgia. "Had the best curveball for two years. Nobody hit my curveball outta the park."

"What happened?" Marla asked.

"I threw a fastball, and this guy smacked a line drive into my right shoulder." Curvy sighed heavily. "Couldn't pitch another curve after that, then they cut me."

"Sorry to hear. The Astros, right? Our family attended some games about the time you were there. Seems like I remember someone yelling your name during a game."

Curvy bobbed his head several times. "Yeah. Those were fun days."

Marla peered at the chair beside the bed and then focused back on him. "Do you mind?"

He waved his hand like it was nothing important while hiding his excitement that a pretty woman wanted to talk to him. "No, no, not at all."

She sat down. "Mr. Morelli—"

"Call me Curvy."

"Right." Marla smiled. "Curvy, what did the man look like?"

"Short, scrawny, gray hair." He motioned his hand around his face. "Not a hundred percent sure it was a guy."

"Say again?" Rivera pushed his gum to the other cheek.

"The whole time he kept talking about medicine and science, stuff I don't know. Sometimes, a kinda buffed-up woman can look and sound like a man, ya know?"

"First time anyone said anything like that," Rivera said. "We'll check that out."

Curvy shrugged. "I can tell you, whoever it was, was damn strong. Slammed that screwdriver clean through my leg."

Marla edged closer to the bed. "I have a question for you that the police didn't ask."

"Yeah? They asked a lot. What's your angle?"

"The man...or woman who did this to you, let's stick with a man for now." Marla tried to lower Curvy's guard by straightening the sheet over his abdomen and chest. "Did he have a round apparatus with a stainless steel or chrome finish?"

Curvy's expression changed. "How'd you know about that?"

"I've seen it...or one like it. It's called a centrifuge." She leaned toward him for a second before sitting straight again. "The person got something from your hip, didn't he?"

"Yeah. It hurts like a mother, too."

"Do you know why that happened?" she asked.

"No. You gonna tell me?"

"He wanted your bone marrow, the bloody slush inside your hip. Did this guy place some of it in the centrifuge?"

"Told you, not sure it was a guy. I didn't see no whiskers. And to your question, I ain't got a clue. I was out."

"Out? How?"

He held his left arm up and patted the bandage just below his elbow. "Shot drugs in me with a needle. Knocked my ass out. I don't like needles. Friends of mine died using them."

"And you weren't conscious when he put that hole in your forehead?" Rivera asked.

"Hell no. I ain't some kinda Superman. I'm guessing if I drilled a hole in your head, it would hurt."

Marla aimed a chuckle toward Rivera. "Yeah, you might be right about that, Curvy." She patted his shoulder. "Oh, sorry. Is this the injured one?"

Curvy quickly changed his grimace to a smile. "All good now. It don't hurt. In fact," he grabbed a full plastic soft drink bottle from the nightstand, "I can still throw." He hurled it across the room, and it thudded against the wall with a loud bang, spraying liquid everywhere.

Rivera raised his eyebrows while chewing his gum. "He's lying in a bed and can sling that thing harder than me when standing."

"Impressive, Curvy," Marla continued to sit near the bed. "About your forehead," she said as her gaze fixated on the bandage. "Did this person inject something into your head?"

"I couldn't see—no mirror, but I felt tape on my forehead and a syringe dangling down. That crazy doctor said the syringe was to shoot stuff inside my head." He tapped the forehead bandage with a finger. "Right here."

He patted his arm. "And there was a second syringe attached to an IV here where he drugged me. When I was out, I dunno know, I guess he shot something in my head."

"Did he say why?"

"Something about making my brain grow bigger."

An icy chill shot straight up Marla's spine as she recalled images of Dr. McCollum shooting stem cells into Crosby's brain, causing it to double in size in a matter of days. She scratched her scalp, trying to make the vision disappear.

Rivera placed his hand on her shoulder. "Are you okay?"

Marla nodded without turning around. "Yeah. Good. Almost."

Rivera stepped back. "Curvy? Tell us where this happened."

With an irritated gape toward Rivera, who interrupted his conversation with the first pretty woman, he said, "Told the cops already. Go out there and ask them."

When Marla gently patted the back of Curvy's hand, he froze. It had been a long time since a woman touched his skin like that.

"Do you mind telling me?" Marla asked.

He didn't move. He didn't want her to move. "The Bluebird Motel. It's over on the west side near—"

"Loop 410 frontage road?" Rivera interrupted. "Blue over white building? I know the place." He smacked his gum and said, "We should go and check it out."

Marla slid her hand away from Curvy before she stood. "Absolutely."

Curvy rotated his palm up. "Are you coming back? I might be able to remember more tomorrow. I could teach you how to pitch a curveball."

Marla threw a sad smile toward him. "Okay. Deal. I'll try to make it back before you leave."

Chapter 10

Rivera exited the highway onto the street under the overpass. Half a block away, The Bluebird Motel, with its two-toned facade, seemed to dance with the pulsating red and blue lights bouncing off the walls. The blazing sun morphed the asphalt into a hot, sticky mess, radiating a pungent odor of burning rubber as if the entire street had been tossed into a fiery grill.

"Damn, this weather is hot," Rivera said.

Marla wiped her brow. "Yep." She counted all the police vehicles. "SAPD is efficient."

"Right. I don't think we could do anything to help the situation." He turned into the restaurant parking lot. "How about a coffee?"

"Sounds good."

After stopping, he took out another piece of gum and popped it into his mouth. "Let's go."

They strolled past the vestibule and tables filled with people before sitting at an empty booth next to the plate glass windows. The air carried a persistent odor of fried eggs and apple pie. Everyone's attention had focused on the flashing lights. A waitress approached with RITA printed in red on a white name tag clipped to her uniform. She slid two menus across their table and asked, "What would you like to drink?"

"Coffee," Rivera said.

"Same for me," Marla said.

"That pot is probably a little stiff. It's been sitting there since mid-morning." She glanced at the counter and then back at them. "I'm at the end of my shift, but I can make a fresh pot before I go."

Crosby crossed Marla's mind. If the coffee wasn't at least two days old, it wasn't ready to drink. "I'll take what you got."

Rivera leaned back. "Me too."

Rita took both menus. "Suit yourself."

They both shifted their attention to the motel and the flashing emergency lights on the police vehicles. Rivera snapped a napkin from the holder and spat his gum in it before balling it up and placing it on the table.

Marla tapped her index finger near the used gum. "I woke up this morning a little queasy. Please deposit that somewhere besides where I plan to drink my coffee."

"Oh, sorry." He snatched the wadded napkin and tucked it under his thigh.

The waitress returned with two cups of coffee. "Anything else before I leave? We have great burgers and serve breakfast all day."

Marla asked, "Rita, right?"

She tapped her name tag and smiled.

Marla returned the favor. "What's going on over there?"

Rita shook her head. "Rumor is, some guy was staying at the motel, and he got Curvy—"

Rivera interrupted. He already knew the answer, but asked to hear what the waitress would say. "Who's Curvy?"

"He's a homeless person who hangs around here. Anyway, he goes to someone's room for a beer, except it was for something else."

"Something else?" Rivera asked. "Sex?"

"It's all a mystery to me, except Curvy's in the hospital and supposed to get out tomorrow. We'll get the skinny then."

Marla spun her cup around to pick it up by the handle. "What about the other person? Did you see him or her?"

"Not sure if it was the same person, but a stranger came in to eat yesterday. He had a funny accent, English or something like that." Rita stopped for a moment. "I think it was a guy. You ever see any of the paintings of the kings from a long time ago? Their rosy cheeks and red lips look kinda girlish to me. Probably because he was from somewhere else. Like I said, England or one of them places around there."

"You served him?" Rivera sipped his coffee.

Rita looked both ways. "We only got one waitress here this week—me. I finally got some help today."

Rivera rested his cup back on the table. "What did this guy look like?"

"Mmm, white, kinda short with gray hair. Had this worn hard look like he had a bad childhood, sickness, or something."

"Hair length?" Rivera asked. "Thin, fat?"

"Hard to tell, with a hoodie on. Covered up most of the head and the midsection, but I'm going to guess more thinner than fat."

"What did he order?"

"Don't recall that, but I do remember he bitched about everything."

Marla handed her a twenty dollar bill. "For the coffees and keep the change."

Rita grinned, stuffing it in her pocket. "Thanks, sweetie."

Marla swallowed hard with the last of the strong coffee. "Let's cross the street."

Rivera dinged the little bell at the motel counter. A woman in her fifties with green streaks sprayed into her hair shuffled while pushing a walker. Her pink, half-rimmed glasses dangled from a gold-colored eyeglass chain around her neck. The smell of unfiltered cigarettes and cheap bourbon cocooned her.

"Need a room?" She waved her arm at the police vehicles. "Don't fret about all that out there. The cops always go crazy around here. I think they found a dead mountain lion or a cougar or something big. Nothing to worry about. One room, king bed?"

Marla raised her badge above the countertop.

"Damn, more cops." She lit a cigarette, and it hung between her lips. "How am I supposed to make a living with a hundred cops up my ass?"

"They came in and talked to you?" Marla asked.

While the cigarette stayed between her lips, she took a drag and blew out smoke. "Yeah. I told them where to stuff their nightsticks."

"That's pretty brave," Marla said.

"Or stupid," Rivera said.

"I've been here twenty-two years, and cops don't scare me. It's their third time down here harassing me this month."

"You're right. I apologize for everything that's happened to you and your business." Marla placed ten dollars in front of the lady. "Did the guy use cash or a card?"

The cashier stood silently, sliding the money off the countertop and slipping it down the front of her dress, inside her bra before speaking. "Card? How'd you know? Everyone uses cash, so...no trace. The stupid cops didn't ask me that question, but yeah, he used a card."

"Am I going to need a warrant for that information?"

She drew another breath through the half-burned cigarette. "Fuck warrants." She held her hand out.

Marla pulled out another bill and turned toward Rivera. "All I have is a twenty. Do you have..."

The woman leaned over the counter. "How many of those you got?"

Marla said. "One."

The woman shifted her attention to Rivera. "What about you? How much you got?"

Rivera shook his head. "I don't carry cash."

"Give me the twenty, lady." She snapped it out of Marla's hand in a second. The cigarette wavered as she muttered, "Damn cheap-ass cops."

A printer clacked under the countertop, and when it stopped, the cashier reached under and plopped a sheet of paper facing Marla. "Here, cheap son of a bitch."

"Don't push your luck, lady," Rivera said.

Marla spun the paper around and read the name. "Michael Smythe. Sounds British."

Marla nodded. "Can you describe him?"

The woman shrugged and shook her head. "I don't remember every person checking in."

Marla held the receipt in the air. "But you remember him using a credit card?"

She banged the legs of her walker down on the floor. "My memory ain't what it used to be."

"Selective memory?" Rivera asked. "Do you have security cameras?"

"Are you freaking kidding me? I'd never have anyone check in if I had proof they were here."

"What about a driver's license?"

The woman scoffed. "Do you know how many John Doe's from 123 Main Street I get?" She flailed her arms around as if swatting an imaginary fly buzzing over her head. "Almost everyone has a fake ID. What other reason would you come here? For a hundred, you want a hooker sent to your room? The St. Anthony Hotel on the Riverwalk would say no, but I got no problem with that."

Outside, Marla breathed in deeply and looked at the bright blue, cloudless sky. Rivera followed her gaze before turning to face her again. His mouth opened slightly as if he wanted to say something, but changed his mind. Finally, he spoke. "We should return to HQ and start searching for this guy." He gestured toward their vehicle in the parking lot and began heading that way without waiting for an answer from Marla. She glanced back at the hotel before following him across the street, choosing not to respond.

Chapter 11

Dr. Wilborn sat in the taxi, and the air conditioner couldn't blow hard enough for her. Her back itched against the frayed fabric. She scooted toward the center, trying to avoid the scalding heat of the sun beating through the side window while considering how to hide her British accent. "Are you sure you have the correct location?"

The cab driver snapped his fingers. "Gotcha, man. I am well acquainted with every part of this town. Lived here my whole life, and there ain't no place in San Antonio I don't know about."

The cab exited the highway onto a narrow asphalt road. Wilborn stared straight ahead at a mirage of wavering water, wanting to feel the ocean breeze and the soft wet Brighton sand under her feet.

The driver interrupted her daydream. "It's to the right and about a mile up. Got no clue why you want to go there, but I'll have you there in three minutes."

She tried miserably to speak with a Texan accent. "Are ya sure it's dry? No water?"

"Hey, man..." he mumbled, "or lady." He raised his voice again. "Less than an inch of rain in almost three months. This town is drier than a tumbleweed. Every stormwater pipe is drier than my ex's..." he stopped to clear his throat before continuing. "Never mind. Nothing's wet in this town. Dead grass, dead trees. We'll be like the Mohave Desert if it don't rain soon."

They drove by small houses to a four-way stop intersection with a laundromat and a convenience store. Dr. Wilborn sensed a wave of anxiety at the sight of three massive ten-foot-tall effluent pipes with colorful graffiti cluttering the entrance. They had locked her up for twenty-eight months in a cell with walls almost too tight to breathe, and now she was heading into a dark hole. The taxi abruptly halted beside a long barren ditch save for sickly yellow grass and limp weeds.

"Twelve bucks. There's a three percent added charge if you pay by card."

Wilborn pulled out Michael Smythe's credit card, but then thought this electronic trail should end, so she stuffed it back into her pocket. "You said you know this town. How can I get a map of the city stormwater system?"

"My bro works for the San Antonio Water Department. It'll cost ya, but I could getcha one. How am I gonna find you once you go inside? Hey, how about I send it to you by email?"

"Send me a text." Wilborn reached around the driver's shoulder with cash between her fingers. "Here's two hundred dollars. Call him."

The driver snapped the cash from Wilborn's hand before tapping a number on his phone. "Bro, listen, I got a guy giving me two hundred bucks to get a copy of San Antonio's stormwater drainage system. Send it to me, and I'll split it with you." He leaned back toward his passenger and laid his hand over the phone. "Said he also wants two hundred."

Wilborn nodded.

The driver smiled. "You got it. Send it to me right now."

"You have a flashlight?" Wilborn asked.

"Sure do. Why?"

"Here." Wilborn handed the driver another two hundred, along with two twenties. "For the fare, the map, and the light."

"Excellent." When his phone dinged, the driver pushed the twenty through a slot in the company's lock box bolted to the floorboard and the other bills in his shirt pocket. "Got it. Sending it to you now. Need help with the trunk?"

"Yes." The doctor leaned against the vehicle when her phone dinged. She smiled upon opening the map attachment.

The driver pulled the trunk from the back. "By the way, where ya from? Ya got one of them foreign accents."

Dr. Wilborn grimaced and waved a hand in the air. "South Africa."

"Hmm. Ain't got a clue where that is."

At the south end of Africa, you ninny.

The driver patted his shirt pocket and smiled. "All right. Here you go." He gestured towards the opening of the concrete pipes. "I've been inside one of them, back in high school. Ten feet tall. Closest to spelunking I ever want to get. Good luck to ya."

Wilborn's heart rate quickened, ears hummed, and neck tightened. The small wheels on the trunk bounced through grass and weeds as the taxi engine faded away. At the pipe entrance, she stopped and unlatched the trunk, removed the revolver, and stuffed it under her belt. "I hope to bloody hell there are Crusties inside like the news reporter said on the tele," Wilborn muttered aloud, then added a smirk. "I could use a brain or two to prod for my experimentations."

Wilborn entered the pipe, ten feet tall and dry as a bone. A welcomed chill filled the air and quelled her nerves. She couldn't believe the news reporter was correct about the temperature inside the pipes. Colorful graffiti covered the walls while a line of dimly lit rectangular inset lights, head high, were set in the pipe's wall. Her finger brushed over one of the metal covers encasing the light, feeling rust so fine it appeared as little more than peppered speckles. Below the lights hung a long black wire strand gleaming lightly in the weak illumination.

Almost thirty feet in, an odor smacking of mold and piss struck her. Crumpled bedrolls and a cardboard box were nearby, and two people sat cross-legged beside each other, one stick thin and the other slumped like a worn-out beanbag. Wilborn mumbled, "Bloody Crusties." She advanced slowly and smiled.

The overweight man wore a wiry black beard and tousled hair. His gray cotton pullover neckline had yellowed from grime and sweat, and his scuffed boots had holes in the soles. The woman sported an orange buzz cut with a ratty blanket half-swathed around her, revealing sorrowful eyes and decayed teeth. Her skeletal face had a deathly pallor as if all the blood had been drained from it. Wilborn surmised she had a hunger for cocaine over food, an ideal Crusty.

"Hey, don't stop here," the man said. "This is our spot."

The haggard female echoed her partner's words, "Yeah! This is our spot!"

Wilborn stopped, lifted the trunk lid, and palmed a pair of handcuffs into her back pocket before holding up a small bag of white powder. "Got some coke." The top snapped down. "Either of you want a dab?"

The guy eagerly nodded. "Yeah, man. Sure."

Wilborn knelt beside the couple. "What are your names?"

"Bambi," the woman answered.

Wilborn smiled sarcastically at this ludicrous moniker. The name Bambi was like naming someone Mary Christmas or Freddie Fates - saccharine sweet sentimentalism gone wrong. A name sounding about as distant from streetwise or hard-case tough as one could get. Long ago, she learned not to question others' motivations. Only people with stable minds gave intelligent answers to those lacking knowledge; those insane would provide no explanation whatsoever because they believed their delusions were true, so why should they bother to explain themselves to anyone? Wilborn grinned again. "Bambi?"

She snarled. "Yeah, Bambi. What of it?"

Wilborn couldn't help herself and asked anyway. "Like the deer? A cartoon character or a stripper name? If I'm giving you some of my coke, then tell me your real name."

"Hey, man. That's what she goes by. All I've ever known her as."

Wilborn smiled at the man. "And what is your name, Thumper or Flower?"

"Bert."

"Bert. Easy, simple." The doctor began again. "Well, Bert and Bambi, I would like a tour of the system." She waved her hand deeper inside the pipe. "Have you been through it?"

Bambi repositioned the blanket over her shoulders. "Give us some of that, and I'll tell you."

Wilborn raised her eyebrows and nodded. "Brilliant Idea. Some now, and after you give me the grand tour."

"You're not from here, are you?" Bert asked. "Where are you from?"

She thought for a moment. If the cops started asking questions about her, everyone she met would say a different place, which would throw the cops off her tail for a short time. "New York."

Bert shrugged. "Ain't never been there."

Wilborn mumbled to herself, Of course not, you simple minded pillock. You live inside a drainpipe.

After Bert and Bambi snorted the coke, the doctor asked, "Do you have flashlights?"

They both nodded.

"Good. Let's go."

The three headed into the depths of the drain, each clutching their flashlight.

"Why is there a line of lights inside here, and does it run throughout the entire pipe?" Wilborn asked. "And what is the black wire under the lights for?"

"Yeah, we like the lights," Bert said. "Not very bright and not sure if they're everywhere."

"Why the wire?" Dr. Wilborn asked.

Bert shined his flashlight on the side of the pipe. "Someone told me when the water rises and hits the wire, an alarm goes off somewhere downtown."

"Like to the police?"

"No. Maybe. I guess, but it hasn't rained in forever, so don't worry about it."

Wilborn let the two lead as if they were tour guides showing off spectacular graffiti and rats scurrying near their feet. Pulling the trunk behind her, the wheels trailed through a thin layer of sand and dirt. She aimed the flashlight beam toward a metal ladder leading to the top of the pipe. "What's that for?"

"A manhole cover." Bert kept walking. "Men can come down through there." There was a break in the pipe where bright sunlight shined above them. "And that?" Wilborn asked.

Bert looked up again. "That's a water grate. When it rains, water pours in from the street through there."

"It ain't never gonna rain again," Bambi said. "How far you aim to go?"

"I'll tell you when we arrive," Wilborn said as the pipe veered to the left. Moments later, the graffiti on the walls lessened, and they found four concrete steps leading up to another level. "There," Wilborn pointed, "why are there stairs?"

"Another big pipe connects there." Bert motioned with his hands. "The flow of water is controlled better by rolling down the steps than using a ramp or a slide."

"Bert is really smart." Bambi shrugged her shoulders, trying to keep the blanket on her. "He went to college and studied physics."

Bert smiled. "Besides, maintenance men show up periodically to inspect everything, and they use the steps to get to the higher pipe."

"A university man. Always like discussions with PhDs in physics."

Bert frowned. "Didn't finish. I left after a few years. I couldn't handle all the crap from the professors."

Wilborn paused before placing the trunk on the ground and pulling on the metal handrail alongside the steps. It didn't budge. "I'm going up to see what's there."

"I'm tired." Bambi wrapped the blanket tighter around her chest and plopped down.

"There's a chain and a padlock across it," Bert said. They don't want anyone climbing inside, so that sign says DO NOT ENTER."

"So, it does." Wilborn slipped a tool from her pocket and stuck the end inside the lock. One good thing from being incarcerated was learning how to unlock any key or combination padlock with ease. After a few seconds of jiggling, the lock opened before she flipped the chain to the side. "Brilliant." She scampered up the steps and shined the flashlight down a straight pipe at least fifty yards long. "This is primo. Bloody good."

"What'd you say?" Bambi asked.

"Come up and have a see." The doctor held her hand out. "Bambi, you first, then Bert."

"We held up our end of the bargain and got you here." Bambi squirmed to edge the blanket closer to her neck. "How about another hit?"

"Well said." Wilborn motioned them toward the stairs and smiled. "After I show you this. Come on, up you go."

Bambi trudged up the stairs, and the doctor nudged the small of her back to guide her along. When Bert stepped up, Wilborn dropped the flashlight. "Sorry, mate. Get that for me."

When Bert stooped to pick up the flashlight, Wilborn reached behind her, pulled the revolver out, and gun-butted the man in the back of the head, dropping him unconscious to the concrete steps.

Bambi screamed and backed away until she felt the cold pipe pressed against her back.

Wilborn spun around, grabbed a handful of Bambi's shirt and aimed the gun at her head. Her speech flipped to a cold and menacing voice echoing off the walls. "Shut up unless you want to die."

"No!" Bambi stepped back as far back as she could go. "We got nothing, no money, nothing, just let us go."

Wilborn barked out orders and shoved her forward. "Don't dawdle, girl. Move!"

Bambi shuddered, her eyes wide with terror, fighting every instinct to turn and run. "Please, let us go." When Wilborn pulled the hammer back, the metal clicking startled Bambi. She timidly shuffled around Bert lying still on the steps. "Okay, okay. I'm going." Trembling, she inched closer until the gun barrel scraped across the short hair on her head. Her eyes cast downward, hoping all would vanish. "Please."

"Snap it up, girl." Wilborn yanked on the blanket with a sneer. "I don't have all day."

Bambi slid her hand down the metal rail to avoid falling. The blanket fell to her feet. "I swear, I promise..." she said, then glanced sideways at Bert, who still hadn't moved. She uttered the standard oath of silence no one would ever keep. "Let us go, and we won't say anything."

With an icy calmness, Wilborn uttered, "Good little Bambi."

Bambi passed the last step, dropped to her knees, and clasped her hands together in prayer. "Anything. I'll do anything. Please don't hurt us."

Wilborn grasped the front of Bambi's short hair and bent her neck backward. Goosebumps shot through her already chilled arms when she felt the gun barrel pushing against her forehead.

A bitter tone oozed out. "If I shoot you here, the bullet will pass through the right frontal lobe," Wilborn's grin grew larger, "possibly stopping inside with only mild damage because it would not have passed through any vital brain tissue, if you had any vital brain tissue. You could survive and still want cocaine every day and live inside this bloody concrete pipe."

Bambi understood nothing of what was said. She winced when Wilborn pushed her head sideways and the barrel slid across her forehead to her ear.

"But here, a bullet traversing the midline, and exiting the other side is universally fatal," Wilborn said.

Bambi shut her eyes and tightened every muscle. Her breathing stopped. She prayed to any god to help her. The cold metal of the muzzle lifted away. Wilborn released Bambi's hair. When she opened her eyes, she had no time to react. A gun butt hit her in the head.

❖

Bambi woke sitting on the ground, leaning against the side of the cold concrete steps, wrists handcuffed to the iron handrail, With her blanket gone, her ninety-pound body, covered with homemade tattoos, shivered in torn gray sweatpants and a sleeveless top. Dirty fingernails were chewed to the quick with jagged edges, and old scratches and dried blood covered the flesh on her arms like an anxious caged animal or a chronic meth addict. Peripheral IV catheters were stuck in her left forearm and the center of her forehead.

Duct tape wrapped around her ankles pulled taut across her skin when she moved her legs, while more tape stretched over her mouth from ear to ear. While inhaling deeply through her nose, she felt grit in her teeth and the taste of adhesive on her dried, cracked lips. She searched for any sign of escape.

Above her, the inlet grate was dark. It was nighttime. The temperature dropped, and the lights along the walls seemed dimmer. She heard nothing, no birds or traffic above her. Cold fear gripped her quivering body, and she realized she was truly alone.

"I'm right here," a voice from nowhere said.

The darkness absorbed Bambi's scream. A sudden bright light stabbed her eyes, making her squint and turn away.

Wilborn's voice came from behind the light. "Don't get your knickers in a knot."

Bambi looked both ways down an empty pipeline and mumbled to herself.

"Bert?" Wilborn knelt beside the trunk with the top raised and her flashlight aimed inside. "He left. Ran out like a whippet with a chill up his arse."

The handcuffs rattled against the handrail when Bambi pulled against them. She shook her head in denial and tried to scream out loud.

Wilborn slammed the trunk lid down while continuing to shine the light on her victim, who struggled to see what her captor was doing. "Don't worry about your man. You are the lucky one." Wilborn knelt near Bambi and patted her forearm near the IV tubing. "You will love me for what I am planning for you. It will be like what John Lennon wrote. Do you know who John Lennon is?"

She shook her head.

"Well, I expected such. He's been dead over forty years, but he composed a wonderful song called The Magical Mystery Tour, and that is where you are going."

Bambi squirmed against the concrete steps. The handcuffs clanking around her wrists echoed down the pipe.

"We..." Wilborn aimed the column of light on her face, giving an evil horror look, then back at Bambi, "we are going to perform an experiment."

Bambi tried to worm herself further away.

Wilborn leaned forward. "It's late at night with no one around, and Bert is not returning for you."

Tears flowed down Bambi's cheeks.

Wilborn sat on the trunk. "You have a choice. If you are a willing participant..." Wilborn reached for the syringe on the trunk lid with one milliliter of a white solution inside. "I will give you fentanyl in your vein. A truly magical trip. Faster and better than snorting mere cocaine, and I can do this multiple times a day."

Bambi whimpered into the duct tape.

"Blimey, girl. You'll thank me later for a wonderful time." Wilborn held up another syringe with twice the amount of solution. "But if you do not want to help me...well, no choice at all really...I must give you this one. There is enough fentanyl in here that it would terminate your life, and I expect after injecting it, you would have one or two breaths before you stop forever." She held both near each other. "Which do you prefer? Magical trips or death?"

Bambi looked at the syringe with the smaller amount and then back to Wilborn.

"I thought so." Wilborn leaned forward again. "Here we go. It's important to keep your arm still with the IV tubing." With a wide grin, Wilborn uncapped the needle with her teeth and knelt beside Bambi. The doctor's tongue pushed the cap sideways as she spoke through clenched teeth. "I will inject the drug into your vein and make all your worries disappear."

A nervous moan grew behind the duct tape as the needle came closer and closer, and soon after, a chill bounded through Bambi's body when the drug entered her vein.

Chapter 12

Special Agent Angelo Rivera held the glass front door open at the DEA office.

"Thanks." Marla stepped through.

"Sure thing."

"Did that coffee taste okay to you?" Marla asked.

Rivera gave a half-hearted shrug. "Guess so."

"It didn't sit well with me."

Michael and Jason, the same security guards who manned the only desk in the lobby for years, observed the two entering the building.

"Afternoon, guys," Michael said.

Jason playfully shoved Michael's shoulder. "She's not a guy. It's obvious she's a girl. Sorry, a woman. What kind of security guard are you? Don't know the difference between a man and a woman?"

"I know the difference," Michael said. "It was a...what do you call those things...a euphemism. I know she's not a guy."

Marla chuckled at them. "Who are you? Rocky and Bullwinkle?" Which earned her blank looks.

"Who?" Jason asked.

"Never mind." Marla signed in.

Rivera asked, "Are those from the 60s?"

Marla smiled. "Right. A cartoon."

Rivera signed in. "So last century."

Michael and Jason high-fived each other. "Whoa," Michael said. "He got you on that one. Yeah, the 60s, last century."

Rivera headed in the direction of the stairs to the second floor as his phone dinged. After viewing the screen, he said, "Secure message. Let's go to my desk."

Marla positioned herself behind Rivera at his desk with a picture of Michael Smythe's British Driving Licence on the computer screen. Marla chose not to mention that two c's were used instead of one, as Americans typically do. The unexpected photograph took both aback.

"This is not the person I expected based on Rita's info." Marla pulled up a chair and sat beside Rivera. "Where's the rosy-cheeked, scrawny, gray-haired man?"

"Right. This round-faced, black-haired man doesn't fit the descript. But he does have rosy cheeks."

Marla felt a wave of nausea and stood quickly. "Damn."

"What?"

"Bathroom. Be back in a minute."

She shoved the hallway bathroom door open and rushed to an empty stall. Falling to her knees, she vomited violently into the toilet bowl until the spasms subsided. The automatic flusher whooshed behind her when she left the stall. At the sink, she splashed water on her face and scrutinized the newest wrinkle in the mirror. At home, Crosby used to approach from behind her, wrap his arms around her waist, and kiss her neck. She felt a deep sadness knowing that wouldn't ever happen again.

Going back to Rivera's office, she took a seat. "Have an idea."

"Are you okay?"

"Hmm." Marla spun through the contacts on her phone before tapping one. The phone on the other end rang.

"Bexar County Crime Lab. David Weidman here."

"David, this is Marla Adams."

"Marla?" He paused for a brief period. "I'm so sorry about Crosby. Honest, if there is anything I can do, please ask."

"Thank you." She set the phone on speaker. "There is something." She threw a little friendship toward him before asking a big favor. "I hope you still like it there?"

"Oh, sure. I love it. They'd have to kick me out of this place. What's up?"

"I want to confirm the ID of the perp from last night's incident at the Bluebird Motel. The name we have is Michael Smythe, but I'm having doubts about that."

"I'm not assigned to that case, but hold on a sec," David said. "I happen to be facing a computer."

Marla heard a keyboard clattering.

"Okay, there. The SAPD sent a copy of Michael Smythe's driver's license, although the English spell it with two Cs. LICENCE. Crazy Brits don't know how to spell." The keyboard stopped clattering. "Hmm. Odd."

"What?" Marla asked.

"It will take two to three days to run DNA tests from blood on a bed sheet and an alarm clock reported from the motel room." Computer keys clattered again before stopping. "An SAPD report shows someone must have wiped the place down but missed a fingerprint, and it's not Smythe's. The print belongs to a British ex-con named Hugo Wilborn."

Marla leaned against her chair. "Wilborn?"

"Right. Is the name familiar?"

"Hugo Wilborn was Dr. McCollum's partner in London. You remember the doctor I hired to save Crosby with the stem cell experiment?"

"Yes, of course," David said.

"Dr. McCollum said Dr. Wilborn was the driving force behind their stem cell research, but he's supposed to be in prison."

"Yeah? You should investigate that, but he's not a he. He's a she."

"Did Rita and Curvy see Hugo Wilborn not Michael Smythe?" Marla whispered to Rivera. She spoke louder. "Dr. McCollum talked about his colleague as he...or maybe not. Thinking back, McCollum always referred to the person as a doctor who would never leave London."

"I don't know about that, but all I can tell you is fingerprints don't lie, and hers are in San Antonio."

"Thanks, David. I owe you one."

"Marla, I mean it. Anytime I can help you with anything, call me."

Marla nodded. "Thanks, bye." She wondered how many secrets the Bluebird Motel still hid. "Run a search for Hugo Wilborn, London, England."

Rivera's fingers rapidly tapped on the keyboard. A British Driving Licence with a thin-faced woman and short dark hair belonging to Hugo Wilborn popped onto the screen.

"What kind of parents name their daughter Hugo?"

"I don't know, but the expiration date is soon. How often are they required to renew?"

"Good question. Type it in the search engine."

Rivera typed in gov.uk. "Every ten years, so that makes Hugo Wilborn's license over nine years old."

"A lot has happened in nine years, rags to almost riches, prison time, loss of a colleague. Do you think there was more than a business arrangement between the two? Perhaps lovers?"

Rivera altered the image on the screen. "If you add a little fat to the face and turn the dark hair grayish…" He tapped the enter key. "You have Hugo Wilborn who is a decade older."

Marla patted his back. "That image is closer to the descript of what Rita said." Rivera rolled down to the next page. "Look at this. The police record reveals Dr. Hugo Wilborn was recently released from prison," he rolled further down, "and a medical license reinstated by the General Medical Council."

Marla slapped the desktop. "They let this goofball out of prison for extortion, and she's still allowed to practice medicine?"

Rivera leaned back in his chair. "Do your time and all is forgiven." He leaned forward again. "How about we check Michael Smythe's info?" He typed on the keyboard. "Well, I'll be damned." He copied Wilborn's edited image and pasted it next to Smythe's photo. "If you glance at the headshots, the cheeks and eye color are similar. There's a difference in weight and hair color, but people often overlook those touchy subjects nowadays. She could pass for him through customs." He typed more. "I'll pull up Smythe's credit cards. Let's see if we can match the motel's receipt with a card."

Marla retrieved it from her back pocket.

Rivera continued typing. "Smythe has a Visa card." A list of details filled the screen. "Whoa. Busy man, or woman."

Marla inclined forward from her chair. "Plane tickets purchased from Heathrow Airport to LaGuardia. We should check customs."

Rivera typed on his keyboard, then said, "It shows Michael Smythe went through US Customs, then loaded on a plane to San Antonio, Texas. Dr. Wilborn is definitely here—"

"And used fentanyl on Curvy," Marla said.

"And maybe others," Rivera said.

Marla stood and paced the floor. "We need to pick her up."

Rivera typed on the keyboard again. "If Wilborn used Smythe's ID and credit card, where is Michael Smythe? I'll have someone contact the

London police department and check this guy's address and wherever he works."

"Good call," Marla said.

Rivera leaned back again and asked, "Why San Antone?"

She tapped the top corner of the computer monitor twice. "Exactly." She thought about the fiasco with Dr. McCollum and his stem cell experiment on Crosby, as well as what Dr. Berghoff questioned at the autopsy. "But why?"

Rivera pushed the print button. "Your McCollum doctor is dead. What in the hell does Dr. Hugo Wilborn, an ex-con living five thousand miles away, want here?"

Marla snapped the page from the printer and responded resolutely to Rivera's question. "I'm sure I'll find out."

Rivera typed faster on the keyboard. "I'll put feelers out for both names in the US and the UK. Anything pops up, we will get it."

Marla's phone rang. "Hello?"

"The windmill is giving us trouble," Cassie said without a greeting. "We need water for the livestock soon."

"What's wrong?" Marla asked.

"I think it's the motor. It was making loud noises, then boom, it quit."

Marla's back stiffened. "Is Festus with you?"

"Sure. He's keeping the cattle close to the water tank. Best damn cattle dog in Texas."

Cassie said, "I wish men would act like Festus and do what they're supposed to do. Men just whine and bitch and moan."

"I'm sure Roger is some help."

Cassie giggled. "Stop it." She cleared her throat. "Sorry, don't worry. I'll keep him. He's still good in the bed."

Roger called out from a distance. "Mrs. Adams, I told Cassie I could patch it up, but she told me she had to call you first."

"I'm stuck downtown for the rest of the day. Give Roger a chance. If he can't repair it, contact Hildebrandt Electrical and Plumbing and have them inspect it."

Cassie snickered at the thought. "Roger can't fix that. He can't fix a bowl of cereal without spilling the milk."

Marla chuckled. "Is there enough water for the cattle?"

"We could stretch it for two days. Roger is asking if he can come to the house and get something to eat."

"Absolutely not. Don't forget about the cameras inside, and if I see him, I'll shoot his kneecaps off."

Marla stuck her phone in her pocket and winced from stomach cramps. "Listen, I better head for the house," she said to Rivera, who hadn't taken his eyes off the screen during the phone call.

"See you in the morning. I'm going to dig a little more before I head back," Rivera said while still concentrating on the information on the computer screen.

Chapter 13

Marla struggled to her truck, feeling like someone was playing kickball inside her stomach. She had to concentrate on opening the door and climbing into the driver's seat. After lying across the console for a minute until the cramps eased, she started the engine and headed towards a nearby pharmacy. Seven vehicles were parked in the lot, and luckily for her, no one at the drive-through window. When Marla pulled up, a mid-twenties man slid open the narrow aperture. "What is your birthday?"

"I need something for stomach cramps and nausea."

"I'm sorry, this is the pickup line for prescriptions. Come inside for the OTC meds."

Marla didn't want to do it, pull rank and show she was a big shot. She wasn't, but she did it anyway. She lifted her badge for him to see. "I don't have time to go inside."

"Oh, I'm sorry. What's wrong?"

"Cramps, nausea, vomiting. Came on suddenly an hour ago."

"Okay, hold on. I'll be right back," the attendant said before disappearing.

When he returned, he handed her a stapled paper bag. "One item will help with your cramps, and the other for vomiting."

She took the sack and pitched it on the passenger seat. "Thanks. How much?"

"On me."

"No, no. That's not why I showed the badge. Nothing for free."

"My car was stolen last week, and the cops found it in an hour. My guitar and amp were still in the trunk. That's over a thousand dollars. This is my way of saying thank you."

She didn't have time to argue. "Okay, thanks."

"By the way, I dropped something else in there for you. Good luck with it."

Marla parked the truck in front of her garage and killed the engine. The cramps had subsided. After opening the door to the house, she called out, "Cassie, you here?"

With no answer, she entered the kitchen and dropped the pharmacy bag in the dry sink. The digital clock said 5:14 p.m. She poured herself a glass of water and drank half. Back pain struck her as sharp as a knife, causing her to hunch over like a bow before the pain abruptly quit. She heaved herself back to the counter and ripped open the sack, bottles clattering in the sink. With a quick motion, she removed the top of the pill bottle for cramping, emptied two pills into her hand, and tossed them into her mouth. They tasted bitter, so she chewed quickly and took a drink before swishing and swallowing. The second box had chewable pills for nausea. She should have latched onto that one first.

The third box was different, rectangular, and flat. A smiling woman's face was on the front—an in-home pregnancy test. "Holy cow. You think I'm pregnant? That's nuts." She leaned against the counter and felt Crosby's presence. Her life bounced back and forth like a fast game of ping-pong: a baby, his baby. Crosby would be with her. The DEA? What would happen there? She already had an HR file thicker than anyone else in the office, which was not exactly a good thing for the newbie on the team. What would she do? Carry a pistol on the right side and a baby on her left? Push a carriage while pursuing dealers and traffickers? Quit and raise cattle? Sit at home and cry with the baby every day?

She stepped into the bathroom, and minutes later the toilet flushed. She emerged with a shell-shocked look and gaped at the red + sign on the strip. "Now what?"

Glancing at her wristwatch, then shaking her head, she capitulated to what she wanted at one time, but not now, not without Crosby's help. "Damn, Dr. Sanborn's office closed forty minutes ago. Guess I'll be there at 8:01 AM."

✦

Early morning winds scudded clouds across the blue sky. Tumbleweeds scratched the earth as they rolled from one end of the county to the other as Marla drove to the medical clinic. When she arrived, five minutes after they opened, the lot was full of vehicles.

Marla tugged on the glass door handle and felt the suction of air against her. Two people were standing ahead of her in line. She did it yesterday and didn't like herself for it, but decided to do it again.

"Excuse me." She held her badge up so the receptionist could easily see. "I need to meet with Dr. Sanborn now."

The receptionist said nothing as the wooden door buzzed. "Thank you."

She veered down the hallway to the doctor's office in the back and gently knocked on the entryway. Dr. Sanborn looked up while holding a medical journal in one hand and a donut in the other. A ceramic coffee cup emblazoned with 'THE DOCTOR IS IN THE HOUSE' sat on his desk.

"Marla? Can I help you?"

She gently closed the door behind her and planted herself in one of two chairs on the opposite side of his desk. "Yes. I think I'm pregnant."

He set the donut aside and wiped his fingers on a paper napkin. "We perform the tests here, but you can also buy them from pharmacies without seeing a doctor."

"I already did, and I'm not sure I like the results."

"You mean it being positive?" Dr. Sanborn asked. "Excuse me for asking, but...Crosby's?"

A flash of anger crossed Marla's face as she rose from the chair. "Who the hell else would it be?"

Dr. Sanborn raised his hands in the air. "Sorry to ask, but Crosby died a month ago, right?"

Marla resumed her seat again and gave the office walls a once over before gently answering. "So?"

"And you were gone for three months before that."

She shifted in the chair uneasily before finally answering, "Yes."

"That would be four months. Was your last menstrual cycle three months ago?"

Marla smirked. "Glad you can still count."

"Glad you still have a sense of humor. So, you might be somewhere around ten to fourteen weeks pregnant. Any nausea or vomiting? What about weight gain? Bloating? Pants tighter?"

"Yes, to all. I ignored the last three. Thought it was stress, eating crap food."

"Any vaginal spotting?"

"Once a few weeks ago," Marla said. "Thought it was my period but stopped after a day."

"Have you been drinking alcohol?"

"No. I made Crosby discard all that before I left, and I had nothing while in Quantico."

A nurse knocked on the door and spoke from the hallway. "Dr. Sanborn, patients are ready."

"Come in, Faith." When the door opened, he said, "Let's get a pregnancy test on Marla and then into a room. Don't send her to the lobby. We'll keep her in the back."

Faith raised an eyebrow. "Yes, sir. One pregnancy test coming up."

The doctor scooted his chair back, and they exited his office. He wrapped his fingers around Marla's upper arm. "We'll get this figured out."

"I promise, it's his."

"Have no doubt."

Positioned on a patient table by herself, she awaited the outcome of the test. Was hers wrong? Was it right? Deep down, this could only mean one thing—she was pregnant with Crosby's baby. Her mind wandered to Crosby's smile, the heart-shaped branding iron he bought her, catching him stepping out of the shower with a towel wrapped around his slim waist, his face grossly swollen from the gunshot to his head, the final bullet hole in his chest. Her phone rang, shattering her thoughts. It was Rivera.

"Hello?"

"Where are you? I have info on Smythe and Wilborn."

"I can be there in twenty to thirty minutes."

"What? You're supposed to be here."

"I said twenty." Marla disconnected the call before Rivera had a chance to reply.

A door latch clicked, and Dr. Sanborn entered the room with Faith behind him, holding an electronic tablet.

The words that followed struck a chill in her. "The test is positive." He pointed at the table where she sat. "Let's have you lie down, please." She lay motionless, staring at the white ceiling. The doctor examined her abdomen and found the uterus enlarged. "Okay, up you go. Faith will guide you to the ultrasound room where Dana, our tech, will see you next. After she finishes her measurements, she'll come find me."

Inside the ultrasound room, she lay flat on her back, praying the cramping didn't return. Dana squeezed a glob of cold green gel on her abdomen, startling Marla.

"Oops. Sorry. Should have warned you." Sitting on a stool beside the bed, Dana smiled while spreading the gel with the ultrasound transducer head. She moved it left and right, then up and down. Her smile flattened. The longer Dana stayed there with no spoken words, the more anxious Marla became about what was happening. While holding the transducer with one hand, Dana typed on the keyboard with the other. Square black and white pictures rolled from the printer.

"Something wrong?" Marla asked.

"Just, um, getting measurements."

More pictures rolled out.

"That's a lot of pictures. Is everything okay?"

Dana pushed away from the machine and moved past Marla. "I'll be back in a minute." She hurried out the door.

While still on her back, Marla lifted her head to see the pictures. They meant nothing, black and white lines in different directions.

The entrance latch clicked again as Dr. Sanborn pushed the door open. His hand brushed across Marla's shoulder with heavy emotion. He straddled the stool and lifted the long line of pictures.

"Dr. Sanborn, talk to me."

"I want to check on something else, Marla." His words hung in the air while picking up the transducer and rubbing it across her lower abdomen. Her heart pounded hard against her chest. When he stopped, he nodded to Dana, who opened a drawer.

The doctor wiped the gel off Marla before replacing the transducer near the ultrasound, then turned it off with the whine of the machine rolling to silence. Dr. Sanborn held Marla's hand as she continued to lie on the table. "This is not good news. You're not pregnant."

Marla sprang up. "Bullshit. I've had two positive pregnancy tests."

"Right, but those only measure a hormone in your urine. You have a mass, a glob of tissue in your uterus that acts like a pregnancy."

"Is it...cancer?"

Dana handed a pamphlet to the doctor, who passed it to Marla. "It's called a molar pregnancy."

She took the pamphlet and crushed it in her hand. "You said I'm not pregnant."

"Not with a fetus. There is no baby inside you."

The pamphlet felt like an indictment of the life she had suddenly hoped to live, immediately snuffed out by a tumor growing within her womb. "So, what happens next?"

"A simple outpatient surgical procedure called a D&C, dilation and curettage. Like a Pap smear, but I remove the contents inside the uterus."

"An abortion? No."

"Not an abortion because there is not a fetus. Read the pamphlet, and I'll meet you at the Hildebrandt Surgical Center at six tomorrow morning. No food after midnight, nothing but a sip of water in the morning. You won't feel much like going to work after, so arrange for the day off."

Alone in the room, she zipped up her pants and then unfolded the crumbled pamphlet before reading the first page. A tear dropped onto the paper. As if on cue, her phone rang. She wadded the brochure and pitched it into the wastebasket before answering.

"Hello?"

"Where the hell are you, Adams?" Rivera asked.

Jumped back at him with an automatic response. "I'll get there in fifteen or twenty!" But the desperation in her voice seeped into her thoughts.

"We've got a lead on Wilborn, and I'm in my Tahoe pulling out onto the street. Tell me where you are, and I'll pick you up."

"I'm in Hildebrandt," she muttered.

The Tahoe engine roared in the background. "Hildebrandt? Did you sleep in?"

Marla didn't know what to say. Her world had turned upside down, and here was Rivera asking about sleeping in. "Had something important to do."

"Meet me at the drainage pipe. I'll send you the coordinates. Get there asap."

Chapter 14

Marla shoved the phone back in her pocket before grabbing the pill bottle for cramps. "Guess there's no need to worry about mistreating a baby." Before leaving the room, she popped two in her mouth, puckering from the bitterness of something like SweeTarts.

Seconds later, she slammed her truck door shut, gunned the engine, and roared off, lights and sirens blaring. She could make it there in twenty-six minutes if the traffic was light. If not, that was why she drove a six-wheeled, all-wheel drive pickup. The median would work if nothing else was moving.

Her timing won out. She flipped the siren off and eased down the two-lane road. Weeds grew amidst limp yellow grass—about the only vegetation alive without water in San Antone.

Well up ahead of her, Rivera veered off the road onto a barren creek bed. He steered around rocks, piles of trash, and leafless broken branches and stopped near three dry, ten-foot-wide concrete stormwater drainage outfalls. These were often hubs for the homeless or others looking to avoid the law. The emergency lights continued swirling on top as he exited his Tahoe. He slipped his dark blue nylon jacket on with bright yellow DEA letters across the back. With a semi-automatic weapon in hand, he entered one pipe in order to evade the glaring sun and waited for his backup.

Marla maneuvered her pickup down the creek bed, swerving around tree stumps and branches the size of basketball goals before stopping alongside Rivera's vehicle. From several houses behind her, barking dogs and shouting could be heard. She had never paid attention to the storm drainage system and guessed Wilborn hoped nobody else did either. When she opened the door, her phone dinged, bring flashlight. She outstretched her hand and retrieved one from the glove compartment.

After Marla zipped up her DEA jacket, she rushed to the outfalls. Rivera removed two pieces of gum from his pocket, stuck them in his mouth, crumpled the paper, and dropped them by his boot. He whispered, "We can discuss why you didn't come in this morning when we're back at the office."

That's probably not going to happen. "You got a plan, or are we winging it?" Marla hoped the medicine would soon kick in for the cramps and nausea.

Without a word, they entered the pipe. Air cooled her neck while graffiti flashed a spectrum of colors from red to violet. Indistinct voices deeper within echoed off the tunnel walls. Marla whispered, "Someone's inside."

"Hand signals only when inside," Rivera replied. "We can thank the City of San Antonio for installing lights along the pipe. I'll take the right side."

"We want Wilborn alive and with a black trunk. I have a boatload of questions for him…I mean her. Is SAPD coming?" Marla asked as she looked behind her for the police backup.

"Supposed to," Rivera whispered. "Nobody here yet, and I'm not waiting any longer."

Marla acknowledged. "Let's go."

They slowly navigated through a world of garbage where rats and cockroaches thrived. Flattened cardboard boxes, a shopping cart tilted on its side with one wheel missing, treadless tires, and desiccated feces littered the area worse than the remnants of an outdoor concert.

After venturing further, they reached a bend in the pipe curving left. Sunshine sliced through the stormwater gates above, creating beams of radiant light in the dimness. A foul odor caught Marla off guard. It was the opposite of fresh air, and her stomach churned from the thick, rank staleness. She wanted to hold her breath for the next thirty minutes.

After a hundred more yards, the pipes shifted right before veering left again. Rivera shut off his flashlight and motioned for her to switch off hers before coming to his side. He raised his hand at the sounds of distant voices. A camping light lit the inside up ahead.

Marla held up a pair of fingers to signify two people.

Rivera nodded.

As they slowly approached the light, voices became louder and shadows moved. Marla and Rivera watched a male and a female kneeling face-to-face.

Marla whispered and signaled forward. "There."

A rectangular case sat behind the male. The male pivoted toward it, lifted an object from the inside, and set it near his foot. The female drank from a bottle, then giggled and leaned forward.

"Shit," Marla said. She covered her mouth as a raccoon scuttled past her.

The female placed the bottle down, turned towards the noise, and saw two figures. She jumped to her feet and screamed.

"Damn it, sorry," Marla said.

Rivera shrugged. "Let's go."

They charged down the sides of the tunnel with weapons leveled at the two. The male hopped up. When a gun dropped on the ground, he reached for it.

Two flashlight beams blinded the eyes of their suspects. Rivera shouted, "DEA! Get on your knees!"

Marla yelled, "Back away from the gun, or I'll shoot!"

The couple squinted, trying to use their hands to block the bright light. "NOW!" Marla shouted. "Back away!"

A mid-twenties man, dressed in a long-sleeved t-shirt and jeans with his dark hair pulled back in a ponytail, sank to his knees and pleaded, "All right, all right. Don't shoot." He left the gun on the ground.

The girl next to him, also in her early twenties, had long blonde hair and wore a sorority sweatshirt, jeans, and a tote bag hanging down to her waist. Fear petrified her, contorting her face, and she neither moved nor spoke.

"Keep your hands on your heads!" Rivera said while striding toward the man, kicking away the gun.

Marla latched onto the shaking girl's shoulder and shoved her down. "On your knees."

Still aiming his weapon at the man, Rivera eyed a row of plastic jugs filled with an unknown content. He chomped on his gum a few times before speaking. "What's in those?"

"Nothing, man. Nothing. Stuff, that's all."

Rivera noticed it wasn't a black case, but two cardboard boxes. Something rattled when he nudged one with his foot. "What's inside?"

"Supplies."

"More information."

"Plastic jugs, straw, plants, stuff."

The girl broke down and hid her eyes, crying. "Please. I don't know why I came. This is the first time. I promise."

Marla had seen people pretend to panic, but this was not an act. Fear gripped the girl. "Nice and slow, reach for your ID. Both of you."

The girl opened her tote bag and held out her college ID. "Please. This is my last year." She yelled at the guy. "You stupid son of a bitch! I hate you!"

The guy reached into his back pocket and pitched his wallet toward Rivera's feet. "Listen, we're not hurting anyone."

Marla shined the light on the girl's ID. "Rebecca Walensky. Rebecca, where's hometown?"

"Barlow. It's a small town in the panhandle of Texas."

Marla thought of her hometown, Hildebrandt, a town with a half dozen traffic lights. "You live on a farm?"

"I go by Becca, and no. I live in town."

"How many live there?" Marla asked.

"A thousand, and I'm the first in the family to go to college."

"Keep your hands on your head," Marla said.

"Please. I don't even know him. We met last night at a party, and he said he had some mushrooms. I just wanted to see what they looked like." She yelled at the guy again. "I hate your guts!"

"Shut up," the guy said. "Don't say anything."

Becca squared her shoulders towards Marla. "I give you my word. I will never do anything like this again. I promise."

"Mushrooms?" Rivera scooped up the wallet and took out a college ID. "That's a lot of shrooms. Are you selling?"

Elon yelled at Rivera, "Hey, give that back! I need it for classes and meals."

"Step back. Your skinny ass doesn't have a chance of taking it from me."

"All right, fine."

"You didn't answer my question. Are you selling?"

"No. I like to get high after class. There is no place to buy quality shrooms, so I grow my own. Nothing wrong with that, is there?"

"Well, yes, as a matter of fact, there is," Marla said.

Becca took her hands off the top of her head and covered her face, weeping harder.

"Stay on your knees," Rivera said. He motioned for Marla to move back, then whispered, "We're not here to bust a couple of kids. Let's make him empty every jug and send them on their way."

"I'm good with that, but let's question him about Wilborn. Maybe he's seen her."

Rivera grinned at her suggestion. "Good idea."

He approached Elon and bent down to meet his gaze. "You understand we can't let you keep this stuff, right?"

Elon nodded. "Yeah, whatever, man. Fucking cops."

"All righty." Rivera stepped back while actively chomping his gum. "The two of you stand and empty every plastic jug."

When Becca stood, Marla handed the college ID back to her. "You promised me."

Rapidly nodding, she stood straight. "I will. I will." She stuffed the card back into her purse. "I promise."

As the two emptied the jugs, mushrooms and straw fell on the ground. Rivera asked, "Ever notice anyone else in here?"

"No," Becca said. "I promise. This is my first time here."

Rivera looked at the guy. "Is that right? Is this her maiden voyage into the abyss, or has she been helping you all along?"

"What if I said yes?"

Marla stabbed her fingers into his shoulder. "Then I'd have to arrest you for being a dickhead."

He continued emptying the remainder of the jugs before speaking again. "Then no, it's her first time."

Rivera nodded toward Elon. "You see anyone lugging a black trunk?"

"I see a lot of people, all kinds, homeless, psychos, vets, people hiding from the law or family."

"You know the drainage system?" Marla asked. "Could you navigate from one end to the other?"

"No, man. I came the way you did and I head back the same way. Elon pointed in the other direction. "That way is miles of tunnels, twisting and turning in different paths."

"So, you do know the system," Rivera said.

Elon stopped emptying a jug. "I...I've been down some of them. I mean, a few here and there, but not all of them. Too many."

Marla asked, "So, you have most of the system memorized?"

"No, three or four...or five tunnels. What about all my jugs? You giving them back to me? I can't afford to buy more."

"More? Why would you need more?" Rivera asked.

Elon shook his head. "Nothing, man. Forget it."

"Tell you what I'll do." Rivera removed a business card from his shirt pocket, held it between his fingers, in front of the guy. "Take this. Give me a legit lead on a scraggly man...or woman with an English accent dragging a black case or bag inside these pipes, and you get the jugs in return."

"You want me to be your snitch? No. I won't do it."

Rivera smashed a jug with his boot and then spun another on the ground to do the same.

"Wait," Elon said. "No more."

When Rivera held his card out, but Elon didn't nab it, another jug smashed under his boot.

"All right. Stop." Elon held out his hands. "Come on, man. I'm broke."

"Are you listening?" Rivera asked. "A trade. You tell me what you hear and see, and you get your stuff back," he pointed at the crumpled plastic, "minus the two."

Elon snapped the card from Rivera's hand and shoved it into his pocket. "Nobody likes a snitch." He spun toward the exit and jogged down the pipe.

Chapter 15

Rivera and Marla exited the drainage pipe, each carrying a cardboard box full of plastic jugs. Their trucks sat alone with emergency lights silently swirling, with no other law enforcement vehicles around.

"You didn't call SAPD, did you?" Marla asked.

"No, I didn't." Rivera dropped his box on the ground with jugs banging against each other. "I wanted this bust to be ours, yours, and the DEA's. This was supposed to be yours. I chose not to let anyone else in on it."

"I don't give a rat's ass who shares the arrest." Marla laid her box on the ground. "Whoever can take her first can have her."

"I'm hungry." Rivera brushed his hands across his pants. "I ate breakfast six hours ago."

Marla realized she hadn't eaten. The cramps were gone, and the queasiness was minimal. Pills for both occasions were in her cupholder between the seats, just in case. "I could eat. Where?"

"La Fonda. I woke up visualizing their enchiladas and extra spicy salsa."

"Wasn't aware of a special salsa."

Rivera winked. "I know a guy in the kitchen."

Twenty minutes later, they stood at the cashier's desk with a girl in her teens holding two menus and cloth napkins with utensils wrapped inside. She smiled and asked them to follow her.

Like a Where's Waldo game, Rivera and Marla scanned the patrons, looking for a little gray-haired person sitting alone. Winning the lottery had better odds than finding Dr. Wilborn in a Mexican food restaurant.

"There." Marla gestured in the direction of the last person at the bar. "Someone wearing a hoodie glanced at us and promptly looked away. A bowl of chips and a martini glass are on the countertop."

"Who drinks a martini here?" Rivera asked.

"An English person."

They both veered away from the employee and headed for the bar. Marla tapped her gun on the side of her belt—strictly habit.

The man stared straight ahead, sipping on his martini. He paused when a hand on each side of him plopped on the bar counter. Pivoting to see two people, he smiled at Marla. "Need something, darling? Can I getcha a beer? They got happy hour for another twenty minutes."

Rivera smiled at Marla, who reciprocated with a smirk.

"Not an English accent," Rivera said.

Marla scoffed. "And not enough teeth."

They both showed their DEA badge to him.

"Hey, I didn't do nothing. I'm just sitting and drinking."

"All good," Marla said. "Mind if I ask your name?"

He sipped his drink before answering. "John."

Rivera said. "May we see an ID?" After reading the man's driver's license, he handed it back with, "Sorry to interrupt, sir. Enjoy your meal...er, drink."

As they sat down, Marla stepped on a bug under the table. "We're like a couple of cockroaches running in circles."

"Curious to find out about the link between Smythe and Wilborn?" Rivera inquired.

"Wow. Forgot. Yes, tell me."

"Michael Smythe, born and raised in London, England, owned a pawnshop and a dozen rundown apartments. He had a colorful scam going. He would rent a room to someone, then every two months raise the price until the renter couldn't pay, confiscate all their possessions as payment, and sell them in his shop."

Marla scraped the remnants of the bug off the bottom of her boot. "How did Wilborn fit in?"

"Before the doctor's incarceration for extortion, she kept something at the pawnshop."

"Rent for twenty-eight months must have been expensive."

"London police sent us info that a taxi took the doctor from the prison to the pawnshop. No stop and collect two hundred dollars. Across the intersection is a pub with a camera aiming toward the street and the store entryway. Wilborn exited a taxi, entered the premises without carrying anything, and remained for twenty-three minutes before emerging with a black Seward trunk. Later that day, she used Smythe's credit card to pay for airline tickets and food but presented her own passport to board the plane. Two days later, the police received a call from FedEx because the shop was locked up and no one answered. Inside, behind the counter, Michael Smythe was dead from a fentanyl overdose, with a hole drilled into his hip, and Wilborn had already gained entry into the US.

Marla caught sight of a portly man dressed in an apron and a white chef's hat coming their way. He clamped his hands onto Rivera's shoulders.

"Angelo, my friend. You came back. And with a date."

"No date." Marla showed her badge. "DEA Special Agent Adams. I'm here for lunch and to review the day's data."

"Oh, too bad for you then, eh Angelo? She's prettier than the last several you brought in."

Marla gave a playful smirk. "Several? Is this your go-to place for dates?"

Rivera couldn't remove the two oven-mitt sized hands on his shoulders even if he wanted to. "I'm here for the enchiladas and your spicy salsa. Don't disappoint me...and her."

The chef motioned to the waiter before returning his gaze to Marla. "My special salsa is very hot today. Be careful with it." He released his paws from Rivera's shoulders. "And bring back your friend. I like her; she brings a brightness to the place."

The waiter set a basket of chips on the table along with two bowls of salsa, one an easy red color and the other, thick, seedy, and dark enough to bite back. Rivera dipped a chip in the red and sampled it. "Hmmm, chopped tomatoes and onions for the masses." He edged the other saucer toward him with his fingertip. He didn't need to angle down to detect the danger. Its simmering spice filled the air, causing Marla's eyes to water. She dared not rub the tear away. Rivera raised the spoon in the saucer, poured the seedy, chunky liquid fire over his chip, and slid the entire chip into his mouth. He continued smiling as he crunched the chip before swallowing. Marla pushed the glass of water closer to him. He scrunched his nose.

"How about you?" Rivera asked, swirling a chip in the salsa. "This one is perfect for you." He raised his eyebrow at Marla.

"How about, no." She scooped a dab of the hot and mixed it with the milder. "Closer to my speed."

Rivera added onto her chip with a teaspoon. "Just a kiss more. Great flavor." He held his index finger up. "All of it. Best to not get any of it on your lips."

With a reluctant sure, she slid the whole chip into her mouth before quickly realizing it had been a mistake. Eyes watering, she frantically waved her hand at the waiter. "Milk. I need milk, now!"

Rivera scooped another chip into the hot salsa and ate it while smiling at her. After swallowing, he drank nothing. "Too much for you?"

"Is he stealing lava from a volcano nearby?"

Deputy Jeffrey Keene strode past the cashier's desk and skimmed the restaurant tables.

Marla stiffened her posture and tapped Rivera's forearm. "Interesting." "What?"

"Jeffrey Keene just entered the restaurant. He is a sheriff's deputy and a very close friend of mine from my years as a police officer in Hildebrandt. I even introduced him to his wife."

Jeffrey nodded at Marla, shot straight to their table, and held his hand out to Rivera. "I'm Deputy Keene."

Rivera shook his hand and responded in kind, "DEA Special Agent Rivera."

After returning his attention to Marla, Jeffrey pulled out the chair between them and sat down. "Heard you're back at work after a month or so."

Marla winced. "Right. My boss asked me for a favor."

"Must have been a big favor after such a short time since Crosby's death. Something only you can deal with?"

"Jeffrey," Marla took a moment to wipe her lips off with her napkin, "what is this about?"

Keene smiled at Rivera. "Do you mind? I have something personal to ask her."

"You're asking me to leave?" Rivera asked.

"Yes, for a little bit."

Rivera peered at Marla as she gave the faintest of headshakes. He faced the deputy again. "I'll stay."

Jeffrey leaned back in his chair. "What is this? A date?"

"No!" Marla almost shouted, grabbing her water glass and drinking from it. "What the hell are you implying? You knew Crosby and you ask me a stupid question like that?"

The waiter placed another glass of water near Jeffrey. "Sorry. You're right, and I apologize." He took a calm sip before continuing. "Does this favor from your boss have any connection to that English doctor helping Crosby?"

It was an uncomfortable pause before she said anything. "Something similar to Dr. McCollum's brain growing technique has surfaced in town, and ASAC Borland requested me to be involved." She had to change the subject but didn't want to ask about his wife, who had become depressed and alcoholic after their multiple miscarriages, so instead, she asked him quietly, "Everything okay with you? How's the sheriff doing?"

Jeffrey glanced back at Rivera. "You sure I can't have a word with her privately?"

Rivera's eyes checked Marla for a response and then focused his attention on the man who had disrupted their lunch. "I'm good here."

Marla threw a resigned shrug at Jeffrey. "I'm not telling him to leave."

Jeffrey snapped his fingers at Rivera. "Fine, sit, eavesdrop, I don't care." Eyes blazing with urgency, Jeffrey spoke his words carefully toward Marla. "Rosemary has not been doing well. She's back to mixing hard liquor and Xanax. Found a tablet of fentanyl in her sweater drawer last week." His finger aligned the salt and pepper shakers together. "At least she's managed to stay away from the emergency department for a month. Even her doctors have given up on her. When she's in the ICU, they pump Narcan and IV fluids in her for two days, then rush her out of the hospital like some crazed addict taking up space." He tilted his head up. "I heard one of the techs call her Rebound Rosie."

"Listen, Jeffrey. I love you like a brother." It hit her when she said that. Her real brother was murdered. "I mean—"

"I know what you mean, and you're like a sister I never had. And a godsend for introducing me to Rosemary."

"I'm sorry, Jeffrey. I wish I could help Rosemary with her problems."

"You can." His voice softened. "That's why I showed up."

Marla looked briefly at Rivera while shifting in her chair. "Oh? Like what?"

"This lunatic doctor from England injected stem cells into your husband's brain and almost cured him, right? I mean, you know, he was talking and stuff three or four days after being shot in the head."

Marla bit the inside of her lip and pulled at her collar as if it chafed her neck. "Get on with what you must say."

Jeffrey reached his hand halfway across the table, but Marla held still. "This week, the sheriff's department learned about the dead druggie at the convenience store with a hole in his forehead and stem cells injected into the brain, and the guy in the hospital; same thing."

"Jeffrey?" She hesitated for a moment. "What do you want?"

"There's word going around there might be another doctor involved in this." Jeffrey locked eyes with Rivera. "Would you mind, please?"

Rivera didn't move.

Jeffrey turned back to Marla. "This perp is hiding in town somewhere, and I want you to find this person, this doctor, and help Rosemary."

When Marla grasped the water glass, the wedding ring on her finger clinked against the clear stem. Instead of taking a drink, she loosened her hold. "First, the perp is a female, and we haven't located her, and second, she's a murderer. You don't want someone like that anywhere near Rosemary. None of her patients have benefited from her ministrations. After these experiments this doctor is doing, the only thing most of them are looking at is the sheet over their head at the morgue. We reckon this person is somewhere inside the hundreds of miles of the stormwater drainage system." She pinched a chip from the bowl, dipped it into the mild salsa, and then dropped it on the plate. She had no appetite anymore. "Remember that guy last year who killed six college girls? He hid in the drainage system for over a week and was a total idiot. This doctor is a smart person and could hide in there for months."

Jeffrey retracted his hand and leaned against his chair. "Okay, yeah, so a female. How about you dispatch all of your agents down there, and I'll have the sheriff send all the deputies, and we'll flush her out like doves in a bush?"

Marla shook her head. "The San Antonio Water System manages almost a thousand square miles of an extensive network of water and sewer mains buried beneath the city, and we'd have to add every SAPD officer on and off duty, which would never happen. Trust me, she'll eventually do something stupid and pop up. That's when we'll snatch her by the neck."

Jeffrey shuffled his feet beneath the table before clearing his throat. "I read a bunch of stuff about Rosemary's condition." He glanced across the restaurant before looking straight at her. "It's because she has a problem in the front part of her brain."

Marla's voice stiffened. "What are you saying?"

"This doctor drilled holes in people's foreheads and injected stem cells. Has to be making the brain perform something beneficial."

Marla closed her eyes, wishing all this would disappear.

"That's what Rosemary needs," Jeffrey said. "The stuff your English doctor used to make the cells grow faster." His fingers slowly tightened into fists, "Crosby's brain almost healed in less than a week. Crazy, right? And when Dr. McCollum died, the Hildebrandt police stuck the vial in their evidence room. I could mix it with Rosemary's bone marrow and give it to her."

"How would you do that?"

"I hadn't gotten that far. Whip it up and make her drink it or shoot it in a vein. Hell, if I have to, I'll drill a hole in her skull and stuff it in her brain, myself."

"That's crazy talk." She slapped the corners of the table. "You can't do any of that. And besides, someone already stole that stuff you're talking about, the protein extract from the evidence room."

"What? Who? Any leads?"

"The Hildebrandt PD says they have none."

"They don't have any idea who?" Jeffrey eyed Marla with a quizzical look. "So, if I happen to find this stolen protein extract and somehow convince this doctor to use it, perhaps, like... let's say we pretend we're trading the protein stuff for drugs or something else, then we could make her mix up the stem cells for Rosemary, and she'd be better."

Marla contemplated what he was getting to. "Maybe, but I'm speculating she blames me for what happened to Dr. McCollum."

Jeffrey's finger drew circles on the table. "Okay, so you bag the protein stuff and pretend to exchange it with the doctor. You know, bait her a little bit."

"Bait? Jeffrey?" She shifted further back into her chair. "You came to tell me you plan to use me for bait? Trade my life for Rosemary's?"

"No. No. Not at all. Not what I meant." He threw an awkward smile at Rivera and Marla. "Pretend, only pretend I...we trade you. Not Rosemary, we arrest her for murder, drugs, and whatever else your boss can think of."

Rivera's chair scratched the wood floor as he scooted away from the table and got to his feet. "I believe it's time for you to go, deputy."

Chapter 16

Bambi shivered, pulse raced, and her ears buzzed. Saliva kept building in her mouth from fear and excitement. She forgot about her right wrist chained to the railing and ankles taped together inside the storm drainage system. Ten feet away from her, she focused entirely on Dr. Wilborn sitting on the black trunk with a syringe in her hand.

"Are you ready? It's one hundred percent love, and you will be amazed." She held the syringe toward her captive. "And you'll beg for more."

When Wilborn stepped forward, Bambi leaned away, holding her free arm close to her body. She couldn't decide. This doctor kidnapped her, but could she be right about the drugs? All Bambi wanted was the sensation of drugs entering her veins and the burning in her nose.

"Don't be a wanker. We can do this easy or not." Wilborn's prison talk interfered. "What'da say we make a run for it?" She pulled the tape off Bambi's mouth. "Bad things if you yell."

Bambi looked down into the barely lit outfall and hoped Bert would return.

"Come on." Wilborn held the syringe facing her. "Let's do it the straightforward way. Makes it more fun, don't you think?"

"You're not going to kill me, are you?"

Wilborn leaned back and waved her free hand. "No, of course not. Not what I want, Love."

Bambi shrunk back against the concrete staircase until she couldn't go further. She swallowed twice from the growing saliva while staring at the syringe. She had cocaine and heroin too many times to count, but never fentanyl. "How can I trust you?"

"Valid inquiry. If you're indifferent to it, I'll permit you to leave because it's the right thing to do, agree? However, as a doctor, you realize I must have documented experimental data." Wilborn mentally measured

Bambi's physique once again. "A weight of forty-five kilos and height of one hundred-sixty centimeters, I have calculated the correct amount of fentanyl to be injected in your vein and make you love the world. In return, you inform me of your cravings and how long until you desire more. That's all. After that, you have the choice to depart."

Bambi licked her lips, tasting salt and the metallic tang of desperation. Swallowing repetitively, she didn't understand why saliva continued to build inside her mouth. She bent her knees, and her ankle and bare feet scraped across the dirt. In acquiescence, she closed her eyes while slowly lowering her left forearm, pretending it was Bert injecting her vein.

Wilborn smiled. "That's a good bird. I'll give you a few drops, and it's up to you if you want more.

Bambi felt a hand on her forearm. With eyes closed, she winced at the venom entering her vein. A hellish warmth engulfed her. A sheet of orange light cascaded over everything before vanishing into black nothingness. Her skin separated from her body, muscles mutated into speckled balloons filled with helium, raising her soul above the earth. Hot ice swirled inside her brain, chilling her, warming her, chilling her again.

"More?" Wilborn asked.

With a deep sigh and a smile, Bambi answered yes.

"Cheers. After this, you'll wake with a sore hip and a headache."

Bambi tried to speak before the warm solution assaulted her vein—her world went cosmic. Bright lights. Sparks electrified every living cell. A thousand million nerves lit up in flames. She saw her heart pump beautiful poison, shoving it faster than a roller coaster charging downhill. The sun flew past, and the whites of her eyes burned. Soaring inches above hell, then shooting straight to the sky, like a rocket man launched into the heavens. A hammer slammed into her forehead, pressing harder and harder. Pins and needles jabbed her scalp countless times. An explosion burst towards a celestial dome.

Bambi woke, sitting on the floor, back against the stairs, with both wrists above her head handcuffed to the rail and tape stretched across her mouth and cheeks. She smelled kerosene from a camper's lantern shining several feet away. Her left hip screamed. Her pants had been pulled down to her knees with a red splotch on the left side of her underwear. When she raised her head, blood oozed down her forehead and the bridge of her nose, slowly dripping on the concrete between her legs.

"It was a bit difficult performing surgery in this tunnel." Wilborn turned the light brighter from a lantern she purchased at the convenience store while Bambi was unconscious. "You were a perfect patient. Did you enjoy the ride? About the drugs, you can have more…much more if you wish." Wilborn straddled the trunk and lifted the drill beside her. "You have a hole in your hip…and forehead. I must admit, I didn't give you all the information about the experiment—fat worthy chance you would have said yes." She waved her hand toward Bambi. "Don't worry yourself about it. I would never inject anything deadly. Want to know what it was?" She waited for a response, but the girl continued to stare with half-opened, drunken eyes. "I injected your own blood, well, a part of it anyway, mixed with my solution of proteins and metal."

When Wilborn said, "The perfect solution to cure the world," her mind flashed back to her childhood home, and her six-year-old sister, Clarise, was screaming inside the kitchen, "Stop it! Stop!" Tiny fists flew towards her foster mother's side as the woman beat Hugo's bare back viciously with a whip made from leather straps.

The foster mother stopped the beating and spun to face Clarise. "Shut that filthy mouth of yours." With one fell swoop, she backhanded the young girl, sending her flying against the cabinet.

Hugo yelled at their foster mother, taking her attention away from Clarise, "Hey, leave my sister alone!"

In an instant, the leather whip cracked across Hugo's waist. "Shut up, or I'll make sure she gets twice as much as you."

Hugo bent over the butcher's block without hesitation and braced for the next set of lashings—anything to save her sister from the same brutality.

For years, Hugo wondered what happened to Clarise. Where did she go? Hugo never expected to hear from Clarise while she was in a London County Council Home. But when Hugo went to prison, she never wrote or tried to visit. It didn't matter because of the cruelty of their foster parents, along with the disrespect and impudence of the General Medical Board regarding her stem cell research, it made Dr. Hugo Wilborn determined to develop the perfect solution to cure the world.

Bambi fell asleep, so Wilborn clapped loudly to get her attention. The sound reverberated down the pipe. "Nevertheless, this should make you a great person, and if my theory is correct, I possess an exclusive task for you." Rising again, she opened the trunk lid. "I have one more thing to present to you." She removed a ten-inch black baton and pushed a button, quickly extending to twenty-four inches long before slapping the lid closed and stepping toward Bambi. "I do not want to use this." Electricity jumped from one electrode tip to the other.

Bambi shook her head wildly and cried out from beneath the tape across her mouth.

"Blimey, girl. Shut up! I have no intention of torturing you." Wilborn kneeled directly in front of her captive. "You must eat and drink, yes? I don't see how you can do that with tape over your mouth. Agree?"

Bambi jerked forward, knees rubbing against each other. Her muffled response led nowhere.

"I'm willing to unbind one handcuff if you promise not to yell." She gestured to the trunk. "I have a bottle of water in there for you." The tip of the baton cracks from electricity. "If you scream," she edged the rod against Bambi's stomach, "well, you don't want me to push this button again." An evil smirk stretched across Wilborn's face. "But if you are well-behaved, you'll get whatever you wish. And don't forget about my gun." Her smirk changed to anger. "If you bugger this up, I'll drop you like an old bag, bitch."

Bambi's eye twitched as she nodded.

"Cheers." Wilborn took a water bottle from the trunk and set it between Bambi's legs, then stepped up the stairs and uncuffed her left wrist with the IV port in the forearm. Bambi tightened her thighs together, quickly twisted the cap off, and guzzled the liquid.

Wilborn moved to face her directly. "Remember." Bambi flinched when the baton's electricity cracked again. The doctor checked her Bremont watch. "You should be proper chuffed to receive another dose soon."

"No, no, please. I don't want to do this anymore. Let me go, and I promise never to say anything."

Still clutching the prod, Wilborn outstretched her arms. "Bambi. You misunderstand me. I'm not here to make you stop. I'm here to create beauty in your world." She lowered her hands. "And no more drilling holes into you. Simple trade. I give you drugs, and you let me finish my experiment. Just a simple injection into your head every...hmm...thirty minutes."

"I get a hit of the fentanyl that often?"

"Right."

She held her arm out. "Okay."

"This time, I inject the stem cells into your brain while you are awake. You must describe to me the sensations, whether it's warm, hot, cold, or if you have a headache, feel happy, or anything else.

"And what about the drugs?"

"You will earn your reward."

Bambi leaned against the concrete stairs and held her left arm close to her abdomen. Above her head, the handcuff on her right wrist rattled against the railing. "I ain't doing shit if I don't get a hit first."

"Listen, you bloody prat." Wilborn smiled and eased her voice. "Sorry, yes, you will receive your reward every time, but the stem cells are first."

Bambi's stare was clear but not sinless, eyes filled with a street-schooled life. "All right."

"No biggie then." Dr. Wilborn opened the trunk again and removed a syringe, holding it loosely in a closed fist. The trunk lid closed. "My solution." She pulled the gun from the back of her pants, and it clunked when dropped on top of the trunk lid, ensuring it was too far for Bambi to reach. She didn't want another episode like what happened at the Bluebird Motel. "I'm trusting you won't try anything stupid. Hold your head still. Ready? Close your eyes and we're off."

Bambi capitulated with closed eyes. She loved cocaine and wanted anything like it, and would do anything for it, but she didn't know this person. Is she going to die, or feel pain, or enjoy every second? It startled her when a hand touched her forehead. She could say stop now, right now. If she decided not to do this, what would happen? She felt a mysterious presence...cool inside her head...no pain, no ache, only something wonderful filling her mind.

"What do you feel?" Wilborn asked.

The coldness of the concrete against her back and legs and the metal railing against her arm increased. "Heavenly clouds filling my head. A distant light, a star, faint and twinkling." Her eyelids squeezed tighter as she bit her bottom lip. "Now pain and pressure."

"Where?"

My tongue hurts, dry. Pain in my head."

"Tolerable?"

"Give me the fentanyl."

The familiarity of the drug rushed into her vein. Every part of her body lit up like fireworks; arms, fingers, nipples. Excited nerves tingled, engulfing her, squeezing every inch of fiber of her being. Warmth filled between her thighs and roared deep into her groin. Her heart raced; breaths increased and then everything stopped and turned to darkness.

A hand wrapped around her neck, pushing her chin up. She opened her eyes and focused on the gray concrete ceiling.

A voice beside her said, "It only took an eyeblink for what I did, but you were out for quite a while." Wilborn held Bambi's head. "You must tell me what you felt."

"Again. Do it again."

✦

The following morning, Bambi woke to find her right wrist handcuffed to the railing. Sunlight shone from a different angle through the grates into the pipe. This time, there were columns of lights along the sides of the pipes. Dr. Wilborn sat on the trunk with legs crossed, holding a disposable cup with steam rising from the top in one hand. "My tea." Her other held a small paper sack. After several stem cell injections, she watched Bambi's actions curiously; she became extroverted, assured, and attentive. "Good morning." Wilborn placed the sack near her. "Food from a convenience shop. I'm sure it's nothing healthy. Something they called a breakfast burrito. Also, bottles of orange juice and water are in there."

Bambi flipped the sack upside down with her free hand, spilling all the items between her legs. One-handed, she removed the aluminum foil wrap and bit into the burrito. "What are you going to do with me?"

"Let you nosh to your heart's content, and then…then continue with my experiment. You have done quite well in a single day."

Bambi finished the burrito in four bites. She grabbed the orange juice bottle with her left hand and pitched it to her cuffed hand, catching it while never breaking her vision with the doctor. Reaching up and twisting the cap off, she flung it at her kidnapper.

Wilborn dodged it while still seated on the trunk. "Excellent results of increased awareness and anticipation."

Bambi drank the entire contents before pitching the empty juice bottle at the doctor.

Wilborn dodged the bottle, then lifted the black baton from her lap and aimed it toward her captive. "Don't make me use this."

Bambi gazed at the spray paint cans littering the ground mixed in with trash. "This is not where we were yesterday. Where am I?"

"Right. We moved down the system, and because of that, I didn't give you an injection of stem cells every thirty minutes. After I moved you, I slept a little while. In fact, you received only twenty-nine. "

"Why move me?"

"Better to keep moving. We'll move again when I want."

"How do you know where to go?"

"I have a map of the city's drainage network. After finding a suitable location, I bloody carried everything here, then carried you over my shoulder. You weigh nothing. I hefted two fifty pound sacks of flour from a delivery truck to the prison kitchen daily, so your scrawny, malnourished body was easy."

"How far from the first place are we located?"

"Not your concern."

The water bottle rolled away from her. "I'm handcuffed."

Wilborn stopped it with her shoe. "Juice? Water?"

"Neither. I'm ready for the stuff."

"Bloody right." Wilborn opened the trunk. "Shall we start again? Stem cells first, then the reward."

"More of that and less drug."

Dr. Wilborn cocked her head. "Less fentanyl? Why?"

Bambi hesitated for a moment, almost shocked to say it out loud. "It knocks the feeling off that stuff of yours, and I'm starting to like it."

A small smile tugged at the corner of Dr. Wilborn's mouth as she thought how thrilled her partner would have been by the idea of their stem cell solution reducing the want and desire of fentanyl. Could injecting the brain, targeting the anterior cingulate cortex, truly enhance the decision-making abilities and attention span, and bring crucial factors in Bambi eliminating Marla Adams?

"I didn't believe Dr. McCollum when he theorized that stem cells would abate the desire for narcotics."

"Don't know that word."

"Diminish, decrease, make something less desirable."

Bambi experienced a sudden rush of power within herself. "I want the first stuff."

Wilborn placed the syringe filled with the stem cell solution on the trunk lid and presented Bambi with a challenge. "We must begin with a test. Take a gander at everything and try to remember all the cracks in the concrete, the angle of the light, where the orange juice bottle lays, and the gravel on the ground."

Bambi nodded and analyzed the area. "Okay, now what?"

Dr. Wilborn removed a black cloth from the trunk and snapped it in the air. "I'll cover your eyes before I move things, then tell me what is different."

"How many changes are you making?"

"You must figure that out for yourself. It is part of the test." She tightened the cloth tight around her head. "There. Can you see?"

"No."

Bambi heard the syringe roll across the trunk. A shoe scraped across dirt. A metal ball rattled before aerosol spraying, followed by a can clattering on the ground.

Wilborn asked from a distance, "Where did I put the syringe?"

"On the left side of the trunk."

"What direction was the needle pointed?"

She thought. "Toward me."

"How many graffiti were on the walls?"

"Six, and you painted three additional ones with a paint can before dropping it on the ground."

"What else?"

"You pushed gravel with your shoe."

"Which direction?"

Bambi snickered. "Right, of course."

Wilborn crept up the stairs and hovered above her prisoner. She asked from behind Bambi's back, making her recoil in shock at a voice so close to her ear. "Raise your cuffed hand." The doctor grasped Bambi's forearm before squeezing the metal cuff against the wrist as tight as possible and then releasing. Bambi grimaced in pain for a brief moment.

Back near her captive, Wilborn said, "I'm taking off the blindfold. Have a gander at the differences."

Wilborn stepped back to monitor Bambi's reaction. "Tell me the last thing I did."

Bambi scanned the room before surveying the doctor, head to foot. Her neck pounded rapidly with each heartbeat, breaths deeper, but she didn't panic. "You untied your shoelace."

"Correct on all counts. How is the wrist?"

She wriggled the handcuff around her wrist. "Hurts, but okay."

"I squeezed as hard as I could. It should be bloody throbbing."

"Not so much."

"Tolerating acute pain? Excellent." Dr. Wilborn picked up the syringe sitting on the trunk lid. "One or two more injections before you have the ability to do what I want you to do."

"Which is what?"

"Want me to loosen the handcuff?"

"I'll use your word. I'm tolerating it."

But Wilborn couldn't leave it at that; she had to test how far her subject would go to get out of this situation and how much pain Bambi could handle before breaking down and giving her exactly what she wanted—absolute control over body and mind. "Your wrist is swollen. I should loosen the cuff."

"Thought you would say that. If it is supposed to hurt as much as you say, then yes. Loosen it."

When Dr. Wilborn injected the stem cell solution into Bambi's forehead, a grin crept across her face while moaning in delight instead of passing out as she had done every time before. After the injection, Bambi said, "I need a shower and a bathroom. I smell."

"After some time," Wilborn said, "most individuals are unaware of their own body odor."

Bambi grabbed her captor's gaze and wouldn't let go. "I can smell me, and you, and the rats hiding in the concrete cracks."

Wilborn blinked twice. "You're handcuffed to the railing. How do you surmise getting a shower?"

Chapter 17

Bambi used her free hand to point down the tunnel. "You said a convenience store was not too far away, right?"

"Correct," Wilborn said.

"Is that the closest exit?"

Wilborn studied the drainage system map on her phone, then gazed down a long, straight pipe. "Yes. The shop where I bought breakfast is this way. After sixty or seventy yards, turn left, and the effluent exit is close to a hundred yards further. Why?"

"At the other place, behind the convenience store, what you call the shop, had a faucet with a green hose connected to it. Most of those stores have that. That's how Bert and I got free water and a shower. I can use the bathroom inside."

"And what of your clothes, the blood on your hip? You rush inside, and the clerk will call the police."

"I'll tell him it's from my period."

"That would be between your legs."

"Guys don't know shit about women. They'll believe anything a woman says."

Wilborn nodded to that response. "From here to there on your own? What makes you presume I would uncuff you?"

"I want the stem cells. It makes me feel good, so no reason for me to run."

"If I release you and you try to kill me, you'll be an absolute ponce trying to mix the solution."

"So, I'll go there, shit and shower, then come back here. You make more playtime punch while I'm gone. Deal?"

"You remember Bert?" Wilborn asked.

Bambi cocked her head in confusion. "You said he left."

"Not entirely true. I have him handcuffed to another railing." Wilborn showed her phone screen to Bambi. "Alive."

"He looks bad, asleep," Bambi said. "Give him something to eat and drink."

"There's enough blubber to stave off starvation. Water, on the other hand…" Another picture of Bert and two empty water bottles appeared on the phone screen. "What do you suggest we do to best solve this?"

"I'll return with food and water for him."

"You have no money."

Bambi disagreed. "I live on the streets. I don't need money."

Dr. Wilborn checked the time on her expensive English watch. "When I uncuff you, if you are not sitting here on your bloody arse in seven minutes, Bert dies with a bullet to the brain."

"Seven is not long enough," Bambi said. "You know I haven't had a dump in two days, and I'm taking my damned sweet time. Lead me to the exit and give me fifteen minutes from there."

The doctor dug inside the trunk for a neutral colored, self-adherent cohesive bandage roll like nurses used to wrap arms after drawing blood and wrapped Bambi's forehead and arm before dropping the key to the handcuffs on the ground. "I will find Bert and kill him if you are not back when I said."

After removing the cuff, Bambi massaged her wrist. "Take me to the exit." While plodding along, she gazed up and down the connecting pipes. "Where's Bert?"

"I know where he is."

They stopped near the effluent exit, where a convenience store with a fuel pump was a short distance away. A low wooden fence enclosed three sides of the air conditioner unit, and a hose connected to a faucet nearby.

Wilborn pushed Bambi's shoulder. "Seven minutes. That is your maximum. You'll hear a gunshot if you have not returned by then."

"Tell me what time it is."

"It doesn't matter. You have seven minutes, and the timer starts now."

Bambi exited the concrete pipe and inhaled, almost forgetting the scent of fresh air. Elation swirled inside her as bright sunlight and the heat of the day slapped the back of her neck. It felt like a lifetime inside the concrete tunnel. Wilborn watched Bambi run with no limp. Anyone with a hip wound should have an irregular rhythm during ambulation, especially running. Was this because the stem cells in the brain blocked pain? Seconds later, Bambi yanked the glass door ajar at the convenience store.

The clerk raised his eyes from playing games on his phone and scrutinized her from head to toe; 5 foot 2, stretching to a hundred pounds, torn gray sweatpants, ragged sleeveless shirt, no bra, erect nipples, unkempt hair, and dirt on her hands and fingers. The wrapping around her scalp caught the most attention, and he was glad for the CCTV cameras in the corners.

The clock above the clerk's head read eighteen minutes after the hour. She wondered how much time had passed since she left the doctor.

"I need to use your bathroom."

"Have to buy something first."

Bambi showed her empty pockets. "I don't have any money. Is it back there?"

"It is, but it's locked."

She made sure there was no one else inside. "I'll fuck you for it."

He scoffed. "I'm not sticking my dick in there."

"A blow job." She could get him off in less than a minute. "I'm good at it."

He hurried to the front door and locked it before nodding toward the back. "Make it fast."

Three minutes passed, and Bambi charged out of the store clutching a plastic bag filled with water bottles and Slim Jims in one hand and a handful of soapy paper towels in the other. She stripped off her pants, shirt, and shoes before turning on the hose. She vigorously wiped the towels over her face, breasts, neck, armpits, and legs before rinsing, causing her to jerk from the cold water hitting her skin. How long has it been? Two minutes? After grasping her pile of clothes and the plastic sack, she raced toward the drainage pipes barefoot in her underwear. The sun was in her face; the entrance was dark. She entered and yelled, "I'm back!"

A baseball bat slugged her mid-chest, knocking her backward. Water bottles bounced against the concrete. Her lungs froze from pain. She tried to force a word, but nothing came out.

The doctor stood over her, holding the bat. "You're late. It's been eight minutes."

Bambi rolled to her elbows and knees. Her breaths were too shallow to say anything. All she thought of was Bert. He needed food and water. She crawled to the water bottles and Slim Jims and placed each inside the sack.

Wilborn tapped the bat against Bambi's back. "Get off your bollocks and put on your clothes. Back to where we were."

When Bambi took a breath, her ribs shot electrical pains through her body. Tears speckled the ground. While crawling, the pain decreased. She controlled it, forced it to dissipate. Standing without eyeing the doctor, she wiped tears from her face and slipped on her shirt, pants, and shoes.

Wilborn noticed Bambi's first steps were short and weak, then became steady and prominent. "I see you are controlling your emotions and pain." Wilborn smiled. "I'm proper chuffed my invention is working. Can you feel the stem cells growing in your brain?" The bat tapped against her upper arm. "But you should have anticipated my actions. This was a test, and you failed the mission by failing the time, so you received the consequences you deserve."

When they returned, Wilborn motioned with the bat for Bambi to sit against the concrete steps. The cuffs clattered on the ground.

"Back on the rail."

Bambi snapped one cuff on the metal rail, but refrained from placing the other on the wrist.

"Now, I said. Snap the other on your wrist."

Bambi watched the bat pointed toward her. She had had her fill of the punishment, but something made her ask, "And what if I don't?"

"You don't get any more injections into your brain."

"I watched you put my blood in the centrifuge, adding and mixing that stuff. It was no problem for you, so I no longer need you. How do you feel about that?"

Wilborn scoffed. "You would kill yourself."

"How about I jerk that bat away from you and use it on you?"

"You've already failed twice." Wilborn pushed the tip of the bat against Bambi's ribs. "Ready to fail again? I won't be so kind." Gesturing toward the open handcuff, she said, "Put it on like a nice twit."

Bambi grasped the handcuff, slipped the chain between her fingers, and tugged with all her might, but it didn't break.

Wilborn jeered at her. "The stem cells don't make you stronger. You're not Superwoman, just an experimental subject who's done about the best you can, and I think I'm done with you. Time I dispose of a failed experiment." She leaned on the baseball bat like a proper Englishman's cane. "I have already selected my next subject, who is willing, and grateful, even providing me additional protein extract to guarantee the success of my experiments. The only vial besides mine was in the Hildebrandt Police Department Evidence Room until he quietly removed it." She swung the bat in a circle before aiming it at Bambi. "Which was the property of my business associate, and that wretched Marla Adams let him die." Pings echoed when the bat tapped twice on the concrete. "Was my partner. Was, being the bloody important word. I have it, or at least my colleague has it. So, this experiment between us has come to an end."

"Wait. I'll be your willin subject." She held the handcuff's open end around her wrist, but didn't snap it shut. "Isn't this what you want? You keep giving me the injections, and I'll do whatever you want me to do."

Near Wilborn, a roach crawled on top of a broken branch. It paused, then went up one side before turning around and crawling down to the other end. Did it want food? Other roaches? Are they loners? No. Writhing herds of six-legged creatures usually sprung from cracks and crevices when darkness changed to bright lights. But this one was a loner, like her. Wilborn had one friend, and everyone else wasn't worth the trouble of knowing. The sole of her shoe scuffed over dirt. Scurrying off the branch, the roach disappeared down a crack in the concrete.

"Hey!" Bambi snapped the cuff around her wrist. "Did you hear me? I said I'll do whatever you want...for the stuff."

❖

Elon Davis held a clean garbage bag containing all the materials to grow his mushrooms. He was still pissed that the cops stole his plastic jugs. He couldn't afford to buy new ones, so he walked into a Walmart Garden section when it was not busy and walked out with what he needed to restart his fungal cultivation. Searching for an area with no stormwater inlets above his head was tedious. The illumination from the street inlets and the row of lights along the perimeter of the concrete pipe was too much. Mushrooms don't like luminosity. An iron ladder bolted to the ground stood vertical and led to a manhole cover. Behind the ladder was a little cubbyhole—perfect for hiding his fungus garden. He broke two lights along the concrete wall with the butt end of his pocketknife and transformed what little brightness there was into utter blackness within the corner.

Voices echoed inside. Sounds bounce off concrete. Did one have an English accent? Placing the bag down, he removed his shoes to silence his footsteps and crept toward the sound. I've got to be an idiot doing this, but I want my jugs back. Moments later, the line of lights along the side of the wall had gone dark. Turning the corner, he nearly stumbled over a bloated body with a scraggly beard and a bullet hole in his gray sweatshirt. Elon covered his mouth and nose with his elbow when the putrid smell struck him. Voices came further down the tunnel. "Damn. It has to be this doctor person." Further down and around a corner, he spotted a short man, or was it a woman standing over a person sitting on the ground. Is this the guy that stupid DEA agent wants? Elon backed away.

Rivera's phone rang as he drove downtown. "Hello?"

"I have to whisper, but I think I found this person."

"Is this Elon? The mushroom guy?" He stopped at an intersection. "Where are you?"

"I'm not sure exactly, somewhere inside the pipes."

Rivera never expected to hear from the guy again.

The revolver hammer clicked near Elon's head. He spun around and gawked at a gun barrel—a black hole that seemed to grow every second.

Dr. Wilborn sighed deeply. "Drop the phone."

Elon released it, and it fell to the ground with a loud clatter while Rivera was still on the phone. Without a sound, Wilborn swept it away with her foot.

"Hey, man." Elon rubbed the back of his neck. His voice cracked. "I'm just trying to grow some mushrooms." "See? Over there. That's my bag with all the stuff."

"Who were you talking to?" Wilborn asked.

"My phone?" Elon pivoted back toward the doctor. "Oh, I mean, a guy that gives me the stuff...the mushrooms. He's nobody. A person living on a farm—a mushroom farm."

"Blimey, you lie like a sack of shit."

Rivera pulled over and listened to the conversation as best he could.

"Nobody knows nothing about nothing down here." Elon stepped back, glancing in the other direction. Could he run and zigzag like people on television to stay alive? "We stick together and, instead, stick it to the cops anytime we can, right?"

Dr. Wilborn smiled while aiming the barrel at Elon's head.

Rivera yanked the phone away from his ear as a gunshot reverberated down the concrete pipe.

Chapter 18

Sheriff's Deputy Jeffrey Keene called Marla.

She wrinkled her nose at the name on the screen before answering on the second ring. "Hello?"

"Marla, please excuse my actions at the restaurant. I went over the line."

She nodded to herself. "Yes, you did."

"After this individual you are hunting is arrested and in jail, I will try to convince the prosecutor to let the doctor help Rosemary. It could be a good thing during a trial, right? Turning over a new leaf, helping someone instead of killing."

"I can't promise this person will survive," Marla said. "Wanted for murder—multiple murders, chances of surrendering are slim."

"Marla, you're not holding back where that special vial is, are you?"

"Are you accusing me of being an accomplice?"

Jeffrey whispered to another person, "She said she doesn't know, and I believe her."

"Are you with Rosemary or at your office?" Marla asked.

"Got to go. I should make another call."

◆

Dr. Wilborn watched the guy zigzag down the pipeline and disappear when the pipe curved right. "Bloody hell. I should have killed him...or made my next subject." She shook her head. "No, I'm ready. No need to waste any more time...or protein extract." She pulled on her collar. It was cooler inside but still hotter than in London. She picked up Elon's phone lying on the ground and ended the call without saying a word.

"What's happening down there?" Bambi called out.

"I told you to stay right where you bloody are, or you get nothing." She moved further away from Bambi while calling a number on the newly acquired phone. Fifty feet down the pipe, a familiar scent, putrid and repulsive, permeated the air, Bert's bloated carcass. Luckily, the air flowed through the water gates, diverting the stench in a different direction from Bambi.

Wilborn phoned, and a voice on the other end asked, "Who is this?"

"Listen, you ninny, you must keep Adams off my back until I'm ready for her."

"I can try, but she does what she wants to do, and she's right most of the time."

"You still holding the extract?"

"Yes."

Wilborn stepped past Bert's body. The smell didn't plague her. She had been around death for decades. "And nobody knows that you have it?"

"Not a single person paid any attention to me. I entered the police station, opened the evidence room door, and took it. These Hildebrandt cops got no clue what they're doing."

Wilborn glanced behind her, making sure Bambi stayed back. "Aren't they supposed to keep the door locked?"

"Yeah, they're supposed to, but they don't." The voice paused. "Are you ready for me?"

"No," Wilborn said. "My subject responded positively, and I believe she's ready."

"So, where is this person?"

"With me." The doctor turned to trek back toward Bambi and the trunk, but stopped.

"What about me? You said you wanted me to do it. You promised me the money that I need."

"Changed my mind. I have someone else, a girl, to do it."

"After this thing you made, this girl with superpowers—"

"No Bloody Superpowers, just smarter than you!"

"And what are you going to do after this thing fails? Come begging me to do your dirty work?"

"She won't fail," Wilborn said. "She's ready."

"Yeah? And when she fails, I won't do what you want until you fix someone else first."

"Rubbish. I can't wait. I must take this Adams person out."

"I have the protein extract vial; all I have to do is stir it up with bone marrow. How about I cut you out and use it on my woman? She needs help."

"Bollocks. You're not making a cake, you twat. This is a very delicate and specialized procedure. Besides, that extract is mine. Do you understand? Mine! Furthermore, you haven't the foggiest how to use it."

Bambi stepped closer to Wilborn. "Where the hell are you?"

Wilborn couldn't let her come around the corner and see Bert. "How the bloody hell did you get out of the cuffs?"

Bambi held the small key in between two fingers. "You dropped this."

Wilborn fired the gun, and the explosion echoed down the pipe. Bambi quickly crouched and covered her head with her hands. "Get your bloody arse back to the stairs and shut up."

"Trouble in wonderland, doctor?" the voice asked.

"No." Dr. Wilborn thought how much solution remained in her vial. She had enough of the metal catalyst for hundreds of doses, but the weak link was the protein extract. "I've read about Adams, studied her for months, and she's smarter and faster than you. And right now, the idiot on the phone can't do shite without at least ten injections in your dithering brain."

"Watch your mouth there, Doc."

"All right, you win; after returning what belongs to me, I'll inject whomever you want."

"Is it painful?"

"You mean the injections in the brain? No."

"And getting the stem cells?"

Wilborn stalled. "If I didn't make you unconscious, then yes, acquiring your stem cells from your hip and drilling a hole in your forehead would hurt."

"Drilling holes in bones sounds painful."

Wilborn stiffened her posture and reined in emotions before a small smile crossed her lips. She could kill anybody with a sharp needle and a syringe. "I said you would be unconscious, you blithering idiot."

"Yeah, great. When your superhero bitch fails, then you do what I want. Okay? Heal my woman first. She's smart, smarter than me."

Wilborn mumbled, "That wouldn't take much."

"What'd you say? Shut up. She's got something wrong with her head, and you'd better fix it."

Wilborn didn't answer.

"Did you get all the cash from the pawnbroker's safe? He always kept at least two mill in there."

Wilborn ignored the guy's plea about some worthless woman. "Yes. All of it."

"You can have the vial, but the money is mine."

Wilborn suddenly realized she could have two after Marla Adams. "If you kill Adams, we'll talk."

"Ass-backward, Doc. I want every penny you stole right now."

Chapter 19

The odor of freshly brewed coffee woke Marla. It was still dark outside her bedroom window.

A metal pan clanked against the kitchen floor. "Shit, shit, shit!" Cassie yelled.

Marla heard another voice. Was it Roger? She grabbed her service weapon on her nightstand and leaped from the bed.

"This is going to wake up Marla," Cassie said.

"Don't worry about her," Roger said.

Marla held the pistol close to her side, her finger across the trigger guard. She paused at the kitchen entrance and eyed the room. The only person there was Cassie in a tattered oversized 1996 Dallas Cowboys Super Bowl t-shirt that enveloped most of her arms, trunk, and legs. She bent down and pitched the bacon back in the pan. Cassie grabbed the panhandle while she spoke to the phone on the counter. "I told you I can't see a damn thing in the dark. I need light in the kitchen."

Roger's voice came across on the speaker. "I'd come over and cook breakfast for you, but I don't want a bullet in my ass. Speaking of ass, why don't you come over here and we can—"

Cassie stared at the phone and laughed. "I should come over and kick your ass all over my bunkhouse."

Marla coughed lightly and turned on the kitchen light. Cassie spun around, holding the pan in her hand. "Ah, good morning—MARLA!"

"Oops," Roger said, "bye." The line goes dead.

"And good morning to you, Cassie, who is alone in the kitchen, even though I detected a man's voice from my bedroom."

Cassie slid the pan back on the stove. "Roger might be dumb, but he's not stupid. You said nothing about me talking on the phone while I was in the house. It's okay if I do, isn't it?"

Marla stepped into the kitchen and laid her pistol on the countertop. "You're not sixteen, and I'm not your mother. I can't tell you what to do with that man, just don't do anything in my bed, or the other bed, or the couch, or the floor."

"I believe you put the fear of God in him, maybe the fear of you, but he hasn't even mentioned once coming close to the front or back door. By the way, no one has ever used this stove, and this pan is brand new."

"Yeah. Didn't feel right cooking without Crosby here." Marla shrugged. "I go by the three second rule."

"Me too." Cassie smiled. "Frying it up a little longer should kill anything on it, don't you think?"

After breakfast, they threw the paper plates and plastic forks in the trash. Marla gazed out the window over the sink. Morning light approached with an endless line of orange rising from the horizon. Purple clouds hung silently in the deep blue sky. A black column of smoke billowed upward twenty miles away.

"That's the Johnson ranch," Marla said.

Cassie looked out the window. "I should call Roger. At the bunkhouse, he's closer."

She called, but he didn't answer. She called again, but still no answer. "We should call the fire department."

"Right," Marla said. "Get dressed. I'll call."

Ten minutes later, they both piled into Marla's pickup. She drove down the dirt road beside Johnson's fence line.

Marla called out, "It looks big. Damn, we need rain."

"It's too big for a trash burn." Cassie pulled her sunglasses off the front of her cap and slipped them on.

"A barn? Old house?" Marla stepped down on the accelerator. "Not black enough for an oil burn."

Marla turned at the crossroad. A single fire department water truck, red lights flashing, drove toward them on the same narrow road. Two hundred yards away, a wooden hay storage unit was fully ablaze.

Roger tugged his cap down further on his forehead while leaning against the front of his pickup. There was nothing he could do. The water truck drove past, and the firefighters climbed out. Within a minute, they were battling the burning pyre.

After the flames were extinguished, Roger inspected the remains, which was nothing. The roof had caved in, and the hay and stored wood planks had burned to ash.

Jake Johnson pulled his truck over to the side of the road. He swung his door open and ran toward the wet, smoldering mess, but Marla blocked him from getting too close.

"I came as soon as I received word the barn was on fire."

"I know you did, Jake," Marla said. "Don't imagine there would have been anything you could have done if you were here."

The firefighters raked through the mess, determining if anything else was still burning.

"I was in San Antone, but I came when they called me."

"Nothing inside worth much, right?" Marla asked.

"Insurance will pay for it. I could use the cash right now." His palms rubbed his face several times, then he pointed back at the smoldering mess. "Inside was the wood Mrs. Johnson and I were going to use to add onto the house someday, maybe double the size of it, but when she got sick with pneumonia and died, I was incapable of doing anything for a long time. That wood stayed there for decades, and sometimes I'd look it over when loading hay, but I couldn't force myself to work on it."

Marla hugged him. "I can get someone here to clean all this up for you."

He released her. "No, thanks. No hurry to take away something of hers."

Marla understood too well.

Cassie tapped her on the shoulder. "I should get our hay out to the cattle." She skimmed over the almost cloudless sky. "No rain means no grass. They need to eat."

Roger stepped forward and adjusted the ball cap on his head. "Mrs. Adams, I can help Cassie if you want?"

Marla stuck out her hand, and they shook. "Thanks, Roger. I like you, but..."

They said at the same time, "Just not in the house."

"Yes, ma'am. Understood," Roger added.

Marla glanced at his waist. "Where's your gun?"

"Oh, left it at the bunkhouse. Rushing over here, I guess I forgot it. Hey, just thought of something, Cassie told me you have enough hay to last six or seven weeks, and I have a buddy on the other side of the county who has extra. I could get him to sell it to you." He made sure Mr. Johnson wasn't close by. "He's struggling with his ranch and losing money. I might need another job soon, and I'm tired of not sleeping in a bed."

"Thanks, Roger. I can't hire you, but you can stay in the bunkhouse for now."

"How about five hundred a week?"

Marla shook her head. "Can't. The best I can do is promise to keep the pantry filled."

He eyed Cassie.

"Don't look at me," she snapped back. "I'm not giving you money."

Roger pushed the brim of his cap down. "Okay for now, Mrs. Adams. At some point, I'm going to need money, but at the moment, a roof and food will work."

Several hours later, Roger and Cassie had finished loading both pickup beds full of hay bales. They drove to the windmill near the water tank. It took longer than either expected as the temperature increased and the sun rose in the cloudless sky. Roger hopped out of his truck, dropped the tailgate, and climbed into the bed. With his work gloves on, he pitched the first bale to the side with ease. "Twelve bales won't take care of all of them, but it's a start."

"Right." Cassie stood next to his pickup while breaking up the bales into piles of hay.

An engine roared in the distance, and a line of dust grew from the dirt road. A deputy's SUV stopped alongside the fence line, and Jeffrey Keene honked his horn before stepping out.

"Who is he?" Roger asked.

Cassie held her hand over the bill of her ball cap, which had Marla's heart brand logo on the front. "Deputy Keene. He's a close friend of Marla. I've met him, and he seems okay. What do you think he wants?"

Roger stood in the pickup bed, lifted his ball cap, and wiped his forehead before replacing it on his head, then pitched another bale on the ground. "Hope it's not what Marla said wouldn't happen. I'm tired of running."

"The drugs?" Cassie nodded. "No. I trust her. She said her boss would bury what he had."

Jeffrey waved at them.

"I think he wants us to go over there." Roger removed his gloves, dropped them on the remaining hay bales in the back of the pickup, and jumped to the ground near the driver's door. "Let's go find out."

They climbed into his truck, and Roger drove close to the fence line. When he turned, Cassie lowered her window.

"Yes, sir. What can we do for you?" she asked.

"Cassie Chandler, right?"

She took a second to answer. "Yes."

"The fire department contacted the sheriff's department about the fire at the Johnson place. They suspect arson. Do you know anything about it?"

"Arson? No, not at all. I was in the Adams house, and we saw smoke from her kitchen window."

"You were with Marla Adams?" Jeffrey motioned toward the driver. "And you. What's your name?"

"Roger Hagen."

Jeffrey nudged his standard issue cowboy hat back a little. "Where were you before the fire?"

"In the Adams' bunkhouse. I saw the smoke and drove to it. It was already big, so I called the fire department."

Cassie said, "We did, too."

"Who is we?"

"Remember? Marla...Mrs. Adams. We were in her house and saw the smoke."

"Hmm." Jeffrey leaned against a fence post. "Hagen? Anyone with you last night or this morning?"

Roger saw Cassie standing still, waiting for his answer. "No. I was by myself."

"Did see anything suspicious when you got to the fire?" Jeffrey asked.

Roger shrugged. "No."

"What do you think caused the fire?" Jeffrey asked.

"Me?" Roger asked. "Could be anything. Dry air? Dry hay? Don't have a clue, but I'm sure you do since you said it was arson."

"I didn't say it was. Suspicion of arson is what I said. How about you come to the station and give a statement about where you were and what you saw?"

Roger yanked the seatbelt strap from his chest before letting it go. "How about you talk to my lawyer?"

Jeffrey pushed back from the fence post. "Since when do you need a lawyer?"

"Since you're pressuring me to go to the sheriff's department and confess to something I didn't do."

Jeffrey rubbed his jaw. "Not my intention. I never said you were involved."

"Good, because I'm not."

"But Mr. Johnson fired you after two weeks of employment."

"Wasn't fired. I left to join the rodeo circuit." He glanced at Cassie, who gave a dirty look in return.

"And he hired you again?"

"Yeah."

"If I asked Mr. Johnson if the two of you had an argument and that is why you left, what would he say?"

"That sounds like an accusation."

Jeffrey rolled his gaze toward Cassie. "If I call Mrs. Adams, will she confirm you were with her in the house?"

"I'd be happy to call her right now if you want me to."

Jeffrey's fingers played with the leather flap where he kept the handcuffs. Cassie and Roger watched closely as he closed his hand into a fist and tapped the top of the fence post. "Not necessary. I'll see her later today." Jeffrey strode back to his vehicle. "Sorry to bother the two of you." He spun around. "Oh, uh, make sure you both stay in Bexar County for the next week."

The two watched the SUV drive away while the tires threw a trail of dust skyward.

"I should get the hell out of Texas," Roger said.

"If you do, the sheriff's department and the DEA will be after you, and being on the Top Ten's Most Wanted is not a list you want to be on."

A herd of cattle stood only feet away from the pickup. Cassie laughed and told Roger the cattle thought the deputy's horn was the dinner bell. As they drove back to the windmill, the cattle slowly eased behind them. After unloading the hay from both trucks, Roger jumped to the ground, and Cassie inspected the water level in the tank. She patted a few cattle on their backs as they ate the hay. The two gave each other a fleeting look. She pursed her lips. He stepped closer, wrapped his hands around her waist, and nudged the small of her back toward him.

"Now what?" he asked. He tried not to glance at her glass eye slightly off-kilter.

She gave him a peck on his mouth. He drew her closer. Her tongue slid past his lips. She explored, she tasted.

Something shoved against her back, almost knocking her down. A calf brushed against her as it headed for the hay, and they both laughed.

"The bunkhouse is five minutes away," she said.

Roger hustled to his truck and started the engine. "I'll be naked in the bed before you can get there."

The back tires of both trucks ground into the dirt and slid sideways as they raced away.

Chapter 20

Marla stood from the back of a room with nine others sitting inside a community center for the Trauma Anonymous meeting. When it was her turn to speak, she trailed to the front and plopped into the single chair, facing everyone waiting to hear her story, like a witness in a courtroom.

"My name's Marla, and...my, um, my life had...is upside down. An arsonist burned down my house, and someone shot and killed my husband. "Sorry, I smile anytime I see Crosby, my husband, even though he's dead." She rubbed the tops of her thighs and exhaled. "Crosby and I were small town cops together, and for a short time, both of us were in the DEA...before he died." Her hand brushed over her mouth. "Never really thought about being a cop when I was a kid."

She decided not to look at anyone and threw a pained stare at the corner of the building. "My little brother was funny, no, hilarious, in elementary school. He always made me laugh, made the whole family laugh. He had a stupid phrase he said a million times a day. It drove us crazy, but I laughed almost every time. 'Dial me in, baby.' He made friends with everyone—everybody's best friend, and he was my best friend until he reached his teen years, then we sort of separated. That's when he simultaneously made me feel cold and hot, angry and happy. We yelled at each other when we shouldn't have." She raised her eyebrows. "I didn't have many friends, ignored boys completely, and was in trouble more often than not. They sent me to the principal's office so many times I had memorized the number of steps from my classroom to there." She licked her lips while staring at the floor. "In my senior year, I became retracted. My few friends became fewer, and when I got picked on, even though my brother was a year behind me, he would defend me and take on whoever he had to." She hesitated and rubbed the corners of her mouth. "I hated it. He tried to teach me how to fight, but I didn't want to learn. I loved him and hated him... couldn't stand him at times." She broke away her stare from the corner of the room and lowered her head. "I didn't know he used drugs. Stupid of me. I saw him every day and didn't see it. Foolish emotions can blind you, then his autopsy report said he had drugs in his system. He had to be using for quite some time.

"But," she snickered, "that's not the worst person in my life. The man I grew up with, my...father, a police chief, he, uh, was cool to me, not letting me in, never giving an inch. He was a competition shooter, a quick draw athlete, at the top of his league in whichever state we lived in."

She paused for a moment before restarting. "He wouldn't let me shoot a gun, but without him knowing, a friend taught me how. I practiced away from my family and became good, better than good. I couldn't tell anyone about the competitions I entered because he would find out about it." She swept her arm across the room. "And because he made me feel inferior and lame and wrong and...pathetic, I said, 'Oh, yeah? Watch this.' I'm gonna go national and win. Win everything, be bigger and better than him, and beat him at his own game, right?"

She scooted further back in the chair. "And when I went to college, I did just that, but I had black stains on my hands and fingers, gunpowder in my hair and face and eyes and ears, and calluses on my fingers and thumbs that cracked and bled. My stomach cramped terribly, and I had diarrhea before competitions...and I loved it. I was fast and lost my fear in life, which excited me, and because of that, I never befriended anyone who came to the meets because they were competitors, each a person impeding me from what I wanted, and I wanted him to understand how good I was, to be there to smile and say, 'Congratulations!'" She licked her lips again. "But the more he ignored me, the more I was determined. The target's bullseye became my focus. I won everything, and I felt lonelier."

Her fingers brushed across her forehead, and she sniffed once. "I kept the trophies at someone else's home, not mine. Until, one day, I filled my trunk with them and dumped everything in his living room." She scoffed. "Stupid, right? But that's when he realized I was better than what he told me. After that, he almost let me in his circle.

"In the Hildebrandt police force, we were always dead even in one-on-one competitions, and I beat him the last two times. I was quick, and he was aware of my speed, and when it truly mattered, during the crucial moments when milliseconds held greater significance than anything else... I'm not sure if it meant anything to him anymore." She cleared her throat. "Or me, either."

Chapter 21

D r. Wilborn followed the maze of the drainage system and exited where she had entered days before. She enjoyed the coolness ten feet underground, but outside, at midday, the sun pounded down directly above her, increasing the temperature by twenty degrees.

Bambi lagged behind. "Where are we heading?"

"Follow me and shut your bloody mouth." The trunk's wheels scratched across the yellowed grass and pebbles at the intersection where a fuel station and convenience store were the only buildings on a corner. They hiked while Bambi held her blanket in her hand. Wilborn was hungry, smelled bad, and tired. The plate glass window had a taxi service sticker with a phone number. She called, and it rang.

"Taxi company."

Wilborn glimpsed at the street signs. "I'm standing near the corner of Vincent and Gibson Streets. When can you send a car?"

Typing in the background caught Wilborn's attention.

"I have a vehicle in your area dropping someone off. He can be there in twenty-five to thirty minutes. What is your name, sir?"

"Wil..." She almost said her name. "Smythe, Michael Smythe."

"Destination?"

She had no idea where she was. "The closest five-star hotel, and I'm in a hurry."

She heard typing on the phone again. "You are in the wrong part of town for that, sir. The closest is nine miles. There's a motel about six blocks from you and a three-star a mile away. I can have someone there in thirty minutes."

"No bloody motels. I want a place with a bar where I can order a martini, a good bed, and a shower. In London, I never have trouble finding a cab in five minutes."

"Five minutes? That's good, but from where you stand, sir, tell me, does it look like Piccadilly Circus? How about you go there and hail a cab? Otherwise, wait for our taxi to pick you up in thirty. I'll ask him to hurry."

The doctor stuck the phone into the pocket as her stomach growled. "Go inside. There must be something edible in there."

When Wilborn opened the glass door, cold air hit her. This city is too hot outside and the bloody buildings are too cold inside. A middle-aged woman holding a plastic sack in each hand smiled and shuffled past them. Three people stood in line to check out, with all noticing the tubing taped to Bambi's forehead. Inside a transparent box, hotdogs slowly spun atop stainless-steel rollers. A shriveled chocolate donut and a bagel covered with sesame seeds sat in the back corner of a "Fresh Baked Goods" case.

"The dogs aren't bad," Bambi said. "I've had 'em."

"Grab one," Wilborn said while towing the trunk, with wheels clicking against the flooring. On the next aisle were rows of crackers and jerky. The doctor snatched something somewhat healthy, a package of mixed nuts, and then waited in line. On the television monitor above the cashier, the local news was on with the sound muted. Bambi blinked at the screen showing a prison photo of Hugo Wilborn, with a tagline reading wanted for questioning on a murder case. Wilborn kept her head low, paid for the food, and then rushed out with Bambi lagging. Snagging the phone from another pocket, Wilborn called the taxi company back and offered to pay extra for a rush pickup. That was when a siren squelched behind them, police emergency lights swirling.

The officer stepped out of the car. "Drop your phone and put your hands on your head."

Wilborn eased the trunk down, then bent down and laid the phone on the ground before standing again and opening the package of nuts. "You Yanks are all the same. What do you want?"

The officer placed his right hand on his holstered service weapon. "Hands on your head."

The doctor shifted the small package from one hand to the other. "You want some?"

"Hey," Bambi said. "How about this? You want this, you fucking cop?" She threw her hot dog at the officer.

He ducked, and when the food bounced off his shoulder, he reached for his service weapon, but decided not to pull it on the twig of a woman standing still. When he turned back toward the other person, a gun muzzle stared him straight in the face.

Wilborn fired the revolver three times, hitting the officer in the head and neck. "Blimey, that's loud." She pulled the trigger again when the man moaned, but the gun only clicked. After tossing the empty revolver to the side, she took the officer's semi-automatic pistol before motioning toward Bambi. "Get in." Wilborn dragged the trunk to the police vehicle's back door, opened it, and shoved it in the backseat.

"Where are we going?" Bambi asked.

"Somewhere besides bloody here." The vehicle charged down the street.

Two blocks further down, a dark green four door pickup approached them with the rear of the truck riding low from chopped firewood filled in the bed.

Wilborn pointed at the truck. "That's where we're going."

The driver eased the truck to the shoulder, willing to let the vehicle with the flashing emergency lights pass by.

When Dr. Wilborn eased next to it and lowered the window, the driver did as well. "Can I help you, officer?"

The struggling engine idled rough from the pickup. Oily blue smoke rose from underneath the cab.

"Put your vehicle in park," Wilborn said as she jostled the pistol in her hand and tried to decide whether it was necessary to kill another.

The elderly man did what he was told, even though confused about the lack of police uniform attire and a girl in the front seat. "What's that on your head?" Ashes crumbled to the ground when he tapped his cigarette on the doorframe. He blew a cloud of smoke toward the sky. "You don't look like a cop, maybe undercover with those clothes on, but why are you driving a cop car? Are you the police?"

Wilborn raised the pistol and fired, hitting the driver in the head. She shoved Bambi's shoulder. "Come on. We're switching."

They dragged the dead man from the driver's seat and rolled him aside.

"There's blood and guts all over the seat," Bambi said.

"No guts. Brains."

"I'm not getting in there."

Wilborn tried to redirect her thoughts. "Help me with the trunk."

The two grabbed it from the backseat of the police vehicle and slid it across the back seat of the pickup.

"Get in," Wilborn said.

"No."

Wilborn ripped the blanket away from Bambi and threw it over the bloody mess on the seat. "There." She hit the roof with the gun. "Get in."

When Bambi sat down, she cringed as the blanket slid in the blood underneath it.

They drove away, leaving a trail of black exhaust behind and the police vehicle with its doors open and lights flashing in the middle of the road.

❖

Rivera's phone rang with the word UNKNOWN on the screen. "Rivera, here."

"That madman almost killed me."

"Who is this?"

"You still have my jugs?"

"Elon Davis?" Rivera asked.

"Yeah. That girl is nuts. She took my phone, and I ran. She shot at me! You hear me? She tried to kill me."

"Are you hit? Do I need to call an ambulance?"

"No. I'm fine."

"Tell me where she is."

"Can't say, exactly. Told you; I ran."

"Why are you calling me?"

"I can tell you where I was. That should help. So, may I have my jugs back?"

"Listen, kid. Why were you back there? Are you growing mushrooms somewhere else?"

"I...no...what? Cleaning up stuff."

"Are you in the same place? Doesn't count if you are."

"No. Different. I'm...what do you call that...spelunking."

"Spelunking is searching through caves."

"Same thing, only bigger holes here."

Rivera changed the subject. "Whose phone is this?"

Elon pointed at the guy next to him who owned the phone to be quiet. "A friend."

"Where are you?"

"At a friend's house."

"Okay. Tell me where you were."

"Near Vincent Park."

"I've been there," Rivera said. "Between 1604 and 410?"

"Yeah. When do I get my property back?"

"When we catch her."

Rivera kept an SAPD police scanner in his pickup. The speaker broadcasted a bulletin of a stolen police vehicle. The information was sketchy, but he heard what he needed—a person with a black case. He drove to the only police station in town and asked to see the video stream. Because the emergency lights were on, both the camera in the police vehicle and the officer's body cam recorded the scene. Two suspects, a cachectic woman and a muscular gray-haired woman, stood near the car. It had to be Wilborn. Red and blue lights bounced off the building, fuel pumps, and the black trunk in the background. The body cam had Wilborn in view. Food splattered across the officer, and the body cam aimed toward the thin woman and then back at Wilborn, who appeared with a gun, pointing at the officer. A second later, the gun fired, and the officer fell. Two more gunshots discharged. The camera inside the vehicle continued to record. The two climbed into the front seat and drove away before pulling next to a dark green 1990s Ford pickup. Rivera wrote down the Texas license plate number. Unintelligible words were spoken and then a single gunshot erupted.

Rivera stuck two pieces of gum in his mouth and pitched the wrappers in the trash as an officer ordered a BOLO, Be On The Look Out, for the pickup truck, then he left the police station for his vehicle.

◆

At home, Marla's stomach cramped as she sat on the toilet, and small blood clots dropped into the water. She was glad Cassie had left to handle the cattle. When her phone rang and the screen lit up, she pushed the speaker button. "Hello."

"What are you doing?" Rivera asked.

There was no way she would give that answer. Her fingers clamped onto her knees as her eyes squeezed tightly. "I..." A bloody glob dropped, splashing cold water on her buttocks. The cramping stopped. She took a deep breath and exhaled. Her shoulders curled forward. Pushing her elbows against her thighs and her hands squeezing against her temples, her head hurt, her soul hurt. She lost something from Crosby. Dead or alive, she still lost it.

"Are you there, Adams?"

She wiped her red eyes and drew in a breath before clearing her throat. "At home, getting ready to feed the animals. I can be where you want later in the day, just not now."

"The mushroom guy called me."

Marla said nothing.

"Did you hear me? The mushroom guy called and said the person with a black trunk shot at him inside the drainage system."

"Go check it out, and I'll catch up with you."

"I did. Wilborn shot a cop, stole his car, then switched to a pickup truck."

"When did this happen?"

"An hour or so ago. I've seen the videos, and the cops have a BOLO out for her. I'll come by and get you."

"Not now. I'm in the middle of...something. Pick someone else up before you go out. She's too dangerous to go after alone, and apparently, there are now two of them on a rampage. You hear me? Don't go alone." She disconnected the call and immediately made another.

A happy female answered the phone, "Hildebrandt Family Medical Office. May I help you?"

"This is DEA Special Agent Adams. Put the doctor on the phone, please."

"Are you needing an appointment?"

"This is an official drug enforcement investigation."

"Oh, my. Just a minute, please."

Off-key music played momentarily through the speaker before the phone clicked.

"This is Dr. Sanborn."

"Marla Adams here, and I'm sorry I threw the DEA card at your receptionist, but I expelled most of what was in my uterus. That procedure you talked about. Do I still need it?"

"I would presume so. Go to the ER and let them check you. Otherwise, you are scheduled for a procedure at the surgical center tomorrow morning."

"I'm in the midst of an investigation. How about you do the procedure now?"

"Marla, this is highly unusual. I don't perform surgeries during midday.

"Don't you still deliver babies and leave the office at a moment's notice?"

"Yes, of course, but this is different."

"Dr. Sanborn, I understand, but a guy is out there killing people. I can't take any more time away."

"You realize you'll need to rest a few days after the D&C."

"How about an hour? I'll sign anything you need to cover your butt."

"It's not me I'm worried about; it's you, your life."

Marla smiled. "And that is why you are my favorite doctor. I'll see you in thirty minutes."

❖

Bambi grabbed a cell phone from the pickup truck's floorboard. "Well, look what I found."

While driving, Wilborn reached for the phone. Bambi moved her hand away. She grasped for it again, but Bambi's reaction time was too quick.

"Give it to me." Wilborn reached for it again.

"Bambi held it away. "Nope. It's mine."

"Listen, you bloody twit," Wilborn backhanded her in the chest, then snapped the phone out of her hand, "maybe you aren't ready for this."

"I'm ready for whatever."

"We'll see." Wilborn made a call. "I have a..." she glanced at Bambi, then back at the road, "an experimental subject with me, and I want to test my subject's decision-making, attention, and anticipation. Nothing too extreme. My subject can't go against one of your cowboys." She listened while driving. "You say Adams' employee is there? The bird? Give me her name." After getting the information she wanted, she said, "Cassie. Brilliant. No, no. I promise. Just a bit of a scrap, that's all. Nothing major. This might bring you closer to the bitch. We'll be there promptly."

Wilborn ended the call and patted Bambi's thigh. "Stroll into a pub, find this bird named Cassie, and start a tussle. I want to see how the stem cells are working."

"What, exactly, do you want me to do?"

"Marla Adams is much tougher. She's DEA. Show me what you can do with someone much easier. If I like it, I'll keep you around. If not, I'm finished with you."

"I want more stem cells before I do anything."

While driving, Wilborn swung her arm toward Bambi for another backhand, but she caught it this time and twisted Wilborn's hand back.

Wilborn winced in pain as the pickup swerved into the other lane. "Blimey, all right. You win." She shook her hand when Bambi let go. "I'll give it to you in the car park."

Bambi entered The Broken Saddle Horn bar at midday and scanned the mostly empty place. Two women sat beside each other at a table.

"Need a beer?" Trixi asked from behind the bar.

"No," Bambi said. "One of those two named Cassie?"

"Yeah." Trixi's phone rang in her pocket. "Hold on a sec." She glanced at it and then stuck it in her back pocket before turning back to Bambi. "The one wearing a ball cap with a heart on it."

Without saying another word, Bambi aimed straight for the table.

"I'll take one."

The voice caught Trixi off guard. "Sure. Whatcha want?"

Dr. Wilborn perched on a bar stool. "A beer. You choose." She swept her hand across the counter. "Purple hair? Kinda different...I mean, for a cowboy pub."

Trixi scoffed. "Pub? Hope you don't plan on blending into the crowd with that accent."

"Not much of a crowd."

"Give it a few hours. This place will fill up."

Across the room, chairs scratched across the wooden floor.

"I said, I don't like your face," Bambi said.

Cassie turned her cap bill behind her and then stood with fists clenched. "You musta tried that line with someone else. Is that why you got a bandage on your forehead? I'm gonna do more than that if you don't get your skinny ass out of here."

Bambi felt a distinct vibration in the air. She anticipated it; the woman's right shoulder twitched, and her forearm muscles bulged slightly. She could almost read her opponent's mind. Bambi had to be perfect to get additional stem cells, but Dr. Wilborn was right. She was no Superwoman. No extra strength, no superpower.

When Cassie swung her right fist, Bambi saw it in slow motion. She blocked the fist and punched Cassie in the nose. Cassie stumbled back, wiping a drop of blood from her upper lip.

"Fuck you, bitch!" Cassie charged at the woman's throat.

Bambi twisted away in front of her opponent and counter-punched her in the eye. Bambi blocked another punch. She decided to end this quickly and slammed Cassie's forehead against the center of the table. Cassie's head bounced like a beach ball. Bambi latched onto Cassie's collar and eased her to the floor.

Adrenaline, confusion, and sadness flared all at once. She had never hit another human. Prior to the stem cells, Bambi would have cowered into a fetal position and begged against violence, but chemistry and medicine make humans do strange things, and she had to impress the doctor. When Cassie got on her hands and knees, Bambi grasped a handful of hair and raised her fist for another punch.

The rack of a shotgun stopped her, cold. "Ease back, girl," Trixi said.

Bambi released the mess of hair, and Cassie dropped onto her back.

"I saw how fast you were," Trixi said, "but you're not faster than the buckshot inside this barrel. Time for you to leave and not come back."

Bambi stepped over the unconscious Cassie and headed toward the door. On the other side of the building, Wilborn finished her beer, waved at the bartender, and followed Bambi outside.

In the car, Wilborn patted Bambi's leg. "That was brilliant, and you are ready for your next gig." She made a sharp turn at the intersection and stopped in front of a row of houses. "It's time to have a gander that stupid bobby, Marla Adams."

Bambi took the cell phone from the console and opened the map app. "Do you know where she lives?"

"I have someone who sent me her address. It's a small town called Hildebrandt."

"Why didn't we go there to kill her?"

Wilborn took the phone from Bambi. "You don't know the layout, how many guns she has, or where her safe place is. The odds are against you, one-on-one." She typed Adams's name and the town of Hildebrandt. "Got you, you bloody ginch."

Chapter 22

Marla packed light, shoving bottles of water, a rolled phone charger cord, and a package of feminine hygiene pads into a thin nylon backpack before zipping it closed. The surgical procedure would take an hour or two. And it's always cold enough to make ice in that place. "Damn, almost forgot." She grabbed a thick pair of cotton socks. I hate bare feet on metal stirrups.

Sharp pains stabbed her in the back, and her stomach cramped. She had to hurry to get to the toilet. After expelling more of the molar pregnancy, she was completely drained. Her eyelids grew heavy. The phone dropped from her hand, banging against the tile floor. "Damn. I fell asleep. I have to go."

A hundred yards from the entrance of Marla's ranch, an engine rumbled in a green pickup as Dr. Wilborn quietly sat in the driver's seat. Bambi had slumped down, knees bent and feet on the dash. She flicked a cigarette butt out the side window, then nabbed the pack left in the console from the previous driver. The odor of burnt motor oil surrounded the two inside the cab.

"I'm bored." Bambi leaned forward and opened the glove compartment. "We could use these."

"Use what?" Wilborn asked.

Bambi removed two walkie-talkies. "These." She considered opening the door and running from her captor, but she would never see the stem cell solution again. She handed one to the doctor.

"Right." Wilborn snatched the device from her hand before pressing the speaker button and hearing Bambi's device click. "Excellent discovery."

Wilborn wondered how much trouble she was in, so she typed San Antonio news on the phone keypad. BREAKING NEWS read across the screen: A police officer and a citizen gunned down less than a hundred yards from each other. "What a load of tosh all this is." A car approached in the rearview mirror. "Get down." She ducked while gripping the police officer's pistol. The vehicle drove past them and the ranch entrance. Bambi chewed on a fingernail like corn on the cob before spitting bits toward the windshield.

"What would you have done if the person in the car had stopped?"

"Me?" Bambi asked. "Nothing. I was listening, and the engine never slowed."

"Listen, you fucknugget. You're not as smart as you think you are. You need a bit more injections for that." Wilborn smacked the steering wheel with the heel of her palm. "Shite."

Bambi lowered her window, ignoring the stink coming from the exhaust pipes. "Forget something?"

"Yes, my contact doesn't know I have a new phone. He might have tried to call me." Wilborn sent a text. HW here. New number, and you need to give me the protein extract.

❖

As Marla hustled outside, she glimpsed Blackie standing majestically in the corral, expecting food, attention, and maybe a ride. She didn't have time, so she called Cassie and left a message saying she would be gone for several hours and please take care of the horses. Afterward, she pitched the backpack in the passenger seat, climbed into her truck, and drove over the cattle guard. As she turned onto the street, Marla noticed a pickup on the side of the road, but she was going to be late and had no time to fool around with vacant trucks in strange places. No time today.

Seconds later, the pickup pulled out and followed.

While driving, Marla's phone rang. "Hello?"

"It's Rivera. Tell me everything is okay with you."

She couldn't lie to him, but she didn't tell every single thing. "No, everything is not good. I'm heading to a medical clinic in Hildebrandt."

"Adams? What the hell is going on?"

"I...I got a problem, and Dr. Sanborn is fixing it." Truth be damned, Rivera didn't need to know any more than that. "I'll finish in about an hour and then meet up with you afterward."

"Wait. I'll meet you there. I can be wherever in a few minutes. What's the address?"

"Talk to you later." Marla ended the call before Rivera had a chance to respond. She wheeled into the outpatient surgical center parking lot and killed the engine. A green pickup lingered a block away.

Marla read the white letters printed on the glass front door.

HOURS BY APPOINTMENT: 6 AM-11 AM M-F

DR. KEVIN SANBORN

DR. BILL JAKOBSON

Marla pushed the blue disability button on the wall, and the doors slowly swung open. To her surprise, no other patients sat in the lobby.

Johanna, the receptionist, smiled at her. "Hi, Mrs. Adams. I'm so sorry you are here, but Dr. Sanborn is getting ready for you in the back."

Marla glanced behind her and then back at Johanna. "Why is no one here?"

"Oh, gosh, we finished hours ago, but still here cleaning up. Well, except Dr. Jakobson. He left to retrieve something from his office but said he would return to give you the anesthesia. Have a seat, and Tina will attend to you in a minute."

Dr. Wilborn drove the truck around to the rear of the clinic and came to a stop. "What could you be doing in there, you bloody tosser?" She ducked in the seat when a Porsche Boxer convertible parked parallel to the building. A man wearing green scrubs hopped out of his car, pressed four digits on the passcode lock, pulled on the gray metal door, and entered.

Wilborn held the pistol out in front of Bambi. "You know how to use this?"

"No, not really. Bert stole a gun once, and we shot it until all the bullets were gone. Where is Bert?"

Wilborn opened the truck door and stepped out. "Come with me."

Bambi waved her off and stayed seated.

Wilborn stepped around the pickup and opened the passenger door. "Get out!" she shouted, reaching for a handful of Bambi's hair.

Bambi blocked Wilborn's hand with her arm. "I may not be Super-woman, but I'm faster than you."

The door swung wider. "Out!" She pointed the gun at Bambi and lowered her voice. "And accompany me to the rear exit."

Bambi rubbed the bandage on her forehead. "Time for my stem cells. I like the feeling."

"We're not doing that here. Go check the sides of the building for another entrance."

The overhead light shined down from the awning above the back door. Dr. Wilborn tugged on the handle, but found it locked. There would be no way to enter quietly. Bambi stood nearby and patted her forehead for another shot in her head. "Blimey, girl. I told you to check around the building. After you kill Adams, you can have the stem cells." The doctor's hand patted the gun. "You're not as fast as a bullet."

"I'm faster than your hand. I'm going around to the other side."

Wilborn focused on the electrical box near the rear exit. "Hey, nutbag. Come back here. Do you know anything about electricity?"

"I live in a drainage pipe. What do you think?"

Wilborn's fist banged on the box twice. "I want to turn off the electricity." Black electrical lines ran into it from above, and below, a gray conduit line fed into a small hole in the wall. Bambi continued to stare at the doctor. Wilborn shoved the girl away. "Go flesh out the building, or I'll bloody well will kill you right here."

Bambi disappeared around the corner to find a large rectangle of thick glass blocks, from the awning to the ground embedded in the wall facing the street. She counted eighteen steps from the edge of the building to the middle of the blocks. She cupped her hands around her eyes and gazed through the glass, giving her a fly's-eye view of the room inside. "Hey, Doc."

Wilborn came around the corner. "What's this?"

Bambi patted the blocks. "After I kill the cop, this is my exit."

✦

Tina wore green scrubs and a smile when she opened the wooden door marked Patient Entrance and smiled. "Are you ready?"

Marla stood. "I guess so."

Halfway down the hall, Tina asked Marla to sit and wait on one of the two chairs lined up against the wall. After scooting back in the chair, she crossed her legs and wiggled her foot a hundred times a minute.

Minutes later, Dr. Wilborn entered the lobby, startling Johanna.

"Oh, I'm sorry. I meant to lock the doors. We're closed."

She peeked behind the receptionist. There was no one else. "Closed? But there's a vehicle out front. Are you still taking patients? I could use a stitch or two. Help get rid of a few wrinkles."

Still sitting in the chair behind the desk, Johanna grasped the telephone handle. "I'm sorry, but you should leave."

"Isn't that Marla Adams' truck out front? The DEA agent? I wanted to talk to her." Wilborn gestured to the parking lot. "About, umm, about someone with drugs, since, well, she's a bobby."

"Excuse me, a bobby?"

"Oh, sorry. A law enforcement person."

Johanna held the phone handle up for Wilborn to see. "We are closed, and if you don't leave, I'm calling 911."

Wilborn waved at her. "No, no. Not necessary. I can catch her tomorrow." She headed for the door, but when she pulled it open, she glanced behind her to see the receptionist defensively holding a pen like a knife.

"Out you go," Johanna said.

After hearing the lock snap behind her, Wilborn spun around and glared at the woman on the opposite side of the glass doors. "You didn't need to do that. I said I'm leaving."

Johanna stood firm.

The building was cold, and when she unzipped her backpack to put on her Spurs sweatshirt, Tina came around the corner, still smiling.

"Let's get you changed." When Tina opened the door, it banged against a row of metal lockers. "Sorry about the mess. We also use it for storage."

In the back and angled catty-corner in the room was a dented exam table with metal cabinets underneath, with IV poles and armless chairs stacked on one another in every corner. Marla cringed at the chrome stirrups sticking out from the end of the table.

Tina pointed at the row of metal lockers the door bumped into. "Place all your clothes in locker number 1." She handed Marla a small key on a stretchable wristband. "Use this to lock it." Her hand patted the stack of flimsy surgical gowns. "Slip one of these lovelies on, and when you come out," Tina gestured toward her neck, "I'll tie you up in the back. Surgery is down the hall."

Marla changed into the gown, leaving her clothes, gun, and phone in the locker. The building's air conditioner chilled her backside, and the floor seemed icy even through her cotton socks.

The surgical table felt like the cold steel tables in the autopsy room. Her body shivered, but was it because of a chill or nerves? Someone placed a warm blanket over her. Her toes curled, and her muscles twitched. She tried to slow her shallow breaths. A sudden need for water caught the back of her throat. When Dr. Jakobson started explaining the general anesthesia, she interrupted.

"No. You are not knocking me out. I have...too many things to do, and I need to be awake and alert."

"That was not the scheduled anesthesia. Dr. Sanborn usually wants a general, but we can put you in a light sleep instead."

"No. I'm sorry, but there is too much going on in this town, and I have to stay awake."

Dr. Sanborn entered wearing his green operating gown, gloves, and a mask, but all she saw on his face were smiling eyes. "Marla? Why are you sitting? You should be lying down and ready."

"Sorry, Doc. I was explaining to Dr. Jakobson why he can't put me completely to sleep."

"Marla, like we talked about before, the procedure takes ten minutes. You would be back awake in twenty minutes."

"And woozy and confused and not for me. Can't you, I don't know the term, make it not hurt while you are down there?"

Dr. Jakobson cleared his voice and gestured toward a corner of the surgical suite. "Excuse us for a moment, Mrs. Adams."

Away from Marla, Dr. Jakobson said, "I'm okay with you performing a paracervical block if that's what she wants. She'd be awake and could get up and walk out."

"Right, but a molar pregnancy complicates this procedure," Dr. Sanborn nodded. "It may take longer."

"Doctors?"

The two turned to look at Marla.

"May we begin? I have things to do."

After Dr. Sanborn explained the procedure and performed a local block of the pelvic area, Dr. Jakobson stood ready to give the anesthesia if the pain was too intense.

She focused on the man she trusted who would do whatever it took to remedy her, then laid her head down. "Let's get this over with."

Behind the building, Wilborn climbed into the pickup bed.

"What are you doing?" Bambi asked.

"I must find something. Get over here and chuck these logs out."

Bambi struggled to move logs onto the ground. "What are you looking for?"

"Bloody hell, where are you?" Almost every log was pitched to the ground. "Where the hell is it?" Wilborn leaped out of the truck bed and opened the backdoor. The floorboard was full of junk. She threw out a handsaw, branch cutters, heavy-duty gloves, a tarp, and a baseball cap, then hesitated and smiled. "There you are, mate. I knew there had to be an axe nearby with all this split timber." Wilborn grasped the handle and headed toward the back door. "This should do quite nicely."

When the phone in Wilborn's pocket rang, she pulled it out and tapped the speaker button. "Better be important. I'm busy."

"Does the extract need to be refrigerated?"

"No."

"What about if it gets hot?"

Wilborn's nostrils flared before answering. "You jumped from cold to hot. Why?"

"It was in my pickup, and it got hot, so I stuck it in the refrigerator to cool it down for a little while. Unfortunately, I forgot about it, and it sat inside for a few hours. Now it's kinda...hazy."

"What the bloody hell does that mean?" she said, pointing the axe at the phone. "Take the vial out and hold it in your hand until it warms."

"Yeah, yeah. Good idea. You promised there's enough to help two people, right?"

There was no telling what would happen if she said she didn't know, so she didn't. "Absolutely. I'm sure of it."

"Because you have to help—"

"Shut up. I'm busy. Do you have the vial in your hand?"

It took a moment for an answer. "Yeah, I guess. It's warming."

"Look at it."

"Okay, okay, better, all clear now. Remember..."

"Remember what?"

"You do her first, then me. When are you going to inject us?"

"I'm not. I have what I bloody need without you."

"No? Then, I want more money for you to have the extract, and I'm out for good."

Wilborn checked the backseat of the pickup, ensuring the Seward trunk was secure. "Are you trying to extort me?"

"Extortion is what you do, get caught, and go to jail. I am selling a product I own to you."

"That is my property," Wilborn snapped back.

"Not as long as I have it in my hand."

"I'm busy," Wilborn said. "We'll talk later."

"Later, and the price increases."

"You're an absolute ponce." Wilborn shoved the phone into her pocket, then charged toward the electric box and unleashed a single hard swing with the axe, hitting the conduit and cutting straight through it. Sparks spewed in every direction, and the light above the door went dark. She let go of the axe and it bounced on the ground. "Get the walkie-talkies. It's time for you to go to work, my little dearie."

The building went dark inside before the emergency red lights dimly lit the surgical suite. A monotonous bell dinged every ten seconds.

Dr. Jakobson glanced at the surgical tech helping Dr. Sanborn and said, "What the hell happened? Kevin, are you done?"

"Yes, wrapping up." Dr. Sanborn pivoted toward the tech. "Get me a flashlight."

Marla lifted her head. "Has this ever happened before?"

"No. Never," Dr. Sanborn said.

"The monitor is down," Dr. Jakobson said. "I can't let her lay here without vital signs."

Dr. Sanborn took the light from the tech and checked between Marla's legs. "Okay, all good. Get her to recovery, and someone open the backdoor and get some light inside this place."

Marla swung her legs off the table and sat up. Her head spun. "Whoa. Dizzy."

Dr. Jakobson caught her by the shoulder when she leaned too far forward. "You should lay back down."

Johanna called 911 when she caught sight of a woman rushing toward the entrance holding something in her hands. The bang of the outside glass door startled her.

Chapter 23

Bambi struck the door with the axe. Glass splintered like spider webs. She wished the stem cells made her stronger. Slamming it against the door again, glass shrapnel exploded onto the floor. Dropping the tool, she reached in and twisted the latch open. "Where's the fucking cop?"

Johanna held the phone receiver in her hand. A voice came from the speaker, "911, what is your emergency?"

Bambi removed the stolen police officer's pistol from her pocket and aimed at the reception desk. She studied the girl behind the desk sitting in her chair, weight, height, slightly twisted to the right with the phone in her left hand. Bambi thought left-handed.

The doping of stem cells in her anterior cingulate cortex worked; attention allocation, error detection, and anticipation of the direction the receptionist would tumble.

"Hang up the phone and get down."

Johanna dropped onto the floor behind the counter on her right side.

Bambi estimated the distance and angle needed to disable the girl. She aimed and blindly fired through the wooden counter. Johanna screamed and grabbed her bleeding left thigh.

Bambi leaned over the counter and chuckled at the girl holding her leg. "You are not the one I want, so you better tell me where the hell is the cop?"

She cried and pointed at the door. "In there."

Bambi ripped the landline phone cord from the wall and walked through the Patient Entrance like she owned the place—because she did. Dim emergency lights lit the hallway. Bambi fired into the ceiling. People in the back crouched with their hands on their heads like civilians running from battle. Employees huddled in the hallway before Bambi fired at the ceiling again. People screamed as they scurried toward the back exit. They pressed on it, but it wouldn't open.

Marla knew what this was, and she was the target. "Get down. Stay down. Don't move." Her head spun when she stood.

On the back side of the building, the pickup's front end braced against the door, with the engine running and oily blue smoke billowing from the exhaust, creating the perfect barricade. Fists banged against metal, and screams called out for help from inside. Dr. Wilborn stood beside the vehicle, arms folded across her chest, ever so pleased at the brilliance of the plan.

Bambi yelled, "Tell me where she is!" Another gunshot exploded inside the building again, and people scattered away from the exit door, hiding in rooms and closets.

Marla staggered from the surgical suite and yelled back, "Everyone go to your offices and lock the doors." She staggered toward the locker room while pulling the wristband off her wrist. Pushing the door open, she turned the key in the lock and latched onto her service weapon. She had to get the attention away from the others. Barely able to say the words, she mumbled, "Come get me." She fired three times into the ceiling and fell backward.

Bambi dropped to the floor and ripped the bandage off. She couldn't concentrate with that on her forehead while calculating the angle of the gunshot sound coming from the other hallway. She thought for a moment—precisely 11.3 feet from the corner. "Marla Adams, Dr. Wilborn wants me to kill you!"

Marla had no idea if this was true, but she said it anyway. Did the words come out, or are they still stuck in her head? "The police...on their way."

Bambi climbed to her hands and knees before rounding the corner of the hall. "Bullshit! I took care of that little reception bitch." She pushed a door open and aimed the pistol at a surgical table with a twisted sheet on top and bloody instruments bundled on the floor. She left the people huddled in the corner alone.

"A little cosmetic surgery? Brow lift? Droopy neck? Come out and let's see what the doctor did to you."

Bambi's attention focused on the white linoleum floor. Drops of blood lined up toward the locker room like people waiting in a queue. She calculated the cop's response. If she kicked the door open, the cop would have the advantage. Surgery minutes ago, bleeding, you're too weak to come out and face me. She rubbed her forehead, hoping the stem cells would grow faster and the brain would work better. Too weak to stand? Is the cop sitting on the floor against the wall with her chest ten inches high, or sitting in a chair, making her chest twenty-seven inches from the floor?

She didn't know how to check how many bullets were in the pistol. She hoped the cop's gun was full when they stole it. *Get this done, so I can get another shot of stemmies.* In a zig-zag formation, Bambi blindly fired multiple shots at the wall before kicking the door open. It abruptly slammed into the metal lockers, startling her, but there was no response. *Come on, bitch. Answer me and return fire. Bullets fired would give me the trajectory angle and exactly where you are hiding.*

The door closed on its own. Bambi fired into the wall, then kicked the door again. The lockers crashed onto the floor, with rattling metal echoing down the hall—still nothing from Adams. The door closed once again. *Is the cop unconscious? Dead? Too easy.*

Bambi would have to step into the room—exposing herself, relinquishing her advantage, but she was too deep in this mess. She wondered what happened to her. Two days ago, she and Bert lounged quietly in their hole in the ground until evil entered their lives. All she ever wanted was cocaine in her nose every day, but now she wanted the indescribable feelings of fentanyl in her vein and stem cells in her brain. She couldn't leave without killing the cop. She had to enter, aim, fire, and destroy.

Am I faster than the cop? The doctor and the stemmies say yes.

She shoved the door against the fallen lockers again and held it open with her heel, yet no reply. Bambi felt something, a vibe; heavier than anything she had felt before, shifting, bouncing, not focused. *Was the cop dying? Confused? Scared?* Bullet holes riddled the walls. On the floor, blood streaked around the exam table.

Behind the table, Marla lay on her side, thoughts swimming inside her head. She had to focus. All she could see was the top edge of the open door. She lifted her pistol, aimed at the entrance, and fired once through the thin metal of the exam table cabinet. The woman Marla had never seen before, who was trying to kill her, screamed and bounced against the door. Marla pushed herself up to a sitting position and saw a scrawny woman wearing a sleeveless shirt with tattoos covering both arms, with blood oozing from a bullet in the right shoulder. She had a small hole in her forehead like Jackie and Curvy.

Bambi caught a glimpse of a scalp behind the exam table. "Hey, bitch." She raised the gun with her wounded arm and fired, missing the table completely. She couldn't hold her arm straight. "Damn you!" She tried to aim toward the head but realized Wilborn's experiment had gone wrong. Bambi was not smart enough. Not fast enough.

Ninety pounds of flesh and bones were no match for bullets. Marla fired twice. Pain shot through the stub of her finger. She missed her mark by a few inches, hitting the girl twice in the stomach instead of center chest.

Bambi bounced against the door and screamed at the fire erupting in her abdomen, then stumbled down the hallway, blood dripping on the floor. The agony and distress would have overwhelmed an average person, but the stem cell injections thrived in her brain, blocking the pain.

Even before she entered the building, Bambi anticipated what would happen. There would be no exit through the front or back door, and she must escape where no one would expect—the glass blocks on the wall. Four wooden office doors lined the hallway; previously, from outside, she counted eighteen steps to the midpoint of the blocks. In her mind, she measured the distance from the back wall, grasped the doorknob of the third door, and opened it, revealing the treasure she expected: a wall of glass blocks. Ignoring the pain, she gripped the walkie-talkie from her back pocket and called out. "Now. Do it now."

Dr. Wilborn dropped the walkie-talkie on the floorboard and pushed the pedal to the floor. The back of the truck smashed into the wall, shattering blocks of glass and furniture in the office. Wilborn shifted into drive and stepped on the gas pedal. The vehicle bounced over debris. Wilborn rushed out from the pickup as Bambi climbed over the wreckage. Wilborn didn't ask how Bambi felt. "Did you kill her? I want to see her."

Bambi waved her hand forward. "We have to leave. The cops are coming."

Wilborn opened the passenger door. She wrapped her arm around Bambi's waist and ignored the screams as she shoved Bambi inside.

Across the street, a woman stood holding a leash attached to a large German Shepherd barking incessantly at Wilborn. She didn't notice the cell phone in the lady's hand pointed toward them.

After shifting into drive, the damaged truck accelerated, spewing glass and brick through the street. The pickup veered down a side street seconds before police vehicles approached from the main road.

Wilborn slapped the back of Bambi's head. "Did you kill her?"

"Get us out of here." Bambi held her shoulder close and leaned against the dashboard. "They called 911." Bambi slumped against the door, blood oozing from her abdomen wounds onto her pants. "Ah, fuck! It fucking hurts!"

"What? Where?"

"Shoulder...stomach." Her skin turned pale and cold. She rocked back and forth, unable to shake the quivering inside.

Wilborn, wide-eyed, glanced from side to side between Bambi and the road, rubbing her mouth with the back of her hand. "Did you find Adams, or did you make a cock up of the whole thing?"

"Shut up. I'm shot and it hurts. You have to fix this."

"Bloody right, I will. Did you kill her?"

"I don't know! I don't care."

"You were supposed to kill her."

The gun clicked. Wilborn glanced down to see the barrel pointed at her. Bambi squeezed her eyes tight and pulled the trigger again and again.

Wilborn shoved Bambi's head against the side window. "You're nothing but a bloody twat."

Black thoughts squirmed in Bambi's head. *I want to go back to Bert and live inside our pipe. We made good money on our corner of the Loop 410 frontage road—sometimes sixty bucks a day—enough to split a hit of coke and a pack of cigs. That's all I want.* It felt like someone kicked her hard in the head.

When Wilborn slammed Bambi's head against the window again, the gun dropped to the floorboard. "Answer me. Did you fuck this up?"

"You're the fuck up!" Her chewed fingernails dug into her arm, trying to push the pain away. "I need help. This is too much."

"Right. Of course. Something for pain."

Bambi cringed. "I need cocaine."

Wilborn pulled a small glass vial from her shirt pocket and held it between fingers. "Here, take this. Cocaine from my trunk. You can have it if you tell me you killed Adams."

"Give me that." Bambi snapped it away, bit down on the cap, and twisted it off. She spat the cap out of her mouth to the floorboard.

"All yours." Wilborn turned a corner. "You deserve it."

Bambi emptied the powder onto the dashboard and snorted it all until it vanished. Her head bounced against the headrest. She shook violently and then slumped forward, dead.

Wilborn scoffed. "Did I say coke? My mistake. A row of one hundred percent fentanyl will kill you that bloody fast."

◆

Rivera crossed the city limits sign into Hildebrandt while chomping on a wad of gum a hundred miles an hour. He studied the clinic locations on his phone map. "Can't you make it easier for me, like every other small town where medical clinics are closer to the hospital? Oh, no, of course not. Instead, there are six spread around town in the shape of a hexagon."

He refused to wait for her in San Antone. That would be too far away whenever she called, and he intended to be there a minute after her call. He never liked people keeping secrets or holding back info, and he wanted to know everything, so she damn well better spill her guts.

While driving past the second clinic, no dually pickups were parked there. Rivera studied the map on his cellphone screen and found the next place was four blocks away when his police band radio screeched and reported a disturbance at the Hildebrandt Surgical Center, address 371 Oak Street, with a dark green pickup driving away in a hurry. One person shot in the leg and stable.

He couldn't be that lucky. Marla was close, in the opposite direction he had planned to go, and Wilborn was somewhere nearby in a stolen vehicle. There can't be many older green trucks in town.

He spat his gum out the window and pulled a U-turn. No need to stop at the clinic. It would be an easy bet; 99-to-1 it was not Marla shot in the leg. Too damn smart, that woman. He dug through the likely scenario; cop cars and ambulances swarming the building like bees in a hive, the pickup gone, and Wilborn missing. The vehicle was too hot to keep, and this crazed, murderous psycho would have to change vehicles again, but where? Wilborn's not a professional car thief, and Rivera doubted the doctor knew how to hot wire anything. Carjacking would be the only way it could happen, and it had to be where traffic was active, not on a side street with houses. There might not be a car pulling out of a driveway for blocks, and Wilborn needed to get out of town, return to San Antonio, and sink back into the drainage pipe maze. Rivera waited at a red light, with busier than expected traffic for a small town, so he scanned cars parked at a strip mall across the street, but none being a green pickup. When the light changed, he eased down the town's main road, reaching the end of town in minutes with no green pickup in sight. He doubled back and searched again.

Wilborn passed through an intersection across town before entering a discount store parking lot. She killed the engine, stepped out, and removed the Seward trunk from the back seat. Two vehicles over, an elderly man had parked and sat in the front seat while looking at his phone. Wilborn rechecked the lot to see if anyone was near as she approached the car, opened the driver's door, grabbed the man's shirt at the collar, and dragged him out of the driver's seat and onto the ground.

"Stay there and keep your head down like a good knob." Wilborn opened the car's back door and slid the Seward trunk across the backseat. "I'll be taking your car." She noticed a fob in the cup holder and a cell phone in the passenger seat. "And your belongings."

❖

Sirens screamed, with two ambulances sitting catty-corner on the street and Hildebrandt PD vehicles surrounding the medical building. The back door was wide open, and people were hovering near the Porsche convertible. Officers jumped from their cars and took defensive stances. A bullhorn squelched. "Come out from behind the car with your hands on your head."

At the front of the building, an officer kicked the shattered glass door open. Two more followed, with guns leveled ahead and boots crunching broken glass.

A voice squeaked from behind the reception desk. "Help." Red lines from pistol sights lasered the air. Johanna cried out, "I'm shot. Please." With king-sized pupils and strained eyes, tears rolling down her face like an angry river, her trembling lips struggled for words. "I'm..." Her voice caught in her throat.

The first officer hurdled the counter. "It's over, ma'am. You're safe."

Johanna coiled on the floor with chafing breaths, her hands wrapped around a bloody leg.

The officer waved the other two forward. "You'll be all right, ma'am. Ambulances are here."

Two officers entered the building and took control of the hallway with years of tactical training behind them.

Inside the locker room, Marla's head swirled—everything good, nothing good. She leaned against the wall. Men yelled out police tactics in the hallway. She recognized the words, the sentences. She lowered the pistol to her side.

The door banged against the fallen lockers. Blood splattered the entry and streaked across the floor behind the exam table. He noticed the top of a head with brownish-blonde hair sticking above the table. "Police. Hands where I can see them."

Marla sat, sprawled against the wall, wearing a surgical gown with blood on her hands and between her legs. "D...E...A." She pushed her pistol forward, scraping it across the floor.

He recognized her as his foot swept the weapon further away. "Marla Adams? Holy crap, are you shot?"

She carried a pained stare into an empty world and didn't respond. The last bit of her husband was gone. It wasn't a baby, but nothing else mattered because it was Crosby's, and she no longer had it.

Baffled words filled the air. She didn't understand. She didn't care. Her teeth bit down on her lower lip as her mind fixed on nothing going right. Praying, begging, and bargaining wouldn't bring him back. She wanted to go home, cry in the shower for a day, and hide under the covers forever.

"Where is she?" Dr. Sanborn asked while rushing from room to room. "Where is she?" The locker room door was open. He stuck his head in. "Oh, Jesus, please. Marla, are you injured?"

Her head barely moved. Still in his surgical scrubs, Dr. Sanborn tapped the officer's shoulder. "I'm her doctor." He stepped around the officer and knelt, facing her. Bright red blood covered Marla's hands and the gown pushed between her legs. Dr. Sanborn called out, "Somebody get a wheelchair, please." When the officer left, Dr. Sanborn looked directly into her eyes. "You saved every person in this building. No one, not a single person died. Do you hear me? Marla, you saved everyone."

Chapter 24

The last traffic light in town flipped to yellow as Rivera slowed toward the intersection. The only thing left was a Dollar General store on the right. After entering, he crept through the rows of vehicles and found a dark green pickup in the second row with doors open. He put his transmission in park with the engine still running. Stepping out, hand resting on the holstered pistol, he read the vehicle's license plate, which was the same plate number on the video. Inside was an emaciated woman, covered in blood with pasty white skin and fixed eyes staring into nothing. He swept between the other cars, finding an elderly man sitting alone on the asphalt.

Rivera holstered his weapon and bent next to the man. "Sir, are you okay?"

"I'm fine, just embarrassed that someone stole my car."

Rivera stood and spun around, noticing a blue car exiting from the lot onto the street.

"Do you have a blue car, sir?"

"Yes."

"Was the person who stole your car a stocky woman with gray hair?"

"Yes. I won't ever forget that face."

He helped the man stand. "Are you sure you're okay?"

After dusting his clothes off, he said, "Yes."

"Go inside the store and call 911. Tell them what happened. What's the make and model of your car?" By the time he returned to his vehicle, the blue car was at least half a mile ahead. He floored the accelerator. The back tires spun as he raced out to the street and then pushed the speed dial button on his phone.

"Hildebrandt Police. What is your emergency?"

"This is DEA Special Agent Rivera following the medical clinic intruder out of town driving a blue four door Ford on FM 25. There's a dead woman inside a green pickup at the discount store on the edge of town."

"What part of town?"

Rivera eyed the screen on his phone before bringing it back to his ear. "Hell, I don't know. I don't live here."

"Recognize a store?"

"Dollar General and I'm heading north."

"I'll send a unit that way."

"Roger." Rivera disconnected the call and placed his phone in the cupholder. "I'm going to kick your ever-loving English ass all over town, doctor. You don't fuck with my partner!"

✦

Wilborn repetitively rubbed her fingers across her lips while glancing at the rearview mirror. The air conditioning couldn't cool enough. Red and blue lights flashed from behind. Her foot pressed the accelerator pedal as far down as it would go, knowing whoever it was would catch up quickly. The car was ancient, like the man she stole it from. As the road dipped and the lights disappeared, Wilborn slammed on the brakes and veered onto a dirt trail. The truck chasing after her raced over the hill and continued straight ahead. For the moment, there was time to hide.

Navigating her way over a dirt trail lined with six-foot-high bushes, like soldiers in formation, the path twisted left, further away from the main road. A two-story house in disrepair stood alone, with scrub brush consuming the front and both sides of the house. Wilborn drove around and stopped near the back entrance. She grasped the doorknob, but found it locked. Seconds later, a rock hurled through the door's glass pane. She reached in, and rusted hinges creaked as the door eased open.

A decade's accumulation of dust coated the kitchen. Tarnished copper pans hung on the wall, and empty wine bottles stood silently on a wooden counter next to a salt shaker on its side. Wisps of cobwebs dangled from overhead lights and drifted aimlessly.

The hot, stagnant air penetrated her being, and Wilborn shed the sweat-laden shirt and pitched it to the floor. Waving the hem of the under-shirt at her waistline, trying desperately to find an ounce of coolness, she longed for the temperatures in the dreaded drainage pipes...and London streets.

Wilborn tugged on a wooden drawer. It was stuck. She jiggled it open as the wood clunked against itself, then shuffled through spoons, forks, and dinner knives. She pulled hard on the second drawer, revealing ladles, spatulas, and cooking spoons. The last one gave her what she wanted—a drawer full of carving knives. Brandishing a thirteen-inch blade, she sliced the air while stomping out of the kitchen, but quickly ceased in front of the open utility room. Covered in arachnid silk were brooms and mops and a single shotgun. She didn't like shotguns—until now. "Why in the bloody hell does every Yank have a shooter?" An open box of .410 gauge shells sat on a counter. Tipping it over and pouring them out, she stuffed several in a pocket before loading one into the single chamber.

After climbing the steps and entering the front bedroom, a limp off-white dress hung from a satin-covered hanger on an open armoire door. Black carbon partially concealed the sides of a fireplace, with a western painting tilted above the mantle.

Wilborn peered out the window. From the house façade, a meandering walking trail led to an unknown place in the woods. Night was coming, and it would be impossible to hear anything until it was too late if someone snuck close by.

Rushing back downstairs, she stepped to the front door and unlocked it. "I'll make it easy for you bloody bobbies to introduce yourself when you enter." Hurrying to the kitchen and grabbing copper pans, she piled them high on top of each other against the front and back doors.

She squinted at the dust floating in the dim light. "What the bloody hell happened to the owners? I like this place. Maybe I'll ship it back home after I'm rich and famous like that idiot who bought the old London Bridge and moved it to Arizona. What a cockup that must have been. To hell with this place. I should burn it down. Get my vial of protein extract, leave this wretched hellhole, and live in a proper home in Kensington near Clapton and Branson and Madonna. We could be neighbors."

Only a few hours remained before dusk. "Best I stay here for the night and pop back into my drainage pipes early tomorrow morning."

Wilborn settled upstairs in the bedroom near the window with the shotgun across her lap, watching and waiting. "Come on, if you're coming. I have a destiny to fulfill."

The sun descended below the treetops, making the dirt trail almost impossible to see. As if on cue, an engine rumbled in the distance. "Fantastic." Wilborn slid the chair back and bent down on one knee, surveying the landscape. There were no headlights, only a flash of red taillights caught her eye sixty yards from the front of the house.

Rivera killed the engine and scrutinized the abandoned two-story house. He called the local police again and reported his location. The Hildebrandt police promised backup soon. Stepping out of his truck, he shoved two more pieces of gum in his mouth before slipping on his DEA jacket and sticking a flashlight in his back pocket. He ran his hand over tire tracks on the dirt trail. "Fresh." Rushing through the bushes, he stepped around the side of the house to the back and saw a blue car. "Your ass is mine, doc." He eased around to the front entrance and gingerly twisted the doorknob. He was stunned when the latch snapped. "Interesting. Unlocked." When he eased it open, copper pans crashed across the floor. "Damn." He glanced behind, hoping for local police backup to show, but he couldn't wait, so he shoved the door open, clattering the pans further. Rivera yelled, "You shoot at a DEA agent, and you get yourself the death penalty! That would be ironic, wouldn't it, doc? You get your own dose of lethal poison in your vein for shooting fentanyl and whatever else you're doing to the homeless. I like it. I'm going to be there and watch them kill you."

The inside was dim, with heavy curtains concealing all the windows. His flashlight's bright beam scanned the entryway and a round five-foot-diameter table in the center of the vestibule, with thick dust-covered candlestick holders, knickknacks, and scattered papers. Cobwebs veiled a tabletop lampshade. His flashlight beam shot up the stairwell, where a massive chandelier hovered from the ceiling, and multiple footprints went up and down the stairs. Does it mean the doctor is on the first floor?

Rivera directed his light towards the hallway and entered the library, with mildewed books lining the walls and a layer of dust enveloping everything.

Dr. Wilborn inched down the stairs, shotgun and knife in hand, and snuck out the front door, only to return seconds later. With the blade gone, she grabbed a candlestick holder. A light flickered in a room at the end of the hallway. She aimed the weapon and crept closer.

A creak of wood alerted Rivera. He shut off his flashlight and shoved a desk lamp to the floor.

Wilborn rushed toward the door and fired at the noise.

Rivera rounded the door and lunged for the gun barrel, pulling Wilborn off balance.

The doctor let go. "Get away from me, you wanker," then flailed the candlestick holder in a wide swath.

Rivera let go and quickly rolled over an executive wooden desk on its side. Wilborn picked up the firearm and stuck another shell in the chamber. Rivera stood up and aimed his pistol, only to notice the shotgun muzzle swinging toward him. "Oh, crap," and he dropped to the floor.

Wilborn fired into the desk, not knowing a .410 gauge shell didn't have the firepower to penetrate through the wood. She dropped the weapon and ran.

Footsteps bounded down the corridor, and copper pans clamored against the base of the stairs. Rivera leaped over the desk and chased the sound into the kitchen, only to watch the blue car kick up dirt as it U-turned and disappeared around the side of the house. He sprinted to the doorway and shot at the vehicle before heading to his car, then crouched and touched the sidewall where a knife had pierced the flattened tire. Minutes later, a police unit stopped behind Rivera's vehicle.

Chapter 25

Roger stepped into The Broken Saddle Horn and headed straight for the bar. Trixi wore the same red beret and yellow suspenders. She flipped a dishtowel over her shoulder and waited for him to sit.

"About time you came back to see me," she said.

"What? You called me to come over. Listen, Trix, I got stuff going on…"

"Yeah? Me too, so you need to drop by my place tonight after work."

"Give me a Lone Star." He slapped a dollar on the counter. "I have to check on Cassie first, so I'll call you after that."

"Cassie wasn't hurt. A couple of punches, that's it."

"She has a black eye on the one she sees with," Roger said.

Trixi opened a beer can and set it down in front of him, then leaned her elbows on the counter. "You're an idiot. The girl punched her blind eye."

Roger drank several gulps before putting the can back on the counter. "She still has a black eye. What kinda place you running here, letting girls fight?"

"Ease off, asshole. I'm the one who put the shotgun in the stranger's ear and stopped your hookup from getting hurt far worse. Do you even know how to say, 'Thanks?'"

Roger finished the beer and placed the empty can on the counter. "I'll call later."

"You can't do what I want over the phone. You get your ass over to my place tonight."

An hour later, Roger wore aviator sunglasses and a backward cap while driving a tractor with a round bale of hay speared in front.

Cassie winced when her hand accidentally brushed across the bridge of her swollen nose. She waved her arms left and right like a ramp agent with orange flashlights directing a pilot on the tarmac. "Whoa! Stop right there," she said. "Drop it here."

Roger lowered the bale and backed away before opening the door to the tractor cab. He smiled. "Don't believe you have ever told me to stop before."

She sarcastically flipped her middle finger. Her face ached when she smiled. "Don't give me any of your bullshit today. We got too much work to do."

Roger jumped from the tractor and tried to ignore the bruising around her glass eye, which stared straight ahead. "Yeah? Like what?"

"Where's your gun?"

Roger grasped the revolver from behind him. "Here. Why?"

"Why don't you have your holster?"

"It's drying." He stuck the gun under his belt. "I cleaned and oiled the leather, so I'll use it tomorrow."

"That windmill is still jacked up, and the cattle need water in this heat and dry air. Get your tools and fix it."

He grasped the pitchfork from the rear of the trailer and dug half-assed into the hay. "They need to eat, too."

"No, best you get the windmill, and I do the hay."

Roger's smile vanished. How about I deal with the hay, and you shut up?"

Cassie shoved his chest with both hands, causing him to step back. "I'm your boss." She poked her finger inches from his face. "And you don't get to tell me what to do."

Roger grasped Cassie's upper arm. "You're not my boss, Mr. Johnson is, and you wanna get your ass kicked twice?"

She swung her fist and punched him in the stomach.

He cringed but still held on to her other arm. "What the hell was that for?"

"A warning."

"I don't need a warning from some shit girl."

When Cassie kneed him in the groin, he let her go and dropped to his knees.

"Didn't see that coming, did you? Looks like I'm a better fighter than you."

Cassie's phone rang in her back pocket. She backed away from Roger before answering. "Hello?"

She grinned as Roger slowly got to his feet. "Hey, Marla? What's up?"

Cassie dawdled near the water tank. "We're dropping hay and fixing the windmill." She watched Roger rub his groin. "Like, stuff you hired me for."

She lifted her ball cap off her head and wiped her brow before placing it back on. "Yeah, yeah. I can be there in a jiff." She glimpsed at her wristwatch. "Okay, thirty minutes. Good." She raised her arm and smelled her armpit. "I'm a little rank from all the work, Marla. I'll run to the bunkhouse where I keep some shirts and jeans. See ya."

She stuffed the phone in her pocket and mounted her horse. "Hey jerkoff, Marla's not feeling well, and she said for me to meet her at the house. You break up the hay and get water flowing. I'll be back to check later."

Still bent slightly forward, he waved her off. "You owe me."

"Oh, poor baby. I'm sorry." She spun away from Roger. "Do your job, and we'll talk about the benefits tonight."

Her horse reared back and squealed, rolling Cassie off and landing on her side. A rattlesnake slithered out of the hay and coiled nearby, ready to strike. She looked left and right. "Where is it?" She kicked, scraping dirt with her heels. It struck her boot.

In a split second, Roger fired, hitting the snake's head. The back half squirmed until it didn't.

"Good God, Cassie. Did it bite you?"

She sat up while holding her wrist.

He extended his hand toward her. "Let me help you."

She caught hold of his hand, and Roger pulled her up like two football players latching on to each other after a play.

She ran her hand over her wrist.

"You're okay, right?"

"I couldn't find it."

"It was on your left side, your blind side."

"Shut up. I'm not blind."

He gripped her upper arms and glared at her. "You're blind in one eye." He let go. "Damn, girl. You got a glass eye and deaf in one ear. That snake could have killed you."

"So, I'm damaged goods to you? Not whole? Missing parts?"

"Hell, no. If I thought that... I'd have...let it—"

"Let it, what?"

"Nothing. Never mind."

Cassie yanked her cap off and slapped the dirt off her jeans, then grasped Roger's shirt, pulled him closer, and kissed him hard on the lips. "Thank you." She pushed away before glancing around for her horse. It stayed about ten yards to her side. "Guess it doesn't like snakes."

Roger licked his lips, wanting more. "Me neither."

She whistled, and the horse trotted to her. Afterward, she blew a half-assed kiss toward Roger. "Thanks again."

"Hey, listen," Roger mumbled. "I, um, I got something to say."

"It'll have to wait. Marla needs me. I'll talk to you later."

◆

Marla waited in her pickup at the surgical center and drank a two-ounce energy drink and an entire bottle of water before pitching the empties behind the front seat. It felt like a boulder had popped out between her legs. She tapped the name Rivera on her phone and it rang.

He ignored the cordial hello and jumped right in. "Almost had the son of a bitch."

"Wilborn?"

"Yep. Tracked her to a retail store on the outskirts of town where she stole a car and left the pickup. I followed her to an old, abandoned house and cornered her inside, but the slippery shit escaped. Now, you better damn well tell me what the hell is going on with you?"

"I'll tell you the whole story when you get to my house."

"I'll be there in ten minutes."

"Angelo, take your time. I'm not quite there yet."

It spooked him. Marla had never called him Angelo. "Ten minutes. Foot to the floorboard," he said.

Marla stopped near her house, killed the engine, and opened the truck door. She eased to the ground, hoping it wouldn't hurt, and it didn't. Festus darted from the barn and stood beside her, eyes bright, itching to play. She leaned forward and rubbed his ears. "Good boy."

The dog shot through the doggie door as she headed toward the house. Seconds later, he returned and dropped his favorite rubber ball next to her feet. Marla grasped the ball and pitched it. Festus charged like a lightning bolt, jumping and catching it in the air, then beat her to the porch before she had time to climb the three steps.

Festus bolted through the doggie door again. When Marla opened the front door, the dog sat beside her leather chair and dropped the ball to the floor.

The extra shot of caffeine and water helped with the pain from where a metal probe should never have been. Shortly after sitting down, Cassie's horse stopped near the house, and Marla heard a thud outside. Crap, forgot to close the truck door.

Cassie knocked on the partially opened front door and entered. "Marla? What's going on?"

Marla checked her clock on the wall as Rivera parked alongside her truck. At eleven minutes, he must have been driving over a hundred most of the way.

When Rivera pushed the front door open, Festus barked once and then stepped closer, waiting for the official password, a rub behind the ears.

Marla plopped into the chair, and Festus sat down beside her. "Both of you find a place to sit on the couch. I have something to say."

"Damn right you do," Rivera said.

Festus caught the mood, stood, and took a defensive half-step forward. When Marla touched the dog's back end, he sat while continuing to stare at the man.

Rivera stretched his hand towards Festus. The dog sniffed, never leaving Marla's side. He redirected his focus back to Marla and spoke softer. "And it damn well better be good."

Cassie jabbed her finger in Rivera's arm. "Hey, watch your mouth."

He circled his finger around his face. "What the hell happened to you?"

"None of your goddamn business."

"Cassie," Marla said with an even voice. "Please...sit."

Her two guests were stunned by the long story of her molar pregnancy and the attempted murder. Marla leaned back, exhausted.

"I'm taking a few hours off to rest. After that, I'll be ready."

"Ready for what?" Rivera asked.

Cassie scooted up on the couch. "Yeah, ready for what? You had surgery. You can't go out rustlin' up bad guys."

Rivera stood. "Why don't you rest up a day or two? I almost had the perp, and she won't escape again."

Cassie stood as well. "Perp? I was joking about a bad guy, or girl, or whoever. You said you shot that girl. She's dead, right?"

"There were two involved—one is Dr. Wilborn, and the other is the unsub. They both escaped somewhere."

"What's an unsub?" Cassie asked.

"An unknown subject." Rivera waited for Marla's permission to continue. When she nodded, he turned toward Cassie. "The girl who ambushed Marla was with Wilborn, a female English doctor, and we believe wants revenge for what she believes Marla did to Dr. McCollum."

Cassie twitched in her seat. "Who's Dr. McCollum?"

"He was an English doctor who tried to help Crosby with the same stem cell therapy after being shot in the head," Marla said.

"Different doctor from the one at the surgical place?" Cassie asked.

"Yes." Rivera leaned his elbows on his thighs and tried to ease Cassie's mind. "Dr. Wilborn is...was partners with Dr. McCollum in a British stem cell research project. Dr. Wilborn—"

Marla interrupted, "Wilborn tried to kill me in the surgical center."

"What are you talking about?" Cassie snapped back. "What in the hell are stem cells?"

Marla straightened in her chair. "Wilborn is taking stem cells from people's hips, mixing them with something, and shooting them into their brains. We think she's doing this to make them smarter and faster...faster than me."

Cassie raised her hand, as if asking permission to talk. "I have no idea what you said other than it sounds crazy. And what am I supposed to do after he kills you? Kick Roger out of my life and go back to Oklahoma?"

"I've got a feeling Roger will follow you wherever you go," Marla said.

"Enough of that," Rivera said. "You stay here while I head to the surgical center to interview employees. After that, I'm returning to the stormwater system to find this crazed lunatic and help bring her in for drugs, assault on a police officer, vehicle theft, trespassing, destruction of private property, and attempted murder."

Marla's phone rang. The name Deputy Jeffrey Keene lit the screen. She didn't want to talk about what he wanted, which was the stem cells for his wife, so she stuck it under her leg. It rang again. This time, she answered and put it on speaker.

"Hi, Jeffrey."

Engines roared in the background of his call. "Okay, you're right. This guy is dangerous. It's all over the police band about the medical clinic, the shooter, the green pickup. Was it you inside the building? And why were you there? I don't think I could take any more problems. Tell me you're okay."

"Yes, that was me in the clinic. Thanks, I'm fine." She pulled the phone away when more engines roared. "Where are you?"

"Racetrack. My cousin has a car, and we're working on the timing, trying to shave another second off the track. Seems like everyone else is doing the same. Sorry, this call is about you. Can you ID the person in the clinic?"

"Sure, a girl who came close to killing me will be hard to forget."

"Jeez, Marla," Jeffrey said. "We might need you for a morgue ID. The sheriff sent out a message to all the deputies. About fifteen or twenty minutes after the shooter escaped, there was a 911 call reporting a gray-haired woman had stolen his car in a store parking lot on the outskirts of town. One of the deputies found the green pickup in the same lot with a body in the passenger seat shot several times. She had a hole drilled into her forehead, and fentanyl powder was scattered across the dash and floorboard."

"Is the victim a thin woman with scraggly hair, a black sleeveless top, tattoos on her arms, and three bullet holes, one in the right shoulder and two in the abdomen?"

"That's her."

"She's the one who tried to kill me."

Rivera motioned with his hand to give him the phone. "This is DEA Special Agent Rivera. Did you say fentanyl?"

Jeffrey winced at Rivera's voice. He was reluctant to say anything after the restaurant incident. "Right. We field tested the powder at the crime scene."

"This is an ongoing investigation with the DEA. The perp who stole the pickup and the car is our prime suspect for international drug transportation. I'll make sure my boss ties in with the sheriff." He whispered to Marla, "This keeps us in the middle of it."

"Let me speak to Marla, please, and take it off speaker," Jeffrey said.

Rivera handed the phone back to her.

"Speaker off," Marla said. She held the phone slightly away from her ear because of the loud engine noises.

"Marla, this is between you and me. This doctor can help Rosemary, and has got to heal her before you take the doctor down. Promise me! You've known my wonderful Rosemary for years. It was you who introduced me to her. You have to save her."

It felt like a fist clenched around her throat, making it impossible to swallow or speak. With a graveled voice, all she could force out was a single word, "K." She took a deep breath before continuing. "But I need something from you."

"What?"

"You were an AP in the Air Force, right?"

"Yes, but it's called the Security Forces now."

"Where?"

"Overseas."

"Have you ever heard about Dr. Hugo Wilborn going to jail in London?"

"I'm not really sure what you're asking."

"Did you know anything about this person while you were there?"

"Marla, I lived my life on an Air Force base."

"Okay. I thought you might still have some connections in the law enforcement community."

Engines roared as cars raced past Jeffrey. "Still not sure what you are asking."

Marla leaned forward in her chair. "I need all the intel on Dr. Hugo Wilborn. Birth, life, everything."

"All that is available online as public records."

"Not that. Was she a troublemaker as a kid, in school, as a doctor, or in prison? Is there anyone she is close to now in the US, in San Antone?"

"I can try, but don't expect much."

"Jeffrey, if you want my help, I need yours."

"Sure."

Marla ended the call and stood. "All right, out you go." She waved her visitors toward the door. "I believe everyone has their hands full with work."

Rivera and Cassie headed toward the front door like they were being escorted off the property.

Chapter 26

Dr. Wilborn was waiting for a red light to change when a police car came alongside. The second she turned to look, the badge flickered in her eye, and the vision hit her again.

Decades ago, Hugo Wilborn stepped into the backseat of a police vehicle after a manslaughter conviction. They took her to a London County Council Home, a hellish place with no chance of a family life—or seeing her sister again.

She never spoke at the trial, never mentioned Clarise tried to prevent their foster mother's daily whipping of Hugo, never said her sister yelled and screamed and grabbed the paring knife from the butcher table and stabbed the woman again and again and again, and never mentioned when their foster father staggered into the kitchen, drunk as usual, and yelled at both of them while slurring his words. Clarise pushed him backward. He stumbled, hitting his head against the sink and falling to the floor. While holding the knife, she bent down next to the lethargic man and, without saying a word, cut the side of his throat and watched a pool of blood grow under his neck.

Eight-year-old Hugo helped her wash her hands and hid her blood-stained clothes in a corner of the basement. She never said thank you. She was too young and too traumatized; at least, that is what Hugo told herself.

When Hugo turned eighteen, the government expunged all records, never letting universities and medical schools know about her traumatized childhood. She can't forget.

Wilborn found her sibling years later in a long term care facility, comatose from head trauma resulting from an attempted robbery of a pub. She visited Clarise every day and promised to bring her back to life and others like her. After years of dedication and the breakthrough of hyperstimulated stem cells regenerating new brain matter, Wilborn was ready to honor that promise, albeit too late for Clarise. Hugo Wilborn's sister had already died.

Wilborn's restless foot bounced on the brake pedal. When the light changed to green, she waited for the cop car to go first. It didn't. An SUV behind her honked, so she eased forward. In her peripheral vision, the police vehicle continued to drive beside her. Wilborn wiped her clammy hands across the pant legs and peaked at the speedometer. The cop stayed close for a block before slowing. Wilborn swept her hand through her hair. "Come on, you wanker. Get out of here." From the side mirror, the police car's turn indicator blinked and eased behind Wilborn. Her hands tightened around the steering wheel. She rechecked the speedometer. Her back tightened, and the revolver in her inside jacket pocket hung heavy. Another car in the left lane sped by them. Emergency lights flashed behind Wilborn. She reached for the gun just before the police car deviated from behind her and charged after the speeder.

Wilborn turned off the main road and stopped a few houses down the street, somehow not bothering her as much as she thought it should. She grabbed the old man's cell phone and sent a message. Calling you, answer it.

"What the hell are you doing?" the voice on the other end asked. "It's all over the police and sheriff's department radios. A woman shooting people in a medical clinic? Are you stupid?"

"Fat worthy chance of anyone getting that woman to talk."

"Where are you?"

"Never mind where I am," Wilborn said. "Is the protein extract still good?"

"Okay, yeah. Clear. I guess so. How do you plan to do anything to Marla Adams with the entire San Antonio Police Force on your ass? They're talking about a dark green pickup on the outside clinic camera. That's you, right?"

Two teenage girls walked their dogs on leashes. Wilborn looked down, hearing them giggle and talk as they passed her most recently stolen car. "I don't have that anymore," she said, focusing on the rearview mirror. One girl turned her head and stared.

"Listen, you are too hot for me to hand you the extract in a public place."

Wilborn watched the girls turn the corner and disappear. "Then I won't help you or anyone who wants help."

"Don't forget, I know all about you."

"You don't know bloody shite about me."

"Yeah? I have evidence about you selling phones in prison. That's another ten to fifteen back inside."

"I was cleared of that."

"You let someone else take the rap."

"As I said," Wilborn snapped back. "I was cleared."

It took a moment for a reply: "All you want is the extract, not me, right? You said you have someone else to kill Adams now, but that wasn't what we originally agreed to, was it? So, you picked me to do it, and you are gonna pay me the bulk of the pawnbroker's money, no matter what."

"Right." Wilborn thought about Bambi rotting in the green pickup. "I do need you."

"I could meet you in the sewer. That's a good place for you."

"It's not a sewer. It's the stormwater system. I need a diversion by getting that twat and her bastard partner off my back, and you're the one who's going to sort that out."

"How's that?"

Wilborn edged down the street. "Time for you to step up and do your proper job."

"Then give me the two million dollars."

"We agreed on one million."

"Inflation is a bitch. I'll cut you some slack, one and a half mill."

"What do you intend to do with the cash? You can't open a new bank account. You do that, and you'll get nicked."

The voice on the phone eased off a bit. "Tell you what, give me all of it, and I'll launder your share for you. I got a guy right here in San Antonio, who, for fifteen percent, will place it in a clean bank account so we can spend it any way we want."

"And I'm supposed to hand this cash to you so you can give it to some geezer? You expect me to trust that you or your fence won't steal it?"

"Yeah."

"You're a fucknugget. I want you to confuse Adams, make her and that shite partner of hers to bugger off. Forget about me momentarily, and that's when I'll strike."

"You can't do anything with that gimp leg of yours."

Wilborn grinned. She had fooled everyone about her injured foot while in prison—the cane, the limp, the slow pace, the practiced deception for twenty-eight months. "Distraction first. After that, you get the cash."

"Are you holding it in that black Seward trunk? Is it getting heavy? Lighten your load and hand over the money."

Chapter 27

Marla's stomach growled, but there was nothing to eat except another peanut butter sandwich and tortilla chips, her go-to meal, every meal, three times a day. Truck tires rolled over the cattle guard as she entered her ranch with the chicken coop and barn closed for the night. Cassie had tied the reins of her horse to the corner column of the porch. After parking, Marla climbed out, and when she entered the house, the smell of garlic, warm butter, and sauteed onions lifted her spirits.

"Cassie?"

"In the kitchen."

Marla moved to the back of the house. Where an empty dining room should have been, a folding card table and two chairs sat. Steam rose from a pot on the stove. Skirt steak covered with a red sauce of tomatoes, basil, oregano, and garlic simmered in a cast iron skillet. "Where on earth did you learn to cook like this?"

Cassie glanced at a recipe on her phone screen beside the stove. She smiled at Marla and pointed the tongs at the counter. "No such thing as a free lunch or dinner around here. Knead the dough. We'll make fresh noodles."

Marla removed the plastic wrap around the dough. "I've never done this before. What should I do?"

"What? Never? Have you been living under a rock your entire life?"

"Maybe. Always used boxed spaghetti and sauce from a jar."

"I'm going to vomit. That's disgusting." Cassie laid the tongs down and grabbed a handful of flour. "Here. Like this." She sprinkled it on the counter and placed the dough on top. She kneaded it for a little while. "Keep doing it, and sprinkle flour every minute or so."

Marla pushed the sliced green and red peppers and mushrooms drying on a paper towel to the side. "Do you have an Italian grandmother?"

"Dated an Italian chef several years ago, but I've never told Roger I can cook. He'd want me in the kitchen for every meal." Her shoulders shivered. "That man taught me a lot about food...and other stuff. Italians know their sex."

"Got tired of him, too?"

"His wife called from Milan. Said it was time to come home."

Marla kept kneading the dough. "Wife?"

Cassie tapped the tongs on the edge of the skillet. "Had no idea he was married. I'll do lots of stuff, but I don't do married men, at least, not knowingly."

Marla's forearm muscles burned. She wasn't accustomed to such activity. "What do you think? Ready?"

"Looks good. Hold the rolling pin like this and flatten it out. After that, I'll cut it into strips. Time to turn the oven on broil."

Marla opened the door. "French bread? Butter and garlic?" She closed it. "Who are you again? The first time I saw you, I picked you out as a cowpuncher who knew her business, but—"

"But what?" Cassie laughed.

"But cooking from scratch? Never."

Cassie's smile decreased. He used to come up from behind, wrap his arms around me, and teach me how to cut the pasta. His cologne was heavenly."

Crosby crossed Marla's mind a thousand times a day, but the closest he was to this type of cooking was listening to George Strait while grilling steaks outside and holding a longneck beer. "Where did you find the pots and pans? I don't have any."

"Sure, you do," Cassie said. "At the bunkhouse. I went there and loaded up. Brought it all back along with food Roger had in the fridge."

Marla burst out laughing. "Roger's food? He's likely to be a little upset when he opens the refrigerator door."

"Nope. He loaded all this stuff in his pickup and followed me here.

"Where is he now?"

"Back at the Johnson ranch. He mentioned being involved in a few projects."

Marla used a towel to dry her hands. "Jake Johnson is not too happy with me right now. Crosby previously sold hay to him, but since the drought this summer and me acquiring more cattle, I need to keep all of mine. In fact, I may be on the hunt to buy extra if it doesn't rain soon."

"Do you suppose he's going bankrupt?" Cassie asked.

"Jake was a major player in the county for years, but after his wife died, he's been kind of off. He might be struggling with the bank loans, and I'll bet the lenders will suck up all the insurance money from the fire."

"Would he sell?"

"I don't think so. The Johnson family has owned that land for several generations. That reminds me: Be ready to help with a new shipment of cattle coming in a few days. I want to buy another hundred."

"Sure. Mind if I stay with Roger at the bunkhouse tonight?" Cassie grabbed the knife and sliced the flattened dough into long strips like she was on a television cooking show before dropping it in the boiling water. She stirred the pasta in the pot with her tongs. "I should buy more cotton socks."

"What do you mean?"

Cassie shrugged. "Don't ask me why, but Roger likes me in nothing but socks."

"Excuse me?"

"Cheaper than buying lingerie. Some guys I dated liked a different color every night." She raised her eyebrows at Marla. "That can become expensive. With Roger, I head to Walmart and buy a three-pack of gray socks, and he's happy. Me, too. My feet get cold at night."

"Time for the peppers and mushrooms?" After Cassie nodded, Marla scooped the vegetables and dropped them into the pan. "Well, everybody has their thing. Oops. Better check the bread." Marla pulled the oven door down. "Ready." She slipped the mitt back over her hand and placed the bread on the hot pad sitting on the counter. "I'll fetch the paper plates and forks."

"What? No, no, no." Cassie waved her hand toward the far side of the card table. "We got real plates, forks, and knives in the cardboard box over there, and the two beers in the cooler should be cold." She rubbed the sleeve of her shirt across her nose. "Men are the strangest creatures on this earth...and then there's Roger." She hugged Marla around the neck. "I don't know what to do."

"Tell me what's going on?"

Cassie stepped back and smiled. "Roger told me he wants to live with me—move in together. Nobody has ever said that to me. I mean, I thought he liked me and all, but he said he wants to stay."

Clasping onto Cassie's shoulders, Marla hoped she wouldn't have to grapple with this drug dealer much longer. "That's great. I'm sure everything will be...great."

"He said he won big money betting on something and plans to buy a plot of land."

"Money? How much?"

Cassie rubbed the heels of her palms over her eyes. "I don't know, didn't ask."

"Listen to me." Marla looked straight into Cassie's eyes. "Do you think it's drug money?"

"Damn it, Marla. You told him to stay away from it or go to jail...so I'm sure it's clean money."

"I should check on it."

"No. You stay away from Roger. Just because someone gets a load of cash, all of a sudden, it has to be drugs? How about he won it fair and square?"

"I'm doing this for you. You should understand before you get involved with him if he's dealing again."

"What are you, my mother?"

"Listen, girl! I'm DEA, and this sounds suspicious."

Cassie pitched her tongs in the sink. "Forget what I said. It's none of your goddamn business what he does." She headed for the door. "I'm out of here, and you can go to hell if you screw this up between us."

❖

Cassie tugged on the reins when the phone rang. While sitting on the saddle, she answered, "Hello?"

"It's Roger."

She glanced at the unrecognizable number. "Where are you calling from?"

"I'm inside Mr. Johnson's house using his phone."

"Why are you in his house?"

"I come in all the time. I grab a bite to eat, a glass of water, take a piss."

"Why are you on his phone?"
"Left mine outside. Quit being so damn snoopy."
"Quit being so damn weird. Why are you calling me?"

Chapter 28

A Bexar County deputy sat at his desk covering the midnight shift and rested his disposable coffee cup on the desktop. Dawn trickled through the window blinds as he dug into a paper sack and snared his last day-old kolache. No sooner had he bitten the pastry than the desk phone rang, and he answered with a mouthful. "Sheriff's department. How may I help you?"

"This is Joe Bass, and I'm reporting a dead cow in the middle of the road."

The deputy swallowed. "A dead cow? Is it blocking the road?"

"I could drive around the first one."

"Excuse me, sir?"

"The first one. After that—No."

"Mr. Bass, how many are out there?"

"Mmm, maybe six. No, I see another on the shoulder."

"Were they run over?"

"Don't see any blood."

"Where's your location?" the deputy asked.

"On FM 82 between the Adams and Johnson land."

"Thank you, Mr. Bass. I'll have someone out there ASAP."

The deputy hung up and reached for the dispatch microphone, requesting assistance from nearby deputies.

"Keene here."

"Have dead livestock outside of Hildebrandt on FM 82. Are you near?"

"Sure. Whatcha got?"

"Cattle."

"As in multiple animals?"

"Right."

"I'm serving civil papers in Hildebrandt this morning. Is it on the north or south side of town?"

"This early?" the dispatcher asked. "Anyway, they're off 82 on the dirt road between the Adams and Johnson land. Do you know where I'm talking about?"

"I'm close."

◆

Marla's alarm clock blared in her ear. She slapped the top of it to bring back the morning silence, then flung off the covers. When she spun to the side of the bed, she was expecting pain in her abdomen but was surprised to find none. After her shower, she dressed, feeling empty and hollow, with nothing of Crosby's left inside her. Metal clattered in the kitchen as Marla turned the corner and saw Cassie drying the pots, pans, utensils, and plates before placing them in their boxes.

"Good morning."

Cassie glanced over her shoulder. "Good morning."

Marla was reserved about what to say next after last night's discussion. "I'm glad you came back."

"Yeah. Roger pissed me off last night, so I decided it was better to sleep here. Still okay if I stay here?"

Marla replied as if the argument between them had never existed. "Absolutely."

"I heard you moving around in the bedroom, so I made breakfast." A browned English muffin popped up from one of the only three kitchen appliances Marla used. "I, uh, cleaned the oven and stove, and only used the toaster and microwave this morning. I know you only want...well, you know, the three things in the kitchen." Cassie wiped her hands on a cup towel. "I'm out to check the fence. I'll swing by later."

Marla almost felt guilty for allowing someone to cook a meal. Using anything other than a cheap toaster, microwave, and coffee maker meant she accepted widowhood, and she wasn't ready for that.

After dropping a K pod in the coffeemaker, Marla tapped the button, and it hissed like an angry panther while spitting out hot, black liquid. Bacon strips crackled in the microwave as she stabbed the muffin with a plastic knife and placed it on the paper plate before slathering peanut butter and honey over it. She opened the large ice chest, where a single bottle of water and a jar of sliced jalapenos sat. After opening the jar, she forked several jalapenos and spread them evenly over the bread. When the microwave dinged, she laid bacon on top, then folded the muffin in half to complete her breakfast—A San Antone Special.

After wiping down the kitchen counter, she opened the front door, and Festus met her on the porch full of electrified energy, ready to herd cattle or chase after a ball a thousand times. Marla bent down and scratched behind the dog's ears. "How was your night, big boy?" She gestured toward the barn. "That way." He shot out, leaping from the porch, and raced away.

Inside the barn, Marla saddled Blackie and tightened the billet strap under the belly just as her cell phone rang in her pocket. Her finger tapped the button. "Hello?"

"Marla, this is Jeffrey Keene. We need you to head to the north side of your land.

"We? Who is we?"

"Sorry. The sheriff's department. You have several dead cattle."

She tossed the reins over Blackie's head. "What are you talking about?"

I can clarify everything when you arrive. Hurry and come out. I'm close to the water tank and windmill."

"Is Cassie with the herd?"

"I don't see her anywhere," Jeffrey said. "You should call and send her over, but we need you here."

Horse hooves clopped outside the barn. Marla gripped the reins and strolled out as Cassie slowed down to face her. Marla smiled at the Heart logo ball cap on Cassie's head. At least she's still willing to wear it.

Marla clamped onto Cassie's leg. "Has anyone called you this morning about the cattle?"

"No, no one. I've been out inspecting the south fence line. Everything looks good over there. I'm planning to head that way now. What's up?"

"We got trouble on the north pasture." Marla slipped her work gloves on, then mounted Blackie. "Let's go."

Fifteen minutes later, as the sun crested the distant hills, Marla and Cassie slowed near the road directly ahead of a cow lying on its side. Marla's gut tightened. Oh my God.

Emergency lights flashed in the grille and on the roof bar of a deputy's vehicle blocking the road.

Dry-mouthed, Cassie struggled to swallow. Several cattle were sprawled across the road. "What in God-forsaken hell?" She stayed in the saddle. "I've never seen anything like this."

Jeffrey met them as they dismounted. "Marla. Come with me."

She handed the reins to Cassie and paced past Jeffrey down the center of the road. "What? How did they get out?"

Marla was counting the animals when Jeffrey gently tugged on her sleeve. "You need to come over here."

She swung her arm free. "What? I have seven dead animals. Let me examine them."

"No. You have more."

Marla bunched her eyebrows. Her face stiffened.

"Come on," Jeffrey said with a wave of his hand.

Marla moved past the road and kicked the cut barbed wire to her side. Over a knoll, she stopped and gawked at what was out there. Every animal she owned lay motionless within fifty yards of the water tank.

"I have no idea what happened," Jeffrey said, "but it looks suspicious."

Marla's eyes bulged. "Ya think so?" She pulled the cap down further on her forehead. "Why are you here? I mean," she searched the area, discovering no one else around, "were you traveling down this road for a reason? The sheriff's department is miles from here."

He backed away while nodding. "Legitimate question. I'm serving papers."

"This early? Shift change is at seven o'clock. You had to be there an hour earlier to gather all the papers to serve this far out in the county. And why is no one else here?"

"Again, a legitimate question. I have errands this afternoon, so I wanted to finish early."

"Is there someone on this road you were serving?"

His face reddened. "No reason for the third degree. I received a dispatch of dead cattle on the road, so here I am."

Another deputy vehicle approached, with dust swirling behind and its grille and roof flashing red and blue lights.

"See? Another unit is coming up now."

"Okay, sorry, a little jumpy." Marla wandered between the carcasses and pushed on a stiff leg. "Rigor mortis. It means they died a few hours ago...middle of the night." She knelt beside one and picked up a stick, then scraped off brow-gray gunk around the mouth. The mixture was a combination of slobber and dry ash.

"Marla!" Cassie yelled. "Marla! Over here."

She swiveled back to Cassie, who stood near a pile of debris. "Did you find something?" Marla hustled over.

"Look." Cassie ran her gloved hand through a scattered pile of ash. "This appears as if someone dropped a bucket load of whatever this is."

The second deputy called out, "Found another pile over here."

Marla crouched beside Cassie and slid her leather-gloved fingers through the mess again. "It feels like wood ashes." Why would cattle eat ash?"

Cassie sniffed it. "Molasses." She brushed her hands across her jeans. "Sugar, too." White crystals glimmered in the residue. "They smelled the sweetness and ate it."

An engine droned from the Johnson land with a trail of dust rising from the ground—a four-wheeler approached them. Roger brought the vehicle to a halt and gawked at the dead animals.

Deputy Keene blocked Roger's way.

When he instinctively slapped the right side of his belt for his revolver, Cassie shouted, "Roger, stop!"

He lifted his hands in the air. "Okay."

Cassie looked at Roger's belt. There was no holster. "Where's your gun and holster? You always carry them."

"I rushed over here and forgot I left them in the bunkhouse."

Jeffrey stepped in front of Roger. "You need to stop right where you are. This is a potential crime scene."

Roger sneered and swept his arm out, pointing at the cattle. "What the hell? There's a lot of dead animals out here. Could this be anything else?" He turned toward Cassie. "How many of them are dead?"

"Where did you go last night?" Cassie asked.

"I, er, I stayed at Mr. Johnson's place. He insisted on me being there early this morning because he went out of town." Roger whispered, "What does this have to do with anything about last night?"

Deputy Keene clamped onto his arm. "Stop right here."

Roger flung his arm free and shoved Keene back with enough force that he stumbled but didn't fall. "Keep your hands off me." He continued speaking to Cassie. "Listen, I'm sorry about last night. We shouldn't have argued." He looked at the dead cattle. "I saw the flashing lights and came as quickly as I could."

"Something killed the cattle!" Cassie wrung her hands and then shook them hard. "I...we don't know what."

Jeffrey brushed past Marla. "Criminals return to the scene of a crime more often than not."

Marla moved nearer. "Are you accusing someone here?"

Deputy Keene sized up all three before shaking his head. "We see this all the time."

Roger faced Keene. "Yeah? Which of us are you accusing? The boss? Did she kill her own cattle?" He pointed at Cassie. "How about the ranch hand? Is that what you're saying? That she planned to kill the cattle, then spend the day drinking beer 'cause she'll be out of a job?"

Jeffrey snapped back. "How about a cowboy slumming off a couple of women?"

"You're a piece of shit." Roger grabbed Keene's shirt with both hands. Jeffrey chopped down hard on his assailant's arms, spun him around, and pinned one arm behind his back. The second deputy rushed over and pulled out his handcuffs.

"Whoa, whoa," Marla said. "Let's settle down and take a breath."

Jeffrey forced Roger away. "You try that again, and I'll arrest you for assaulting an officer of the law."

"And I should call the cops and have you arrested for pretending to be an officer of the law."

Marla plopped a hand on each of them. "You two children, shut up. These are my cattle...my problem. I don't want any bickering." She spun around toward Cassie. "Get the front loader and a chain and drag the carcasses off the road and back on my property."

"Yeah, good idea," Roger said. "I'll help." He motioned for Cassie to climb onto the four-wheeler behind him.

As the four-wheeler rode toward the bunkhouse and the engine noise diminished, Jeffrey asked Marla, "Rosemary is not doing well. How about just you and I track down this doctor, and leave that other agent out of it?"

"Jeffrey, look around you. I'm preoccupied with other things right about now."

"Do you think you know where she is?"

"Rivera almost had her right here in Hildebrandt."

"What happened?" Jeffrey asked.

"Had her trapped in an abandoned house on the north side of town, but the slinky bitch disappeared. Now she's gone. My guess is she slithered back up into the drainage system."

Jeffrey inched closer to her. "You know which part?"

Marla shrugged. "Maybe."

"Tell me where you assume she is. You take care of the animals, and I'll find the doctor."

Marla removed her phone from her back pocket, opened an app, and showed it to Jeffrey. "We are almost certain she possesses a map of the San Antone stormwater drainage system—miles and miles of it. Rivera and I interviewed convenience store employees, taxi drivers, and others near Dr. Wilborn's location. She had always stayed within a few miles of the airport. After fleeing from Rivera, she probably headed to the closest outfall in that vicinity." Marla circled the area with her index finger. "That would be ten miles from where she was before."

"Is SAPD looking for the car?"

Marla shrugged before closing the app and sticking the phone into her pocket. "It's a guess, but it's all I've got."

"How long until you're done here?" Jeffrey asked.

"It'll be a while before we drag the animals off the road and then the vet has to gather samples."

"Okay," Jeffrey said. "You stay as long as necessary, but I expect Wilborn to return to her previous location. It seems like that has become her 'home base.'"

Why do people use air quotes? "Sure, whatever you want," Marla said.

"I'll head to where you suggested first," Jeffrey said.

"You should call for backup. Wilborn is dangerous and armed. Do you want me to send you the app?"

Jeffrey marched toward his vehicle. "No. I know the place." When his door closed, the emergency lights continued flashing. He spun the car around and left, disregarding the idea of going to the closest drainpipe exit. The diameter measured only six feet instead of ten, and he knew that only a desperate, ignorant person would go there—and Dr. Wilborn was neither.

Chapter 29

While Marla waited inside the veterinarian's office, the television screen on the wall displayed the local weather report, with a meteorologist pointing at the Gulf of Mexico.

"There is a Category 4 hurricane targeting the Texas coastline." With a broad red arrow pointing below Houston, it and angled northwest. "It will make landfall north of Brownsville this afternoon and turn toward San Antonio. Anticipate heavy rain and winds for a few days." A list of expected rainfall popped onto the screen, with Corpus Christi receiving eight inches, San Antonio with six, and Austin with two.

Marla smiled. After almost three hot months of severe water restrictions, relief was finally on the way. She called the office, and they transferred her to Rivera's cubbyhole.

"Special Agent Rivera here."

"It's me. Expect me to be late."

"Why?"

"I have…I have…all of my cattle are dead."

"Dead? How?"

"I don't know yet."

"When will you find out?"

Her voice leaped an octave. "I don't know that either. I'm at the vet's office and hope to learn something soon. What are you doing?"

"Finishing my report about missing Dr. Wilborn. Borland is itching to get it. He asked if you were involved. I told him no."

The receptionist announced, "Mrs. Adams, you may enter now."

"Have to go. I'll call later."

The side door buzzed, and memories of the surgical center flooded back. Dr. Grimes, the owner of Hildebrandt Veterinary Large Animal Services and Hospital, opened the door and extended his hand to Marla. They shook, then he gestured toward the laboratory.

He snatched a lab report from the printer and offered it to her. "Arsenic."

Marla paused and analyzed the paper. "Are you sure? How could a hundred cattle have ingested arsenic?"

"No doubt that is what killed them. High concentration in the blood and urine and inside the rumen. I'm glad you had me collect the samples as soon as you did."

"Why?"

"Arsenic breaks down rapidly. With a high blood level and ash in the rumen, the animals had been eating it for several hours. Mrs. Adams, when was the last time you checked on your cattle?"

Cassie checks them every day, so yesterday was the last. I got the call about the dead animals on the road this morning before she headed out there."

"So, nobody checked the cattle for about twenty-four hours?"

"I'd say that's about right."

The laboratory analyzer dinged, and the printer kicked out a page.

"Everything has been good so far except the arsenic," the vet explained. "This is the last of the tests." He read the newest report. "Hmm, wait, this is odd. They also had copper and chromium in the blood."

"What does that mean?"

"There should be no legitimate reason for those metals in the blood, but there is enough there to poison them with these as well."

"Three metals? That's crazy."

"Two metals. Arsenic is a metalloid."

"Okay, but why chromium, copper, and arsenic?" Marla asked.

"Wait a minute...when you said it like that..." Dr. Grimes stepped to his computer. "I attended a conference last year, and one lecture was about strange animal deaths." He typed on the keyboard. "I'm a nerd about lecture notes. I keep everything." He kept typing. "Here it is, Guess What Killed Them? was the title, and I remember the room was packed. The forensic pathologist who taught at a vet school up north was a dynamic speaker, and everyone loved his presentations. He always brought interesting topics for us."

He scrolled down to the fourth example, The Death of a Herd of Deer. "They were poisoned with chromium, copper, and arsenic." He stood back and let Marla view the screen while he read the lecture summary. "The deer ate wood, pressure treated with CCA, chromated copper and arsenic. It's a chemical produced decades ago and utilized to resist termites and fungi. The lumber industry ceased using it in the early 2000s because of several cases of arsenic poisoning."

"Still don't understand." Her eyes opened wide. "Oh, damn. The ashes. Cassie said someone mixed in sugar so they would eat it."

"Right," Dr. Grimes said. "In the lecture, a house burned down in the forest, and soon after, a herd of deer ate nuts, plants, and seeds that had fallen into the ashes. The arsenic level was sky high."

"Like my cattle?"

"Like your cattle."

"Cassie was right. Someone dumped two front loader buckets full of burned wood with CCA, knowing it would kill the cattle."

"But from where?" Dr. Grimes asked.

Marla thought about Mr. Johnson's ranch. "Jake Johnson had a fire in a hay storage unit with stacked wood he kept for decades."

"Heard about that fire. Bad. Could have been disastrous."

"After the fire, there was a pile of rubble and ash, and the planks were twenty plus years old, so they had to have been treated with CCA."

"Makes sense," Grimes said.

Marla examined the laboratory reports. "But Jake wouldn't poison my cattle."

"No, Mrs. Adams, I don't believe he would. Too nice of a guy."

"He's always been helpful to me, especially after Crosby's death. But he inquired if I wanted to sell my hay and land so he could raise more cattle." Marla rubbed her dry lips with a finger.

"I can't see Mr. Johnson trying to force you from the cattle business and make you leave."

"People are strange animals, and they do strange things."

"But why?"

Marla stood. "Wait." She tapped the table with her finger. "Not leave. The opposite. If I'm here, right here, I can't be somewhere else. Someone wants me to be here."

"Here?" Dr. Grimes asked. "Not following you."

"To be away from what I'm supposed to be doing, hunting a killer, a fentanyl dealer. This crazy-ass doctor wants me off the trail so she can backtrack and kill me, just like when you hunt a grizzly."

"That's scary, but you must dispose of the carcasses soon. They can't sit on your pasture and decay."

"Right." Marla reached into her back pocket for the phone and called Cassie.

"Hello?"

"I want you to drag all the carcasses together and burn them today, then bury the remains."

"Um, yeah, sure. I can do that. I'll call Chief Verdon at the fire department and have them on standby. Marla, what are you planning to do?"

"I'm going after the son of a bitch that killed my livestock. Is Roger with you?"

"No. He left for the day."

"And went where?"

"Listen, it's none of your business what he's doing."

"Cassie, the cattle were poisoned, and I want to talk to everyone. Where is he?"

"Even me? Do you think I had something to do with your cattle? What about Mr. Johnson? That crazy old man most likely did it because you won't sell your hay to him. What about the cartel? They probably want revenge for what you did to them. Or that deputy, or the sheriff, or your boss? What about them? Are you going to question all of them, too?" Cassie ended the conversation before Marla had a chance to respond.

"Well, that didn't go over like I wanted." Marla made another call.

"Special Agent Rivera here."

"They were poisoned with arsenic," Marla said.

"Damn! You think it's somehow related?"

"Hell, yes. I'm sure this crazed doctor killed them. Wanted to divert me...and you from her."

"It worked. We're back to a cold trail."

"Is there a BOLO on her from SAPD?" Marla asked.

Rivera accessed the DEA's secure website with the password. "Sure is. They'll probably detain every blue car in town."

"That's a lot of cars."

"Let's hope they'll get lucky."

Marla's phone rang while still talking. "Have to take this call. It's the medical examiner's office calling me."

"All right, keep me informed."

Marla answered, "Special Agent Adams here."

"This is the Bexar County Medical Examiner's office, and Dr. Berghoff asked me to call you. He is ready to perform the autopsy on the body you inquired about."

Marla rubbed her hand over her mouth before replying. More dead things. "Thank you. Please tell him I can be there in…um…traffic…twenty minutes."

"I will." The woman disconnected the call.

Marla's phone rang again. The screen displayed WORK. She answered, "Adams."

"This is Sandra Vogel, ASAC Borland's assistant. He wants you and Special Agent Rivera in his office at the top of the hour."

Vogel relocated from Jersey to San Antonio after the previous assistant got into a bit of trouble and was murdered. She brought a northeastern accent with her, not to mention her attitude.

"Can't," Marla replied. "I'm on my way to the autopsy of the Hildebrandt Surgical Center shooter. I can make it there in an hour."

"You sure you want me to tell him that, Sweetie?"

There's that attitude again. "I'm committed to something else and already on my way there. And, yes, if you feel obligated to go in there and explain to your boss that I am out doing my job, then I guess you better get right on that."

"I will, and you better do yours."

Chapter 30

"Welcome back," Dr. Berghoff said to Marla. "Ready?"

Marla shook her head. She didn't want to be back at the medical examiner's office. "No, but let's do what I came for. The brain."

The autopsy technician helping the medical examiner was a prominent veteran of the procedures, and he let her do most of the work. She had short steel-gray hair and hazel-green eyes. A short-sleeved green scrub top revealed tattoos of a cross, a snake, and a scalpel over muscular biceps and forearms that could out bench press anyone her age. With a flick of the switch, the bone cutter buzzed like a chainsaw while she skillfully directed the saw blade around the circumference of the skull and chattered away about various topics.

"I've been cutting bone and pulling guts and lungs and hearts and brains for years. Never bothered me." She scoffed. "Some people's stomachs turn and get queasy with the idea of seeing the inside of a body. I never did. When I was six or seven, a first grader, I saw a dead raccoon on the street. It must have just happened because there was blood all around it, and the head split wide open. That's the first real brain I ever saw. I'd seen photos and drawings of animals in books, but this was the real deal for me, and I lit up like a Christmas tree. After that, all the kids called me Raccoon, and it stuck through high school, so the only people who talked to me were nerds interested in science, like bio and chem. When they taught the health class in middle school, I had a greater understanding than the teacher and made it known to her. That'll get you in a boatload of trouble. I got to where I ignored most people. Adults were shitty to me, worse than kids my age, if you can imagine that. Never married. Couldn't give a rat's ass about what anyone thought. Kinda eliminated second dates, if you know what I mean. So, I said the heck with them, and I live my life among the dead. They don't bitch, or cry, or tell stupid jokes." She released the trigger on the saw and stuck her fingers between the separated bone. The top of the cranium moved slightly. "But I do have a soft spot for the little ones, especially infants that are only a few days old—the one or two pounders. Those kids don't tell stupid jokes. If you can believe it, I'm also a certified neonatal intensive care sitter. They settle right in the crook of your arm if you hold them just right and give them a bottle. Kinda snuggle up to me."

She laid the saw on the chest and used a bone spreader that looked like a tool from The Game of Thrones to separate the cap from the rest of the skull. Inside, the meninges tore with the sound of wadded Saran Wrap being pulled apart. After placing the skullcap in a stainless steel bowl, she kept talking.

"See, nothing to it—nary a peep. I do like the dead. My favorite people to be around...that is after the month-old babies." She finally smiled. "They are just too cute."

Meticulous with the scalpel, she reached under the brain and cut the spinal cord, freeing the medium cantaloupe sized organ from the body, and carefully placed it on a disposable pad spread across a stainless steel table.

Marla winced at the pink-tinged brain with clotted blood vessels snaking in multiple directions. She closed her eyes briefly before nodding at the doctor to continue.

Dr. Berghoff dissected the brain, exposing the anterior cingulate cortex (ACC), an area positioned behind the prefrontal cortex. He noted the ACC was fifteen percent larger than average, with ecchymotic hemorrhages from repetitive injections injuring the tissue.

Back in her truck, she took a few notes about Bambi's gunshot wounds, the almost healed hip wound that was only days old, the hole in the forehead, and the stem cell modified brain, before rushing back to the DEA building. When she entered ASAC Borland's office lobby, Sandra Vogel sat behind her desk and sipped a can of diet drink from a straw before setting it down on top of an assisted living booklet. Marla figured family was the only reason a Jersey girl would come to San Antone. Parent? In-law? Didn't matter. "I'm here."

Without saying a word, Sandra leaned over her desk to adjust her nameplate which read "Administrative Assistant," then pressed a button on a black box. With her misplaced accent in the central part of Texas, she announced, "Special Agent Adams is heah."

In the DEA, there are no Mr. or Mrs. or Ms. Everyone goes by a title.

Rivera startled Marla when he stood from a chair near the corner of the room. "You're an hour late."

"I am not." She glared at the administrative assistant. "I told her I had to go to the shooter's autopsy before coming here."

"And?"

"Same thing. A hole in the hip and the forehead with that concoction shot inside the brain."

Borland's voice came over the black box speaker. "I'm in the middle of something. Have them wait in the breakroom."

Sandra wrinkled her nose at the two as she grasped her can and sipped her drink. "Wanna wait?"

Rivera motioned toward the hallway. "Come on, I need to get something from my office."

Marla smiled. "You mean cubbyhole." She pointed at Borland's door. "He's the only one with an office."

"True enough."

They headed to the rear of the building, where plate glass windows let the sun's heat penetrate everything inside. Everyone sat in their own little cubicle with different mementos stuck on their corrugated walls, each expecting their project to be priority number one. She passed by a vacant workstation and paused at Quinton Wales' spot.

A 2x2 inch photo sat in the back corner of the desktop. Marla reached over and picked it up. Quinton Wales and his wife smiled at a restaurant on the Riverwalk, captured in a selfie. He blamed everyone for her death and for destroying his family, and he wanted everyone to pay for his misery.

"Adams?" Rivera called out from several cubicles away.

She dropped the photo on the empty desktop.

"I got what I wanted." Rivera signaled toward the doorway. "Break-room."

Marla entered the room and saw an overflowing wastebasket in the corner, with paper coffee cups spilling out. Stale donut holes lay scattered beside the sink. On the table were a half-full sack of kolaches and an opened plastic container of yellow mustard. The bottle felt cool, so she snapped the top closed and returned it to the fridge.

"Want a cup of coffee?" Rivera inserted a pod into the machine and pressed the brew button.

"Yeah. Sure."

She had no desire to be in the breakroom or the county medical examiner's autopsy room, but she had been to both today. The postmortem replayed in her mind.

Rivera interrupted her thoughts when he set the cup on the table. "Are you all right?"

She blinked, then looked up. Before answering, she sipped her coffee. "Why?"

He wiped the counter down with a wet paper towel. "You seem distracted."

The cleaning solution on the paper towel threw her thoughts back into the autopsy room. The sterile metallic smell of the room filled her mind. After this one, she doesn't want to be around another again, but she probably will.

"Hey!" Rivera lightly squeezed her arm. "Talk to me. Are you feeling okay?"

"No, yes. I...maybe. No firm leads."

"Remember? I'm here to help." Rivera pulled a chair back and sat down. "What's going on with you?"

Marla straightened her shoulders. "Wilborn has disappeared after turning someone into a monster, and she may be doing it again, passing fentanyl out like fairy dust." A headache crept up the back of her skull. "And now...Borland. What does he want? We're getting hit from both ends."

A rap on the wall gave Marla a jolt. Sandra poked her head around the doorway, grinning like the cat that got the cream. "Time's up, dolls. ASAC Borland's waitin' for ya both."

When Marla entered the office, she was dumbfounded at who else was there. Why the hell is Borland's immediate boss in the room?

Special Agent in Charge Davies sat quietly in one of two winged-back chairs. Both arms rested on the armrests, and his left index finger and thumb twisted the temple of his glasses side to side.

A little more than a month ago, he sat beside her in the hospital surgical waiting room, talking for hours and hoping for good news about Crosby. He said he would do anything to help. But today, he positioned himself with distant eyes and a professionally blank facial expression.

Borland nodded toward the couch between the chairs. "Have a seat." He waited until both sat before asking, "Where are you on the Hugo Wilborn investigation?"

Marla sighed. Borland knew the answer. He had received their written reports, and she was sure Davies had read them.

Rivera went first. "Sirs, at present, we are still in search of the suspect."

Borland interrupted. "There have been three additional fatalities linked to fentanyl."

"Excuse me, sir," Marla said. "How can you be certain it's from our suspect?"

"SAPD have reported homeless found dead around the stormwater system, with holes in their forehead and broken bits of rainbow colored fentanyl tabs close by. Crime lab says they are the same as the dust on your shooter's clothes."

"I just came from the medical examiner's office and Dr. Berghoff didn't mention any new corpses to me," Marla said.

"He probably hasn't had time to do them yet," Davies said.

"Where were the vics found?" Rivera asked.

"Mostly south of the airport," Borland said.

Rivera leaned toward Marla. "Makes sense. That's the location where we found the mushroom guy, and when he contacted me, he was less than a mile from where we first encountered him."

Marla glanced at Davies, who remained seated while acting distant and aloof, then redirected her attention back to Borland. "I'm unclear about the purpose for being here, sir."

Borland fired back. "The media wants answers, and I'm..." he glanced at Davies and raised his eyebrows momentarily, "We are backed up against the wall."

"It's not my fault someone came after me. Do you reprimand every agent who is fired upon?"

Borland continued to sit while answering. "In the last six months, we've only had two incidents of agents being fired upon."

"Only two?" Marla snapped back. "I believe it's three, two agents, but three shootings—me at the clinic, and my husband was shot twice." Marla stood. "The cartel shot him once and a second time...." She rubbed her hands over her face. "And you are well aware of that incident."

Davies raised his hand and spoke softly. "Enough. Adams...Marla, please sit."

She stood for what felt like an eternity. Her toes curled and uncurled inside her black shoes before she gave up and plopped down.

Davies crossed his legs while still twirling the eyeglasses between his fingers. "You're a good agent, Adams, but you might need help on this—"

Marla leaned forward. "You asked me to come in during my family medical leave. You wanted a favor from me, gave me full rein, and now you want me to withdraw?"

"This is unrelated to your FMLA. You can return to it anytime you want. I want to emphasize that we are not taking anything away from you. We want a third agent assigned to this case."

"Rivera and I can handle this just fine."

Marla's phone rang. She was glad it was Jeffrey. "It's the sheriff's department. I asked Deputy Keene to check on a place for me." She aimed her phone toward each of them with Keene's name displayed. Borland nodded. She answered, "Adams here."

"I'm stopping somewhere else before I go where you suggested."

"Excellent." Marla gave Borland a skeptical glance. "So, you are tracking someone inside the stormwater pipe?"

"Marla, no. I'm not there yet."

"Hang on. We can be there shortly."

"I have no idea what you are saying."

"Right." She slipped her phone in her pocket and looked at Borland. "May we go, sir?"

Borland eyed Davies, who nodded once. "Keep us informed."

Marla charged out with Rivera behind her.

Rushing down the stairs to the lobby, Rivera said. "I thought we were getting canned. It's damned lucky Keene called you. What did he say?"

"He told me he was running an errand before heading where I suggested."

"You've got to be joking. You made it sound like he had the perp."

"I did it to escape the charades upstairs."

He clamped onto Marla's shoulder, keeping her from exiting the building. "Where are you going?"

"I have no clue. We're at a dead end again."

He released her arm. "True."

"Angelo..."

This is the second time she has said my first name. What the hell is she going to say next?

"The slaughter of the cattle, the mass poisoning, was a move to distract me so Wilborn could set me up for an ambush. I have no doubt Wilborn is working on another attack, and given that the next diversion could be to kill you as a further distraction...warning. This lunatic is smart, prison smart—knows how to kill, and we could walk into a trap that takes both of us down."

"In hindsight, going after her in the abandoned house by myself was not the best idea. If I had waited for a police unit, we could have covered both doors and trapped her. But I was pissed at her for the ambush at the medical facility. You don't hold any secrets back, and I won't either. Agree?"

"Agree." They shook hands and smiled at each other. "I'm heading back to the ranch. Have some business to tend to."

"I got things to do, too." Rivera rushed out the side door toward the parking lot.

Marla hesitated before pushing open the main exit door. The rumble and buzz of traffic from Loop 410 behind her flooded in, but the scorching temperature and bright sunlight caught her off guard. She pivoted half-circle, ready to go back in; instead, she leaned her head against the building and let out a deep sigh. After collecting herself, she knew Cassie wouldn't make the first move, so she crouched down on the curb, pulled her phone out, and sent a text. Need help.

Yeah? Maybe look up your ass. Lots of bullshit there.

She snickered and rubbed her nose. "That's my girl." All I can say is I'm sorry for what I said.

It was sorry.

Marla held her phone with both hands while texting back. Still need your help.

Why?

Lots of reasons, but mostly the new shipment of cattle coming. Reconsider staying?

No reply.

Still huddled on the curb, she texted again. Meet me at the barn?

Still no reply.

She laid her phone beside her, then pressed her trembling fist against her lips. Brushing her hair away from her forehead, she released a hollow laugh and whispered words that would go unheard.

◆

Marla stopped her truck near the barn. She climbed out and skimmed the area for Cassie's horse, but saw nothing. Blackie whinnied inside and Marla smiled. "Do you smell me, big boy?" She opened the door, and both horses shuffled inside their stalls. "Daisy, girl." Marla rubbed the horse's nose before reaching into the bucket and handing a carrot to the horse. She sidestepped to Blackie. "Hey, good looking. You must know it is your girlfriend's turn, right? We have someone to talk to down the road."

When she led the horse outside, she looked for Cassie once again. She glided her hand along the horse's neck. "We need to do this every day, just the two of us." After saddling Daisy, she mounted her and rode toward the Johnson Ranch. Jake's contaminated wood poisoned her cattle. He said he was out of town, but where? Was there any proof he was gone?

When Marla approached Jake's house, he stood on the porch, smiling and waving. He grasped the reins and wrapped them around the post.

"An unexpected pleasure, my dear. Hope everything is okay."

Marla dismounted and shook his hand. "I'm good. All good with you, Jake?"

"Oh, sure. Come on in and have a glass of iced tea."

When she entered behind Jake, she noticed nothing had changed from the last time she had visited. A 3x5 picture frame with a photo of Mrs. Johnson was positioned on the coffee table near the rocking chair, with a ball of yarn and two knitting needles in a wicker basket on the other side.

"Come into the kitchen. I made a pitcher of fresh tea. Still like it with sugar?"

"Of course."

"It's a fact, people are getting away from sweet tea." He put the lid on the canister. "They're going to unsweet, but I can't do that. Need my sugar."

Marla snickered. "What's this world coming to?"

"I'm glad you came by. I want to let you know that anytime something happens around the place, text me, and I'll come as soon as I can." Ice clattered inside the glasses before he poured the tea. After handing one to her, he pointed toward the dining table. "Please, sit."

"And same for you, Jake. Anytime you would like to contact me, text me or call. I'll do what I can for you."

"That's great. What's new?"

She sipped her tea. "Ahh, perfect." She took another sip. "I haven't had the chance to say how sorry I am about the fire."

He nodded several times. "Well, thank you. It's been tough. With the lumbar gone, it sort of confirms…" he raised his chin and sniffed, "that I'm never going to build what she wanted."

"Jake, I'm deeply sorry." She sipped the tea again. "None of my concern, but is the ranch doing okay? I'm worried about you. It's no secret cattle prices are low, crops are lost, with nothing growing in this heat."

"Yeah." He sipped his tea. "It's getting tougher. Insurance is dragging its feet on paying, and the county commissioners said the site was a hazard and too close to the road. They expect me to clean up the mess, but it costs money to do that."

Marla placed her glass on the table. "I did have a question. When did you leave town before the fire?"

Jake stopped looking at her. "The, uh, the day before."

"To see family? I hope everything is okay."

"Yeah, sure. Everyone is good. Why?"

"I'm sure the police confirmed all that. You know, where you went."

"What are you saying? You don't think I had anything to do with it, do you?"

"Jake, it's the cop in me. I like all the loose ends cleared. Where did you go?"

"My ex-daughter-in-law's house. She never calls, only texts, and she sent one that she needed help with one of her children. I jumped in the truck and drove two hours to her house."

"Thought you said everyone was good."

"When I got there, she said she never sent me a text. I drove back later that day. She's a little odd, so I didn't push the idea she should look at her phone. I'm guessing she sent it and erased it."

Marla waved her hand. "Right. Pretty odd, indeed. I had another question about the fire and the ashes."

"Listen, I am so sorry about all that. Honestly, I don't know what happened. I've told the police, the sheriff's department, and the insurance company everything."

"Oh, right. I'm sure. But, uh, did anyone from the sheriff's office come over here to the house?"

"No. I met them where the fire had happened."

"I see. You know that a couple of bucket loads of ash were dumped on my property near the water tank a few days after the fire. Do you have any idea how that got from your place to mine?"

He slid his glass to the side. "Don't know what you mean?"

"I had Cassie check the front bucket on my tractor for ash, and nothing was visible. Would you mind if I checked your tractors?"

Jake sat straight in his chair. "You think one of my tractors carried the ash to your place?"

"You're in the clear, but it had to be a front loader carrying the ash to my place, or dumping into the bed of a truck, right? May I?"

"Sure. We can ride over to the shed in my pickup."

They went out the back door to the truck. Jake climbed into the driver's side, and when Marla opened her door, a shotgun leaned barrel up on the passenger's seat. Jake pulled it closer toward him as she sat down and closed the door.

"Don't worry, the chamber is empty. I carry it for the rattlers."

Marla gently latched onto the barrel. "I'll hold it for you while you drive."

When they arrived, three tractors sat under the shed, two new ones and one almost old enough to be antique. Marla swung open her door and kept hold of the shotgun. She checked the chamber and racked it until all the shells popped out before leaning it against the truck. She headed straight for the closest one and checked the bucket. It was clean, as was the next. The older tractor sat away from the newer ones. Sweeping her hand across the bucket, she felt a fine dusting of ash on her skin. Dried mud and ash covered the tire tread. She brushed her hand on her jeans. "Where do you keep the keys to the tractors?"

"At the house."

"How often do you use the older one?"

"I load the large round hay bales with the bigger ones. The older one, I carry light things in the bucket from time to time, but I haven't used it in at least a week, maybe two. It's still sitting in the same place."

"Anyone else use the tractors? What about Roger?"

Jake shrugged. "Yeah, probably. He moves stuff around."

"Come look at this, Jake. I'm sure this is the tractor that dumped the ash on my property."

The two bent down, and Marla showed the dusting in the bucket and the ash covering the tires.

"You said the key for this one is in the house?"

"Right, but you don't need a key for that old thing."

After she stood, Jake did the same. "Explain," Marla said.

"It's fifty years old and can be hot-wired pretty easily. Sometimes I forget the key and don't want to drive back to the house. It takes a few seconds, provided you know what you're doing."

"Hmm. Guess I don't know much about how to do that. Who would?"

"Anyone working on a farm or ranch, mechanics, old car enthusiasts."

Marla sat up straight. "Like race car mechanics?"

"Sure."

"Take me back to the house, Jake."

Marla's phone rang. "Hello?"

"Rivera here. Have some new info for you."

"About the doctor?"

"No. About your good buddy, Deputy Keene."

"What about Jeffrey?"

"Did he tell you he was in the Air Force and where he was stationed?"

"I knew he was in the service. He said Europe."

"Not even close. He was based at RAF Croughton Air Force Base in Northamptonshire, England, and he was there during the first half of Dr. Hugo Wilborn's internment."

"Not sure where you are going with this?"

"Marla, your buddy volunteered at the prison where Wilborn was incarcerated every weekend. There's a good chance they met."

Chapter 31

Wilborn banged her fist on the backdoor of The Broken Saddle Horn. "Get your bloody arse out here."

Trixi opened the door with a short-barrel shotgun pointed at Wilborn. "What the hell are you doing here?"

"I need your help—"

"And I need you," Trixi glanced both ways down the alley, "to get out of here."

"Listen, Connie—"

"My name is not Connie, it's Trixi. Connie is long gone. I'm Trixi."

"Stop being a bloody plank. You're Connie, my cellmate for two years. Did you bloody forget it was me who helped you escape?"

"Don't you forget. You weren't the only one helping. God love my brother, but he's a dipshit some days. That place dragged my ass down from the second I entered."

"I treated you right. You got extra food and fags. Even got you a bloody phone to talk to your brother."

"Yeah, but you had your reasons to get me out," Trixi said. "Besides, he's the only thing that kept me sane for two bloody years!"

"And you're here only because I paid you plenty of cash to send me everything about Marla Adams."

"Okay, so what? I came back to the States and did what you paid me for. I sent you letters about her. So, now you're here, and I'm done with you. Thanks for busting me out, but don't confuse yourself believing I'm your lifelong bezzie mate."

When Wilborn grabbed Trixi's arm, cold steel pressed against the doctor's abdomen.

"Listen, Dr. Feelgood, at point-blank, this will cut you in half. Best you let go."

Wilborn released her grasp. "I need a place to hide the money and the equipment."

Trixi shook her head. "Not here."

"Where?"

"I know a place sort of close to the airport. It's not used much, so you can hide it in a corner."

"Where?"

"I need a hundred grand," Trixi said.

"Sodding hell. I paid you already." Wilborn furrowed her brow. "Why?"

Trixi motioned back toward the bar.

Wilborn howled at her. "You can't buy a place that sells alcohol. You're a felon. Hell, you can't buy anything that's not with cash, you're an escaped convict!"

"Thanks for reminding me. The money is for me to be a silent partner in this place. Cash in my pocket every month."

"No. No more money."

Trixi pushed the barrel against Wilborn's abdomen. "Then let the homeless in your precious storm drain steal your money from you."

Wilborn glared at her for a moment before answering. "Fine. I'll get it to you tomorrow."

"Now." Trixi nodded toward the blue car behind Wilborn. "You have it in there, right?"

After digging through the trunk, Wilborn returned holding a small sack with bundles of cash. "I need a gun."

"Since when do you like guns?"

"I don't, but the other one ran out of bullets."

"Put more in."

"Don't know how."

Trixi drew a handgun from behind her belt near the small of her back. "Here. It doesn't have a bullet in the chamber. You have to rack it first."

"What do you mean?"

After explaining it to Wilborn, she held the pistol out. "Don't rack it, or I'll pull my trigger and you won't feel anything after about a second."

Wilborn took the weapon and dropped the sack of money between their feet. When Trixi glanced at the sack, Wilborn quickly racked the gun and pointed it at Trixi's chest. "You mean like this?"

She continued to point the shotgun at Wilborn. "Won't do either of us any good if we're both dead."

"I need the other vial."

Trixi leaned forward, her eyes focused on the pistol, and latched onto the sack with her left hand. "That would require another deposit."

"Do you have it here?" Wilborn asked.

"Bro has it after he stole it from the Hildebrandt Police Department Evidence Room." She shoved Wilborn back with the shotgun barrel. "Get in your car and go hide your sci-fi junk."

It took thirty minutes of bumper-to-bumper traffic for Wilborn to reach the destination Trixi mentioned. She pitched the empty revolver in the bushes, then picked the lock on the wire fence gate and the metal door to the building. She pulled the pistol from her pocket and then flipped on the light. The fluorescent bulbs buzzed above her. The brick structure was larger than she expected, a hundred feet long, forty-feet wide, and forty-feet tall, with no windows, a light film of dust covering the floor, and no footprints. Twelve-inch orange-painted pipes hung from the ceiling to the floor, with a few gray metal storage cabinets scattered about. Cobwebs covered old newspapers, painter's cloths, and flattened cardboard boxes in the back corner. She flung a cloth to her side, found a dingy white tote bag with a drawstring top, and stuffed folded newspapers into the bottom, then opened the trunk and counted thirty thousand dollars before placing the money on top of the newspaper and pulling the drawstring closed. "That should look like a proper fortune."

Afterward, Wilborn shoved the trunk into the corner and covered it with cardboard and painter's cloth. At the door, she glanced back to the corner, then toward the street. No cars were passing by. With cobwebs everywhere and no footprints, no one had been inside for quite a while, so she kept the door unlocked and the padlock off the fence gate, never knowing if she might need to escape in a rush with her money and equipment. She opened the vehicle's back door and pitched the bag on the seat, but then changed her mind. "A bloomin' Crusty could nick it just as well as I could. Best I chuck it in the boot."

A few miles down the road, traffic congestion caught her off guard. "What the bloody hell are these Yanks doing?" Dr. Wilborn gripped the steering wheel with both hands and pleaded for a miracle to shift all American drivers into the right seat, like a proper English vehicle.

I have to get off the streets and back underground, but where am I?

A plane angling off in the sky caught her attention, and she wondered if its destination was London. A glaring sun radiated heat through the windshield, and the air conditioner couldn't keep her cool enough. She longed for a British rainy morning. Bright red lights flashed ahead of her—taillights. She slammed on the brakes, and tires skidded on the asphalt. With fingers cramped on the steering wheel, she let go and tried to shake off a twitchy feeling spreading across her arms and neck. A white noise buzzed louder in her ears. After taking a deep breath and the car in front gone, she glared at the yellow fuel icon flashing on the dashboard. She lowered the side window as another plane rose into the sky. "That is where I bloody well need to be! Heading back to England!" The fuel icon seemed to brighten. "I should return underground, not to the airport." The traffic light changed. "But I'm not sure I have enough petrol to get there." Slowly driving while scanning the buildings on each side of the street, she hoped to find a fueling station. "There. About bloody time. A shop with petrol."

After parking next to a pump, Wilborn tried to determine the difference in the price from UK and the States, liters versus gallons, dollars versus pounds. It didn't matter. "I've banjaxed this entire day." She slid Michael Smythe's credit card into the pump, but nothing happened. She tried it again, still nothing happened. Taped to the pump, a piece of paper read TAP USE ONLY. "Brilliant. Stuck in a muckity carpark and have no idea what the bloody hell that means."

She opened the boot of the car, filched a hundred dollar bill from the cloth bag, and stuck it in the front pocket. Another car arrived on the opposite side of the pump, music blaring, the bass pounding every second, vibrating the ground and teeth. Wilborn returned to the vehicle, latched onto the fob in the cup holder, and clicked it once, producing a small beep and locking the doors.

When it was her turn at the register inside the convenience store, Wilborn grabbed a bag of chips. "This and six liters in that blue car."

"Six what?"

"Liters. Wait, blimey, two gallons." She slid the hundred dollar bill across the counter.

The cashier picked up the bill, held it in front of the overhead light, and inspected it briefly. "We don't get many of these. Gas and chips will be eight dollars and eighty-four cents." He counted the change and placed it in Wilborn's hand before pointing at the car across from hers. "Watch out for that driver. He's a mean teen."

Wilborn caught sight of something under the glass counter. "Give me that."

"You sure? It could make it worse for you."

"I said, give it to me." She pushed the bills and coins back. "Now!"

The cashier plucked a six-inch hunting knife in a sheath and laid it on the glass counter.

"Keep the change...and the chips."

Wilborn stepped out, pulled the knife from the sheath, and held the blade behind her back.

The teenager smiled and said, "Hey! I ain't got enough money to put gas in my car."

Wilborn slowed without saying a word.

The teen changed from a smile to irritation. "You hear me, bitch?"

Instead of walking to her side of the pump, Wilborn aimed straight at her soon-to-be opponent.

"Hey, old fart, give me some money!"

Wilborn glared straight at the kid, then rushed towards him.

The kid raised his shoulders and hands like a gangsta on a music video. "What the fuck are you doin'?"

Wilborn swung the knife blade in the air several times. "Get the bloody hell away from me."

The kid backed up behind his car. "Back off, bitch."

Wilborn pounded the teen's side window with the knife butt. It shattered, raining broken glass on the seats and floorboard. "I sliced up pieces of shite like you every day in prison. You are nothing to me." She stabbed the front tire, air hissed around the blade, and then noticed something interesting in the driver's seat: a 9mm pistol. She reached in and took it. When Wilborn's car chirped once, she climbed in and drove away as fast as possible.

A block later, after a traffic light changed red, she stuck the knife into the sheath, pitched it and the 9mm pistol onto the passenger seat, and then lowered the windows. Sweat dripped down her neck and armpits. "Bloody wanker. I should have gotten petrol."

The fuel gauge lit red. The engine sputtered and died. Pushing the ignition button did nothing but let the motor crank without starting.

Wilborn looked in all directions while sitting alone at the intersection before opening the trunk and removing the cloth bag. She flipped it over her shoulder and plodded toward the curb, then paused before returning to the vehicle, opened the front passenger door, and took the knife and pistol. When the traffic light changed to green, the blue car, with its doors and trunk open, didn't move.

Darkening clouds grumbled above, and the wind swirled her gray hair. Dr. Wilborn rushed behind a building and opened the stormwater drainage system map on the old woman's phone. With a light mist filling the air, she raised her face upwards and welcomed the moisture. She missed London weather.

As her fingers moved the map on the screen, she realized she was half a mile from where Bert and Bambi had been. There was no remorse for the girl. Her fault. She could have said no to the cocaine when we met. No to the fentanyl, and I would have found another bloody Crusty.

Dr. Wilborn's shadow disappeared. "About bloody time this hellhole has a cloud in the sky."

A siren yelped close by. She peeked around the corner of the building where a police vehicle had stopped behind the blue car. She spun back and hurried down the alley. Near the next intersection, someone had parked a green Toyota Camry next to the curb with the engine running. A young girl sat in the driver's seat with her hands over her face. Wilborn stepped closer and tapped on the window. The startled girl turned to look. Smeared mascara streamed down her cheeks.

Wilborn smiled as the girl lowered the window partway. "It seems as though you ran over my foot."

"What? How?"

"You didn't see me standing over there, and I had to move, but you still hit me."

She opened her door and looked down at the woman's feet. "I'm so sorry." The girl stepped out. "How can I help?"

"I don't believe I can walk anywhere. Would you mind taking me to a medical clinic?"

"Yes, yes, of course."

"Help me place my bag in your back seat."

The girl pitched the bag in the middle of the seat and held the door open. "Do you need help to sit?"

"I prefer the front passenger seat. There may not be enough room for me in the backseat."

"Oh, okay."

Wilborn leaned against the side of the car. "Go around and open the door."

When the girl rushed around to the right side, Wilborn climbed into the driver's seat and closed the door. "Thanks." The car lurched forward and drove away.

Fifteen minutes later, Dr. Wilborn drove the stolen vehicle past a large shopping center and veered onto a narrow road. Steady heat and rising humidity took their toll, with armpits stinking, clothes stuck to her skin, and heat rolling from her collar. "Maybe Bambi had a good idea about delving into a cold water hose for a shower. Degrading. Even in prison, I had a proper daily shower. A hotel would be better, but I'm sure every business in town has my photo."

There it was, a large stormwater outfall. Wilborn eased off the side of the road and hid the vehicle behind a handful of trees. While holding the bag in one hand, she entered the ten-foot diameter pipe. Her body chilled as the temperature decreased a few degrees inside.

"How did this go all to pot?" Cold sweat lingered on her temples. "This has been a major cockup. I should forget the skank and leave this God-forsaken country, but I must first hold the protein extract in my hand. Right, the extract; I must have it today." A beamy smile spread across her face as she chuckled. "And I have the *million* right bloody here in this bag!" Her voice echoed down the pipe. "I should tell the bastard I'm willing to help whomever he wants. Have him come to me, and when he does," she swung the knife neck-high and jabbed a would-be person twice before spinning around and kicking empty air, "I'll kill him and take the vial. Give the wanker nothing. That's what he deserves."

When sunlight flooded the tunnel from a stormwater grate above, she slid the blade into its sheath and dialed a number on the phone.

A voice answered, "About time you called me."

"You want the money?" Wilborn asked. "Give me the vial and it's yours."

"What about Adams?"

"Listen, dickhead. The extract is the only reason I'm in this bloody country. I must have it to further my research."

"Thought you wanted the DEA agent dead. You said she killed your partner. What's his name?"

"Dr. McCollum." Wilborn paused. "It's getting difficult. What is most important to me is the vial. With it, I can save this idiotic world and all the stupid people."

"I'm guessing you are miscalculating the amount inside the vial. There's not enough to save the world. And besides, you said your partner, excuse me, your dead partner, was the one who made the extract, not you, so how are you getting more after you screw around with a few other brains?"

"I'll keep a little, and once I perfect my experiments, dozens of companies will eagerly pay me." The British government will want it. I'll meet King Charles and the Prime Minister."

"You might be getting ahead of yourself there, Doc, but whatever. Tell me where you want to meet," he chuckled on the phone. "Coffee shop, restaurant, Walmart? How about the San Antonio Detention Center? I'll bet I could find a way to get you inside. You could call his Royal Highness from there."

"You come here."

"And where's that?"

Wilborn dropped to the ground. Even inside the pipe, the temperature was higher than in London. She pulled on her sweaty collar. Bloody heat, Christ.

"I asked you, where do you want to meet?"

Was she ready to give up her position? Would he arrive alone or with others to steal the money? There is only one way to get the vial. "Come to the pipe south of a golf course and a big shopping area."

"Is it beside a major highway?"

"Yes."

"That sounds like The Quarry Market. Is that where you are?"

"How the bloody hell am I supposed to know the name of it?" Wilborn asked.

"Okay. How far inside are you?"

"Deeper than before."

"More specific, please."

"I'll drop you a pin on the map." Wilborn pulled her sweaty shirt away from her skin again.

"I got something to do before finding you," the voice on the phone said.

"Come alone, or you get nothing." The line went dead before any reply.

Chapter 32

Deputy Jeffrey Keene called dispatch, "Keene here. I'm out for an hour."

"10-4. Everything okay?"

The Sherrif's department was tight. Everyone knew each other's family and, essentially, their personal problems.

Jeffrey tapped his steering wheel with his fingers before answering. His wedding ring clicked on the plastic. "Mmm. Personal. Meeting a Pastor."

The dispatcher didn't reply immediately. "About Rosemary?"

Never believing in coincidences, passing a church halted him from speaking. He often confided with his Pastor about her, and maybe he should go again. After clearing his throat, he answered, "I'll check back in when finished."

"10-4."

He glanced at the partly cloudy sky after making a right at the intersection and heading home. Random raindrops spattered the windshield as the car entered his neighborhood. There were no children outside. Just as well, she would stop on her porch, fall to her knees, sob, and beg and curse God at the same time, all because children were laughing and enjoying themselves. Rosemary had stopped his family from visiting since his brother had children. Three pregnancies; three miscarriages. They...Jeffrey had to do something before Rosemary became pregnant again.

He turned into the driveway, killed the engine, and stepped out. The handful of raindrops falling had ended. Weather-stressed trees dangled brown leaves, barely shading the yellowed front yard grass and dying flowers. The heat and lack of rain punished everything and everybody.

He twisted the doorknob and called out, "Rosemary? I came to check on you. Do you need anything?"

No one answered. The house felt like a furnace, with the fireplace ablaze and hot air spewing from the central air vents. The thermostat was set at ninety degrees. He flipped the heat to cool and lowered the temperature to seventy. The living room looked the same as when he left hours ago, with lights off, unfolded clothes spilling out of a tipped over laundry basket, a plate with a half-eaten piece of toast and dried scrambled eggs sitting on the coffee table, and a muted television in the corner illuminating the walls with a game show. He made his way into the kitchen, noticing the sink full of dirty breakfast pans and dishes and the hot oven with the door open and baking the room at 475 degrees. There was nothing inside, so he switched it off. He noticed her seven-day pill box on the counter next to the coffeemaker. He meticulously filled each day's slot with her correct meds, but she hadn't taken any.

"Rosemary? Where are you?"

He peered out the windows to the backyard. Her favorite chair stood empty. Inside, next to the backdoor, was her two-gallon plastic watering can. It was full. He entered the bedroom and paused. After unbuckling his service belt, he lowered it to the floor before treading to the bed. Rosemary lay on her side while facing away. Her wet hair dripped sweat down her neck from wearing her long-sleeved pajamas and cotton robe. Using both pillows, she stuffed one under her head and the other tucked close to her body. In a scattered pile were his papers from RAF Croughton Air Force Base in Northamptonshire.

"Hey, babe. Are you okay?"

She didn't move.

"Rosemary?"

He gently placed his hand on her shoulder. She didn't move. "Rosemary? Say something."

Her deep breath placated his fear.

She mumbled a sentence as if it were one word, "What do you want?"

"Is there anything I can do for you?"

Her only movement was a deep sigh. "I want to go back."

"Back where?"

"England. London. We were happy there. We had friends, I had a job, and we did our volunteer work. Here? I don't have friends. No job. No one wants me here."

He shook his head. "That's not true. But I meant like something to eat? Want some water? It's hot in the house, so I turned off the heater."

She swiftly pivoted and settled on the side of the bed. With her eyes wide open, she glared at him and shoved her finger into his shoulder. "You took all my stuff, my drugs. I like it hot, and I don't want any of your damn water!"

Jeffrey moved closer, leaned forward, and encircled his arms around the back of her neck. He touched his forehead to hers. "I'm sorry. I wish...wish for something, for you to be happy."

She buried her face in his chest and wrapped her arms around his waist. "I want children. I want them now." She let go and rubbed her watery eyes on his shirt. "I want them more than anything." She caught hold of his belt buckle and pulled the belt loose.

"Wait, Rosemary."

She unbuttoned his pants. "I want it now."

"Rosemary, no. I'm working."

She sniffed hard but never looked up as she grasped the zipper.

"No. Stop." He grabbed his pants so they wouldn't fall to the floor. "This is not how it's supposed to be."

She shoved her hands against his chest. "And how is it supposed to be?" She rolled back on her side, away from him. "Get out. Leave me alone." She flung her hand in the air. "I need a man who can give me children."

Jeffrey squeezed his lips tight, then zipped his pants up and buckled his belt. She lost the pregnancy, not him, but he couldn't say it. He never would. "You must snap out of this, Rosemary, and take the medicines your doctor prescribed. You can't be on street drugs and get pregnant. It would not be good for the baby."

She sat up again. "What baby? We don't have a baby." She scooped up most of the papers on the bed and stormed toward the living room. "Get away from me." She latched onto his service belt lying on the floor. "Go. Now. Leave me alone."

Jeffrey followed her. "Rosemary, I promise to do something. I'm working on a plan to help us with this problem."

She spun around while still holding the service belt. "Problem? So, I'm a problem to you?"

"No. That's not what I meant."

She pitched the belt and gun into the raging fireplace. When she threw the papers toward the fire, Jeffrey's ID badge from His Majesty's Prison Service burned. "How about this—you're the problem!"

Jeffrey dropped to his knees and leaned toward the fire. The scorching heat made it impossible to reach in and grab the belt. He quickly snatched the poker and when he slid it under the belt, water slammed down his back.

Rosemary held the watering can in her hand. When she pitched the empty can to her side, it banged several times on the wooden flooring. "You'd rather save your gun belt than me." She headed back into the bedroom and slammed the door behind her.

With his shirt sticking to his back, Jeffrey hooked the belt with the poker, carried it to the backyard, and laid it on the ground. With the leather smoldering, he touched the pistol, but it was too hot, no way to know if it was safe. After cooling, he extracted the magazine and the shell in the chamber. "I'm tired of messing with this damn doctor. I don't care what she wants to do to other people, but she damn well better fix Rosemary right now." Jeffrey changed into a plaid shirt and jeans, opened the gun safe, and removed his western gun belt and revolver. Climbing into his vehicle, he started the engine. "Hog-tie her, handcuff her, throw her in the trunk. I don't care. That damn doctor does what I want, or I'll kill her." He backed out of the driveway and gunned the engine.

Chapter 33

Roger opened the door on the second floor of an apartment building and stepped out. Behind him, Trixi stood at the threshold with one hand on the door and the other rubbing Roger's shoulder. He turned around and kissed her on the cheek.

He patted the gun stuck under his belt at the small of his back. "See ya later."

"Behind you in about two minutes. Have business at the bar."

Roger checked his front pockets. "Have to wait for Mr. Johnson to pay me."

"Come by. The next Lone Star is on me."

"You could make it a Shiner."

While slowly closing the door, she said, "Don't push your luck, cowboy."

The lock snapped shut. Roger shuffled down the stairs, past the swimming pool where a dozen people lay in the sun, drank beer, swam, or all the above. When he reached his pickup, he found Cassie, wearing boots, jeans, a western shirt, and a ball cap with a heart logo, leaning against the driver's door with her ankle crossed over.

"You want to explain to me what you are doing upstairs with that woman?" She uncrossed her ankles and stood. "Or you going to make something up really quick?"

Roger held his hands out. "No. Nothing like that. She bought me breakfast, and I needed to talk to her about...some stuff."

Cassie approached him. "Stuff? Like what kinda stuff?" She threw a punch into his chest. "Tell me. Tell me what's so damn important."

"Nothing about you."

"Oh, so now you know what's important in my life. You some kinda guru? Know all? See all?"

She threw another punch toward his stomach, but he blocked it. She swung again, and he spun her around and bear-hugged her.

"Ease it down a notch, would you?"

She jammed the heel of her boot into his foot.

"Damn it." He pushed her forward. "What's wrong with you?"

"What's wrong? You're an idiot. Are you going to lie to me or tell me straight up you fucked her? Did you do it on the bed, or the couch, or the floor? Maybe you did her on the kitchen table. Maybe all those places."

"Oh Jesus, Cassie, you're the sick one. I would never do that."

"Oh, right, because you plan to be with me. Only me?"

"Because she's my sister."

Cassie's jaw dropped. She stepped back and blinked several times. "What in the hell?"

"We've been close our entire lives, but she sort of left for a couple of years, and I moved close to her while she was...busy. When we moved here, she started working at the bar, and I at the Johnson Ranch."

"So, you're not..."

"No! God. She's my sister, and I'm not a pervert."

❧

Trixi parked in the employee section of The Broken Saddle Horn Bar and entered through the side door, lugging a paper sack with handles. She made sure a small blue packet sat under bundles of cash before knocking twice and pushing the door open with the back of her hand. A blob the size of Jabba The Hut sprawled behind an old desk with scattered papers as he puffed on a long, thick cigar. Behind him were his cigar humidor, cigar cutter, lighter, and two canisters of lighter fluid.

With no facial expression, he said, "Trix, come in. Do you have something for me?"

She placed the sack directly on the desktop. "Here. Like I said I would, fifty thousand, and now we're partners in this bar." She laid a piece of paper facing him with Secured Loan written on top. "Sign here, Buster Benson, and the money is yours. Don't forget. The bar is collateral, and if you don't pay the loan back with interest in thirty days, this place is mine." It was a bluff. She knew she couldn't own anything.

He took a deep draw from the cigar and blew the smoke high in the air before resting it on the ashtray. He glanced inside to see stacks of hundred dollar bills, then grasped the sack handles and placed it on the floor to his side. "In fact, there's no need to worry about anything." He slid open the top drawer, removed a pistol, and pointed it at her. "Not much reason for you to get paid back at all."

"You planning on shooting me...here in the bar? The cops would shut this place down."

"I would say you were trying to rob me, and to protect myself, I had to shoot."

"Hmm." She pushed the fob button inside her pocket, and blue smoke rose from the sack. Buster did what she expected, frantically dropping the gun and reaching for the money. That was when she unraveled a garrote from her wrist, stepped around the desk, swept the weapon to the floor, and wrapped the wire around his neck. He was too fat to get out of the chair. While she leaned back, he reached for her with his little T-Rex arms wavering in the air—until he stopped moving. She seized the sack and placed the secured loan paper inside, then opened the bottom drawer where he kept his untraceable money and dropped all the bundles of hundred dollar bills in the sack. "Nice of you to give me a legitimate accelerant, Buster."

She grabbed a facial tissue from a box, and picked up one lighter fluid canister, squeezed a few drops on Buster's collar, before laying the canister on its side, where fluid leaked onto the papers. She moved the cigar from the ashtray and dropped it on the scattered papers. "The poor soul." She pushed Buster's head down toward the desk as far as it could. "He fell asleep and burned the place down." With a pencil, she stuck it inside the barrel and moved the gun back into the drawer. "Now, I have to find another job." She opened the door and looked back over her shoulder to make sure the desk had ignited.

Chapter 34

Jeffrey didn't drive where Marla said to go. He pondered the odd tendency of criminals to gravitate back toward what they perceive as comfort, even if it means sinking into a hole deep enough to be buried and forgotten. The rain increased as he veered off Highway 281 onto the frontage road. Ahead to his right stood the Alamo Quarry Market, a designer's dream. Once an abandoned, dilapidated brick building with tall smokestacks blackened from decades of carbon-filled smoke, it transformed into a decorative, brightly lit mall bustling with customers buying goods from around the world.

Rain continued spattering the windshield while he gazed out at the heavy clouds. Before reaching the parking lot, he switched to a side street leading away from the market. The two-lane road narrowed across a small limestone bridge. Despite the Texas drought, thousands of colorful silky flower puffs interweaved among acres of flat ground comprising clumping grasses, wildrye, and buffalograss—and a large diameter stormwater outfall in the center. Last month, he read a police report of twenty-plus homeless people hiding in this pipe. Instead of making arrests, the SAPD ensured that the individuals in need were fed, clothed, and accepted into shelters around town.

A mile away, the Olmos Dam stood nineteen-hundred feet long and sixty feet tall. The government had constructed it in the 1920s to hold back billions of gallons of water after a disastrous flood killed over two hundred people and devastated downtown San Antonio. In 1998, eleven inches of rain pulverized the city in one day, and the dam saved downtown.

Jeffrey veered across the open field where a brown pickup truck sat alone. *She must have stolen another vehicle, but I got you.* He instinctively grasped his microphone. "Keene here." *Wait. What am I going to say? Can't reveal the location, dispatch would send help.*

The dispatcher replied, "Go ahead."

"I'm checking back in."

"All okay with you? Saw the Pastor?"

He had forgotten he used the excuse to see someone at a church. "Right, and...um...near the airport."

"Why there?"

Jeffrey rubbed his hand over his face. Damn, shouldn't have called in. Now what? "I see a vehicle on the side of the road. Going to check it out."

"Plate number?"

Crap! "Um, no plates. They're gone, missing."

"I'll send backup. Give me your location."

"No. Don't need help. I got this. It looks like an abandoned vehicle sitting for quite a while."

"Be careful. A thunderstorm is brewing in the southeast section of the county and moving north."

"10-4." Jeffrey dropped the mic onto the console. "Now what?"

He smiled when his phone rang and the name on the screen was Marla. "Hello?"

"I've been thinking about where Wilborn could be. You might be right about her heading back to the area south of the airport."

That made Jeffrey's decision easy. It would be best if he and Marla found Wilborn together, just the three of them, to work out what everyone wants. And if things don't go right...then ...people get hurt. "Are you familiar with the stormwater outfall south of The Alamo Quarry Market?"

"A grassy area just off a two-lane road?"

"Yes, and I believe I found the doctor, and you need to hurry, so we can arrest her and make her help Rosemary."

"That's pretty damn good luck finding someone when everyone else in town is looking, too. You need to be careful because, don't forget, she has a gun."

"I'll be okay with you as backup."

"I'm thinking about Rosemary, and you don't need to do anything stupid. Wilborn's desperate."

"She's a scrawny piece of shit, and I can handle myself." He knew what she would say if he went alone. "In fact, forget it. Stay away. I've got this. And she will do what I tell her to do."

Marla remembered Rivera's call about Jeffrey being stationed in England. "Tell me. Have you met her before?"

"I...I...a figure of speech. Come meet me. Just you and me on this. Okay?"

Jeffrey ended the call and exited his vehicle before palming the truck's hood, which was still warm. He left his emergency lights flashing—a habit, good or bad, but trained to leave on. Every time an incident happened in town, there were several emergency vehicles, all with their lights running like it was Christmas. He reached back inside the SUV to turn them off, then stopped. Leaving them on, local police backup may show, and he didn't want that, but turning them off and Marla may not come to the right spot. He adjusted his western style gun belt and then pointed the flashlight straight into the abyss.

"I'll check the area out before she gets here. Why in the hell would the city insert lights along the sides? Do the homeless illegally sleeping in here need a night light? Whatever. It's good for me, so I don't care." He turned off his flashlight. The dry pipe, covered in colorful graffiti, shot straight and long toward The Quarry Market. "This could be a quick find."

After trekking for a while, Jeffrey came to a T junction breaking off to the right. He checked his phone for the stormwater map, but there was no reception. He waved it head high in the air, but still no bars, no glory. "Damn. Now what? Which way?" A stream of water trickled through the center line of the pipe, picking up pieces of paper floating like boats without rudders. "But this doctor is an odd character. Would she go right or straight?" With not a single sound coming from either direction, Jeffrey trudged straight ahead.

◆

Marla returned from Jake Johnson's place to her barn when her phone rang again. She dismounted Daisy and answered, "Hello?"

"Rivera here. What's your plan with the deputy?"

"I just got off the phone with him just a little while ago, and we're supposed to meet at the stormwater outlet south of The Alamo Market."

"Do you think this is a setup?"

"Not sure."

"I'm on my computer at the office right now and see the spot on the city map." Rivera logged off. "Meet me there."

Marla unsaddled the horse. "I can be there in fifteen."

With his phone pressed against his ear, he rushed downstairs. "Me too."

Rivera slowed his Tahoe and parked behind a sheriff's department SUV with the emergency lights still flashing. He unwrapped two pieces of gum and shoved them in his mouth while sticking the wrappers under the left windshield wiper blade. Why would the deputy leave the lights flashing on his vehicle? It's like a large Vegas neon arrow saying, Enter here. The odds were even that bad shit would happen.

Several feet in front of the SUV sat a brown pickup truck. He exited his vehicle and pulled on the pickup's door handle, but found it locked. He cupped his hands and looked inside through the driver's window, seeing nothing significant.

Moments later, Marla parked beside Rivera's truck. As she climbed out, a light rain dampened the brim of her DEA cap. A multitude of native grasses, mid-calf in length, wafted in the breeze. Dead trees stood naked with broken branches nearby. "What's with the jeans inside your boots?"

Rivera patted the side of one boot. "Old work boots, ugly but waterproof. I've marched through ankle-high water with nothing seeping through this leather."

Marla's phone chimed. It's Jeffrey texting me. I'm in deep and wanted to make sure I can still message you. Let me know when you arrive and I'll return. She replied with a single word, Okay.

Marla opened the weather app on her phone. "Damn."

Rivera asked, "More from the deputy?"

"No." She pointed her phone screen toward him. "This shows heavy clouds filling the radar. To the east, the remnants of a category two or three hurricane are approaching us. The app says fifteen to twenty inches of rain today and tomorrow." She studied the sky; lead-colored clouds hovered above them.

"Have we ever had that much?"

Marla shook her head. "I'm not sure."

"Well, one thing is for damn sure." Rivera knuckled the logo on the sheriff's department vehicle door. "That deputy friend of yours is inside, waiting for you."

"Take it easy on him. All you have is conjecture."

"All I have is fact! He's working with Wilborn and drawing you in for the kill." Rivera motioned toward the pickup truck in front of the deputy's vehicle. "Do you know who that belongs to?"

Marla saw where the missing license plate should be. "Not sure. With the missing plates, it may be Wilborn. Ready?"

"Are you sure you want to go in? I mean, this crazed doctor wants you dead."

"What?" She adjusted the cap on her head. "This won't be the first...or the last person who wants me dead. Dr. Hugo Wilborn has a bag of fentanyl, and we need to get it."

Rivera continued chewing his gum. "And what about the, you know, the stem cell stuff? Is that why Keene is in there?"

"I want the fentanyl and Wilborn in jail, and we'll arrest Keene if he's involved. Come on, let's go."

Rivera sized up the darkening sky. "You're right. A Big Ass rain's coming."

A wind gust lifted her hair off her collar. "Yep." She drew her pistol. We need to hurry."

They entered and turned on their flashlights.

A chill weeviled across Marla's neck. Along the side of the concrete pipe was a spray-painted quote in multiple colors, "Abandon all hope, ye who enter here." Marla hoped it was a college English major showing off rather than being truthful. "These lights on the sides of the pipe seem dimmer."

"Definitely brighter where we found the kid with the mushrooms, but that was closer to the airport. It could be a different power substation. Hell, I don't know, maybe The Quarry Market is sucking power away from these lights."

Minutes later, they came to the same T junction Keene had encountered. "Which way?" Marla asked.

"I read somewhere," Rivera aimed his light to the right. "people turn at a crossroads when lost. Lefties turn left, and right-handers turn right."

"Really? Never heard that. Do you think Wilborn ever heard that?"

Rivera shrugged. "Let's find out." He veered right. "This way."

Marla followed as water trickled down the sides of the tunnel from the inlets ten feet above. A thin stream of liquid lifted dry dirt and crushed leaves around the soles of their feet, then almost imperceptibly flowed the opposite way they were going.

❖

Jeffrey had ventured only once through this drainage system and didn't like it. Deep underground, no immediate escape, the quiet, the cold. He shook it off and stormed ahead, hoping to hear the doctor's voice soon. His enthusiasm waned. The rain poured a little heavier through the inlets, and the flickering lights on the sides began to irritate him. Why the hell have water alarm wires with no place to hide if it goes off?

Extending his feet apart to keep water from sloshing over his boots and the bottoms of his pant legs, he wheeled around to scout the area. I should have gone right.

He paused at another T junction in the tunnel. "This could transform into a maze pretty damn fast, never finding my way back." Thunder rumbled above his head, and the lights dimmed. He turned on his flashlight and gazed down the long, straight pipe, while slowly advancing. He mumbled to himself, "Nothing. Absolutely nothing but emptiness. I should have waited for Marla." He turned around and ran back to his SUV to find another SUV with government plates and Marla's Dodge dually pickup truck parked behind him. He texted her again, "Where R U?"

They stopped at another T junction. Marla glanced at her phone before showing Rivera. "Should I tell him?"

Rivera shook his head. "No. He's inside somewhere. If you say yes, then he may run back to the trucks. We need to catch him off guard, not announce our position."

Marla typed a reply, "Almost." She expected a quick response but he didn't reply.

"Let's go right," Rivera said.

"Bullshit." Jeffrey ran straight into the pipe again and turned at the T junction. He paused when he arrived and the second T, then charged straight ahead. A minute later, a Y appeared, with the pipes decreasing to six feet in diameter, and the row of lights ending.

The tunnel went pitch black when Jeffrey shut off his flashlight. He switched it on again. "Damn, which way? He glanced over his shoulder. "Which way back?" As the walls closed in and the temperature dropped, his chest tightened. "Soldiers pray in a foxhole, and I should too, inside a place deep enough to bury me."

Fifty feet later, the tunnel Y'd again, with a dim light and distant voices on the left side. He whispered, "Found you, you asshole." Was she injecting someone with the stem cells? He had to stop the doctor before using all of it. Rosemary needed her share.

Jeffrey aimed the light ahead and called out, "Wilborn?" When he entered the left side, it wasn't the doctor, but two women in their twenties sat with legs crossed, face-to-face, with a butane camping lantern lit beside them. A female, blonde-haired, with random streaks of turquoise, ignored him while injecting something from a syringe into the brunette's arm.

"Hey." Jeffrey shined his light on the two. "What are you doing?"

The brunette shut her eyes, and the blonde concentrated on what she was doing. The brunette tilted her head back and moaned. The turquoise-haired female dropped the syringe beside her, opened a takeout box, and bit into a hamburger.

With a mouthful, she asked, "What the hell do you want? Go away."

The brunette eased onto her back.

"I'm a sheriff's deputy, and you need to evacuate from here," Jeffrey said. "It's going to rain today, and water will be in these pipes."

"No way you're a cop, not in those clothes."

He forgot he changed out of his uniform.

The blonde took another bite, then held the burger away from him. "This is our place, so tell that freak to stay away."

"Who?"

"Some bitch gave us a hit, so now she has this fantasy she owns us. She grabbed my tits and squeezed hard. Tried to tear off our clothes. She slapped me, so I kicked her right between the legs, and we ran." The blonde aimed the half-eaten burger at Jeffrey. "You get the hell out of here."

He stretched his hand toward her. "Let me help you out. There may be trouble soon."

"Get away from us, or I swear, I'll kick you in the balls."

"Do you know how to find your way out of here?"

"Yeah, yeah. Don't worry about us."

Jeffrey directed his light at the blonde. "Which way?"

Her smile displayed black, broken teeth and a shiner under her left eye. "You're lost, aren't you? Go back the way you came, or...better yet, go past us and turn left, then left again, then right. It takes you to the market. That's probably the best way for you." She pointed down the tunnel.

"Don't go back that way, go this way, and if you see a shithead with her cunt hurting, tell her I said, 'Fuck off.'"

"The woman you saw, did she have a black trunk, an accent, perhaps from England?"

"Who knows?"

"Does the tunnel get smaller?"

She smiled again. "No, man. We got here fine. You wanna get out?" She pointed down the tunnel. "Go that way. Left, left, right."

Jeffrey moved past them. Left, left, right. He paused when he heard her whisper, "Asshole."

As Jeffrey headed down the tunnel, things shifted, graffiti faded away, and the diameter decreased to four feet. He dropped to his hands and knees, condensation dripped from above his head, and black mold crept up the walls. The water flow increased, rolling over his hands and wrists. His revolver slid out of the holster and clattered on the concrete. He stuck it back inside. "She lied, and I'm screwed." He looked behind him and knew he was lost.

"The only thing to do is go back." He twisted around and headed back toward the women. Without saying a thing, he passed by them.

The two women cackled. "Oh, sorry. Did I send you the wrong way?" They both laughed. "This time, I promise, go right." They laughed again.

"Bullshit." Jeffrey turned left and entered an eight-foot tunnel. His flashlight shined on something unexpected—a three-step concrete stair with a metal railing and the pipe rising higher. Adjacent to the stairs was a metal ladder rising to a manhole cover above him. Disposable syringes lay near his feet. Are these from Dr. Wilborn or the two drug addicts?

✦

The temperature cooled inside as Marla and Rivera cautiously trekked onward. Thunder echoed through the inlets above their heads. A steady stream of water handcuffed around their ankles while graffiti morphed from calligraphic gangland writing to artistic flowers and quasi-landscapes.

Above them, an explosive crash with a bright blast lit up the inlet grates. A thunderous roar shook the tunnel as the lights along the side flickered.

Marla ducked. "What the hell?"

When the lights stabilized, the inlet nearest them continued streaming water into the pipe. "Lightning must have struck close to us." Rivera glanced at his father's watch. "We've been down here too long."

Marla tapped the weather app on her phone again. "We're too deep underground for a connection."

Rivera tried to ignore that thought. "Heavier rain is coming. We should leave."

Marla rubbed her forehead. Taking a quick look in both directions, she realized they were too far underground for calls. As water streamed between her legs, she said, "We should go a little further; shouldn't be too much more."

"Which one are you talking about?"

"Wilborn." Marla stumbled with the answer. "I don't know."

"Damn right you don't," Rivera said, "and we better be ready for Wilborn and Keene together."

"Okay, got it." Marla stuffed her phone into her back pocket. "I understand and confirm. We watch for both and keep moving."

Within a hundred yards, the pipe branched into two-eight-foot diameter tunnels, with no inlet grates above their heads. They turned their flashlights back on.

"Now what?" Rivera asked.

"I say we continue," Marla said.

"Then we keep going right, so we don't get lost."

"Look," Marla said, "there's more graffiti painted on the left, meaning more activity, more people, and maybe a better chance of finding the doctor."

Rivera shined the flashlight on his watch again. It's been twenty-four minutes inside. We could be in a boatload of trouble. He aimed the light down the empty tunnel. "All right, left it is."

Less than a minute later, they reached another Y; this time, the tunnels decreased to six feet in diameter, almost head high.

"Do you know where the hell we are?" Rivera asked.

Marla briskly rubbed her nose. "We'll figure it out."

Distant voices came from the left tunnel. When Rivera turned off his flashlight and Marla pointed hers toward her feet, they saw the light motioning further down the tunnel.

Marla turned her light off and whispered, "We may have found Wilborn." Voices carried through the murk, but they were unclear. "We're too far away to make out what they're saying, but you may have been right all along. It must be Wilborn and Jeffrey." Marla said. The lights along the tunnel walls were gone, plunging them into darkness. "Let's ease up closer."

As they crept toward the voices, the words became clearer. Twenty yards later, the tunnel bent forty-five degrees. They both peeked around the corner to witness two people facing each other, arguing, while flashlight beams shined across the sides of the tunnel.

Rivera took out his cell phone and pressed the record button.

Concealed in the dark, Marla knelt on one knee and watched the two. When the light brushed across the woman's face, she recognized Wilborn from the prison photo—short but not scrawny. She was muscular. Did Jeffrey know the doctor at the beginning of her incarceration before she bulked up? It didn't matter if he knew her or not. What did was that Wilborn had a bag of fentanyl somewhere, and more immediately, she held a gun in her hand.

Wilborn's flashlight silhouetted the man. But what drew Marla's eye was the old-fashioned holster hanging low on his hip with a revolver inside.

Deep underground, the humidity in the tunnel thickened with the smell of stale air, sweat, and garbage. The hair on the back of her neck stuck to her skin as a single drop of perspiration trickled from her armpit down her side. Something's not right. She whispered to Rivera, "Both are armed, and they seem to be arguing. They're on edge about something."

"We need to take them." Rivera's brow furrowed as he hissed back, "Surprise is our only advantage."

Marla's phone vibrated from a text. She aimed her screen toward Rivera and whispered, "Calls aren't going through, but texts are."

It was from Jake Johnson. I was cleaning the area where the hay storage unit burned when I found this mixed in the ashes. It was a photo of a burned leather holster, with barely legible letters on the side, RH.

✦

Jeffrey stepped to the top stair and pointed his flashlight down the middle of the tunnel. Something moved. A dark wave came toward him, inches high and a hundred yards away. High-pitched sounds bellowed out from the concrete pipe. A stampede of tiny red eyes reflected against the light; dozens more moved up and down. He couldn't focus on the mass. It was coming too fast. When ten yards away, he saw it. "Oh, holy mother."

He grasped the metal railing and flung himself over it as a flood of rats raced down the stairs, swerved right, and disappeared down the tunnel.

Seconds later, a rumble grew from where the rats came. With one hand gripping the metal handrail and the other clutching the flashlight, Jeffrey illuminated the dark, vacant pipe. Flashes of white grew closer. He recognized it. A horn blared—the water alarm. "Oh, motherfu...." A deafening explosion rocked the room as water burst out from the pipe with the force of a raging river, slamming against the walls and creating swirling rapids that threatened to engulf everything in its path. The powerful current tore at Jeffrey, instantly drenching his body and causing him to slip his grip on the handrail. His heart raced as he struggled, his fingers desperately clung to the rail. With every passing second it became harder to hold on while struggling to keep his head above water. Mustering all his strength, he propelled himself towards the metal ladder, but another sudden surge slammed against him. He hooked one foot under a rung and pulled himself closer, numb and aching fingers grasping onto the rail for dear life. Each rung felt like an eternity as he climbed closer to safety. Finally, with a last surge of adrenaline, he reached the top.

Three hundred yards from where he originally entered stood a square concrete catch basin with a round manhole cover on top. The heavy metal cover lifted a few inches and scraped the concrete as it slid to the side. Jeffrey stuck his head out into a heavy rainstorm as cold water soaked his body. The ground reverberated under his feet as he looked down the manhole to the turbulent, rising water. After climbing out, his boot sunk inches into the soaked ground. He reached for his revolver, but was missing. It had fallen out of the holster. Seconds later, water belched out of the manhole.

He rushed back through the grass and mud toward a ten-foot outlet where thousands of gallons of water gushed out. He shook his head, expecting the doctor and the miracle cure for Rosemary to have drowned by now.

The rains pounded, and the wind swept against Jeffrey in every direction while slogging through the muck toward a different outfall where he had parked. Rising water flowed into the grille and over the hood of the brown pickup. But thirty feet back and on higher ground was his SUV and behind him were two other vehicles, Marla's Dodge Ram Dually truck and an SUV with government license plates, all with the water level halfway up the wheels. He ran toward the outfall, with the stormwater gushing. "She can't be dead." His heart pounded faster. "I have to help her."

Chapter 35

The man in front of Wilborn shifted and Marla immediately tensed when the flashlight illuminated the man's face and western gun belt with a silver medallion gleaming on the side of the holster. A silent prayer burst in her head, Oh, Holy Mother of God....

Rivera glimpsed Marla and then back at the perps. In a strained whisper, he asked, "What?"

She briefly looked at the two again. Her boot skittered across gravel as she latched onto Rivera's sleeve and hauled him backward.

Wilborn ceased talking as both pointed their flashlights to the ground.

"Did you hear that?" Wilborn asked.

Roger turned his head toward the noise. "Yeah...something. Probably an animal scrounging around."

"No. Go check it out," Wilborn said.

Marla recognized the man. Damn, Cassie. What in the hell are you going to do? It was Roger Hagen, and the silver medallion on his holster meant he didn't leave for rodeo riding, he left for fast draw competitions, and men are faster than women.

Then it hit her. Jeffrey and his race car buddy knew how to hot-wire a car and a tractor, but he didn't kill her cattle. He didn't lie. He was busy delivering county summonses. She remembered Jake Johnson telling her he left town because his daughter-in-law sent a text. She denied sending it, and Jake thought she deleted it. That didn't happen. Someone sent a fake text to make Jake leave town, steal his tractor, and dump the ash on Marla's land. Jake said it and it went over Marla's head. He said anyone on a farm or ranch. Roger Hagen worked for Jake, and he had to have known how to hot-wire the old tractor.

"The son of a bitch killed my cattle." The sole of her shoe scratched the dirt.

Roger aimed his flashlight down the tunnel and drew his revolver faster than most people in the world. Marla and Rivera ducked back behind the forty-five-degree angle of the tunnel. Both gripped their guns, prepared to shoot. A small animal crossed from one side of the pipe to the other, froze in place, then scurried down the pipe. Roger holstered his revolver. "It's nothing."

"You didn't go very far," Wilborn waved her hand, perturbed. "Keep going."

Roger blocked Wilborn's view. "We're already too far in the system. And what if it rains more?" He waved his light beam across the wet tunnel walls. "It could flood. We should get out of here."

"Don't worry about me." Wilborn held the flashlight in one hand and a pistol in the other, still aiming it toward the ground.

Roger extended his hand. "Give me the money."

"Shut up!" Wilborn yelled. "Everything's gone rotten. I've changed my mind. Give me the vial, and I'm done with this cockup."

Roger directed his flashlight towards Wilborn's chest. "You're out?" He arched an eyebrow in disbelief. "That's pretty chickenshit of you."

Wilborn's fingers clenched the gun grip. If Bambi were alive, could she out draw this buffoon? Could I surprise Roger? A quick bend of my elbow and fire before Roger pulls the revolver out of the holster. "And what about you? When I arrived in this God-forsaken city, your sister told me you couldn't kill anyone, so you left town."

"Not totally true. I had something to do, but I came back."

"For me? For the money? Or for that tart you're shagging?"

"I left for two days to enter a competition." He patted the silver medallion. "Almost won the whole thing. And as far as who I came back for, you can be damn sure it wasn't for you."

The water flowed heavier from an inlet grate forty feet away. The doctor shook her head and spoke a little louder. "The experiments are what's important to me. That Adams woman will kill me if she sees me."

"Hmm," Roger said. "The tables have turned. You're scared of her."

"Shut your arsehole."

Marla and Rivera inched toward Wilborn and Roger. Rivera's phone kept recording the conversation as the rising water level rapidly reached over the toe box of his boots.

"You've got nothing to worry about," Roger said. "I have her little ranch girl wrapped around my finger. Listen, I can keep Adams under control. I've learned a lot about her since coming into town, and she's nothing but hot air."

"You bloody idiot. She's not after you. She doesn't even know your sister was my cellmate for a year."

"How do you know?"

"Because you're not in jail or dead."

Roger tilted his head. "Yeah, probably right. But..." He patted his holster again. "If it comes down to it, I can take care of myself. All I have to do is wait for the right opportunity to take her out, but like I said, before I do anything, you gotta fix Cassie's face. She's blind and deaf on one side. Damn good in bed, but she looks weird. Grow her a new eye and an ear, and I'll give you the vial and your revenge."

"You're like a turd floating in a hot tub. I can't flip a handkerchief in the air and magically conjure up random body parts." She cupped her hand. "I want the protein extract now." Wilborn caught Roger glancing at her pistol.

The thought of the blade in her back pocket crossed Wilborn's mind—pitch the gun to the side, make Roger shift his attention away from her, then grab the knife and slice his throat—but what if Roger didn't look away? It would be suicide.

"Where's your stash of mad scientist stuff?"

"You're starting to grate on my nerves."

"Yeah? Okay, I'll amend it to, 'Where's that science kit of yours like the high school kids play with? Better? You need to tell me so we can get going on Cassie. Is it down here?"

"No. I have it hidden."

"Buried treasure? Now you're a pirate?"

"Opposite. It's hidden way above ground."

Roger smiled. "The Olmos Dam?"

"How the bloody hell do you know anything about the dam?"

"It's a mile from here, right? How'd you get there?"

"Less than a mile." She pointed in the direction of The Quarry Market. "Idiot blokes waddling to their vehicles in a large carpark, glowing like they have sunshine coming out their arses...and yet there I was, waiting for them."

Roger kept his right hand on top of his holstered revolver while keeping Wilborn's gun in his peripheral vision. "How'd you manage to break into the dam's station house?"

"I was in prison for two years and learned to pick a lock, just like your sister did."

Roger snickered. "Yeah...Trix told me about that girl. She'll be there teaching others for the next decade. Hey, there was no car where I entered. Where did you hide it?"

"Not too far away. You didn't park next to the outfall, did you? Someone could spot it and call the police."

Roger cocked his head and narrowed his eyes. "Don't worry about my truck. You have the million dollars here with you, right?" He held his hand out. "The deal you made with Trix in prison was I kill Adams, and you give me money, but since you came to Texas, you've been a bigger jackass than even what she told me, so that's gonna cost ya."

"You can't have more. I need the rest of the cash to leave this shithole and vanish."

"Not going back to London?"

"Bloody not. They'd arrest me in the airport."

"What the hell are you talking about? All along, you were going to be the greatest doctor of all, and London would throw a celebration in your honor. Look that up. It's called Delusions of Grandeur. As a doctor, even a nutso like you should know that."

"I'm not bloody nuts, you wanker."

When Wilborn raised her right hand, Roger drew his revolver in less than a second and pointed it at the doctor's chest before she had a chance to blink.

"Better drop that to your side there, doc. If you're dead, you won't be able to snatch your Nobel in Medicine."

"Blimey. This is rubbish." Wilborn lowered the weapon. "Who is nutso now?"

Roger eased his revolver back into his holster. "Do us both a favor and stick that thing in your pocket. You ever try that again, and I'll pull the trigger."

Wilborn stood rigid and mulled over how to kill Roger without making a sound. In the end, she pocketed the gun to calm Roger's concern and held the bag of money in front of him. Once he reached for it, she would grab the knife from her back pocket and slit Roger's throat. "Very well. You take the amount we agreed on and give me the vial."

"And Adams?"

"Forget her. Give me the vial."

Roger lifted his hand off the revolver, stuck the flashlight under his right armpit, and dug into his pocket. "All right. I'm a man of my word, a million it is." He held the vial out between his fingers, then pulled his hand back from her. "I want a handful of those fentanyl tabs, along with my money."

Wilborn sidestepped and removed a bulging sack from behind an iron ladder that extended upward to a manhole cover. "One million, all here. The fentanyl is at the dam."

Murder for hire was enough for Rivera and Marla. He shut off the recorder and stuck his chewed gum onto the concrete wall. "Ready?" They stepped out from the dark corner, leveling their flashlights and service weapons at the two perps.

"DEA," Marla called out. "Hands up. You're under arrest."

Wilborn targeted her flashlight toward the voices.

It stunned Marla how fast Roger drew his revolver. "My, my." He flashed an iridescent smile as charming as any blockbuster actor would on screen. "What a pleasure to see you, Mrs. Adams."

Marla aimed her pistol toward Roger. For the first time, he didn't seem like a bumbling cowboy. He looked dangerous. When she gripped the handle firmly, pain shot through the nub of her fifth finger, and she wished it back. Frustration and self-loathing boiled within her, unable to forgive herself for being caught off guard and shot by an unknown assailant. "Both of you, drop your weapons and raise your hands."

Roger slipped the vial back into his left pocket.

"Well fuck my chi," Wilborn said. "Marla Adams came to me? You murdered Dr. McCollum, and you think you are going to get away with it?" The sounds of the planes grew louder.

"I did no such thing. Your partner was a cocaine addict and in over his head with a Mexican Cartel boss. Everyone knows what happens when you do something stupid like that."

"You kidnapped Dr. McCollum, my partner...my lover, to save your dying, rotter husband." Wilborn's face reddened, nostrils flared. "But you let him die...you let both of them die."

Marla took a step, ready to beat Wilborn senseless, but kept her cool while keeping her aim on Roger. "Drop your weapons."

"How about I drop this?" He released the flashlight from under his arm, and it clattered to the ground.

"Like you dropped your holster in Jake's fire? He found it."

"So what? A little fire didn't hurt no one."

"And my cattle? You poisoned all of them."

"Just cattle. I'm sure insurance paid you quite well for them."

The rumbling above their heads reminded them of the international airport just miles away.

While still holding the gun, Wilborn laid the sack of money on the ground with water swirling around the bottom, then took one step toward the ladder up to the manhole cover. "Let's ponder this a minute."

Roger took two steps back from Wilborn as water sloshed over his cowboy boots.

Marla bit the inside of her cheek as she kept her aim on Roger. "Now is not the time to try something stupid." She waved the barrel toward Dr. Wilborn. "Back over to your buddy, or I shoot. Won't bother me to put a bullet in your leg or chest."

Rivera pulled out his handcuffs while continuing to aim at Wilborn. "Throw your weapons on the ground, hands behind your head."

Roger raised his left hand slightly but continued to point his revolver at Marla. "Okay." He said, stepping back toward Wilborn. "Not sure how you think all this is going down." Roger scoffed at the situation. "No need for gunfire, okay? Watch me. I'm placing my gun back in the holster."

"No! On the ground!" Marla snapped at him.

Roger ignored the command and slid his revolver back into the holster. "Mrs. Adams, it seems you need a new herd of cattle. How about we say you happen to find a little cash down here...and nothing else?" With his palm resting on the gun grip, Roger focused on Rivera. "And what about you, Mr. DEA agent? Since you are a government employee, your salary is a bit on the low side, right? A vacation, all expenses paid would be nice. No one would find out."

Roger kicked the sack, and it rolled on its side, with cash falling out. He latched onto a bundle of one-hundred-dollar bills. "All cash. All yours. Spend it as you wish." He pitched it toward Rivera, who kept his aim on Wilborn as the money splashed into the rising water. Roger kicked the bag again to grab another bundle, but noticed folded newspaper had fallen out. "What the hell is this?"

"Don't get so petty bourgeois," Wilborn said. "Concentrate on what's important, the two DEA agents in front of you."

"What's important is you were planning on screwing me over." Roger drew his revolver and aimed toward Wilborn. "How about I turn you over to the Feds right now?"

An icy gust of air rushed past Marla, pushing her hair away from her neck like a chilled kiss. The surrounding pressure suddenly rose so fast it bear hugged her chest. Panic bubbled up within her as she realized where the wind was coming from—the tunnel.

"Where the hell is the fentanyl?" Marla shouted over the roar that grew louder until it sounded like a thundering diesel locomotive barreling toward them. The ground shook, and another explosive gust of stale air from the tunnel pushed all four off balance. A horn screamed around them.

Rivera shifted his sight toward the empty pipe. "Marla? Holster your weapon, now!" He instinctively reached for her arm when a wall of water exploded out, battering their bodies against the concrete wall, and thrusting them into a raging torrent that swallowed them whole.

Chapter 36

Marla slammed against the hard concrete, scraping her body across the unforgiving surface, twisting and turning uncontrollably as the water pulled her helplessly under. She reached out for anything to keep her afloat, but all she felt were her arms swirling through the tumultuous water. A glimmer of light struck her face as her head pierced above the churning waves, and she gasped for air. Around her, the storm's angry torrent burst from huge pipes, filling a once dry creek bed.

"Rivera!" Marla cried out as the nascent river sucked her under again. The icy water stung Marla's skin, and the force of the current slammed her back against a submerged tree trunk. She could feel the bark, rough and splintered, digging into her, scraping against her body, and the pressure of the branch pulling against her belt as the taste of metallic mud and algae filled her mouth. The branch twisted her further underwater. Her hands slapped at the water, her throat tightened, and with the last of her breath escaping, her lungs burned for air. Her vision blurred from the murky water as an image of Crosby's outstretched hand in her mind tempted her to give up and be with him.

With a sudden tug, a hand grabbed her collar and pulled her up from the water. She gasped for breath and saw Rivera leaning over the branch, holding onto her shirt, and snapping the wood free from her belt.

Together, they fought through the downpour until they reached higher ground. Completely drained and unable to speak, they collapsed onto their backs, inches from the rushing water and relentless rain beating down on them.

Rivera raised his arm and rubbed the watch on his wrist.

Marla chuckled. "Still working?"

"Hell yeah. Keeps on ticking."

"How about with a hurricane dropping a foot of water on us?"

"No prob."

Marla forced herself to sit and appraise the area while the blackening clouds rolled overhead and thunder pounded the sky. "We came out of a different way."

Still on his back, Rivera raised his legs and let the water flow out of his boots, over his already soaked pants, and onto the wet ground. "Damn good thing we did. We would have surely drowned going that way."

"Not sure where our vehicles are. Probably underwater by now."

Rivera sat up, raised a hand over his forehead, and scanned the wet grassland. "Over there, at the bottom of the basin. That must be where our trucks are...were. If so, you're right. They're damn sure underwater."

"I wonder where the doctor and Roger are and if they're alive. And what about Jeffrey? Where is he?"

"I don't know about any of that, but I do know we have to get out of here," Roger said. "This area will flood fifteen feet pretty damn quick."

"To where?" Marla asked.

Violent trails of lightning zigzagged like daggers across dark gray clouds, churning into a tempestuous mass. Its electric fury filled the air with a pungent smell of ozone. The storm raged with a ferocity that could knock even the strongest tree to its knees. "We have to go there." Rivera pointed toward the looming dam through a barrage of wind-whipped rain crashing upon them with unrelenting intensity. "Wilborn said she had her stuff inside the dam station house. It has to be the trunk with the fentanyl and the medical equipment."

The water level had risen ankle deep in a few minutes.

"The road!" Marla yelled. The roaring thunder and howling wind almost drowned out her shouting. She touched her scalp and felt the cap had washed away. "I remember it curves around to the front of the dam. Let's go."

Marla wiped water off her face several times. "Look out there about a hundred yards to the left. How did Roger and Wilborn get that far away?"

"They're in trouble," Rivera said. "That area is already flooded, and they're stranded while hanging on a branch."

"Let's get out of here," Marla said.

Slogging through the soggy grass, mud squelching under their feet, they made their way toward the road in drenched clothes. Wind and rain swirling from every direction.

Marla's hair stood on end, and she felt a thousand ants crawling over her skin. A deafening thunderclap exploded, with an instantaneous worldwide camera flash hotter than the sun. A second later, a violent shockwave belted across the ground, knocking them over like bowling pins.

Rivera grabbed Marla's arm. "Go. Get up. Move."

Fifty feet away, the heavens electrocuted a tree, splitting it in half and shattering debris across the road.

Marla rolled onto the shoulder of the road. The chilling rain beat on her back. "Need a second."

"No." Rivera jerked her up and urged her forward. "Got to get out of here."

Her soaked clothes clung to her body like a second skin, slowing her down with each step. Rain pounded against her like miniature ball bearings. With each ounce of energy left in her, she pushed herself forward, determined to reach the dam. Yet, when she reached the US Highway 281 overpass, and the rain quit beating her, she stopped and placed her hands on her sides. "Wait a second."

That was when Rivera's mocking voice bellowed out, "Slow Adams. Too damn slow. I beat you here by ten seconds."

"Give me a minute and I'll be ready." Marla leaned forward and grasped her knees.

"Bullshit, Adams. We should get to the dam before they do."

"How do you know they're still alive? They've probably drowned by now."

"You were trained for this. Stand up and let's go."

She surveyed the dam, five stories tall and almost two thousand feet long, with the station house towering on top. To enter, they would have to run to the opposite side. While under the bridge, a waterfall of rain pounded the asphalt road steps away. She wanted to sit and wait for it to ease up.

Rivera leaned opposite her, his face inches from hers. "Come on, Adams. We can get there in ten minutes. What are you? Some wimp ass newbie?"

That did it. Without saying a word, she charged headlong, with cold rain pelting her face, and ran as fast as her aching body would allow.

◆

The rain slashed in from all directions. Dr. Wilborn and Roger clung to a large floating tree branch like two rats holding on for dear life, knowing that if it broke, the raging waters would drag them under. Howling winds screamed in their ears, and strong gusts whipped their faces, causing their soaked clothes to flap wildly, pushing them ever closer to the distant, looming dam. The tension between them was as taut and electric as the lightning above them, each word a charged bolt aimed at the other's heart.

Roger slapped the back of Wilborn's head. "You weren't giving me the money, were you?"

Wilborn's eyes narrowed in anger, with lips pressed together as she hung onto the branch. "Shut your gob. I did it because I knew they were coming, so I wouldn't hand over a million dollars to Adams."

"That's bullshit. You didn't know they were down there."

"Rubbish. I did it to protect you."

Roger laughed as the branch wavered in the water. "You're dead."

"Take a gander at me," Wilborn shot back, "clearly, I'm not."

"No?" Roger slapped Wilborn's wrist. "Your expensive watch is not moving. The water drowned it. It's dead."

"Blimey hell." Wilborn ripped it off and hurled it into the raging water.

Roger yelled, his voice swallowed by the roaring waves. "Guess it's your lucky day."

Wilborn wrapped her arm tighter around the branch. "What the bloody hell are you talking about?"

"Over there." Roger pointed toward the dam. "Do you see that metal ladder up ahead? It leads straight up to the top. We can climb up to the station house and grab my money."

"Bloody hell it is." Wilborn's hand shoved Roger's chin. "Your money is behind us, up Shit's Creek, I'd say. Find the sack, that's where yours is. Where's my vial?"

"Paddle faster, you worthless bitch, or we both die."

The two fought against every flare of the wind and wave that threatened to drag them further from the ladder.

Roger lunged for the metal post and missed. He pushed the branch away and snagged the rung. "First one up gets the vial and the money."

Wilborn latched onto Roger's pant leg and yanked him back into the water. She clambered up the ladder to the top and over the railing, sprinting toward the wire fence where she had picked the padlock earlier. In one swift motion, she flung open the gate and rushed to the metal door of the building, pleased with herself that she was smart enough to leave it unlocked.

Roger was stunned at how fast Wilborn, ten years older than him, could run. He hopped over the railing as the door to the building closed. He groped the empty holster and realized he had lost his expensive competition revolver in the water.

Inside, the room was black, and Wilborn pulled the pistol from behind her. She wasn't sure whether it would work after being in the water. She felt a glimmer of relief when her hand grazed the knife still in the sheath.

Roger flung open the door, illuminating the heart of the dark room, and entered. Before his eyes adjusted to the darkness, Wilborn charged with the knife. With Roger's quick reaction time from years of fast draw practice, he latched onto Wilborn's wrist and redirected the blade, cutting his skin and muscle rather than plunging into his gut. Roger swung his other fist into Wilborn's chest, knocking her off balance and skittering the knife across the floor.

Wilborn crawled away as the door slowly closed until the latch clicked, enveloping the room in darkness once again. "You've been nothing but a wanker since I met you. Give me the vial!"

Roger scrambled blindly to find shelter behind a cardboard box, holding his belly as the warmth of blood trickled between his fingers.

A menacing voice filled the darkness. "All right, you blithering piece of shite. Give me the vial."

Did Wilborn find the knife? Pain radiated in Roger's stomach with each breath.

Feet shuffled in the dark, then silence. Wilborn's voice pierced through the darkness from a different direction. "Come out. Show yourself. How'd you like a tab of fentanyl right about now, cowboy? I have some in my trunk, over there in the corner."

Roger gritted his teeth, muttering in frustration while lying on the frigid, unyielding floor. "To hell with this life of crime and violence." He rubbed his bloodied hands over his pants. Get out of this place and forget everything here. He couldn't shake the vision of Cassie's face out of his mind. *No, damn it. Stay right here...with her. Done with running all over this country for fast draw competitions that don't pay squat. With a million dollars, I could buy old man Johnson's place. But if I kill the bitch, I could have two million.* Reality hit hard when he tried to move, and a pain shot through his abdomen. *I'm kidding myself. How am I gonna buy cattle and equipment? The Feds will confiscate the cash, leaving me with nothing.* He coughed, bringing up a wad of foul tasting mucous. *The knife must have gotten me deeper than I thought.* A deep breath made him cough again, and the pain in his abdomen caused him to double over in agony.

When Wilborn moved, her foot stepped on the knife. She placed it inside the sheath before shouting from the oppressive darkness, "Hey, fucknut! Are you still alive? Give me the vial, and the money is yours."

"Go to hell! You didn't do much to me. I'm taking all the money and leaving you high and dry."

Wilborn yanked the pistol from her pocket with seething rage. *The bloody hell he is.* She fired a shot at the ceiling. A flash of fire erupted in the dark, filling the room with the taste of charred ozone. The explosion deafened her for a moment as she tossed the weapon onto the concrete. *I hate these things.*

Roger heard the gun clatter on the floor. *She dropped it. Empty?*

"Get your arse out here, you twit, and give me the vial!" Wilborn picked up the pistol and wedged it between the small of her back and belt. "That knife wound in your gut...you'll bleed out." She reached for the phone, but it was gone. She lied, anyway. "I still have a phone that works. I'll offer a trade—an ambulance call for the vial."

◆

Marla and Rivera sprinted a quarter of a mile down the midline of the road, from one end of the dam to the other, pushing their legs to their limits until they finally reached the driveway atop the concrete mass. Rain pelted them as they gasped wet air deep into their lungs.

She swept drenched hair away from her face and noticed the partially open gate. "Wilborn must have beat us here. The city employees wouldn't leave it open."

Rivera picked up the padlock, then pitched it aside. "Only one way to find out."

A gunshot resounded from inside the building.

Without hesitation, Rivera drew his pistol from its holster and shook it. "You still have yours, right?"

Marla followed suit, releasing the magazine from her pistol and shaking out the water before snapping it back into place. "Ready. Let's go."

They hustled past the gate towards the station house entrance.

When Rivera grabbed the door handle, Marla grasped his arm and shook her head. "There's no back door to this place, One entry. And remember, she's armed. I go left, and you take the right."

Rivera eased the handle down and cracked the door open before closing it again. "Total darkness. Did Wilborn cut the power?" He reached for his flashlight, but it was gone.

Marla did the same. "Mine's gone, too. The light switch should be shoulder high. I'll reach for it as we enter."

Headlights swerved from the street and raced straight for the fence. An engine roared.

Chapter 37

"God dammit! Get the hell out of my way!" Jeffrey yelled from inside his SUV as he barreled toward them. A driving rain bombarded San Antonio. Windshield wipers swished rapidly back and forth. "Wilborn belongs to me—for my Rosemary!" The vehicle smashed into the fence, shattering the grille and headlights and spidering the windshield glass. The gate flew over the vehicle's roof as he floored the accelerator and the engine whined higher.

Marla and Rivera lunged to the side as the vehicle slammed into the building, sending bricks flying and crumpling the metal door frame. Thick steam poured out from under the crushed hood. Lightning cracked above the building, and splintering light penetrated the damaged wall.

Wilborn came around the side of an eight-foot-tall, gray-painted box, pointed the pistol at the vehicle and closed her eyes. She fired a single shot, piercing the broken windshield and shattering the back window. She covered her ears after the sudden explosion and muzzle flash. "Fucking rotting whore! I hate this bloody thing."

Marla and Rivera skirted around to the right side of the damaged vehicle and returned fired.

Wilborn dropped to her knees, covered her left ear, and shot again, breaking the rest of the back window. "Damn it. That's too bloody loud!"

Jeffrey reached inside the console and removed a pistol. He struggled to open the driver's door, but it wouldn't budge, so he leaned to his side and kicked it hard until it banged against the broken brick. He jumped out and let off two shots.

Marla yelled at Jeffrey on the left side of the damaged SUV. "What is that gray thing?"

Wilborn spun to the other side and fired again, shattering the driver's door window.

Jeffrey flinched. "I've been here, and it's nothing important." He spun around the back of the vehicle while Marla and Rivera returned fire, piercing holes into the center of the tall box.

Jeffrey met up with Marla and Rivera. "Listen. I kinda know the layout. Last year, the water department gave the sheriff's office a tour and showed us how the gates of the dam work. That is a storage unit, but behind it is another shorter one that contains buttons and knobs to control the water flow." He pointed toward the far side of the building where six parallel vertical metal pipes, ceiling to floor, each painted orange, were connected to a waist-high square box with a large wheel valve. Two boxes glowed with green lights, while four burned red.

"Those must be the pipes for pumping the water from the flooded side," Marla said.

"What are the boxes on the pipes?" Rivera asked.

Jeffrey said, "Those are electronic valve controls regulating flow from one side of the dam to the other, dictating downtown and the Riverwalk's water supply. When there's a change, the main station is alerted."

"Police Station?" Marla asked.

Jeffrey shook his head. "No. The Water Department."

Wilborn called out, "Adams, you twat, hurry up and die, so I can save this stupid world!"

Marla glanced at Rivera and Jeffrey. "Would that be the definition of a lunatic?"

Roger crawled further away from Wilborn. His hand bumped against a broken piece of metal and stuck it in his pocket. He called out as best he could. "I'm switching sides. This bitch is crazy. She stabbed me."

Marla peered around the vehicle's damaged front end. "Come out with your hands up."

"Bring the doctor over here to me, and we won't shoot," Jeffrey said.

Wilborn spun around and fired, then turned back behind the tall box after hitting the SUV's already steaming radiator. "I'll kill all of you wankers."

Rivera fired several rounds into the box.

Jeffrey shoved Rivera's shoulder. "What are you doing? You can't kill the doctor. She has to help Rosemary."

"You idiot. She's not surrendering to us. How about I empty my magazine into that steel contraption, and we end this right now?"

On the opposite side of the eight-foot gray storage unit, a bullet had shattered the top hinge of one door, revealing the inside where light shone through bullet holes and tattered bright yellow and orange San Antonio Public Works Department clothing hung. Wilborn slid back from it to a smaller, four-foot-tall black box with a nylon cable threaded between two door handles. "Let's have a gander at what we have here."

Roger said with a weakening voice, "I'm hurt. I need help over here."

Marla called out, "Stay there."

Rivera said, "Tell me where Wilborn is so I can take down this crazed psycho."

"No." Jeffrey clamped onto Rivera's wrist. "You can't kill her."

Rivera swung his arm free. "I can't tell you what will happen if the perp resists arrest."

Banging metal against metal from behind the tall gray box silenced their discussion.

Wilborn pounded the gun butt against the nylon cable. Wait, you idiot. I'm the bloody wanker. She grasped the knife and sliced through the cord. That was proper easy. When she opened the doors, her eyes met an array of switches and lights, but the most important were the six levers in a row, clearly labeled GATE OPENINGS, with only numbers two and five raised, letting water flow, while the others remained lowered and closed. In one swift movement, Wilborn flipped the other four levers upright, causing yellow emergency lights hanging from the ceiling to flash frantically and an air horn blaring in a rhythmic pattern.

"What's happening?" Marla asked.

"It's time for the reckoning." Dr. Wilborn stood in front of the box while holding the gun in the air. "And this will all be on your bloody—"

Wilborn's words were cut short as a body slammed into her from behind, sending them both crashing to the ground.

Marla pointed to the middle of the building. "It's Roger and the doctor on the floor. She aimed her pistol at them. "I can't get a clear shot. We need to move closer."

As soon as she took a step, the building rumbled as the red lights connected to the four pipes changed to green.

"Oh, hell," Rivera said. "The water gates are opening."

Panic engulfed Marla as she sprinted outside and watched all six gates spill thousands of gallons of water into the San Antonio River. She ran back inside, adrenaline bursting through her.

"She's flooding the river, downtown, and the Riverwalk. Hundreds, maybe thousands, will drown if we don't close those valves."

A muzzle flash ripped through the air when Wilborn fired a shot into the ceiling. "I've got your Yank traitor, and he's going to die if you don't let me out of this place." Wilborn pinned Roger in a chokehold with her pistol pressed hard against his temple. The acrid stench of blood and gunpowder hung in the air.

Roger's bloodied shirt clung to his body, wet and sticky. Each movement felt like sandpaper scraping his skin. He gritted his teeth and tried to turn away. Wilborn tightened her grip and pushed the hot barrel against Roger's skin, burning a round mark on his temple. With all his might, Roger forced out defiant words. "She ain't got shit. I still have what she wants, the vial, the precious protein extract." He elbowed the doctor as best as he could, but it meant nothing.

The grip of the pistol rammed into Roger's temple. "Give it to me," the doctor growled in a low, menacing voice, hot breath tickling Roger's ear. "Give it to me now, or you die right here."

"Take me with you," Roger bade. "I was bullshitting when I said I switched. They don't want me."

"You think you're coming with me?" Wilborn squeezed her arm around his neck harder, causing Roger to cough and gasp for air. "You've banjaxed everything for me from the beginning, and now it's time for payback." Wilborn aimed her gun toward the SUV and shouted, "Bloody right, Adams. The three of you come out, drop your weapons, and let me have a gander at you."

Marla gestured for Jeffrey to sneak around to the other side of the vehicle. She yelled out toward Wilborn, "The deputy's hurt after he ran into the building. Give us a minute."

"Rubbish. You got two seconds, or this bloke is dead."

Marla, Rivera, and Jeffrey stepped out from around the vehicle, their pistols leveled at Wilborn.

"Stay right bloody there." Wilborn tightened her grip harder and pulled Roger backward.

But Marla refused to back down. She knew they had a chance if they kept speaking to the doctor. "Let's talk this through." She stepped cautiously closer, gun leveled, finger on the trigger. "There's only one way out, and that's past us." Marla aimed as close to Wilborn's head as possible. But the last time she shot at a person with her little finger half gone, she hit the attempted murderer three inches off center. Three inches would be Roger's head or neck.

Rivera and Jeffrey flanked her on either side.

With a deranged expression, Wilborn aimed her pistol squarely at Marla. "Stay put! Don't move a bloody inch." The doctor pushed the muzzle harder against Roger's ear. "Or he's dead."

Roger fought to keep his balance as the doctor dragged him backward. "Where do you think you're going? Back to the corner? How are you getting out of here?"

"No biggie for me. I've been inside before and know how to get out."

Roger choked out his insolence. "You think there's something in the corner?"

"What do you know about that?" Wilborn kicked the gate opening levers, shattering the inside of the electrical apparatus and sending sparks and smoke into the air.

"You're one dumb broad, Hugo Honey," Roger said. "Who told you to come here and hide your trunk? Trixi did, my sister, and she came and took everything. She wiped you out, and we'll split it while you go to hell."

Every muscle in Marla's forearms and hands tensed with her aim. Her finger eased the trigger back, then released. She couldn't be sure. "Let him go, Wilborn. Your delusions are over."

Wilborn dragged Roger further back into the depths of the building. Something was wrong. Someone uncovered the Seward trunk. She shoved Roger onto the floor, then opened the trunk. Everything was gone except a note. Needed money. T

"Bloody hell!" Wilborn kicked the side of the empty trunk.

Roger jumped on Wilborn's back and the two rolled to the floor. He straddled Wilborn and punched her in the chest and face.

Wilborn slammed her fist into Roger's side. His stomach muscles cramped, and he rolled off. She jumped to her feet and glanced at a three-by-three-foot square opening on the floor, an entrance to an outside catwalk, crossing from the back of the building to near the door. She had placed the trunk nearby, knowing her last line of defense was to drop it through the opening and escape, but now it was empty. She aimed the pistol at Roger.

"Look who's the fool, now." Roger grabbed the shard of metal from his pocket and plunged it into Wilborn's foot.

Wilborn screamed, then fired, hitting Roger in the chest. She staggered down the catwalk.

Jeffrey cried out, "No. No. Doctor, are you all right?" He rushed to the corner and found Roger flat on his back. "He's dead." He kicked the empty trunk with his foot. "Where's Dr. Wilborn's equipment? Where's..." He gazed at the aperture on the floor. His eyes widened, realizing what it was. He had forgotten about the catwalk during the building tour last year. Without a second thought, he raced past Marla and Rivera toward the SUV and the damaged door.

"Jeffrey?" Marla asked. "Where are you going?"

"It doesn't matter," Rivera said. "We have to stop the water flowing out from the gates."

With the San Antonio River already swollen dangerously high, Marla had to decide whether to go after Wilborn or save the city. She made her choice; Jeffrey needed help and the crazed doctor had to be stopped.

"Adams!" Rivera pointed at a wheel connected to the closest pipe. "Damn it, come on, I can't do this alone." He grasped one wheel tightly and strained to turn it. The pressure of the flowing water was too intense to handle by himself. "Come on!"

Marla glanced in Rivera's direction before turning back to where Jeffrey had disappeared. He knows where Wilborn went. Don't wait. Get Wilborn and everything stops. Get her now before she kills more people.

"Hey!" Rivera said.

Marla turned toward Rivera and stood still.

"Adams, get over here, now!"

Jeffrey, take care. Steeling herself, she squared her shoulders and nodded firmly toward Rivera. In her mind, she set Wilborn free. "All right. I'm coming."

Together, they grabbed the wheel, and with their combined strength, they forced one gate closed, and the light changed to red.

Jeffrey sprinted around the corner of the building and clambered down a narrow metal ladder onto a wire mesh floor. Standing there was Wilborn, gun in hand, pointing straight at him. The swirling gusts of wind knocked both against the rail.

"Please, I'll do whatever you want," Breathless, Jeffrey begged. A drop of salty sweat trickled to his lips. "Just heal my wife. That's what you've done with that other girl at the clinic, right? You fixed her. Do it, and I can hide you from the DEA."

"You want me to use my stem cells on your wife?" Even though this man was in law enforcement, he could vouch for her after declaring the experiment a success. "What's wrong with her?"

Jeffrey smiled. He would finally get what Rosemary needed. "She's depressed, sad. We lost babies, miscarriages. Do something to keep her pregnant all the way through."

"I've never done anything like that." Wilborn continued to aim the pistol at Jeffrey. "I heal brain injuries."

"You make things grow, right? Brains and other stuff. Make her..." he waved his arms wide, "her womb better. You're super smart. You can do that."

Wilborn spun through the female anatomy in her head: eggs, ovaries, fallopian tubes, uterus, cervix, smooth muscles, blood supply...nothing similar to the brain. But if the two are willing to try and the woman doesn't die, her stem cell therapy might expand to many parts of the body, not just the brain. Wilborn shook her head. "I don't know."

When Jeffrey stepped closer, Wilborn aimed the pistol at Jeffrey's chest. "I believe in you. You can save her. I'll pay you whatever you want and say you are the greatest doctor in the world."

"There are no guarantees. I'm not even sure she would live through all of it." I would be famous. "But I must have the vial from Roger before starting any procedure with your wife."

"You got it. I promise."

Blood dripped from Wilborn's shoe as she limped one step forward. "And one hundred thousand dollars."

Jeffrey's smile escaped him. "What? I don't have that, but I can take you somewhere to fix your foot. A quiet place, not a hospital. An x-ray tech who fixes broken bones on the side."

"That sounds like rubbish."

"I don't have that kind of money."

"Well then, move aside."

"No."

The wind and rain swept around them. Wilborn changed the gun from her right hand to her left and reached for the rail. Jeffrey reached for his pistol and rushed her.

Marla heard a gunshot outside. She let go of the wheel. "That's Jeffrey out there. I have to go."

Rivera grabbed her arm and yanked her back. "Get over here! The city is flooding, and I need help turning these wheels."

Marla struggled in which direction to go. "I...I...I should check on the gunshots." *Damn it, Jeffrey. Where are you?*

Rivera forced her hand on the wheel. "Turn, now!"

She frantically turned it as hard as she could, praying Jeffrey would return any second. But he didn't.

Emergency sirens blared outside. Red and blue lights flickered into the darkened building, yet Jeffrey was still not in sight.

After the last wheel stopped turning, all the lights on the boxes had changed to red and the spillway closed, Marla barreled outside past the damaged vehicle with a pistol clasped in her hand. The brightness of the sun glaring into her face surprised her, except it wasn't sunlight—it was headlights. She raised her hand to block the bright illumination trained on her face. The long day had turned to dusk, but the rain and wind refused any respite to anyone or anything.

A police officer yelled, "Drop your weapon and get on your knees."

Soaked to the core again, a tempest of wind pushed her off balance. She gazed across the police vehicles. Officers stood with their service weapons drawn and pointed at her. "I'm DEA Special Agent Adams! Inside is another agent." She scanned the area for Jeffrey. "Has anyone seen a sheriff's deputy?"

An officer called out, "I recognize her. She's good. Weapons down."

Marla made her way to the edge of the building where a metal ladder descended, its rungs slick with rainwater. Wind and rain shoved her against the building and then the railing. She stepped down, holding her breath, and peered through the catwalk wire mesh at the still water in the channel leading towards downtown and the Riverwalk. Thousands of unsuspecting people would never realize how their lives nearly changed for the worse. Off to the side, on a concrete slab thirty feet below the catwalk, Dr. Hugo

Wilborn lay motionless with her limbs distorted and her skull smashed like a pumpkin hurled from the third floor.

Something in the middle of the catwalk caught her eye, a mound of sorts. She rushed ahead, heart racing. It was Jeffrey curled on his side and Wilborn's pistol next to him. She knelt down and rolled Jeffrey onto his back, revealing a red stain on his shirt. Blood mixed with rain fell through the wire mesh into the water below. It was a tragic scene all too familiar to her—a victim with a gunshot wound to the center of the chest. As the rain pummeled San Antonio, she pressed her clenched fist against her forehead and gazed at the lifeless body in front of her. The chaos behind her of police and Rivera's voices was a cacophony of blame and accusations, but their words were nothing more than meaningless noise to her. Her husband, Crosby, had been killed because of her, and now Jeffrey Keene died trying to help his wife—and her. He was as close to what a brother could be. She laid Jeffrey's arm across his chest. "They both died because I left them behind. I let them die." She leaned her head back and let the rain wash over her face. "No more," she whispered to herself. "There will be no more love." She dropped her head down and spoke into the empty darkness. "Not ever again."

Chapter 38

The wind flicked Cassie's hair over her face. She didn't bother to sweep it away. Festus positioned himself beside her, rock still, waiting for a command. Cassie sat next to a fresh pile of dirt six feet long and three feet wide, with a simple headstone; her lips quivered as she reached out and laid her palm on the mound. She glanced back toward the bunkhouse a hundred yards off when she thought she heard the front door creaking open and Roger's boots scuffing the porch. Closing her eyes, she could almost sense his smile and the sudden jerk of his body from a bullet.

A mockingbird perched on an oak tree limb above Cassie's head. Its melodious voice sang for a lost loved one. She gazed up at it and smiled as it fluttered its wings and flew away as quickly as it had come, leaving her alone once again.

While raising her face into the sun's warmth, dust plumed upward across the open range and faded with the wind; it was time to leave.

Each day the world moved on, giving life, taking it away, taking everything, gorging on life like hungry wolves consuming every soul.

People live, people die, people lie.

A quarter mile away, Marla rode Daisy toward an oak tree with a glorious canopy the size of a house. Moments later, she stopped and swung down from the horse, then removed her ball cap, swept her hair off her forehead, and replaced it on her head. "May I?"

Cassie continued to sit and nodded with a whisper of a smile.

Marla flipped the reins over Daisy's neck and then scratched Festus behind his ears. "People will say they are sorry. People still say that to me." She bent down on one knee near Cassie. "Your heart hurts. It's the worst pain you will ever have." She closed her eyes and saw Crosby, a bullet hole in his head, blood trickling onto thirsty ground. "You don't want to live without him, but you do. When you decide to love someone, you give away the most precious thing you own, but you get more in return. I continue to think of Crosby every day and the worst decision I ever made."

Cassie wiped a tear away with the edge of her finger. "What do you mean?"

Marla sat on the ground and grazed the palm of her hand across the roughness of the tombstone. "I left the police department and went to Quantico to be like Crosby," she paused, then spoke again, "but I could never be him. I was gone for three months, and he died before I ever saw him again."

"You saw him. You tried to save him."

Marla shook her head. "Not as the Crosby I once knew. I made a vow to love and comfort my husband for the rest of my life, but I didn't. I abandoned him. Was it envy? I don't know."

"No." Cassie drew her knees near her chest. "He was shot while under-cover."

"True, but he went deep undercover because of me, all because I left town. He wouldn't have stayed away if I had been there to support him." Marla scooted closer to Cassie and wrapped her arm around her friend's shoulder. "I can't tell you the blackness inside you will disappear. Mine hasn't. Hope it never does." Marla pulled her knees up near her chest, too. "Crosby always wanted to be a rancher. The DEA was his way of making enough money to buy cattle and land. And now, here I am..." she eyed the horizon, "no husband and no livestock." She stood and brushed the dirt off her jeans. "That was his dream, so now it's mine." Marla laid her hand on Cassie's shoulder. "And I'm going to need your help."

Cassie raised an eyebrow at her. "With no cattle, doing what?"

Marla's half-smile radiated in the summer sun. "Got another hundred head coming, and I need a ranch hand, but you have to promise me no drugs."

"That's a no-brainer. I'm never touching any of that stuff again."

"Great." Marla reached out to help Cassie stand. "Deal."

She didn't make a move towards Marla. Instead, she hugged her legs and rested her head on her knees. "If you don't mind, I want to stay with Roger for a bit longer before deciding my next move."

Marla adjusted her cap on her forehead before reaching for the reins. "Understand. Let me know if you want to stay."

"Hey."

Marla pivoted back.

"The cap...a new logo, right?" Cassie reached out her hand. "Mind if I try it on?"

"Even better." Marla grinned widely, opened her saddlebag, pulled a new cap from inside, and snapped it open. "Here you go."

Cassie fine-tuned it until it felt comfortable. "Feels pretty good."

Marla tilted her head. "Looks good on you."

Cassie leaned back, hands resting on the fresh mound of dirt. "Of course, it does."

They both chuckled.

Cassie tapped the logo with her fingertip. "What's in the center?"

Marla smiled. "Right. New business, so new brand. A female gender image inside a heart."

"Interesting."

"I'm starting a female cattle ranch, all women."

"Besides you, who else?"

"Hoping you would still be a part."

"So, just two?"

I hired another, Trixi Hagen."

Cassie's opened her eyes wide. "What? The bartender? Roger's sister?"

"Yep. After the bar burned down, she had no place to work. Seems nice and a hard worker. She'll be number three. After she's ready, I'll buy another hundred head." Marla mounted Daisy. "Come back to work when you're ready. I really could use you."

As Marla headed toward her home, Cassie swept the dirt off her palms as the wind rustled her hair. She read the inscription ROGER HAGEN, COWBOY etched into the tombstone. The field of grass behind her quivered in the breeze. The mockingbird returned and sang to her, and with that, she stood, brushed the dirt off her jeans, and mounted her horse. Festus swiftly bounded up on all fours and did several figure eights. Cassie adjusted her new cap. "It's time to go to work."

THE END

About the Author

Patrick Hanford has lived in Texas most of his life. He graduated from the University of North Texas, Texas College of Osteopathic Medicine and recently retired from family medicine after more than thirty-five years. He interjects his past experiences of daily medical clinic life throughout his stories.

With three novels published and *The Creation of Marla Adams* reaching Amazon best selling status in four countries, he has continued with the Marla Adams series.

He lives with his wife, plays golf, walks in West Texas wind, and travels from one end of Texas to the other visiting children and grandchildren.

Acknowledgements

I am grateful for the endless support and guidance from my family, friends, critique partners, beta readers, and arc readers throughout the multiple rewrites of the third installment in this series, *The Pursuit of Marla Adams*. A special thanks to my exceptional editor, Cameron Chandler, who has a keen eye for developmental editing and is exceptional at pinpointing areas that need improvement. I hope we continue to collaborate on future novels.

I also want to acknowledge the Write Right Critique Group members, the professors at Texas Tech University who helped me with the British language, and Texas Tech HSC physicians. A huge thank you goes out to Dr. Mirla Avila, a neurologist who reintroduced me to the intricate neuroanatomy and physiology of the brain's anterior cingulate cortex, and to Steven Boyland for his assistance in explaining San Antonio's stormwater drainage systems and Olmos Dam projects.

A special mention must be made to KJ Waters, who helped design an incredible book cover and provided valuable advice as well as unwavering support throughout this journey.

Writing fiction allows for complete creative freedom, where authors can choose to tell the truth or fabricate anything they desire. While most roads and landmarks mentioned in this book - such as the Olmos Dam, airport, and highways - are actual places in San Antonio, everything else is simply born from my slightly off-center mind.

P lease visit my website at www.patrickhanford.com.

You can find me on social media at:

Facebook: PatrickHanfordauthor

Instagram: @patrickhanford.

Twitter: @patrickjhanford

If you'd like to receive the first few chapters of my next book, please sign up for my newsletter on my website. I'll share occasional updates on my writing, upcoming releases, sales, and special offers.

www.ingramcontent.com/pod-product-compliance
Lightning Source LLC
Chambersburg PA
CBHW072104300726
48975CB00003B/689